STUMBLING UPON MOWGLI

a novel

By
Nicasio Latasa

INKWATER
PRESS

PORTLAND • OREGON
INKWATERPRESS.COM

STUMBLING UPON MOWGLI

Chapter 1

The night before Cosmo and I left for Mexico I could not sleep. I had no idea we were going any-where at the time, no clue what the next day would bring besides meeting Cosmo at the beach before work to go surfing, but I was restless and the air felt astir. It reached out with icy hands, the bed morphed into an army of slithering insects, and tired eyes fix-ated on the stillness of our bedroom walls. Karana rested like a newborn baby after a good cry. I walked to the kitchen and drank a glass of water. The rain simmered into a gentle tap dance upon the fiber-glass awning covering our back porch. Sleep would not come, I realized. It was many things. It was J.P.'s death, it was Karana's silence, it was my place in the world. Maybe I did not know it consciously then, but somewhere locked beneath the entrails of submission and regret I sensed the presence of a powerful force from which I could not hide. I decided to go out into the night. My truck started up and headed past dark store fronts, through green stop lights, and halted when the asphalt ceased to go any further west.

Low tide sank into the jaws of the sea. A cruel, midnight sky devoured blackened saltwater and spat out acres of desolated sand. A purged, barren wasteland littered with beaten appendages of lifeless seaweed, despondent piles of damp tree limbs, trails of garbage, plastic, and wilted cardboard usurped the usual, friendly hospitality offered at the toes of the sea. Wiggling digits, playfully free, transformed, discovered evil alter egos and stalked the land of soil and concrete. Swirling winds somersaulted amidst baritone roars of angered thunder. The storm began small, itching, twisting, clawing at the guts of the atmosphere. Surge propelled surge. Clouds swelled and the storm built into a frenzied torrent which expelled Hershey Kiss size teardrops upon a thirsty planet.

The altered shoreline yearned for its liquid life force to return, to cease the damaging ebb sucking all familiarity, all possibilities, all dreamed and invented into a cataclysmic oblivion. The vacuity hit me square in the mouth. Sweatshirt hood pulled down over a gray and black beanie shielded the cold, the emptiness, the lack of stars. Restless thoughts, which called me to walk the edge of the ocean well into the early hours of the morning, guided my steps. For a moment as the storm gathered strength for another deluge the rain slept. Soon all would change. Nature snarled alive and robust, churning in a free flow of expression an innate prowess poised to unleash a liberated downpour of spirit and power, exposed, and direct.

I envied the storm. How fortunate to know its true essence, the very core of its existence, and then release that entity without hesitation, without doubt.

To know it would expel an unreserved gush of emotion on full display, frothing, breathing, howling, and inspiring awe at its every twitch propelled a bitter spark of jealousy in the pit of my stomach. I was mute, slightly dragging the tip of my left shoe on the concrete of the shore walk for reasons I could not fathom. I never walked like that before, funny; all the while the grit of sand scraped between rubber and the wet cement creating an ominous screech in the air. As I watched the tide creep back I did not realize how much like the storm I was at that moment. Maybe because I did not think I was capable of such a release. That the upwelling reeking havoc on my organs would not split open a distended belly and release its contents to the world. Let it rain guts, heart, soul, and bone. A prayer existed, a hope, far too many wishes, but I grew overly comfortable to remain confined inside a puffy cloud always smiling, always penitent, but afraid to commence into a true downpour of emotion. I thought I could keep going. Keep trudging along, keep moving, but like a gathering storm it was only a matter of time before I let go. Nothing extraordinary happened. No wild premonitions or visits from angelic prophets. I only gazed at the darkness of the sea, but somewhere in my trance I imbibed an arcane taste from the sweet ooze of triumph. I felt like I could make the world right again, sane again, competent again, not that the world ever possessed any of those elements in the first place, but it seemed possible. A fools dream, but a good dream, a worthy dream.

The water crept up and swallowed the trash, the

kelp, and the dismembered limbs. I navigated from concrete to sand and found a six and a half foot branch of traveled driftwood. I held its knobby composition in two hands like King Arthur wielding Excalibur and waved it towards what little showed of Orion's Belt. A buckle loosened, the stars relaxed. The universe slithered into my grasp. So many nights without sleep, so many dreams left in a mess of cosmic dust, but standing on the ravaged beach a modest pour of strength reached an apprehensive soul and filled it with enough courage to set off on an emancipating voyage.

I am not sure why I remember that walk with such vivid detail. Maybe I give it more credit after the fact as I search for what inspiration prompted me to leave in the first place. I did not know it. I could not fathom it, yet the sea grinned as it pushed foam further up the beach. My system shifted subconsciously and set the tumblers in motion as a light sprinkle began to fall. Mother Ocean felt it; she twisted the belts of time while I tightened the strings of my sweatshirt hood so it sucked against my cheeks. I staggered to my truck with an odd hope that by the next day the whole world would change. A wave crashed, thunder rumbled somewhere over Palomar Mountain and I made my way to the warmth of Karana resting easy underneath our blankets and fell into a peaceful sleep unaware that the next morning would unleash the storm that had been brewing in my belly for far too long.

Chapter 2

Somehow I knew the train would come to a shrieking halt. Call it willpower, premonition, luck, call it a mere stroke of serendipity, yet however a label would get anointed to the breakdown that occurred, the result was imminent, or at least I believed so in my mind. Maybe silent prayers that escaped from reticent jaws did the trick, or perhaps the telepathy I attempted on blurring trees and totem-like telephone poles to uproot and spill in a flurry of wood and leaves and cables upon the steel tracks. I knew the conductor would probably pick up the intercom and go through a rehearsed diatribe about how the loco-motive was experiencing technical difficulties and they were trying to get to the bottom of the problem as soon as possible. Soon after we would hear an apology for the postponement followed by a hope that all the passengers could bear with them during the delay. The engineers and doormen would sort through switches and wiring, computer screens and instrument panels searching for a cause that hindered the eight car, mode of transportation. They would dig into the memory banks of problem solving, possibly the brake line, a blown fuse, a loss of power to the main frame, but my doubts loomed about the crew ever finding a mechanical glitch. Cosmic forces felt diligently at work and the apparent signs screamed as distinct as the hooting of an oncoming train whistle.

I should have never boarded in the first place. I felt it beforehand, but could not avoid the overwhelming pulses surging through a body unfamiliar with acting upon radical compulsions. All needed to be done in proper order, sorted and drawn out, cautiously laying down directional tile towards the next logical step. The proper etiquette had to commence, piece by piece, line by line, and then, only then could the next decision proceed. It stood as a delicate balance on the jagged fence of ambivalence. Careful and fastidious continued a tessellated pattern of mundane cowardice I could no longer tolerate.

A frenzied artillery of cell phones flipped open and sent an attack of invisible signals out through the walls of the debilitated train car. Next lap-tops opened up and the striking of keys began to propel e-mails through cyberspace. Who knew how many waves of technology impaled all of our bodies as they danced around us on invisible pathways. I thought to call for a second and inform my employers of the predicament, but reluctant fingers refused to strike the eleven digits on a cracked and faded, silver cell phone. I turned instead to the window and watched the rain pour down flooded with thoughts about why I was at the mercy of public transportation, but the answer came quick in knowing that Southern Californians could not drive in the rain. It became an undisputed fact every time the roads got wet. Morning traffic reports became inundated with countless accounts of crash sites and stories about spun-out vehicles banking into center dividers whenever it began to fall. Better to stay off of the road during a rainstorm in our section of the country.

Honey drops of moisture came into view ten feet from the window; they paused for a second with a flutter of wind and crashed into a damp piece of tinted glass. It was a brief life, created in the belly of a dark nimbostratus cloud, formed into droplets, and released shortly thereafter like a parachute jumper freefalling to the earth below, only to end its existence in an abrupt splat against the cool of oval glass and metal train. Sad to think the same fate awaited many motorists as they woke from their encumbered homes and were released upon the wild streets at a rushed pace only to collide with another pile of glass and metal. Cosmo's words haunted inert bones and led me to question why I sat on the paisley, fabric seat at all.

It was raining harder than two hours prior when my truck came to a halt at a stop sign back in Oceanside. The ocean peeked out in between two large houses where the cross street of Oceanside Boulevard ended at a slight graveled hill. A caramel hue overtook the blue-green radiance of the sea as local run-offs and the San Luis Rey River merged with the murky waters. It brought to mind the coffee I consumed earlier that morning, diluted and filled with cream and sugar poured from the heavens.

I continued to drive towards the harbor. Garret, the morning Deejay on the local 94.9 radio station was on his soapbox about the real independence and freedom to play good music. He stressed the importance of not playing a song just to sound edgy and hip, but to actually enjoy and respect the tracks he spun on the radio. He then proceeded to tell the early rising audience that **Rage Against The Machine**, a band they frequently played, probably would have never existed if **Public Enemy** did not come first. Before I could decipher if he really said **Public Enemy**, the base hit and Chuck D's commanding voice exploded out of the speakers. A smile emerged and my head bobbed as I cruised along the coast.

The harbor looked tattered and too dirty to enter. Dark clouds congregated on the horizon, accompanied by a sharp breeze which carried sand on its wings and disseminated speckled granules across the asphalt. Cosmo's steel-gray, Toyota pickup truck rested in a middle spot facing the ocean at the north jetty parking lot. How many mornings we met there just after the first rays of sunshine for an early morning session I could not count, or put into lucid perspective. His truck parked in a similar position with the stereo blaring and as always was there well before me.

As I pulled up next to him I lowered the volume on the radio to a whisper as Garret introduced "Bank Robber" from the **Clash**. No booming sound reverberated out of Cosmo's truck, nor did bursting laughter or excited hoots, just a reiterated drone of raindrops drummed morose tunes on the hoods of our vehicles. He rolled down his passenger window while I emulated the motion and put down my driver side window as well. A chill bit my cheeks and over-powered the hot air blowing out of the ducts in the truck. We exchanged nods, but no words exuded as the drumming mollified.

"Hey," Cosmo finally said.

"Hey."

"You ready for this."

"Are you still planning on going through with it?" He did not respond, but his left eyebrow rose and his head tilted up, which extended a slightly dimpled chin to accentuate his intent. A few of his sun-bleached locks spilled out of a black beanie. I knew the answer would be yes before I asked and I wished I could have taken it back the moment it escaped my lips.

"Don't feel forced to go man; it's totally fine. You know I can pull this off by myself." Cosmo did not change expression at all while he spoke, which meant he really would not have blamed me for not wanting to paddle out. Never one for small talk or to say things out of pity, Cosmo more than anyone I ever knew said what he meant. I knew he would have absolved me and not held a grudge if I decided to stay in the warmth of my truck. Erratic dashes of rain landed on the back of my left hand and dove towards my bones. The cool impalement brought about a shiver at the thought of entering the water. Even though the underlying tones that swam in my guts and desired to stay glued to the cloth seat and remain sheltered underneath the bower of the steel fortress that pro-tected goose pimpled skin from the cold, I would not let him go alone. I would have never forgiven myself.

"I was just checking with you because of the storm. I am ready for whatever you need."

"I'm glad. The words refuse to form on this inept tongue of mine, and thank you comes out overly cliché, but I appreciate it more than you know."

"No worries. You don't have to thank me. I am....," but Cosmo cut me off before I finished by putting out his hand and manufacturing a crooked, half smile indicating nothing more needed to be said. The act of speaking did feel unnecessary amidst the frigid air and our pending adventure as words dissipated faster than the steam from our breath. I decided to get out of the truck and keep my mouth shut until Cosmo requested conversation.

Two icy hands recalled the process of turning a damp wetsuit right side in without thought. A pattern repeated and etched into memory as familiar as the loop, swoop, and pull method of tying a pair of shoes. The ocean screamed alive displaying many facets of a never ending repertoire. White caps and large surf created an ominous seascape and teemed with ferocity. Mother Ocean appeared disheartened and expelled her grievances in arrays of crashing foam.

The beach was empty. A few months down the road when summer reined the spot would overflow with bodies and tents. Kites would take to the air, lifeguards would stand posts upon mint green towers, scraps of trash would drift from blankets and scatter about as people from two minutes to two thousand miles away congregated and plopped themselves upon the sand. Young boys would transform in seconds as they became infatuated with watching girls

move about in bikinis. A busy circus would commence of noise, varied characters, and tomato pasted
sun burns, but on a chilly morning in late February
the crowd consisted of five: Cosmo, myself, and three
huddling seagulls nestled close in the sand.

"Are you all packed?" Cosmo shouted through his
window. I was interrupted from my gaze upon the
beach to notice him still in his truck as rain dripped
from my hair.

"Packed for what?"

"To go."

"Go where? I thought we were going surfing."

"We are, but not here. Not now. Not in this."

"Then where? Remember I need to be out of the
water by seven-thirty to make it to work on time."

"You mean you didn't call in?" Cosmo asked with
a slight crack in his voice. Instantly I knew that I
missed something and became plagued with an overwhelming feeling that I let him down somehow.
He liked for people to think, not to make them
uncomfortable or beneath his wisdom, but to search
for answers that were right in front of them if one
could stop and put the pieces together. I put nothing
together, no problem solving, just stood like an idiot
in the rain.

"So where did you have in mind?" I sputtered out.

"I just can't do it here. He loved this town, his
friends, the community, but he had plans to be free of
the rat race this place had become. He felt truly alive
at his favorite place down the coast. That's where he
really wanted to be, isolated, on the cusp of the ocean
with nothing but wide open space to fill his eyes."

Cosmo stared towards the sea, sailing with scraps of driftwood and marshmallow waves unaware that I hovered in the wet weather. I knew I should have returned to my truck, but I lingered and waited for an answer. Shivering from the cold, the piercing wind, the thought of coming up with an excuse for not showing up to work and struggling with the myriad of possible plans swimming around Cosmo's brain, I stayed put. His expression, the direction of his words were leading to one possible destination, and as my mind actually began putting something together it became apparent that I would need to request more than one day off from work. How could I have missed it? Three days prior at the funeral, what were his words? "Tuesday morning meet me at North Jetty, we need to send J.P. off right." How one dimensional of me, something Cosmo always pushed to get out of my system and the reason why I began doing crossword puzzles, to think it was as simple as showing up and paddling out. My mistake for not accounting for the fact that nothing with Cosmo ever followed a path of solitary dimensions. I should have known better.

Cosmo watched my mind at work, a gift he used since the day we met, and eased back into the seat of his truck. His shoulders relaxed and a smile came to his face. "I want to get on the road by three. I still have a few things to button up and should be done with them around one or two. I'll wait until four o'clock, if I have not heard from you by then, well then, that is just the way it is going to be, I guess." His tone impaled my chattering body and reached into a cavernous valley of emptiness.

"I'll do my best, but it's not going to be easy. I mean how many days are we talking here? Two? Five?"

"Not sure. As many as it takes."

"And I am just supposed to walk up to my boss and say I need to leave now. And, oh, by the way I'm not sure how long I'll be gone, but it will probably be around, oh, as long as it takes. Then I'll have to call Karana next and explain to her that I'm going to disappear for a while with Cosmo, which ought to really freak her out. She might assume that I might never come back."

"I already called her."

"What? When?"

"Two days ago. Figured I better tell her of my intentions. I even invited her along because of how much uncle J.P. thought of her, but she declined."

I looked like someone slapped me in the face. Red and stunned I landed on the door of my truck. "Well what did she say?"

"She said you need to go as much as I do. Actually that you need this escape more than you know."

"Even if I loose my job?"

"'Better than losing you to a job that your heart is not really into,' she said." Slapped harder and my head rang. The rain threw punches, the wind snapped bone, and I faced an incursion of which I possessed no defenses. Cosmo's smile turned into a chuckle and it agitated me.

"What is so amusing to you about all of this?"

"You are. Get out of the rain; you look like a fucking drowned cat. I'll see you at three." He laughed and put his Toyota into reverse. He drove off and I could not move, petrified by everything that his purposed journey entailed. The request for time off would not go over well, especially on such short notice, plus Karana and I were in the middle of a trivial spat and I did not want to leave without appeasing the situation at least a little bit. I could not believe she actually told Cosmo that I needed to go, that she basically told me to go. I finally climbed back into my truck and noticed a text message form her on my phone. I did not feel in the mood to read it and drove home to get ready for work as **Modest Mouse** climbed out of the speakers.

TWO HOURS LATER I sat stranded in the rain. My tentative plan consisted loosely of getting to work, I was hoping on time, some definite ass kissing, maybe a lie or two about how long I would be gone and then hopefully back on a train to get home and pack. But that seemed crazy. Cosmo could be so crazy. Why the hell could he not wait for a weekend or tell me straight out at the funeral instead of hiding it in some coded message? At least then I would have had a head start on trying to eke out a few days off of work. We were busy and it was the end of the month, always the craziest time. I wanted to blow it off, forget it, walk into work and finish up the month.

Conversations continued on an assortment of phones. They opened a door for smokers to step outside and have a quick puff underneath an umbrella. Men and women discussed imminent big deals, what to ship out before DHL arrived, losing money because the conductor could not keep a train going straight on a delegated track. The ties were so ironed and prim. Black jackets, business dresses, business suits, gelled hair; the talk was all the same. I looked down at my shoes; the right one unlaced, and realized I was no different. That was my life. The existence I somehow had drifted into. I was someone I thought I would never be. My only solace came from knowing I did not carry a briefcase. The train car spun into a tornado and a sense of vertigo panged my stomach. Clutching my cell phone I opened it up and decided to read Karana's message.

"You know who you are
And you have been missing
Go and find yourself
I love you"

The pain that stabbed at my insides when Cosmo told me he had spoken to Karana returned to my bones and a whirlwind proceeded in my mind. I wanted to question everything; my clothes, my thwarted complacence, my station in life, but I knew it would not solve anything? The moment was much simpler than all of that. Cosmo needed me to go. And I knew Karana was right, I needed it as well. Plus, why had the train malfunctioned in the first place? It was not just a momentary pause to let another train pass by, no, the train broke down just as every stirring molecule in my blood knew it would. You hear that signs are everywhere, pointing, directing if we could open our eyes long enough to see them. Was it a sign? Was it fate giving me one more chance to escape my penitence towards incessantly following within the lines? Call it mystic, call it arcane, call it mere coincidence, but I could no longer deny the alluring obviousness of the moment. I pushed out of my seat and headed towards the smokers. An attractive woman with streaky, most likely dyed-blonde hair asked me for a cigarette as I approached the door. I gruffly got out that I did not smoke and parted the huddle of umbrellas and tobacco clouds and charged into the rain

I heard an Amtrak employee yell at me, something about having to re-board the train, but I was gone. My mouth opened and swallowed nature's life droplets as I cleared the tracks. The voice disappeared, the train vanished, and I stopped, dropped my head back and extended my arms. I stood outstretched underneath a cathartic baptism of flowing showers. What was to come? What adventures were ahead? Everything was possible in that moment. My jacket hood finally came up to cover my drenched hair. Mud splattered steps guided towards civilization as the phone came to my ear.

"Hey baby.........

"I love you...........

"Yes I am going to Mexico."

Chapter 3

The cab ride from San Juan Capistrano to Oceanside cost a flat rate of fifty bucks to go roughly twenty-two miles and I arrived home soaking wet and out of cash. While I packed, the job I walked out on never came to mind. Instead, as I fumbled through camping gear, layers of clothing, and which surfboards to bring along the only thought that penetrated the thick layer of clouds surrounding my head came in the form of Karana. I took the last of the peanut butter from the pantry and could smell her in the empty house. I watched her silhouette gallivant upon the walls moving in offbeat, elated convulsions to a country song I would never catch the name of, I caught sight of the knife that sliced her index finger nearly to the bone when she was cutting tomatoes from our garden, and at once I missed her. I threw the plastic jar and a handful of Emergen-C's into a Rubbermaid container and closed it shut burdened with thoughts about what a horrible time it was to disappear.

I called Cosmo from the cab and it took all I could manage to hold him off until 2:30 which only allowed a moment to say a quick good-bye to Karana on her early day off work. I told her so much in a return text message. When we talked at the harbor he mentioned that he wanted to leave by three, but after telling him the train story he welled with excitement and could not wait to get going. She walked in at ten after two with the hood of her jacket over her sandy-blonde curls. I tried to speak, but words cluttered on the tongue like a backup on the freeway, stalled and nowhere to go, and for what seemed like an entire minute we just stared at one another. Finally she broke the silence.

"What time is Cosmo coming to get you again?" she asked removing her saturated hood. Karana often asked questions she already knew the answers to.

"I was able to get him to wait until 2:30."

"So about twenty minutes then?"

"Yeah, give or take." I looked at the floor. "You knew this was coming, how come you didn't tell me?"

"Because I knew you would have talked your way out of it if you had more time."

"Am I that predictable now?"

"No, but on this one you would have definitely rationalized, but don't do it. Be content with your decision." I wanted to say something clever, something lasting and absolving that she could hang onto in my absence, something that might lighten the air and let us part on a good note after days of not resolving our conflict, but she read my thoughts and stopped me before I could get a word out.

"Let's leave everything as it is o.k.," she continued. "We don't have the time and I do not want to pressure you to spit out a fabricated answer." She took off her light-blue coat and draped it over the couch. Her eyes returned from the furniture and found mine, which I am sure looked lost and confused, then instantly she moved her hazel lenses to the wall and proceeded to talk. She often used the tactic of casting off her gazes when trying to placate my concerns and I could never tell if she was being completely honest with her diverted eyes. I pondered her validity as she continued. "Hopefully this trip will bring you to a place where you feel comfortable enough to give me an honest answer, either way, no matter what the outcome. Take this time. Cosmo wants you to make this voyage. Though sending you off alone with him might not be the most intelligent thing in the world to do, for who knows what will happen while you spend that much time with Cosmo, but I know this is what you are supposed to be doing. And as I wanted to extend in my text message this morning, go and enjoy this time. You have been working non-stop. Your patterns are too repetitive as of late and I know that is killing you. Go and breathe the open air. Explore and say hello to the man you are, the man I love, the man I will be patiently waiting for when you return."

Still at a loss for words I pulled her into my chest and squeezed our bodies together. She smelled of fresh rain and sunk into my bones like a warm fire. I could not let go. Many days had passed since we held each other with such vigor and even with the lingering agitation between us she returned the embrace with equal strength. Perhaps it was the situation, perhaps her tone, perhaps I finally let myself feel vulnerable enough to release emotions that festered inside of me, but no matter what force orchestrated the moment my tear ducts opened up and liquid poured from my cheeks and mingled with her already damp hair. The sobs were uncontrollable and not related to any one particular thought. I loved her, I knew it, but could not understand in that perfect moment of complete exposure and comfort in her arms why I could not answer her directly. Why I side-stepped serious questions. Why could I not come to terms with the reality that there was not a better partner on the planet to share my life with? The questions seared my skin and brought streaming tears to a halt as I could no longer stand the ambivalent ogre that held onto such a precious creature.

I wiped my cheeks and separated from her. "You are amazing," I managed to say. "Not sure that I even deserve you."

"Don't say that," she said and took the sleeve of her sweatshirt to dry off the remaining moisture on my face. "That is an awful thing to say. That's like saying I'm a moron for wasting my time on a complete waste of time, which you know you are not. Just give me a kiss and promise you will be safe, and that you will come back to me."

I took my time and stared into her eyes; deep, understanding eyes which gave me their undivided attention. Classified as hazel on her driver's license her eye color always tricked me. Their chameleon act made me nervous when we first started dating, because I was afraid she would catch me off guard with the question of detailing her exact shade. With a bit of luck she mollified my fears at breakfast one morning three weeks after our first date. She picked up a slightly charred piece of bacon and took a bite while studying my face. "Your eyes can almost be called hazel like mine," she said. I almost choked on my orange juice while trying to respond. Most days I called them brown, other times gray, but staring into the depths of her irises before saying goodbye they seemed to emit a strong trace of green. The green flashed like the surface of the sea in dense coves off of Highway One in Big Sur and radiated a sense of invitation and warmth. A near jade set of alluring gems exuded serenity, a peace similar to one of those sublime coves, yet so much could hide beneath such dreamy beauty. From the exterior all appeared calm, but currents surged, predators roamed, cold impaled with white shark fangs, all elements churned under a soothing carapace. Whatever sea of emotions stabbed her guts in that embrace she left them tacit and reached for my lips concealing any internal commotion. The kiss was brief and lacked passion, but our wrapped bodies made up for its lack of zeal.

"I love you," was all I could get out. No promises of my safety, no oaths of returning cleansed and refreshed, just three hackneyed words re-used throughout modern history escaped into the stillness of our rented home and transformed the sea beneath her ribcage into a raging tempest.

I left Oceanside in a fog. I climbed into the Scout numb and unreflective about my charge off of the train. We crossed the Mexican border at 3:38 in the afternoon. Sporadic showers played hide and seek all the way from Oceanside to the crossing point at San Ysidro, with each downpour less brusque than the one before. Our gear remained dry underneath the protection of the hard top covering J.P.'s old International Scout while a fourteen foot Boston Whaler attached by trailer hitch and harness paddled along behind us open to the elements. The small, aluminum boat would slow our progress and limit the number of roads we could travel down along the way, but its purpose and accompaniment on the journey was set in stone as its destiny stood firm on the blue waters of the Pacific a few hundred miles south of the border.

The wait to get into Baja could take no time at all depending on what hour we crossed through it. Passing through before three P.M. on a Wednesday our lane piled up with only five cars in front of us, which made our total wait time about one minute and thirty seconds. The procedure for getting across was fairly simple. We pulled our vehicle over large, steel alligator teeth that came up from the ground and could probably rip the tracks off a D-9 tractor if we tried to reverse over them. Not that we could back up anyhow with the volume and speed of a parade of cars that lined up behind us. After crossing the jagged fangs a stop light with one red and one green light stood in front and to the left as a guard with his back to the vehicle and perched about six feet off the ground monitored the incoming swarms. If the light rang and shined green it would say "Pase" and on with our journey, but if the light rang and blared red we would have to pull over to the right hand side where teenagers and young men armed with M-16's checked through our belongings and asked questions about what items we brought into the country. Over many years of making the trek across the border I was only pulled over one time entering Mexico. The questions were brief, spoken solely in Spanish, and responses of "acampar" and "surfear" so near to the English versions registered with the young soldiers who waved me on with open grins and shoulder-strapped weapons. No such ordeal replayed itself as Cosmo and I received the green light and our caravan of truck and boat trailer jumped over the alligator teeth and welcomed the adventure of a new country.

We began the ascent up a steep, extended grade which lead to the Tijuana beaches and the toll road south through Rosarita and Ensenada and a sudden pang almost stopped my heart. I made a mistake. I never should have left. Karana told me to go, but I suddenly felt like it was only an act she was playing. She was not telling me just to go on the trip, but telling me to go for good in her own subtle way. Thoughts pestered me. I was my own ruin. Passing small houses littered with graffiti, iron bars, and stacked cinder-block I could hardly breathe. Rain ceased to fall for the time being and underneath my breath incantations flowed out requesting Cosmo to turn the truck around. He could not hear the muttering over "Against the Grain" by **Bad Religion**, but somehow he sensed the unease radiating from my rattled frame. He extended his right hand to the volume knob and lowered the music. Cosmo sang out as the volume decreased.

"What's up buddy, you all right?"

23

"Huh."

"You look a little peaked and that you might be mumbling to yourself over there or something."

"What are we doing Cosmo? What am I doing?"

"Driving into Baja and staying out of the rain."

"No I mean why am I in this vehicle with you. I have this sudden slap across a sunburn of guilt nearly suffocating me right now. Karana's face haunts the roadways as we travel along and I keep seeing her hidden displeasure as we said goodbye." I paused for a moment and licked my lips. They were not dry or in need of any attention, I was just stalling for what I really wanted to ask him. I could no longer hold it in. "Honestly Cosmo, no profound analogies or theories please, do you really need me to be here?"

No response followed while the Scout hummed around a large swooping curve towards the first toll booth. I could not tell, but the silence seemed to expel anger. The volume remained low on the stereo with only faint words decipherable on the continuing MP3 player. A white sign with blue lettering came into focus as we pulled into a toll booth lane behind a mid-nineties red Nissan Sentra. It was spotted with black flakes where paint peeled from its body and blew into the wind. Autos were 23.00 pesos or $2.30 U.S. according to the sign. Cosmo pulled some loose cash and a few coins out of his ashtray and wadded it up in his hand. The Nissan sputtered on and we pulled up to the window.

"Buenos tardes senor," Cosmo said forking over the money.

"Buenos tardes," the man replied. He wore a navy

blue jacket and a matching San Diego Padres hat. "Mucha lluvia hoy, no?" the man asked as he handed over a receipt.

"Si, mucha lluvia," Cosmo responded. He was right; there was a lot of rain that day. We drove through the toll and Cosmo veered over to the right next to the public restrooms. Adjoined to the restrooms sat a small store no bigger than a normal bedroom. Two young girls stood behind the register. I did not need to go to the bathroom, but I was getting hungry. I picked at some leftover pasta before Cosmo picked me up, but I had yet to eat a solid meal for the day. Sabritas potato chips sounded good, but since we were across the border and nearing dinnertime I felt like I could wait for some real food. Cosmo did not move or motion to unstrap his seatbelt and the Scout engine hummed along as the only noise to fill the void of silence besides the faint trace of music.

"I'm not going to beg you," Cosmo finally got out. "If you are going with me you are going on your own volition, but make a choice here and now. I'll go back to TJ and drop you off at a taxi station if you want out, but tell me now." He looked into the store as a plump, Mexican man entered. I thought for a second he might follow the gentleman and pick up something to munch on, but instead he waited for my response. I could not quite tell if he was upset or just being direct and honest. Whatever his emotion I suddenly felt like a frightened child on his first night sleeping over at a friends house. How pathetic he must have thought I was.

"Look, man, I know it took a lot for you to get

this far Dano. I mean your job, Karana, I know it was not easy and I appreciate the effort, but you have done the hard part. I want you on this journey, you know that or I would never have asked in the first place, but if it is just too much then let me know. I will think none the less of you."

Just as I faced the same words a few hours earlier in a rainy parking lot, he again would not think any less of me, but again how would I ever be able to live with myself after the fact. The confusion swelled. Was I going to lose Karana? What would I do for work if they did not take me back? I became faced with such an uncertain future that only one day before felt solid and definite. A rash decision, an escape from a stalled train and there I sat just south of Tijuana with everything I had been building for possibly lost forever. And to top it off he wanted a decision right then. The road back was so close. All it took was another escape from a Brown International Scout and I could go back and try to rectify my careless behavior.

"How long, seriously man, do you think this will take?"

"I know what you want, but I can't give it to you. I wish I could but I can't." He decreased the volume on the MP3 player to nothing and continued. "I need this to be a journey with no absolutes except for eventually reaching the ultimate destination. I know you would feel more comfortable with a timeline, but that's not what this trip is about. And like I said if that doesn't suffice, then I have no problem getting you somewhere where you can get a ride back home. But let me ask you this, how long have you been pent up in that office? How close are you and Karana to setting a date for your wedding? How are you feeling about your place in the world now that you are thirty? Sometimes we need walkabouts, my man, to cleanse our souls and give us a better perspective about this planet we live on. On the cusp of so many things in your life this might be a perfect opportunity for some of that perspective before you make so many life changing decisions."

I knew he was more right than I would let myself admit, but I wondered if he was trying to influence me. Cosmo could convince a mouse that it was a ferocious predator capable of slaying giant beasts when he set his mind to it. I felt I was the mouse and he was trying to convince me to jump into a battle that I was ill prepared for. I thought for a second and tried to pick out any over manipulations, but then it hit me. If Cosmo really wanted to persuade me to continue on he could have brought up J.P. The whole trip revolved around his memory after all. He could have used the obvious fact and inundated me with an overflow of guilt, but he did not. He never even mentioned J.P and I admired him so much for that.

The words mutated and formed in the stomach, but encountered trouble making it to the voice box. For some reason I felt selfish at the thought of agreeing, for seeking out my own pleasures while the life I left behind carried on and dealt with reality. Yet I made it that far, he was accurate about that being the most difficult part. Already across the border, leaving then would have meant that I quit after we already started. If that was the case I should have never got in the Scout in the first place. I silently prayed that I was just over thinking and Karana meant every word she said. Then I swallowed the useless uncertainty and apprehension buzzing in the air and turned to my friend.

"I could sure use a beer and some tacos about now," I said. He laughed and unbuckled his seatbelt.

"I got to take a leak first and then we'll grab some grinds."

"What did you have in mind?"

"Come on, you're disappointing me. You think we'd pass through without visiting Rina's."

I gently slapped my forehead. "Not sure how I let it slip my mind. I guess it has been too long. God I have not seen her in forever. She has to be getting up there in age by now."

"She never reveals her real age. You know that. I'll tell you what though; it does not look like that woman ages a bit."

"Does she still stock Bohemia's?"

"I'm sure she would run to the market and pick some up for you if they are out. You know she will take care of us. Maybe about twelve tequila shots for you as well stress boy."

"How about you go piss on your shoes smart ass."

"How about I just piss on you." Cosmo pretended to unzip his pants and then hit me in the shoulder. His play taps hurt because he left his middle knuckle slightly higher than the other knuckles so that on impact the blow furnished a textbook Charlie horse. He perfected the technique from years of his uncle J.P. practicing on him and while I rubbed the point of impact it struck me that J.P. would take the journey as charred ashes at the bottom of an urn instead of at the wheel cursing like a sailor. As Cosmo headed towards the bathroom I could not help but think of how much he missed his uncle. With a dad missing since the age of fourteen, the only person close to a father figure in his life no longer existed in physical form. A chill rumbled through my body, but I quickly warmed up to the fact that I made a decision to remain on the trip and that Rina's food already tasted hot and magnificent on my tongue.

Chapter 4

A hangover in Mexico is as common as waiting for an extended period of time at the border when returning home to the United States, which always happens, especially after getting into a bottle of tequila. The tongue stuck to the roof of the mouth and I felt as though I walked through an arid desert for three straight days without water. With a pounding head nothing sounded quenching, not water, not soda, not food, and I wailed like a sick sea lion wishing I could take back the last shot I for some reason felt was necessary to chug down when I was already over-polluted with liquid courage. The only cure that ever seemed to work with any consistency was going for a surf. It seemed impossible as a member of the living dead, but the saltwater, the fresh air, the coolness of the sea would enter my pores and go to war against the hangover as if the elements were T-cells fighting a virus. Cosmo and I were hurting and in need of the oceans healing powers the morning after our visit to Rina's.

Rina had fed Cosmo and I a hearty meal complete with fish tacos, rice, beans, guacamole, homemade salsa which burned my mouth and left a strong taste of cilantro on the tongue as it went down, and fresh albacore ceviche in lime juice. The food tasted as delicious as it had during my last visit two years prior. Cosmo and J.P. introduced me to Rina's restaurant and cantina on my first trip to Baja with them. It became a necessary stop on our way down the coast. The food, the company, the big screen televisions showcasing sporting events and boxing matches, as well as a blaring jukebox and on occasion talented local musicians that played their hearts out on Rina's little makeshift stage, not to mention the overall vibe which allowed us to feel right at home made Rina's all too enticing to pass up when heading into Baja.

She greeted us with her usual firm embrace when we entered the door. Our shoes made light tracks of water and mud on the mocha colored tile from the day's earlier rainstorm. The familiar odors of burnt tortillas and onions mixed with stale liquor and sawdust consumed my nostrils as we took a seat in a red-leather booth nearest to the bar. A barely visible sun nestled into the sea when we arrived and Cosmo immediately made arrangements with Rina about a place to stay for the night in the adjacent, quaint hotel she also operated.

With our food on the way we finished our first beer and went outside to pull the Scout around the corner to unload some of our gear into our room. When we returned to our booth we found a full bottle of tequila and a bowl of sliced limes placed on the table. Rina poured out free shots to her customers all the time and often left a bottle on the table for her regulars. She liked to sit down and sip on a shot or two as patrons told her of their latest adventures in life; like who was getting married, who was getting fat, who passed on to the afterlife, and always, always, she asked for any inside information on the Los Angeles Lakers. She listened intently like a grandmother and laughed with her entire body, limbs shook, breasts were in full motion, head tilted back, and in infectious shrills that reminded me of the high pitched yip of a coyote. Along with framed pictures on the walls in her cantina of bull-fighters and early nineteen hundreds photos of how Rosarito used to look before the rise of big hotels one could find posters of Kobe Bryant doing a reverse slam dunk, Magic Johnson kissing the NBA finals trophy in 1988 after a second consecutive championship, and Kareem performing his famous skyhook, along with various banners and pendants pertaining to the purple and gold. We told her that Kobe was holding up fine with his ruptured pinky finger and that the addition of Pao Gasol to the team would hopefully bring the Lakers another championship.

She scolded my absence. I blushed and apologized for my hiatus. She also told me that she would not let me in the door on my next visit if I did not bring Karana along with me. On my last trip down the two women met for the first time and they hit it off instantly. Rina had said Karana was the love of my life and that if I let her get away the possibility for love would elude me forever.

Rina thanked us for the visit and promised that we would be safe in her country. Tourism was down with all of the recent violence that made the news in the states. In our haste to leave I forgot about the mass murders and kidnappings that bombarded our newspapers. She blessed our journey and told us not to worry, because her people were beautiful and peaceful. I promised that Karana would be on the next voyage and I gave her a convincing hug, then we toasted to love, to life, and to a night without rain.

The shots flowed, Bohemia beers disappeared fast enough to avoid getting warm, and in the morning we paid for our over indulgence with raging headaches. We wanted to get an early start on the road, but in our condition we slept in later than we hoped. After spicy eggs, beans, and tortillas for breakfast, which I nearly regurgitated when I went to the bathroom to wash my hands, we finally got on the highway around nine in the morning. It was really my fault. Even when he felt awful Cosmo could rally and get himself going. He convinced his body that everything was fine and somehow managed to carry on like nothing in the world ailed him at all. He already packed up the Scout and ordered breakfast when I finally dragged myself out of bed to join him at the table. He sat quietly and read his book.

Cosmo read anything he could get his hands on. He dove into every genre. After testing out of high school a year early he continued his education in libraries around the world on his many surf trips. He asked professors for lists of their favorite books when we took classes together in college. His television rarely came on, and when it did it usually aired something from the History Channel, The Discovery Channel, or Animal Planet. He watched movies quite often, but could not tell you what sitcoms were on the air or which reality show belonged to which star. No matter how many books he took with him on a trip he always made sure to bring along a Hemingway novel as well. He did not always read it, but kept one with him just in case he needed to satisfy a feeling that came to him while on his travels. He was into the **Green Hills of Africa** at breakfast.

I had my head out of the passenger window imbibing the coastal air as we headed out of Rosarito en route to a break named Salsipuedes just north of Ensenada for a mid-morning surf when we left Rina's. The hangover brought on strange emotions. I felt regretful, though I did nothing wrong besides drink a little more than I should have. I also felt a longing for things I did not possess. A man that I wanted to be, but was no where near becoming. Then through the breeze J.P. came to mind. His smile, his laugh, his absence on our voyage weighed on my thoughts. After we exited the water a palpable void would encompass the scene. We would not find J.P. sucking down a beer and frothing at the mouth to critique our surfing.

"You do have arms don't you?" he would ask. "For god's sake swing those things around a bit. You look like the damn tin man in need of some oil. Don't you understand that rotating your arms, shoulders, and head leads the rest of your body into a complete turn? Loosen up. Looks like you are surfing with a stick up your ass," he always commented or said some version of the statement whenever he watched me flounder about in the ocean. The first sound of it often slapped me with a twinge of insult, but more times than not he hit the nail right on the head. He cured a few of my mechanical glitches over the years. I learned to place my front foot at more of an angle and slide it towards the inside of my board while riding with my back to a crashing wall of water. He also loathed my proclivity to race out of the pocket and get too far ahead of a wave. I could always hear him screaming in my head to slow down and stay locked in the meatier sections of moving water to maximize my talent.

The first time we met he called me a pansy-ass. I sat in Angelo's fast food restaurant at the south end of Oceanside biting into a large cheeseburger when I heard a deep voice shout out my name. "Is there some pansy-ass named Dane in here?" a large man with a thick, black mustache roared out. In the middle of a bite I could not speak right away and the man started towards the door. I swallowed my food and squeaked out that my name was Dane much the way a shy student would speak on the first day of school when a teacher mispronounced their name. He tromped in my direction with a determined look on his face and sat down at my table. He looked angry, but in control, and I could not tell if he wanted to kick my ass or tell me if someone in my family had just died. The six foot and four inch frame took a seat between me and the door. I could not escape him. I could not figure out what I had done. His hair coiled at the ends into slight curls and his tanned, almost red cheeks burned underneath the halogen lights.

"So you ready to go there buddy?"

"Sir?"

"Don't call me sir smart ass. Damn I love the

onion rings here." He dipped two monster size rings into my pool of ketchup and chomped them down without asking for permission. A bit of red sauce stuck to his mustache. He grabbed a few more rings and I wanted to tell him to leave, but his presence intimidated me. I decided to wait and let him explain why he stole my food and unsettled my nerves when I did not even know who he was. He belched and looked out the window. "Are you going to finish that burger or not? It's time to get on the road."

"Huh?"

"Huh nothing, on the road. Cosmo got tied up and told me to come get you. He will meet up with us down in Rosarito."

"What?"

"Gee you have a lot of words in that vocabulary. What, huh, sir must be teaching you all kinds of complex theories out at that college of yours."

"Excuse me?"

"There we go two words at a time not bad. I'm uncle J.P. And don't take anything I say personal; I'm just messing with you." Cosmo and I became friends only a few months before that first meeting with J.P. It took days of rationalizing to finally agree to head into Mexico with him, but he never said anything about a crazy uncle. Common sense told me to bolt for the door while I took another bite of my burger and thought about what kind of lunacy I let myself fall into. J.P. sensed the tension and bellowed out a full laugh. His dimples sucked into his cheeks and the gruffness disappeared.

"Don't worry I'm not going to eat you. I'm going

to hang with you guys for a few days on your trip and when you turn around for home I'm going to go a bit further down to my favorite place in the world. Ever hear of La Escondida?"

I took a breath and felt relived. "Cosmo mentioned it once, but I've never been there."

"Well maybe on the next trip you can sneak away for a few extra days to come check it out."

"Yeah, that sounds cool."

"Good. Grab the rest of that burger and let's go." I threw my trash away and took two large bites to finish off my burger. J.P. grabbed my bag off of the ground and I watched him limp towards my surfboard. I did not notice the uneven walk on his way in, I was too nervous, but in a relaxed state I caught sight of his debilitated movement and rushed to get my board before he tried to carry them both. It was hard to tell which leg he favored more, but it appeared as though the right leg received a bit more coddling. I offered to take the bag, but he glared at me. The message came out very clear; he despised pity and unnecessary help.

We loaded my board into the Scout and started down the road. "This here is my Baja-mobile. It will go anywhere. I got that little boat attached which might give us some trouble, but not too much. What do you think?"

"I like it."

"I act like a hard ass sometimes, just my personality. Got to make sure you are alright though. But what the hell do I know. Cosmo thinks highly of you and that's good enough in my book. He has a great judge of character, way the hell better than I do. You should have seen some of the outright bastards and straight bitches of women I have hung around with in my day. Don't know what I'm thinking sometimes." He paused and shifted into fifth gear as we gained speed on the freeway. "Anyway I would have thought you were a lame-ass, weenie from the looks of you."

"Well, umm."

"Just screwing with you again, gees. Loosen up Dane. You can't be a worried, mister stick up your ass in my car." I laughed. It was a true laugh; the guy struck me as hilarious once I got over being intimidated by him. "Can you do me a favor there Dane?"

"Yeah sure."

"Climb back there and get into the cooler for me would you." I made my way to the back seat and peered into the rear hatch area. Underneath the cooler lid rested a full bed of ice filled to the top rim.

"What am I looking for in here?"

"Should be a few quarts of beer in there. Pull one of them out."

I dug through the ice and found a thirty-two ounce bottle of Coors beer. The lid slammed down and I navigated my way back to the front seat. J.P. opened the center console and pulled out two plastic cups and a bottle opener as we glided down highway 5. "Shouldn't we wait until after the border to open this up," I asked.

"Nah, don't worry about it. No one is going to fuck with me. Open it up and pour it out."

"Will the whole thing fit your cup?"

"What do you think I got two cups out for? So

you could stare at an empty cup while I indulged myself?"

"Well I didn't want to assume."

"Look this is the way to roll into Baja. Besides that much beer would get warm way too fast drinking it on my own. Split that bottle up. Stop being such a pansy-ass," he said and we both laughed. I did as I was told and stuck the empty bottle underneath my seat after handing J.P. his cup. We sipped the icy beverage and charged into the dark. I felt invincible with J.P. at the helm and believed his bold statement that nothing would meddle with us on our adventure. He sounded convincing in the way a super-hero would claim to be on the way to save the day, only he was more of anti-hero figure than the likes of Superman or Spiderman. We made it to Rina's in good spirits after we finished off a second bottle and steered our way over to the bar. His limp made him tough and approachable at the same time. Rina ran up to him and they started to dance. The bartender yelled his name and carried out the P like a soccer announcer would scream the word goal after a score. He was a rock star without the posse. The locals smiled and visitors snuck in and struck up conversations with him while we waited for Cosmo to arrive. That was my very first impression of him. A lion, yet a teddy bear, respected, and well-liked.

My head out the window ten years later and I felt as though I had lost my own uncle. Cosmo had not revealed the entire details of his passing. I restrained from asking, but I did want to know. I also knew that it might be too painful, too soon for Cosmo to discuss the whole ordeal. He found him. Found him cold and dead. He called 911. He took care of all of the paperwork. He called family members and friends. It was all so close, all so much. I knew J.P. suffered from heart problems and arthritis. I also knew he drank heavily and occasionally dabbled in hallucinogenic drugs. The whispers passed through the funeral. "It was a heart attack. It was an overdose," but nobody knew for sure. Cosmo kept the facts to himself. He told everyone that J.P., which stood for John Paul, needed to rest and that his tired body could go on no longer. I let it stay a mystery and did not prod him any further even though I knew there was much more to tell.

We exited the toll road at the Salsipuedes turnoff and pulled onto a windy dirt road. The bumps did not sit well with my hangover. We paid five dollars to surf for the day and parked on the bluff. The high cliffs surrounding the bay kept the wind from affecting the waves and we took in a view of near sheet glass. My skin embraced the sun and appreciated its presence after the last few days of rain and cloudy skies. The dissipated storm left behind a decent swell in the water. Cosmo tracked the swell before we left and said we might get lucky and follow it down the coast, because it emanated from the northwest. I sensed that I would be challenged by the surf, by Cosmo, by my own demons, but a peace came with that sense. I would face those challenges. I had to; I was left with no other choice.

Cosmo brought an urn out of the Scout and set it on the hood. It stood about fourteen inches tall and bulged out in the center like a Buddha belly. The urn looked blue in the car, but when exposed to the sun it took on more of a grayish hue. J.P. kept a kiln in the basement of his apartment. Every so often when the urge overcame him he spent hours throwing clay and creating various pieces of ceramic art. He displayed a raw talent for the craft. He never refined his visions, his creative trinkets, and let them stay in primal form straight out of a moment of inspiration complete with defects and minute flaws. He gave most of his artwork away as gifts for birthday's, wedding's, or during Christmastime. The particular urn Cosmo chose to serve as the vessel to carry J.P.'s ashes was a favorite of Cosmo's. J.P. made it the day Cosmo was born. He wanted to give it to Cosmo's mother and father as a gift for bringing a child into the world, but decided against it because he was not satisfied with his work, but it was not a bad piece for the fourteen year old J.P. that created it. The urn came out slightly oblong with a tiny crater caved in it near the base and so he decided to keep it for himself. After Cosmo heard the tale of its creation he asked J.P. if he could have the urn one day. In typical J.P. fashion he told him, "Maybe when I'm dead." The urn, the aluminum boat, and an old cowboy hat were the only things Cosmo wanted out of J.P.s belongings. He took them without asking, but no one argued against the deed, everyone knew J.P. would have wanted it that way.

After he changed into his wetsuit Cosmo grabbed his board under his left arm and a small bit of ashes in his right hand. He headed down the cliff and I followed closely behind him. Cosmo waded up to his chest and dropped his head. The tide was high and rose close to the base of the cliff. The rocky beach rumbled as water drained back into the sea. Cosmo did not say anything out loud and let the ashes fall. They floated on the surface for a few seconds until encroaching white wash dunked them below the surface. He looked back at the cliff, down its contours and jagged shapes, and then caught sight of me. He gave a smile that looked half happy and half relived then jumped on his board and headed towards the surf. It was not much of a ceremony, but the grand finale would not commence until we reached La Escondida, a place dear to J.P.'s heart. Cosmo just wanted J.P. to surf with us the whole way down.

The waves were a bit lumpy and took some effort on our part to make it through the soft sections, but they crested in the chest high range and we surfed with only one other guy in the water. He sat well outside of the lineup and I only remember him catching two waves during the session. Cosmo was in his usual, incredible form. It never mattered if it was his first wave after a raging hangover or his fiftieth wave in a marathon session, Cosmo always made surfing look almost too smooth, too soulful, and that it was as easy as getting out of bed in the morning. His first two turns neared the ridiculous as water exploded off the back of a shoulder high right while he flew down the line. I shook my head in appreciation and turned around for a wave of my own. J.P. was there, I felt it. Felt him laughing at me as I fell on my first wave while trying to emulate Cosmo with a gouging turn. "Get that stick out of your ass," I heard echoing in my ears as clear as the glassy water that sparkled before me.

Chapter 5

Ensenada resided twenty minutes south of Salsipuedes. The town was known as the third largest
city in the state of Baja California. A home to a large
harbor which accommodated a wealth of cruise ships
and fishing fleets, the city also thrived on a regular
flow of tourism. Ensenada was founded in 1542 by
a Portuguese navigator named Don Juan Rodriguez.
For many years it remained a small fishing village,
but being the home of the only deep water port in
all of Baja it became a part of standard shipping
routes that linked the town directly to major cities
in Mexico as well as ports in the United States and
Asia. The town grew. Popular cantinas sprang up and
became well known around the world. Hussong's and
Papas and Beer stood out as the most renowned bars
in the city and their bumper stickers and tee-shirts
could be spotted all over the globe. From high class
seafood dining to street tacos on a corner at all hours
of the night, Ensenada catered to a variety of travelers. The town also served as the last major city on
the map before heading deep into the unpopulated

terrain of Baja California. After Ensenada shopping markets decreased in size as did the ability to get a hold of a wide assortment of items. When planning a long journey into the deserted coastlines and dry landscapes it was always a good idea to stock up on any supplies that might be hard to come by further on down the road.

Highway 1 stretched down the length of the state and ended in the town of Cabo San Lucas at the southern most point of the peninsula. A trip all the way down Baja would narrowly surpass one thousand miles from the border city of Tijuana to the tourist rich Cabo San Lucas which thrived on the blending of the rugged Pacific Ocean and the clear blues emitted from the Sea Of Cortez. An abundance of surfers and fisherman make the journey throughout their lives. In many ways the trek beckoned much like a pilgrimage or a right of passage. Narrow, pothole infested roads wind through arid deserts and rolling hills. Once south of Ensenada, veering off of Highway 1 would almost always lead to a poorly maintained dirt road. An ample amount of these so called roads rattled like washboards and contained large ruts, which made driving down steep declines quite risky when searching for waves or an empty inlet to fish. We blazed off the majority of our miles on Highway 1, but our real adventures began when heading off road.

Even more than paying a visit to Rina's bar and Cantina Cosmo loved to arrive in Ensenada. He spent almost half of his life across the border and much of that time occurred in the friendly confines of Ensenada. His eccentric grandfather fell in love with the town in the late sixties and purchased a modest vacation home at the south end of the city. From the time of his birth Cosmo traveled across the border with his parents and a wide variety of relatives at any opportunity that presented itself. A short, two hour drive and suddenly he became immersed in another country, a different language, and a relaxed, simplified lifestyle that ran polar opposite to the rushed pace of scurrying back and forth between school, surf contests, baseball practice, and all of the events a popular child attempted to attend. The home did not possess much monetary value, but it meant the world to Cosmo. It became his home away from home. The house did not contain a television and the electricity and water ran intermittently at best. His family often cooked dinner over open fires and played games by candlelight when the electricity failed. He read books, walked to the beach and surfed alone, and picked up the Spanish language with a fluent tongue.

Cosmo was fifteen when his grandfather passed away. His mother and uncle J.P. fought to keep the home instead of selling it off and splitting up the money. They succeeded at keeping their remaining siblings at bay for a number of years. Cosmo's Uncle James moved to Washington and his Aunt Diane lived in Colorado which made the home in Ensenada obsolete for the both of them. Cosmo's mother, Madeline, knew she could not keep them off of her back forever and she tried to convince her kin that Cosmo needed the escape to Ensenada more than ever after her divorce to Cosmo's father and the news that he had wound up in prison shortly after the split. Though not entirely won over, Diane and James conceded to the pleas of their sister for the time being.

The home acted as a refuge, another world, an inviting dreamland where Cosmo erased the absence of his incarcerated father. He could be anybody or nobody, and he relished in the anonymity of creating a new version of himself upon each visit. As soon as Cosmo received his driver's license he began taking his own voyages to his favorite town. By the time he turned nineteen he figured out all of the ins and outs of the local nightlife. He knew which bars to hit up at the most opportune times. He knew where to find the prime happy hour locations, the best spots to dance, the cheapest drinks in town, and where to mingle with the most beautiful women. He also became localized at the popular surf spots on the north end of town.

At twenty-three years of age his family sold the house. An ongoing battle against increased vandalism and crime in the neighborhood drove everyone in the family away from visiting the casa, even uncle J.P., with the lone exception to the rule being Cosmo. I made trips with him as often as we could in the last few months of ownership. We would depart on a moments notice, sometimes in the middle of the night. After hitting up the local bars upon our arrival we would retire to the comforting tiled floors of the casa de Ensenada.

As difficult as it was, he finally accepted reality on our last journey on a Friday night in late September. All of the windows on the back patio, even through the black, iron bars that protected them were smashed in. The locks on the security door were compromised to the point that his keys did not work. We entered the house through the living room window where deft vandals removed two iron bars and were welcomed by a pungent odor of stale urine and rotted food. We found holes kicked into the walls, graffiti written in splattered messes with household cleaners out of the supply closet, the book case thrown to the ground, silverware scattered across the floor, counter tops ripped from the kitchen, and ashes from a fire on the living room tile. The family never left anything of value inside of the house, but looters came looking anyway. Cosmo kicked a few things around, spat out frustrated curses to the familiar walls of his youth, and we left, never stepping foot inside the house again. The loss did not dissuade Cosmo from the love of the town, however, and he illuminated into an excited child whenever he rounded the last bend and the large ships of the harbor came into view.

We surfed for three and a half hours at Salsipuedes and made it into Ensenada for a late lunch. We ate at Cosmo's favorite taco stand around the corner from Hussong's. I went to the restroom while Cosmo ordered for the both of us. An ice cold Corona and a plate of tacos sat on the bar upon my return. My first bite came across the taste buds with a bite of onions, heat from a blended salsa, and a sweet tasting meat.

"Mmm, this is good. What is it, carnitas," I asked.

"Nope, not carnitas."

"What then, because I know it's not chicken?"

"It's sesos."

"Sesos, what's that," I asked taking another bite, "I've never had sesos before."

"Sesos are good eating. You like them then?"

"Hell yeah they are delicious. Why are they so sweet?"

"Because, sesos means brains, you are eating a brain taco. A very rich meat."

I dropped the taco immediately. Our surf session cured my hangover from the night before, but instantly my stomach turned flips once again. "Please tell me you are not serious."

"Totally serious. What's the big deal? You said yourself that they were delicious. I think they are, look." Cosmo opened up the taco and revealed bits of brain then quickly closed it up and took a large bite. "See, no big deal. I thought you liked them."

"That's before I knew I was eating cow brains. I feel like I'm going to puke." Cosmo laughed and the cook behind the bar chimed in. The chef wore a dirty apron and a hefty beer belly. His smile displayed a missing tooth on the top row and a spotted mustache draped down towards his chin.

"El esta infermo?" the chef asked.

"Si," Cosmo returned.

"Antes or despues?"

"Despues Oscar," Cosmo responded and the two laughed again.

"I know he asked if I felt sick, but what else did he say?"

"He asked if it was before or after you knew."

"Why. What's the difference?"

"It's a huge difference. Finish your food."

"I'm not going to eat that."

"Don't worry the other tacos are just carne asada. Eat up."

"I don't know if I can." I inspected the rest of the tacos and the meat looked much like the typical carne asada I grew accustomed to eating. My stomach danced to an unbalanced rhythm and I tried to appease it with a long swig from my beer. I got to the bottom of the bottle and ordered another one. Cosmo giggled during his meal and it bothered me, because I knew I overreacted. The taco did taste wonderful before he exposed the contents to me. My mind told my stomach otherwise once the word brains shot from his mouth. How did that happen? It tasted the same before and after the revealing of its identity, but the information stored in my brain changed the very taste because pre-disposed knowledge alleged that the taco should have tasted disgusting. I no longer wanted to be subjugated by such petty rationalization. I walked out of my job, perhaps my life, and I needed to stop drowning in seas of apprehension. I picked up the half eaten taco and held it in the air for Cosmo and Oscar to see. With my free hand I took a drink from the fresh Corona then bit down. I cleared the trash, the pre-determined outcome, and tried to savor the unique flavor of the meat. Cosmo and Oscar both cheered.

"How is it the second time around," Cosmo asked.

"I would not call it my favorite, but it's not bad."

"Well alright. You want to try lengua next. Tongue tacos?

"No thanks, I think I will stick to this for now." We all laughed and Cosmo and I finished our meals. At about three in the afternoon we paid our tab. Cosmo suggested we stay the night and cruise the town for some fun. I argued at first, but I knew it would go nowhere. Cosmo needed at least one night in the town that brought him of age. I enjoyed Ensenada almost as much as Cosmo, but we were already on our second day of the trip and in that time we had only eclipsed a grand total of seventy miles south of the border. At that pace our journey felt like it would take an entire year and J.P. would never find his rest in the sea.

We checked into the Tortuga hotel and got cleaned up. The attendant at the desk gave us each a complimentary beverage ticket when we paid for our room which made our first stop for the night the hotel bar. The quaint bar room contained only the bartender and one elderly gentleman who smoked a cigarette and quietly watched a soccer match. Cosmo ordered a Negro Modelo with a shot of Patron tequila and I stuck with a Corona. The bartender introduced himself as Carlos and he spoke excellent English. He attended a technical college on the hill just north of Ensenada and planned on becoming an engineer. He loved American women, especially blonde's, and divulged into a few of his success stories he experienced with frisky tourist's. "They love me cos I am tall, dark, and handsome," he said with a laugh. "Well I'm no very tall, but es better. I'm closer to their chi-chi's." He told us that club Banana would be our best bet on a Thursday night. He also said to mention his name to the doorman Marcos, because they had been friends since grade school. Cosmo tipped him well and on our way out of the door he informed us that we might see him later at the club because his shift ended at ten.

We hit the streets and aimed straight for Hussong's. It felt odd wearing jeans and a sweatshirt to fend off the cold. Nearly every visit to Ensenada in my life occurred during the span from late spring to early fall and the usual attire consisted of shorts, tee-shirts, and sandals, and although it was almost spring a sharp chill ran through the air. The extra layers made Hussong's stuffier than normal. Cosmo looked exactly like J.P. as he parted the hordes of people standing around the bar to order us a round of beers. In any establishment, no matter how large the crowd, J.P. used to make his way right up front and grab the attention of the barkeep immediately. Cosmo followed J.P.'s example and within a few minutes we plowed through our first beer. A foul odor, perhaps of cracked sewer pipes or from festering alcohol spilled from intoxicated hands, funneled through the sawdust floors and timbering voices while we pondered ordering round two. Cosmo could elbow his way through the wall of people that grew larger by the minute to purchase another round, but we decided to move on. I wanted something quiet; Cosmo wanted to rage on.

We decided to stop at Tony's. Cosmo gave a high-five to the doorman when we entered through beaded curtains. The drummer for the band at Tony's also posed as a deejay between sets and the dance floor swayed to his latest selection. A short waiter with a lazy, right eye and a large smile led us to a semi-circular booth. He wore a black vest over a white shirt accompanied with a bow-tie and a waist apron. He appeared drunk when he spoke, but took down our order with great determination. The waiter returned before we settled into our seats and set down two Corona's and two shots of clear tequila.

"Tequila es on the house amigos," our waiter said. Tony's handed out free shots with the first round of drinks. I pushed mine aside while Cosmo gave me a scowl.

"What's the matter with you?" Cosmo asked.

"Nothing, I just don't feel like tequila again tonight that's all."

"You are on vacation remember. What the hell do you have to do tomorrow?"

"We have to get on the road. Down south, remember?"

"And we will, no doubt about that. Let's have some fun in the meantime."

"I am having fun."

"Well I'm not taking a shot of this shitty tequila alone."

"So don't take it then."

"Really, you are not going to have one with me?"

"Really."

"And waste this wonderful concoction just before Fernando is ready to come back on stage."

"Don't go there, leave Fernando out of this." Fernando was the lead guitarist for the band at Tony's. He took care of us whenever we came in. He made sure our servers kept the beers flowing and often dedicated songs to our table. Fernando would learn the names of each person in our party and screamed every name out loud before he roared into a song. He played a mean solo on "Hotel California." We thought the world of him.

"Come on, for Fernando."

"You suck. How can I say no now?"

"Feranaaaaaaaaaaaaaaaando," we yelled and slammed down the barely tolerable liquid. Cosmo got up with his beer and cruised around the establishment. He often followed a similar routine on a night out. He would wander around with no real destination in mind except to seek out what the night had to offer. Fernando and the band returned to the stage and rolled right into a song that brought the locals to the dance floor. Halfway through the first song we made eye contact and I raised my beer to him. He grinned and yelled an "aye aye Dane" into his microphone. I pointed to Cosmo on his walkabout and Fernando screamed out his name. The tequila worked on my senses and the urge to dance swept over me. Our lazy eyed waiter dropped off another beer as the band jammed on. Cosmo disappeared for twenty minutes and finally resurfaced on the dance floor with a gorgeous brunette. She appeared in her early twenties and wore eyes ready to search for the stars. She and Cosmo floated in that direction.

After the song ended the two dancers came over to my booth. The woman waved across the room and two good looking women picked up their drinks and sat down with us. Cosmo introduced his dance partner as Celeste and the other two went by Jennifer and Stacy. The girls arrived that day from a town just outside of Tempe. All three of them attended Arizona State University which celebrated a spring break the following week. They planned on staying in Ensenada through the weekend and making their way back to Rosarito on Monday to kick off Spring break with a mass of raging students. "Getting started on your spring break a little early," I asked.

Celeste did not hear the question due to her rapture of Cosmo. Stacy looked a little uncomfortable and constantly shuffled in her seat, but Jennifer answered with a kind, polite voice of sincerity.

"Yeah we are. We wanted to get in as many days as possible to let our hair down. We finished our mid-terms yesterday and got on the road early this morning." She smiled and revealed the whiteness of her teeth. Her skin emitted a faint trace of pale that could quickly tan in just a few hours of sun. I hoped the weather would clear for her.

"Ever been here before?" I asked.

"No, none of us. We always go to Rosarito, and that is where we are headed on Monday, but I convinced the girls we should try something new. I always wanted to check it out down here."

"How do you like it so far?"

"Not bad, a lot more locals out and about than in Rosarito, but it's refreshing. It's nice to go to another country and feel like you're actually in another country. In Rosarito it often feels like you never even crossed the border."

"I know what you mean." Fernando screamed out our names and led into a new song. Celeste wanted to dance again and pulled Cosmo from his seat. Stacy glanced off in various directions and looked for somebody more interesting to walk through the door. Jennifer's auburn hair ran straight and long. She raked it back as if to tie it up in a ponytail then let it spill on her shoulders. She did not jump out as drop dead gorgeous at first glance, almost coming across like a fuzzy photograph, but as she spoke and her honest laugh exuded over Fernando's guitar her attractiveness came into focus. She was beautiful and an unfamiliar urge inside of me wanted to pull her on to the dance floor. Jennifer began moving in her seat to the music and then elbowed Stacy in the ribs as if to tell her to loosen up. The spinning disco ball switched from silver lights into streaming rainbows.

We watched Cosmo and Celeste on the dance floor. Jennifer gave out a scream as they twirled to the music. "He can move."

"Yeah, he definitely knows how to let go."

"Is his name really Cosmo?"

"Yes and no."

"How do you mean."

"Well, his middle name was supposed to be Cosmo. Somehow on his original birth certificate they mixed up his first name with his middle name and instead of Jason Cosmo, he became Cosmo Jason Sawyer. His parents decided that the error was some type of sign and left it as it was."

"Interesting. And your name is Dane, right?" Jennifer asked.

"Yes it is."

"And where did your parents get that name from?"

A laugh erupted from my chest that I could not corral. "What's so funny," Jennifer asked.

"Nothing, not many people ask about my name, that's all. My parents went to Europe on their honeymoon. They went all over the place. Italy, Spain, Greece, France, but they absolutely adored the citizens of Denmark. They claim the Danish are the warmest and friendliest people they could have ever hoped to meet. I guess they wished for those same characteristics to exude out of their son and branded me with the name Dane."

"Well I think they definitely screwed that one up," she said. I agreed with a wide grin and she burst out laughing. I chimed in with her. Stacy smiled and I thought she might actually join in on the conversation, but I realized her joy emanated from a group of good looking men who entered the bar through the beaded curtains. The four men, most likely in their late twenties, were seated across the dance floor from our booth. They appeared established in some type of successful life back in the states, brokers, bankers, salesman, lawyers, I could not tell, but they definitely seemed to be enjoying themselves. Stacy batted her eyes and scooted as far away from Jennifer and me as she possibly could without falling off the end of the padded seat at our booth. Fernando screamed, Cosmo followed with a howl, and then Cosmo and Celeste returned to our group. Celeste needed to use the restroom and motioned for her girlfriends to follow her to the ladies room at the far end of the bar.

"A woman's duty," Jennifer stated and stood up to join her friends. She gave me a glowing smile and turned towards the restroom. Cosmo signaled our waiter to bring a round of drinks to the table and inched closer to me.

"You having fun now, brother?" Cosmo screamed as he leaned on my shoulder.

"Yes I am. That Celeste is very hot. It's amazing how the gorgeous ones always fall blindly towards your ugly ass."

"The curse my brotha, the curse. But hey, that Jennifer is smoking hot her damn self. She is fully into you. I can sense it."

"She is pretty, damn cute. And a tad sarcastic, I like that."

"Well then, what do you think?"

"What do you mean, what do I think. I'm engaged remember."

"Yeah, but I can sense a strong connection between the two of you."

"Oh yeah, and can you also sense the ring on Karana's finger? The promise and devotion I declared to her. Can you sense that Mr. I will see where the night takes me?" I finished the last of my beer and stared at Fernando and the band wailing away on a song I would never know the name of. The keyboardist went through the motions, but the bass player and the drummer displayed an effusion of joy as they throttled away at their instruments. I could play a few chords on the guitar, nothing profound or complex, but I enjoyed the feel of strings and wood in my hands. Watching the band I could not deny the envy that brewed in my belly at their ability to guide an instrument through the melodies of pleasing music. To make a guitar sing, to make the drums pound a rhythm that made everyone want to move their hips, to navigate the veins and arteries of an instrument with such command that my soul, my entire existence, would release their innermost secrets through the striking of improvised chords. As much as Cosmo attempted to turn my thoughts elsewhere I wanted to think about nothing but the band and the pulsing music.

I hoped he dropped the topic during my fascination with the flowing sounds, but to my dismay he had only just begun. "I respect the ring and the promise man; I do, but come on now. Where are we, what are we, what is the night? You are not married yet. Technically you are a single man in a foreign country enjoying the night before him. Nothing wrong with that. Nothing wrong with taking this moment as it comes. She digs you and I can tell that you dig her. That's perfectly fine."

"What is fine, oh wise one?"

"Shut up ass clown. It's fine for you to take advantage of tonight. Karana will never know and never needs to know. It's a man deciding if he is taking the proper steps towards his future. One last night of passion to get out of his system. To let him know if he is making the right decision to choose one woman for the rest of his life, that's it and that's all. Tonight is right now, marriage is for the rest of your life."

"So it is."

"So it is. And I still can't believe that you want to go through with it."

"Why do you have to say shit like that?"

"You know why, because of how against marriage

I am. Sorry, but I have to be real. It's the death of the self. You end up ruining each other. Everything you wished and hoped and dreamed for becomes this blur of bullshit and a coalesced, imaginary common goal. In reality though it has nothing to do with a common goal, nothing at all." Our lazy eyed waiter set down drinks for five, did a half bow, and stumbled towards the four gentlemen that caught Stacy's eye. "All you end up doing is sacrificing and doing things you would have no interest in doing in a thousand years," he continued, "and the only reason you do them is because you are married. You have a certificate and license, big whooping deal. Marriage is for people who do not know what else to do. They have some fun as young adults, they experience a bit, then they get to thinking, hmmmm everyone gets married about now, I guess that's what I should do, and they do it. Not because they truly believe in their hearts that they should, but because they think that is what society requires them to do. That at some point everyone has to do it or their life is not complete. Who cares if love is not involved really, just get married because that is what you are supposed to do."

Cosmo took a large swig from his fresh beer. The girls still had not returned from the bathroom. I wished for them to come back so I did not have to respond to Cosmo's long winded diatribe. He brought up many valid points to prove his hypothesis, but he did not convince me to acquiesce to his bitter argument. My parents still shared the same bed. Their love for each other often embarrassed me as it still carried the original spark that ignited the day they shared their vows on the cliffs of Torrey Pines. I knew pure and true love existed. I also knew it was rare. Though I was an idiot, Karana was my rare love; Cosmo could not talk me out of that, no matter how tauntingly Jennifer's slim figure flirted with my senses.

"I need to ask you something. Something very personal as a friend I trust, though sometimes I'm not sure why I do."

Cosmo laughed, "O.k., shoot."

"How can you vomit all of this on me? You introduced Karana and I. You have witnessed our blossoming relationship. You have treated her like a sister, before, and after our courtship of one another. How can you tell me now that it is alright to cheat on her, to sew my royal oats as they say, while you have been one of her biggest supporters?"

Cosmo imbibed his drink and looked towards the band. He knew the girls would return any minute and wasted no time with an answer. "I say these things to protect the both of you. I love the both of you. I don't want to see you destroy one another. It happens man. Love gets ugly. The people you were, the dreams you wanted to achieve, you will at some point begin to blame each other for your combined shortcomings. It happens, it happens all the time. Your flicker for changing the world and striving to make a difference will morph into what color paint goes best in the bathroom or what kind of kind of wine perfectly accentuates a fish dinner. You won't be able to help it in your kindness for one another. You will let each day pass into the next and then wake up at fifty years of age asking, where the hell did the last twenty years go? I don't want to see that for either of you, I like you both too much."

I took offense even though I should not have. When he drank his brutal honesty grew more intense. He often drifted into semi-stream of conscious soliloquies like an activist poet shouting at a rally when liquor flowed through his veins and before he could take a second to realize what effect his words were inflicting on his ill prepared victims his verbal barrage already impaled a deep wound. I witnessed people reduced to tears or ready to rip his head off after one of his rants on more than one occasion. Yet, no matter what, even when drinking, Cosmo always managed to keep his cool. He never took any of the insults thrown back at him personally and he did his best to console those he brought to the point of weeping. I was not about to let him get the best of me and fired right back at him. "And I suppose you know all of this from your grand experience. From your endless revolving door of one night stands and perhaps, if lucky, a few three week long passion filled romances. You say all of this because you are afraid, scared to truly put your heart in someone else's hands. Preach on Cosmo, preach on, but I don't agree with you."

He smiled. I could tell he enjoyed the battle of words. It took a few years to understand this about Cosmo, to realize that during his rants what he wanted more than anything was for someone to return fire with a clear head. He pined for intelligent discussion and would argue in opposition of a topic just to keep a conversation going even if he believed in the exact opposite of what he was arguing for. I could not tell if he was playing devil's advocate as the band wailed on, partly because of his conviction, and partly because of our indulgent alcohol intake. My head swam and the weightlessness of intoxication distorted my sense of reality. He continued, "Maybe I'm wrong. Maybe you are right and I'm afraid. Maybe you have it all figured out and I'm just a Bedouin Shepherd roaming the globe in search of an invisible flock. But what do we really have in this life Dane? What do we actually have at our disposal? It's just this moment, man. That's all. It could all end tomorrow. Not to sound morbid, but it's the truth. We might get sideswiped by a trucker who falls asleep at the wheel tomorrow on one of those scary-ass roads south of Ensenada. Then what, what did we waste? What opportunity passed us by? This moment, this breath, this instant is all we have, take advantage of what is before you."

My beer lost its flavor. The girls made their way towards our booth. Celeste bounced along to a song that sounded reminiscent of a Mexican Polka. The four men of Stacy's desire ogled the women as they walked by. One of the men yelled in their direction and Stacy stopped to hear him out. She grabbed Jennifer by the arm and inched within earshot as Celeste dreamily floated by. A strand of hair fell across Jennifer's face while she waved to our table. Cosmo and I both waved back and he elbowed me in the ribs.

"Last chance Dane. Those guys seem pretty interested."

"Do you really believe that marriage doesn't work, ever?"

Cosmo laughed faintly with his tongue curled

onto his teeth. "Oh man, I have your head all screwed up don't I?"

"So what, are you saying that you are just trying to get a rise out of me?"

"I am only saying that it's stuff you should think about before you take the plunge and decide once and for all to ruin each other's lives. Two people who have so much potential to offer the world, but will bury that potential in the fallibility of actually trying to please each other for the betterment of marriage. What a farce that is. No one on this planet can even please themselves and we have the audacity to think we can combine two lives and somehow it will all make sense. Good luck pal."

I fought conflicting urges that enticed me to smash in his nose with a pummeling right hand and watch the blood ooze down his face or to heed his advice and walk over to Jennifer and sweep her off her feet. Stacy sat down near the man who yelled out to her, but Jennifer remained standing. She leaned on the booth with both of her hands and laughed with her full body to an apparent joke. I thought of her figure, her exceptional smile, and pictured the two of us naked and alone back in the hotel room. She called my name in a passionate scream while our inter-twined bodies twisted in a mess of limbs and sweat. I could feel her warmth, the bliss of being received in-between her slender, athletic legs, and the moans of pleasure while we explored each other in drunken ecstasy.

Flavor returned to my tongue. I chugged down the remaining half bottle without breathing and slammed it on the table. Jennifer and I made eye contact through the stumbling bodies that tried to make sense of a fast paced rhythm Fernando and the band fell into. A wave washed through my system, an icy wave, a devious tsunami, and I wanted to ride it straight into Jennifer's skin, but the wave crashed before I could ever make sense of it as Karana's laugh somehow cackled over the music. She danced her way into my conscious like a sudden twist in a dream and I awoke to the agony of her absence. She would have loved to dance the night away in a flood of free tequila and live music. I laughed to myself as I thought of her trying to keep pace with the band. She was offbeat as usual, but she bounced, a wide grin adorned her countenance, and she spun in full gratitude of the moment.

I stood up from the booth as Celeste slid in next to Cosmo and whispered into his ear. A large bill in pesos found its way out of my pocket and on to the table, but Cosmo shoved it away. "Save it," Cosmo said and rose with me. Apparently Celeste was ready to dance again.

"Thanks asshole, and thanks for trying to destroy my marriage before it begins. I appreciate that."

"No problem. Anything else I can do to save your life, you let me know."

"You're such a dick."

"Come on, like I thought for one second you would ever go through with it. You are so done you might as well be the Jurassic Era. You make antiquated strides every day Dano. Besides, you think Jennifer would have even let you get near her, please. I still don't know what the hell Karana is thinking hanging around an ugly ape like you." He hit me on the shoulder and broke into a wide grin. "Sometimes though," he began before gulping a large swallow of beer, "sometimes it's good just to get those mental images working. To let them drift and dream and see where they take you. And you did, I could see it, and then you came to, in the recognition of your true feeling, which is obviously Karana. Don't let things fester, let your mind travel through the incessant flow of mysteries and downright crap that travels out there. You will filter through the shit and come out clean on the other side every time, because you are who you are, but a little mind journey never hurts."

"Come on Cosmo let's get out there," Celeste pleaded. It was amazing how quickly I went from wanting to break his teeth to wishing I had a pen to write down his inebriated words of wisdom. He loved to push towards the apex and see who was left hanging on after his surge. So many times I thought I would slip and crash towards oblivion in our friend-ship, but somehow, someway, on the brink, where Cosmo kept his cool and I floundered like a fish on the deck of a boat I managed to hang on.

"Good night you two," I yelled out to Cosmo and Celeste.

"Good night dear," Cosmo screamed back, "don't wait up." I flipped him the bird and started towards the exit. Jennifer took notice as I approached her in her new seat in Stacy's lap. Their full drinks sat untouched at Cosmo's booth as a hoard of beer bot-tles littered their new table.

"I hope the sun comes out for you," I said to

Jennifer and strolled out through the beaded curtains. The walk back to the hotel felt reassuring in my bones. Cold air funneled down the windpipe and into appreciative lungs. A step staggered every so often, but the cool buzz moved my feet back to the Tortuga hotel. I tried to place a call to Karana, but my intoxicated ears could not decipher the Spanish tongue that delivered my instructions. Instead I sank into my pillow with a vague sensation of a soul breaking loose, a world spinning in new directions. I was anyone; I was no one, much like Cosmo in his youth on the tourist friendly streets of Ensenada. My status unknown, my future uncertain, and a journey full of adventure waited behind the wheel of our old Scout the following morning.

Chapter 6

W e stopped just outside of Ensenada at a small
roadside gas station. Although we were not on
a schedule of any kind it felt like we were behind.
Cosmo did not seem to care. I feigned that it did
not bother me either, but it was a lie. I still worried.
I fretted over how long we would actually be gone,
about how long Karana would wait for me, about
what I needed to repair when I got home. Cosmo
had returned to our hotel room sometime just before
sunrise. He slept a grand total of four hours before
I woke him up. I did all the work, I loaded the car,
re-fastened every tie hook and tow hitch, and then
checked us out of the Tortuga hotel, but on my way
back to the room to drag him out of bed he met me
on the stair well. He let out an extended yawn that
came across only as a formality. He did not seem tired
at all.

"Thanks for loading the car Dane."

"No worries."

"Let's grab some coffee and get going," he said
nonchalantly. I almost asked him how his night went

with Celeste, but thought better of it. He never spilled the sleazy details about a night he shared with a beautiful woman and would simply emit a shy smile when asked about one of his escapades. Celeste would be no different. He opened her eyes. She envisioned rare dreams and they let the night sweep them away. I was sure it went well for the both of them

Cosmo went inside to buy beer and ice. I looked up from the gas pump to watch a red-tailed hawk swoop no more than twenty feet overhead and land on a pegged telephone pole behind me. The bird shuffled for a few seconds to settle itself. It dug a piercing beak into its feathers then came to a stationary position and stared directly at me. An eerie dose of fear crept into my skin during the intense leer and I was concerned that I might have transformed into a helpless rabbit or an unaware gopher and within seconds sharp talons would rip into my flesh. Blood would ooze upon the dusty asphalt and run freely down my limbs. I would become just another pathetic victim twitching and kicking the last spasms of life before succumbing to a traumatic death beneath the clutches of a lethal predator.

The pump clinked and stopped at three hundred and twelve pesos, about thirty-two dollars. We could have waited and topped off much further down the road, but Cosmo thought we might make a few detours before the next station and he felt that we could use every drop of gas that we could fit into the tank. I blinked during the disruption, but could not unlock my gaze from the majestic creature perched above me. I wondered if the bird was the grim reaper incarnate acting as a guide to my ultimate demise. An anxious energy radiated, froze my feet, my motions, my urge to up and flee, and insisted that I stay put until the flying visitor decided my fate.

Clouds separated and drifted over the mountains. It had not rained since our first night two days prior. It looked as if the recent storms were ready to take a break from the west coast and the creeping sunshine was almost enough to warm my bones. Why fear? Why swirling thoughts of malcontent? The stare intensified and I could almost make out the dilated pupils of its eyes. The bird saw right through me. It knew me. It tracked me down from the entrails of my past or from some distant future and sat poised to come in for the kill and end my meaningless existence or to let me grab a hold of its feathered being and take flight across the universe. Either outcome felt possible. I would have waited there, for the moment, forever.

Another blink and wings extended. The streamlined body dropped from its crest and gave two powerful flaps then tucked in. Come get me. If I had wasted too much, if I existed as a pitiful excuse for a human being who meant nothing to the pounding drums of the world then the creature would finish me off. That termination I would have deserved, it would have been justified. Yet how I craved to fly, to spread my clandestine wings and soar, but the choice did not belong to me. The hawk honed in just above the pump. Here came the agony, the severed flesh, the magic ride across the stars. My hair rustled, body shook in full tremors, and an explosion ran through my chest. I opened my eyes and the bird was gone. Miraculously I found no hole in my thorax or abdomen. Impossible, something passed through my body, for that I was certain.

Silence consumed the fuel station as longing eyes searched the horizon for the vanished bird of prey. The hawk's absence instantly panged with a lump of discontent. I was certain that I would have experienced my last few breaths on the planet or taken flight to the highest peaks and lowest valleys on the wings of my personal prophet, but neither scenario occurred and a sense of disappointment swelled as I observed my dirty sandals planted in the same spot they sat thirty seconds prior. A dual trailer semi-truck blew by the station and lifted everything within reach on its tippy-toes then released all of us on parachute gusts as it headed down the road. The sudden burst of warm air rained down like the refreshment of a cleansing shower, and I bathed in its soothing caress.

I released the pump from the Scout and returned the accordion limb to its proper home. My hand trembled as I screwed the silver gas cap three clicks to the right. A feigning steady left hand climbed on top of the right to assist in finishing the task. The dust smelled of crispy potatoes, the two lane highway stretched into a cavernous sea of black and yellow, and Cosmo made his way out of the store with one case of cold Corona's and a case of warm Pacifico along with a tan strap of leather that resembled a belt slung over his shoulder.

"What the hell has come across your face? Looks like you have seen a ghost or something." He set down the beer to open the back hatch while I gazed stupefied at the horizon. Cosmo moved with ease while he released the back latch then raised its weighted door and propped it open with an old shovel handle out of J.P.'s basement. "I traded my Padres hat for this belt, what do you think?"

"I didn't see a ghost. Or at least I don't think I saw a ghost. Can birds be ghosts?"

"So that means you don't like my belt then. Oh well, I find it impressive enough. Hand-made quality here man. No matter. What the hell do I know if birds can be ghosts, what do you think?

"Huh."

"I said, what do you think? Can birds be ghosts?"

"But that's what I asked you."

"Yes, and I said hell if I know, or something like that."

"Cosmo, that bird knew me."

"What bird?"

"The one that almost ripped my heart out of my left kidney while you were inside paying for the gas and buying beer."

Cosmo thought for a second. "What do you mean it knew you?"

"What?"

"I mean how do you know? Did it say hey Dane what's up, or something weird like that?"

"No, I'm being serious here. It stared at me, then through me, and I felt as though it knew my every thought, my every dream, my slew of disappointments. It locked in on me like a fly on shit, or a sniper on his victim, and then it released. It spread its gorgeous feathers into a marriage with the wind and came straight for me. I was done for. I was dead. It sped through my organs and then it was gone as if it was a ghost, a dream, a silly vision. But, it couldn't be, no, it was none of those. I'm sure it was not a spirit of sorts, but it was something."

"Something meaningful perhaps?"

"Perhaps."

"Perhaps not."

"Perhaps. Damn, I'm starting to talk like you in these random, profound parables."

"Sorry Dane happens I guess."

'I guess so."

"You ready to go?"

I took another peek at the horizon. My hawk was gone or at least in any physical shape that my lenses and irises could gather and send to my brain, but it flapped its wings somewhere in the distance and I sensed that we would meet up again before our trip was over. I turned to Cosmo. "Yeah, I'm ready."

"Cool, I'll drive. You look too shaken up to take over right now. Here, drink this. He handed me an ice cold Corona and I sucked down the golden liquid into my welcoming function of a human body. It seemed a bit early to begin drinking, but the cool beer numbed the spinning wonder that danced beneath my ribcage. The Scout sputtered a bit at the turn of the key, but she cranked over soon enough and we were back on the highway in no time headed down a black and yellow infinite abyss.

Chapter 7

A light switched on. Heavy feet tried to remain quiet as he tip-toed to her bed. The young girl pretended to be asleep on her stomach as he sat down beside her. He gently nudged her shoulder, but she did not move. He tried again. "Patty, wake up sweetie," but the girl only moaned and rolled on to her side. With her back to him, her father glanced at the walls. Gone were the fantasies of a young girl. He could no longer find the traces of the Cabbage Patch Kids, no more Care Bears or My Little Ponies, and no more Strawberry Shortcake. A young woman blossomed. Rock posters littered her walls. Names like Pearl Jam, Nirvana, and the Sexy divas of En Vogue transformed the innocence of a young girl into the desires of a young woman. Calendars flipped so fast. He wanted to choke the passages of time. Leave her as she lay. She had not yet become that young woman. Some-where beneath the sheets rested the same little girl who pined for her daddy. The same little girl who held his hand when she felt scared, the one he read stories to about princesses and talking animals, his precious one. She turned thirteen in a month and he did not know who to buy for, a young child of sugar and spice or a young woman who liked boys and talking on the phone. He kissed the back of her head. He helped create the beautiful child. He loathed all the apprehensions in his life. His lack of spontaneity, his broken dreams, but he knew she outweighed all of his failures. She was his greatest gift to the earth.

"Wake up Patty I have to talk to you."

She groaned and opened her eyes. "What Daddy I was sleeping."

"No you weren't you big faker. I could tell you were awake."

"How could you tell?"

"Because I know you too well, that's why. What happened to your night light? Didn't it have a princess on it of some kind?"

The girl sat against a light tan wall with her blanket pulled up to her chest. Her father sat side-saddle across from her. She studied him for a second. He looked much older than he did before she left for school earlier that morning. The day aged him like a rotten grape in the sun.

"That was a Belle night light from Beauty and the Beast Dad. I'm not that little anymore. I'm a teenager remember."

"Not yet you're not."

"In a month I will be. But I consider myself a teenager already."

"Why? Why do want to grow up so fast."

"Because being a little girl is stupid. People always want to dress you up like a doll. Adults won't tell you anything important, and leave you out of everything, because you are too young to understand them, they say. Not to mention I can't see half of the bands I wish I could see, because of age limits."

Her father smiled. I never pondered such ideas at her age he thought. At twelve, going on thirteen his world revolved around baseball games, bicycles, and coming up with enough change to buy candy at the local market. He wondered how she already contemplated the world at large. The coming and goings, philosophies, and meanings of life came out of her young lips like he used to spit out the starting lineup for the Los Angeles Dodger's when he was a boy. He sat dumfounded at the wise soul that sat before him.

"I think you are old enough to understand things. Actually, you probably understand them better than I do. The world is a crazy place. It baffles me all of the time. Just when I think I make sense out of something it goes and changes on me." He looked back at her posters. The blond haired kid wore very sad eyes. He looked as if his heart carried a heavy burden full of pain and despair. That is how he felt, dismal and indifferent, but he tried to stay upbeat for the sake of his daughter.

"Dad, what's wrong."

"Why do you think there is something wrong?"

"Come on Dad."

"What?"

"Why did you wake me up to talk?"

"You know I wanted to talk about stuff, about your life. Hey aren't volleyball tryouts coming up soon."

Patty kicked off her covers and jumped from her bed. "You see this is what I'm talking about. You are stalling because you think I am too young to understand something aren't you. I know something is up Dad. You and Mom hardly talk to each other anymore and you look so sad right now. You know me well Dad, but I know you too." She walked in front of him and stared into his face. "Dad tell me what you came to tell me, please."

He let out a deep sigh, "It's not that I'm keeping it from you honey. I guess I'm having trouble telling it to myself really. Sweetie, how do I say this besides saying it outright. Mom said she is going away for awhile."

"Away? Dad just tell me. You said the same thing when I was eight when my cat Merlin died. Where is she going? On a vacation? Where?"

"I can't get anything past you can I? Patty, your Mom said she is going to live at Aunt Sharon's for awhile. I think she wants a…" he dropped his head and for the first time in years he let tears escape from his eyes. He wanted to be strong for his daughter, but his emotions swelled like a raging torrent. Patty sat down next to him and put her head on his shoulder.

"A divorce dad is that what mom wants?"

"I don't know honey. I don't know anything anymore. I'm sorry. Sorry I'm not a strong man, a resilient man, but I feel like I have an empty hole in my chest." He wiped his tears and took a deep breath. He looked at his daughter. His wonder escaped him. He no longer saw the young girl, the enchanted fantasies, and instead focused on a young woman wise beyond her years. She looked at him the way his mother did when he was a child. He knew that Patty did not gain her wisdom through her distant mother or from his own knowledge. No way possible. She was born with innate gifts beyond his comprehension. "She did not exactly say the word divorce, but I have a feeling that is what she is thinking. Mom said she needed a break to sort some things out. But what am I thinking I shouldn't be talking about myself? Are you alright Patty?"

She took her time before she responded. She saw it coming for months. Her mother made comments, her dad moped around, and the air in the house felt stale for some time. Her best friend's parents had split up two years prior and the patterns appeared hauntingly similar. The thought hurt her. The idea of having to choose, the likelihood of two separate households, the possibility of being forced to get to know a step-parent, but subconsciously she had been preparing for the moment for over a year. In her previous visions she saw herself crying uncontrollably when she heard the news, but faced with it a different feeling came over her. She felt an arcane sense of relief as well as incurring a deep well of regret for her father. He looked destroyed. How did he not see it coming? Maybe he did. Maybe he just hoped it would never actually happen.

"Where is Mom?"

"Wait, you didn't answer me."

"I think I'm ok dad, but how are you?"

"You are not supposed to ask that I am. This is

such a horrible burden to place upon you at such a fragile age."

"I'm not a doll Dad."

"You're right. I need to collect myself. I'm not sure where your mom is right now. She just up and left after she told me the news. She had a bag with her, but most of her stuff is still here. I asked her if we should tell you about the whole deal tonight. She sighed and scratched her fingers on the table. I think she was crying. Then she got up, strapped her bag over her shoulder and said "you do it if you want." Then she was gone."

"That bitch."

"Patty."

"What dad. How come she could not come and tell me herself?"

"I'm sure she will in time, Sweetie. Tonight was pretty emotional."

"I don't care. How do you think it is for me?"

"I know it is hard."

"Not you Dad, her."

"Oh."

"She always does this. She always runs out. Remember when I broke my arm during my soccer game? She would not even ride in the car with us, she couldn't handle it. And remember when I wanted to play volleyball instead of taking piano lessons and the big fight it caused. She took off in her car and made you deal with it. Why can't she just stand in front of us and deal with it."

"I'm not sure I have an answer for that Honey."

Her father noticed intensity in her eyes. She

purged a mass of emotions. It stabbed his guts to listen to her spill out such sorrow and discontent. He wanted to give her a hug and make it all stop, but he knew she needed the release. She directed her fierceness towards him.

"Why do you let her push you around Dad? She walks all over you. I see it all the time. You just accept it. She is horrible to you. She treats you like a stray dog."

"Now Patty, be fair."

"It's true and you know it. And you just sit there and take it. I'll tell you something, Dad. I'm glad she is gone."

"Come on now Patty you don't mean that."

"Yes I do. I mean it with all my heart." Tears streamed down her cheeks, but she kept going. "She acts like she never wants to be here with us, like we make her life miserable because she has to put up with us. Let her go to Aunt Sharon's for all I care. Let her go to Antarctica, I don't care if I ever see her again." Patty began bawling and her father held her tight. He wanted to pass along some consoling words, but decided it would be better to just let her cry. The night brought a flurry through her system and she reacted however it flew out of her body. His strong girl in anguish, it tore him apart.

He held her until the sobs eased into a controlled breathing pattern. The tears made a pool on his shirt just below the collar bone. He brushed back her hair and kissed the strain on her forehead. "My brave little girl, do you feel better now?"

Patty snorted and wiped her face with the sleeve

of her left arm while her father searched for a box of tissue. "Don't worry Dad, I ran out of tissue a couple days ago."

"Oh. I'll go get some out of my room."

"Dad, I'm fine."

"You sure?"

"Yes I'm sure." She got up and looked out of the window while her father rested against the door jamb. Somewhere in the night her mother began flipping the pages of a new life without her. She already seemed like a stranger as Patty tried to picture her face. The soft skin, the traveling eyes, the sandy-blonde hair, she seemed nothing more than a passing image in a magazine. Who was that woman? Patty contemplated her mother as an idea came to her.

"Dad, you have to tell me something."

"Of course darling. Anything you need you just let me know."

"Why did Mom have to name me Patricia, same as her?"

"I guess she felt the name needed to be passed on. It was your great-grandmother's name as well."

"I don't want to be Patricia anymore."

"But you are Patricia, you can't change that."

"But I can change my name."

"You want to change your name, Patty?"

"Yes I do."

"What's wrong with Patricia? Don't you like your name?"

"There is nothing wrong with the name itself; it's just that she gave it to me. She wanted me to be like her. I don't want to be anything like her anymore."

"But that's ludicrous. It's on your birth certificate. It's what everyone knows you by. You are my Patty."

"No I'm mom's Patricia. She always uses Patricia when she's angry. Dad you know my real name, my favorite name from my favorite story that you have read to me so many times."

"You are not serious."

"Yes Daddy. I want to be Karana from **Island of the Blue Dolphins**. She was brave. She was strong, and she could take care of herself. She was from a lush and beautiful island. I have wanted to be Karana since the first time you read it to me. "

Her father put both hands up to his face and slowly raked them into his dark brown hair. Patty's rebellion pleased him, but he could not reveal it to her. He needed to act as a parent in control of a tumultuous time in his daughter's life. He bit the inside of his lower lip and removed himself from the door jamb. "Patty, honey, you are upset and you have every right to be. I feel for you honey, I do, but give it a couple of days. Maybe this will all blow over. Your feelings will simmer down and maybe your mom will come to her senses and she will be back with us. Just give it some time Patty. You should get some rest, and we can talk about it after a good night's sleep."

"I don't need to rest," Patty snapped back. "She's not coming back Dad and you know it. I'm not a Patty, I never have been. It has never sounded right to me. Dad, please, for me, please Dad."

"Patty."

"Karana dad."

"Look I know all of this has been rough on you,

and I'm so sorry, but it has been very tough on me as well. I am losing my wife, my friend, your mother." He sighed and rubbed his eyes. "Can we please continue this in the morning? Perhaps we will both be a bit more rational."

Patty wanted to argue, but she saw the despair on her father's face. "I'm sorry, Daddy. Sorry Mom doesn't love us anymore."

"She still loves you Patty. She loves you very much. I know you do not see it right now, but she does. She just fell out of love with me I guess. I'm sorry I could not keep her here."

"It's her fault, not yours." She hugged her father. He smelled of the cucumber-melon botanical soap in their hallway bathroom. Patty breathed deep and tried to imprint the scent into her memory. He kissed the top of her head and said goodnight. As he walked towards the door Patty said "I love you," and crawled into her bed. Her father switched off the light and said "I love you too, Karana," then went downstairs to fix a drink.

Karana's mother never came back home to live again. She filed for divorce several weeks after walking out on her husband and daughter. After the settlement was finalized Patty's father let her officially change her name to Karana. She told me that it was the first semi-radical thing she ever remembered her father doing. He possessed many pleasant qualities, but she never understood his lack of ambition to follow his dreams or ideas, especially since they came to him in floods. His biggest fault in her eyes, though she adored him to no end, was that he always accepted complacency. He never strayed out of the box, never swam upstream, and seemed content to file right in line, which would have been fine if he did not always pine for something better in his life. According to Karana, if you liked your life, excellent, be happy with it, but if you wanted something more then chase after it. Do not sit around and wish for it to come. Make your dreams come to you.

When Karana and I met I was a dream seeker wrapped in a litany of her father's pleasant qualities. We soared, we traveled, and we plowed through each day like tomorrow would never come. We were happy. I was happy. She was happy. We were happy with the choice of one another. Then I began to follow in line much like her father. Responsibility got the better of me before I truly needed to be responsible. Instead of furthering my education or starting out near the bottom at a job I truly cared about I took a position based on instant salary. It worked at first. We went out to dinner all the time. We moved in together and saved for the future. It all appeared extremely bright. We figured it all out. And then something died. It festered and rotted inside my guts while I pondered my position in life everyday as I sat below the pallid walls of my office cubicle. Did we rush? Patience fit upon us like an old pair of shoes and it seemed improbable that we sped our lives up before we knew what happened. Truth told, I did, and Karana had nothing to do with it, but instead of speeding it up really, I simply took the easy way out.

The money flourished, the security rooted, and I thought that the hollowness of my job duties would take a back seat to the opportunities instant success would grant upon us. I was wrong. The job aided many things, but it dulled my soul. Karana on the other hand enjoyed her job to the fullest. She sought out her career. She walked it like she talked it. She was finishing her Master's degree when we started dating, and in the time of our coupling she completed school and was hired on as a counselor at a nearby private high school. Karana adored her students and the ability to help them seek out their futures. She also found a plethora of faults in the educational system and vowed to amend the seeping wounds. Passion effused from her conversations. She saw change and believed she could help bring about that change. She made a difference in a lucky child's life every single day with her beliefs in the good of mankind.

I envied her enthusiasm and love for her work. I approved contracts and punched in numbers, the lack of élan in my occupation stirred an instant mixture of melancholy and regret each time I told someone what I did for a living. Many people would have begged for the opportunity I was given. They would have found elation and pleasure in their work. It would fit them. It no longer fit me, but I became ensconced, afraid to step away from the security blanket swathed around the routine of nine to five. Karana could see the misery and told me to quit if the job made me unhappy, but I stayed. She feared I was becoming exactly like her father. Someone who dreaded taking a risk, taking a step away or a step back to find who they were and a life they wanted to live. Of course I denied it, but she was right. I was becoming her father. I was stuck. That was why we were fighting. That was why she told me to go along with Cosmo to Mexico. She wanted to dislodge me, to open up my lead curtain eyes and discover the man she fell in love with so we could walk down the aisle in harmony.

I owed her more respect than to wither away in front of her while she imbibed the juices out of life. I owed her the fight. She deserved someone who followed his dreams, not a man who sat around wishing for something more without ever acting upon it. As we traveled down isolated roads and made camp on empty beaches I set out to capture the man who possessed the courage to follow his dreams. For me and for the woman with the passionate soul, the wise soul, the heart effusing with compassion, the heart constructed with valor and strength. I owed her the fight, and I knew that anything less than returning to her from the dust of Baja California willing to take a chance for the sake of our lives together would have been an absolute failure.

Chapter 8

We made good time on the single-lane highway after filling up at the gas station. Mid-morning on a Friday far from a major town posed no threat of traffic to the Scout as we hummed along the road. Occasionally we got stuck behind a large semi-truck hauling vegetables, fuel, or lumber, but we blasted right on by the massive trucks during the straightaways or on the rare passing lanes that sprang up intermittently. My body remained jittery from the encounter with the hawk. I tried to sit still, but could not cease engaging in perpetual, nervous actions. I turned up the music on the MP3 player, and then turned it down. I played with the locks, the windows, my fingernails, the sandals on my feet. I wanted to flush the whole experience from my mind at that moment, not to discard it completely, but rather lock it in a dark cavern somewhere until I could let some time pass from the incident to try and comprehend what actually happened. Maybe a ghost, a vision, a distortion, a misconception, perhaps nothing at all, but the moment needed profound contemplation and the mood in the car did not seem fitting.

Cosmo spotted the known landmark, a boulder which stood about seven feet high and painted completely white. Young lovers marked the rock in spray paint and created hearts with initials inside of them or went to the full name approach and wrote statements such as, "Mario amo Isabel." Below the rock rested three wooden crosses adorned with penned dates and hordes of decayed flowers. They acted as sacred monuments to loved ones who died in a tragic car accident. The landmark sat on the west shoulder in the middle of a blind curve in both directions. Many scenarios could have played out. Maybe a car tried to pass around the curve and smashed into an oncoming vehicle, or perhaps one vehicle pulled out of the turnoff and thought the road looked clear and another speeding car whipped around the curve to collide with it. It was hard to tell, but at one point in time the curve ended three lives and most definitely altered the lives of many others.

Similar monuments appeared up and down the winding, narrow, reaches of Highway 1. Sometimes the crosses blended in with the scenery, sometimes they caught my eye, and when I did notice I always felt a stab of sorrow, a sense of frolicking spirits, in knowing we passed right over the exact spot where an unfortunate soul took their last breath on the planet. I wondered what they would think of the monuments back home. People would most likely complain. We were a culture afraid of death. We did not want to be reminded of it any more than necessary. Tuck it neatly into the confines of a somber but lush cemetery and forget about it. One day death reigned as the ultimate tragedy. The next day it would be forgotten, swept under the rug of denial. The Mexican culture on the other hand kept death among them. They accepted its existence and marked its lightning strike right out in the open for all to remember, for all to mourn. I said a silent prayer to the altar as we turned right onto the dirt road.

After about twenty-five minutes of bouncing up and down and every which way, the Scout and the poor little Boston Whaler skipping behind us plowed through the potholes, rocks, stretches of sand, remnant puddles, and brought us to the ocean. Cosmo called the spot Pop Rocks for the sudden emergence of large sea rocks in the line up during shifting tides, but the map named the area Punta Azul, or Blue Point. Pop Rocks produced better waves during the south swells of the summertime season, but could still get really good if the swell approached with a strong push from the west. We knew the current swell possessed a hint of west in it so we thought we would give Pop Rocks a try, but to our dismay the waves did not concur with our theory. We exited the Scout and watched the surf for twenty minutes. A north wind stirred the texture of the sea and the waves broke all at once, offering no more than a second or two of ride time upon them.

"Bummer," I said, "It's all walled out."

"Yeah it sucks. The wind is not helping either."

"Do you think when the tide starts to go out it will get a little better?"

Cosmo studied the surf. He wore light brown shorts, black sandals, and a black hooded sweatshirt pulled over his ears. Born in Washington State, Karana always made fun of Californian's like Cosmo and I who at any sign of cold would bundle up with sweatshirts and beanies, and yet would still wear a pair of shorts and possibly a pair of sandals with the abundance of warm gear. Cosmo looked perfectly normal to me, I wore a very similar outfit, but I knew Karana would make a sarcastic comment about the two California kids if she saw us standing on the shore at Pop Rocks. "Nah, the tide going low won't do anything. This place breaks better on a high tide anyway."

"It was worth a shot."

"Yeah, I guess so."

"What do you want to do now," I asked hoping to move on. We talked about camping at Pop Rocks if the waves cooperated, which would have been my first time staying the night there, but with the dismal outlook before us and plenty of daylight available I wanted to re-locate to a new spot. Pop Rocks carried a negative stigma in the surfing community relating to nefarious rumors of banditos reeking havoc and surfers gone missing. Cosmo said he never encountered anything even slightly out of the ordinary while camping at Pop Rocks, but his professions did not ease my worries. The crosses on the main road screamed over the sea. I did not want to meet those shrieks face to face.

"Well I want to surf."

"Me too," I said and inched towards the Scout.

"Want to get on the road then find some place else?"

"Yeah, I'm down. Let's do it."

"Maybe we should bust out some food and have a little lunch first?"

"Nah, I'm good. Rather get on the road and find some waves."

"Well let me grab something to snack on then before we get going."

"I'll drive if you want so you can eat on the road. You must be exhausted anyway from your late night."

"Are you sure about that Dane, sure you want to tackle the beast?"

"Shit man, I have been behind the wheel of the beast before."

"Yeah, but not towing a boat."

"Give me the keys ass hair."

"They're in it tough guy."

I ground second gear on my first shift, but the Scout became familiar soon enough. Searching for waves during surf trips or back at home could often transform from a simple ride to the beach into a scrupulous chore. Many aspects became involved. Wind condition, tidal position, swell direction, and the number of people in the water as well as a slew of other factoring variables could effect a decision on whether to suit up and paddle out or to get back in the car and keep searching. The word skunked would get passed around as a way to describe an unsuccessful search. Skunked came across overtly taboo, a distinction you never wanted to discuss aloud or make mention of in fear that it may actually come true. Much like talking to a baseball pitcher in the middle of a no hitter surfers conceal the word beneath their lips out of a dreaded superstition of breaking up what could end up being a perfect moment in time. We got skunked at Pop Rocks, but neither of us mentioned it out loud because of the exuding optimism that arose after we witnessed plenty of swell in the water. We knew we just needed to find the right spot for the swell to line up with.

We thought about going down a few different roads, but we kept on driving until we reached the turnoff for Las Cuevas, The Caves. I stopped the Scout as soon as we got onto the dirt road. The road to Cuevas took longer to reach the ocean than the road to Pop Rocks by about fifteen to twenty minutes in each direction. That being the case it would take us at least forty to fifty minutes to find the sea. At one point in time J.P. glued an older, digital wristwatch to the dashboard just above the vent knobs. It read 1:18 in the afternoon. With the sunset to commence sometime after 5:30 we knew that a trip down the road to Cuevas at that time of day meant we would almost certainly camp there for the night. We briefly discussed the pros and cons of a night at Cuevas and decided to go for it. Cosmo made three peanut butter and raspberry jelly sandwiches with a white plastic fork and cut them into halves. We split the halves and chased them down with cold beers as we continued on the bumpy road in hopes of a decent surf session.

Cuevas offered a stunning view upon arrival. The protected cove emitted a crystalline mixture of tur-quoise and emerald water glistening in the afternoon sun. Concrete colored sand stretched the length of the beach and gave way to thirty foot cliffs on each end with small sea caves carved into them from incessant wave action. The cave at the south end opened up to the height of a one-story house and the width of a semi-truck. At low tide one could walk from the sand on through the cave for about twenty feet without ever ducking their head and reach the fringes of the sea, but at high tide the cave drowned in seawater making a trek through it impossible. As recent as five years before our trip we could collect abalone right out of the cave, but word passed, people followed tire tracks, and repeated travelers stripped the spot of anything edible, even the sea anemone population dwindled from their plentiful abundance in years past. The north cave barely qualified as a cave at all due to its diminutive size. On hands and knees one could crawl through the sandy bottom, pyramid shaped crevice for about fifteen feet until it opened to the ocean. During a big swell the pounding surf sent a thunderous roar echoing through the cave and caused the sensation of being dropped in the middle of a storm cloud when sitting at its entrance.

Two men in a small fishing boat tugged at a net about a hundred yards offshore. We parked the Scout at the edge of a rugged path that led to the beach next to a black, Jeep Wrangler with the top off and covered in a thick layer of dust. The Jeep displayed Colorado plates and an Aspen Local sticker on the right side of the rear bumper. We could see the main break from the beginning of the trail peeling off a few good waves. The size did not appear to make it into Cuevas when we arrived, but it looked fun and we could not wait to get in the water. Of course, the goal in searching for surf in Baja revolved around finding an empty spot to ride with only those in your party, but whoever drove the Jeep could not be seen in the water which meant plenty of vacant waves to play upon.

A plump lizard, probably a horny toad, hissed and scurried under a faded, green base of a yucca plant as we started down the trail. We opted to head straight out for a session instead of setting up camp right away. Empty waves and pristine conditions could transform in an instant and we thought we should take advantage of the scene presented to us. Morning clouds dissolved into the horizon as the sun beat down on our wetsuits during our ten minute hike to the beach. The trail emptied out in the sand about a quarter of the way down the beach from the north cave. I scoured north, then south, looking for the owners of the black Jeep, but could not locate them anywhere. Two sets of footprints made casts in the sand just above the waterline and aimed towards the south end of the beach. Cuevas offered three main peaks to surf on the quarter mile stretch of sand, one right at the end of the trail which often closed out, another two-thirds of the way down marked by a ten foot high, jagged chunk of terrain that dislodged from the cliff above, and the last one near the entrance to the south cave which usually produced the best waves.

We passed the second break and the large chunk of earth and noticed a man and a woman sun tanning on their bellies. They looked like peeled potatoes slathered in oil and their bodies glistened in the sunlight. As we got closer to the couple we noticed that the woman previously removed her bikini top and set it beside her to avoid any unwanted tan lines. They appeared to be asleep so we quietly stretched out the kinks from a day on the road and paddled out into the surf. Cosmo left the remains of J.P. in the Scout. He wanted to see what our fellow travelers were up to before he held another brief ceremony in the presence of the sea.

J.P. liked to shore cast at Cuevas, but he never really caught much there. One time I remember him pulling in a decent size halibut, but more times than not he reeled in an empty line. He said the water enticed him to keep sending out his bait. He adored the color, the usual protection from the wind, and would plop himself down on a chair with a cooler full of beers for hours at a time catching no more than a good buzz. I looked on the beach for him, as if his death was only a dream, a bad joke played by Cosmo that he adherently stuck to, and I saw him casting out and then cussing vehemently because his hook, line, and sinker did not hit either of us when they dove into the water. I tried to remember his many portions of advice he threw my way and any caveat he blurted out if I defied his expertise and put my focus back on the waves.

A chest high set came in and I picked off the first one. I went backside on a left and pulled off a two feeble turns until I hopped out at the shoulder still a bit stiff from the car ride. As I gathered my board and paddled back towards the line Cosmo got to his feet and faced a steep right. Next he stalled his board and then disappeared underneath the curl of a crashing lip only to resurface two seconds later. Gracefully his board carved off the bottom of the wave, rose up the face, and arced into a fluid turn that popped his fins over the lip and sent a translucent halo of water rocketing into the air. He then proceeded with a very similar maneuver and as the wave came to a close he corralled his momentum on top of the crashing water and floated sideways across it until he casually glided down the broken wave.

His surfing always looked effortless, almost too at ease. He possessed the ability to surf with more speed than anyone I had ever witnessed, yet exude the deception of moving in slow motion at the same time. Descriptions of his style invoked words like smooth, soulful, or fluid. People often said his body acted in total unison with his board and all of his limbs. Cosmo appeared more comfortable cruising in the surf than on any other place on the planet. It seemed as though his entire life made sense in the clutches of a wave, but as he described it, "life absolutely makes no sense while surfing and that is what's so great about it. You let go of life, of worry, of expectation, and the hierarchies of society. Sometimes the best sense is no sense at all. To live completely emancipated from the chains of the mind. I am fortunate enough to become enveloped in this disconnected bliss and I wish to be nowhere else, or to think of anything else, I feel as though the universe flows through me while playing in the ocean."

He did not always find such bliss in the sea. At a time surfing sat on his chest as a monolithic onus.

As a youth Cosmo picked up surfing like most people learned how to walk, which led him straight into competitions. At first he enjoyed the events, a group of boys and girls budding with adolescence playing all day in the surf and on the beach. He flirted with girls and made friends with teens up and down the state of California. As his skills increased so did the magnitude of the contests and the pressures of competition. Cosmo dreamed of becoming a professional surfer, to earn a living by means of traveling and surfing in contests around the globe, but as a natural born non-conformist the strictures and schedules of appearances and photo shoots sucked the luster from his perceived fantasy of what a career in professional surfing would entail. He just wanted to surf, whenever he wanted, how he wanted, on whatever board he desired, but the responsibilities of a pro did not always allow such freedoms.

He once told me that blowing his knee out before qualifying for the world tour might have been the greatest blessing in his life, though at the time seemed the most tragic. It took eight months of constant rehabilitation and great determination from Cosmo to get his knee back into surfing shape. After all of the hard work and dedication he put forth to get back in the water stronger than ever it surprised many people, including myself, when he announced that he would not continue his quest to qualify for the world tour. In his time away from the water any remnants of the competitive bug that once drove him towards stardom evaporated from his body. He did not blame anyone who could do it, he envied them really, but in his absence from the contest scene he realized that the competitive edge did not drive him the way it did for many other surfers.

I could not help thinking about what could have been as I paddled back in position for my next wave. Cosmo's surfing blossomed with age. He understood his rails. He knew that less amounted to more when it came to movement. He scarcely wasted a flailing arm, an extra hop, or an exaggerated turn. I knew he could still compete and do well if he desired. Surfing's world champion, Kelly Slater, was in his mid-thirties and still excelling at the highest level, but deep down I knew Cosmo shed the skin of the competitor at the ripe age of twenty and never once did he look back.

The surf industry offered a variety of ways to make money without going through the grind of a year on tour and Cosmo took full advantage of what was available to him. He went on boat trips to tropical islands like Bali, Fiji, Tahiti, and the Maldives which were sponsored by major surf companies that hoped to film spectacular footage for an upcoming surf flick or to capture photographs for the next spotlight issue in a surf magazine. The surfing world had grown from a bunch of broke daredevils just looking for a good time in the sea to mega corporations like Quicksilver and Billabong whose stocks could be publicly traded on the open market. If one possessed enough talent and a hint of strategy, they could discover loopholes that would keep them traveling and even paid a bit of money. Cosmo exuded both. He also wrote free-lance articles and occasionally took photographs for the major surf magazines while also appearing in a variety of magazine shoots and surf videos. In many ways his childhood wish came true. Cosmo was every bit the professional surfer he hoped to be without the burdens of competition. He traipsed around the globe on a moments notice surfing the best waves with the best surfers in prime locations all on someone else's dollar.

We surfed until the sun reminded us that night would swallow the day. With the moon not quite three-quarters full the tide would remain moderate which allowed us to set up camp on the sand. We each brought our own, small, two man tents and set each one up on either side of the fire we got going just before dark.

The sunbathers made camp one hundred yards down from us in almost the exact same spot that we noticed them for the first time. Their names were Hillary and Campbell and they were on a voyage from Aspen, Colorado. They got into Campbell's Jeep one morning to pay a visit to Southern California and kept on going. They shared some fresh albacore with us that they purchased from the fisherman we spotted when we first arrived. We missed the opportunity to buy fresh fish while we were surfing and appreciated the gesture. Cosmo returned the favor by introducing both of them to an almond tequila he bought in Rosarito. They were instantly hooked on the sweet liquid and Campbell pulled out a joint from his pocket. He sparked it up and passed it to Hillary and she in turn handed it to Cosmo. He respectfully declined, and so did I. The couple was baffled. Two roaming surfers in Baja turning down free tokes of marijuana in the open air caught them off guard. Cosmo had his reasons for not indulging in marijuana, an herb that changed the course of his life. I on the other hand occasionally dabbled at a party or in a sporadic moment, but it was so infrequent that I could take it or leave it when offered to me. Cosmo held no contempt for those around him who smoked the herb; it did not bother him at all, he was only living by a promise he made to himself when his father received a five to ten year sentence in a federal prison.

Hillary asked questions as often as she could. She wanted to know all about our journey in the finest detail. Cosmo did most of the talking, but more or less generalized his answers due to Campbell's constant interruptions. Every time Cosmo or I got going on a topic requested by Hillary, Campbell would butt into our statements to let everyone know he was there. He found it necessary to do one better than us on each subject we discussed. If we made mention of the Scout, he spat out the capabilities of his Wrangler and the many other vehicles he owned, when Cosmo spoke of a surf trip to Costa Rica, Campbell bragged about the three houses he owned, one in Aspen, one on Oahu, and one in South Carolina right on the water.

Arrogance spilled out of Campbell's mouth and I found it easy to dislike him, but I considered the situation before drawing final conclusions. He did not appear much the camping type, which contradicted a glowing Hillary at ease underneath a blanket of stars and two men, at least a decade younger and as comfortable sitting around the campfire as we could have been in our own living rooms. Plus, the palpable connection that formed instantly between Cosmo and Hillary burned as bright as the roaring flames separating them. Campbell might have been too stoned to notice, but I caught on and secretly crossed my fingers for Cosmo to behave.

Campbell was exactly the kind of person Cosmo would have loved to go into a verbal war against, but the fight did not surface in him. They jarred back and forth only slightly, but not in a manner typical of Cosmo. Maybe Hillary's presence distracted him, maybe he just needed some sleep, but either way he drifted somewhere distant that night, somewhere lost in an ocean of thought miles from the rest of us.

We offered the couple another shot of almond tequila. They slammed it down and said goodnight. In less than twenty seconds all I could see was the illumination from their bouncing flashlights. The roar of the surf and the past two nights of binge drinking placed a heavy weight on my eyelids. I loosely held an empty beer bottle in my hands. Cosmo offered me another one, but I needed to rest. He put his head back on the fabric of his camping chair and said goodnight. I unzipped my tent and wondered about his tone. He spoke as though frustrated by something. Perhaps he wanted to talk, or needed get something off of his chest after Hillary and Campbell retired to their camp. I took a glance at him as he stared at the stars. The seven sisters made an appearance almost directly overhead. The clear skies meant the night would pierce our tents with cold fangs. I almost asked him if everything was alright, but decided against it as I thought about the warm confines of my sleeping bag. He would speak his mind when he felt the urge, for that I could always count on for certain, Cosmo speaking his mind when he needed to.

Chapter 9

I am drifting atop a popcorn cloud. Flesh looks orange so close to the sun and mirrored against an ashen lining of my astral transportation while I shimmy like a stick figured pumpkin. The skin of the earth disappears and nothing impedes the cream colored island of fluff as it glides into a light-blue oblivion. Who am I? Where am I? Above the equator, near the polar caps of Antarctica, over the Rockies and spilling into the Pacific Ocean, I cannot tell nor do I care. My vision of nothing yet filled with everything. The entire world is tangible, alive, frolicking about as I sink into the coconut Jell-O cushions supporting my body.

My cloud maneuvers inverted circles around a vapor trail left behind from a speeding F-14 Tomcat. I lick the wind. I am the wind. I am the atmosphere. I am the beating drum of thunder and awe. A red-tailed hawk soars just beneath the marshmallow bower eyeing an afternoon snack of squirrel, or rabbit, or coiled venomous rattle snake. Its keen eyesight, around eight times more powerful than my feeble eyes, surveys all movement below. The urge to call the magnificent flier a "she" resonates on the tongue, but my education lacks the ability of identifying birds by their sex. How is that done anyway? Somewhere it seems that the size of a bird of prey marks their gender, with the females being the larger of the species. She appears large, beautiful, and liberated; her name will be Lola, a name that emanates from days past in a bird show at the San Diego Wild Animal Park. Whether Lola was the hawk that flung open a door from a miniature blimp and darted furiously to an outstretched, gloved hand of a khaki clad trainer, or the girlfriend of the garrulous cockatoo in the comedic portion of the show I cannot recall, but either way she sings out the name into the wind. Fly Lola, fly.

She hones in, straightens her piercing beak, clenches razor sharp talons, and commences into a freefall towards the earth. Her speed increases as brown and red feathers ruffle in a streamline of velocity. A winged bullet shot to the terrain below becomes a smear of waning black ink darting down an empty canvas.

Suddenly I worry about her. Will she be able to stop? She is going too fast to ever hit the brakes. She will incinerate into a ball of orange flame, a fiery phoenix set forth on a kamikaze mission of certain peril. I miss her instantly, sheer feathers disappearing, and those eyes, wise eyes, gleaming eyes, inviting yet pernicious, will never again squint in the glare of the sun or lock in on unsuspecting prey. "Stop Lola, stop. Call off your apparent suicide and return as the captain of this cloud," but she cannot hear the screaming words deafened by the wind.

Eyes close; she plummets and collides with the earth. Salt hits quivering lips as tears jump from swollen cheeks. Eyes reticent to reopen and imbibe the view of blood, dust, and scattered feathers, yet fleshy lids rise to an unexpected sight. There is no flattened carcass; no disseminated body parts sprawled in a mangled heap, just a hole about a foot wide, narrow and showering iridescence. My cloud elevates and the globe shrinks. Stinging light runs deep into the bowels of the earth, beneath the outer crust of shifting plates and ocean floors, piercing further through the impervious, rocky mantle, swims amidst the magma flow of the outer core, and picks up enough of a burst to explode through the solid inner core. Instantly a ray of light shoots through a slit on the opposite side of where Lola penetrated the armor of the planet, and she emerges. A blur of fluff slowly eases into a glide and a shriek escapes, echoing off the stars. I am in love.

I want to follow her in flight. Flap my clumsy arms and dive towards oblivion. I walk to the edge of the cloud and look straight ahead at the glowing sun. Two hands come together poised, ready to fly, to flee, to drift about the universe aimlessly on no more of a plan than a shift in the wind. A deep, slow breath in, then a calm breath out and I take my eyes from the sun to look below. Sweat forms, legs wobble, and a bass drum explodes in my chest. First the pounding beats slow and with great force, a cavalry approaching over a bluff miles away. Then it hits my throat. I choke. I gag on the air. Lola waits, soaring, but I do not move. She can no longer bear to look at me, at my pathetic corpse frozen and unable to heave off of the stationary cloud. She catches a gust and banks to the west. My fingers reach for her as she flies by, but she passes just out of reach as I sit too frightened to make the extended lunge necessary to say goodbye. "Wait Lola. Please give me a minute to unthaw, to build up the courage to take this terrifying leap," but she does not hear me as the brilliant sun swallows her image on the horizon.

Hesitant coward sinking to the earth, "please kill me

now. Steal all the oxygen from my searing lungs. Jam spears through my defeated heart." The cloud bumps into the land and I am covered in mud. A putrid ooze grinds in my teeth and spills out of throbbing ears. The pigs laugh and snort and shit on my soiled skin. The sty reeks of rotten meat and festering outhouses. Hell begins its fury. The swine continue parading through the muck, urinating on my hair, my back, and I roll to one side. My limbs will not move and only half of my left eye is not completely smeared in mud. It scans the area for Lola, but she is gone and so is the sun. Ebony clouds expunge streams of tar. The left eye closing quickly catches a ray of light. It is Lola's entrance into the earth still glowing amidst the showering apocalypse. Shit on my lips, maggots between my toes, and a laugh echoes from a foreign chamber at the thought of Lola's freedom. Limbs still idle I crawl with my chin and floating, bony knee-caps towards the showering of light. The heat and power of brilliant illumination wrap around my body and two, mud-crusted, repulsed eyes open wide.

Chapter 10

I opened my tent to a shimmering, slick sea. Next to the charred embers of our camp fire sat an empty tequila bottle. Cosmo must have stayed up for quite some time howling at the moon and the shining Zodiac. I stretched out for a second and put on my wetsuit. Smiling waves enticed stiff bones to paddle towards their generous offerings. I made sure to keep quiet as I raced past Campbell and Hillary and dipped into the chilly water. A morning session alone always restored my faith in the universe. The new sun, the smooth waters, an inkling of rebirth, a portal of fresh possibilities dominate the quiet. Serenity overcomes and Mother Ocean shows that she is even more beautiful when just waking up from a long nights sleep.

I picked off waves when I felt like it. Half way through my session a pod of dolphins swam over to catch a couple of waves and check out the guy in the funny looking, rubber suit. I counted nine of them, but there could have been one or two more. They played in the surf for over five minutes and acted like a group of buddies I invited over to share a few waves with. After each wave I caught I would paddle back out to a scene of five to nine playful creatures heading straight for me on the next incoming wave. Each time, I closed my eyes and ducked under a wave and prayed that they would not crash into me, and each time I resurfaced unharmed to watch the dolphins already in position for the next set. They circled around me, swam underneath my board as if saying goodbye, and then headed out to sea.

When I decided to go in I found Cosmo by a small fire cooking breakfast. He commented on a few of my waves and handed over a plate of eggs and bacon. I asked about his head with a forced laugh. He looked at the empty bottle resting in the sand. A long sigh erupted and he formed a devious smirk.

"What are you grinning at," I asked biting into a piece of bacon. It carried the flavor of burning pine and ocean breeze.

"You know."

"Know what?"

"You mean you didn't hear Hillary come back over here last night?"

"No, I crashed out. Oh shit, you didn't did you?"

"No, no relax, we just talked for hours until we emptied the bottle."

"Good we don't need Mr. Cool over there causing a big scene."

Cosmo dug into his eggs and added more pepper after his first bite. "She is one cool woman, I'll tell you, Dano. Did you know her parents named her after Sir Edmund Hillary, one of my idols? I sure hope we meet up with them again after they head out." A haze covered Cosmo's dreamy eyes and we did not talk while we finished breakfast.

Hillary and Campbell walked over around noon to say their goodbyes. Campbell said they were heading further south and that we might meet up with them at another junction. Hillary looked like a child whose parents came to pick her up early from a friend's house. She wanted no part of getting back into the jeep, but she tried her best to feign excitement in Campbell's wishes. In the dark I could not make it out clearly, but daylight revealed the age difference between the couple. She looked radiant in her mid to late twenties and Campbell definitely wore the years of someone in his mid-forties. They sped off, kicking up dust as Campbell spun out his wheels.

With the swell still building we decided to camp one more night at Cuevas. It would not accommodate a large swell, but while moderate it would produce the cleanest waves within a long stretch of coastline. After lunch Cosmo and I got out the fishing poles and threw our lines in the water. We did not catch anything in the afternoon sun, but the gentle lapping of the waves and the clear waters brought on a content peace.

We enjoyed a fun session in the surf before the sun went down. For years Cosmo constantly harped on me about my refusal to launch airs while surfing. I would go on about how so many kids possessed little-to-no-style because of the aerial assault that took captive the surfing world. After dropping in, many surfers would race down the line as fast as they could until they came into contact with a breaking section of a wave and launch themselves into the air without ever executing a turn or being in sync with the moving wall of water. Cosmo would laugh and tell me that I was getting old way too soon. "If they are done as a part of your surfing arsenal," he would say, "then they are perfectly acceptable. But, I do agree with you, if that is all one does, bust airs, without learning to lay their board on rail or how to throw a gouge of water, then that person is definitely lacking for style, no matter how spectacular his or her airs are." Heeding his advice I attempted airs more often. That evening I pulled off a clean front side air with a slight grab from my right hand before calling it a night. Nothing beat getting a deep tube ride, but I did receive a great shot of adrenaline after landing a well executed air.

We got the firing roaring after we deposited a few dried out yucca plants into the flames. Dinner began to digest avocado, black bean, and lobster burritos. Our stomachs were grateful for trading an old wetsuit jacket for a few lobster tails. The fishermen wanted to give us a hoard of other forms of seafood, but with limited ice and only the two of us dining we knew the food would go to waste and requested only the lobster. We boiled them in a stainless steel pot over the fire. A few cold beers, fresh lobster dressed with a bit of garlic salt, and nothing but the waves and instrumented crickets emitted noise into the dark sky.

In somewhat of a food coma I barely noticed that Cosmo had not spoken a word since handing me a plate before we sank into our food. He seemed on the verge of tears and ready to get into a brawl with the crackling fire when I looked over at him. He held the stoking stick in his hands like a sword, right hand on top of the left, waiting to impale an approaching intruder. Cosmo rarely looked angry or disconsolate, normally adorning his face with a look of contemplation when not speaking. The rare look frightened me for a second as if he knew something that I did not. Did he know of a legendary Chupacabra in our parts that snuck up and sucked the blood out of unsuspecting victims? Did I say something to offend him? I could not figure out his change in mood after the enjoyable waves and pleasing food we gobbled up just a short time before. Noticing his empty beer I walked over to the ice chest and pulled out two brown Pacifico bottles and started towards him with a cold peace treaty in hand. Before I reached him he began to speak.

"I'm not sure why I didn't get in the car with you and Karana to go to the concert that evening," Cosmo began.

"Huh. What evening?"

"When J.P. died."

"Oh," I said barely audible. I handed him the fresh beer and crouched down near the fire.

"We bought those **Pinback** tickets so far in advance and I was all fired up to see them." He paused and took a deep breath. I sensed that he was on the verge of saying something really heavy. His mannerisms were controlled, but I could tell he might have trouble getting through his anecdote. I sat as still as possible and tried to avoid making any sound. He continued, "My mom would probably say I had an intuitive feeling overwhelming my senses and I caught the flow of a major event colliding with my universe. Might have been that, might have been that I had not heard from J.P. in a couple days, which broke the habit of checking up on him as often as possible, and whether it was a telepathic sensation or just a logical hunch I knew I had to go see him before the show and just meet up with you two later. He definitely had not been doing well as of late."

"As you know his joints went bad in his mid-twenties," he went on. "Swelling in his knees, wrists, and elbows slowed down his mobility and became classified by doctors as some type of acute arthritis. He went through the normal routine of painkillers and possible cures that began with basic aspirins and then from there he graduated onto any kind of medication that ended in "zine," "prine," or "line." Then came the holistic options and natural remedies ranging from rattlesnake venom to an all wheatgrass diet. The pills never seemed to ease the pain, he never followed the natural routes with any consistency to produce long term effects, and the only time the aches ever seemed to mollify to a point of tolerability was when he got good and sauced. I knew it would not cure his ills, so did everyone else that knew him. In fact in many ways heavy drinking most likely exacerbated his problems, but in that much pain, with so much life craved to live and a raging stubbornness thicker than the Amazon Rain Forrest, everyone around him acquiesced to J.P.'s habits in order to let him still participate in activities he loved to do. Fishing, shooting pool, dancing with a pretty woman, even bowling became frequent events he could handle along with the help of some Wild Turkey, or Jack Daniel's, or maybe just a cold Budweiser. Any attempts to sway him away from his tactics were futile and the only war I ever won with J.P. was to get him to drink my favorite local beers from the Stone Brewing Company. J.P. cherished their smoked porter.

Then preceded the debilitation of his heart. A triple bypass at the age of thirty-six caused doctor's to remove three segmented blood vessels from his legs and attach them to his aorta as alternative routes around the blocked arteries. Left weakened by the surgery and with three new scars covering a tattered body his physicians read him the list of actions he should no longer partake in: alcohol, cigarettes, strenuous activities, recreational drugs were all stressed to be abstained from. J.P. flashed his intoxicating, dimpled-moustache smile, signed his paperwork, and left the hospital with no plan of altering any of his previous patterns. After the surgery I did try to intervene only to hear replies of "piss off smart ass, and while you are talking so much why don't you talk to Al at Pig Liquor and pick me up a fifth of gin." He attempted these outbursts with as much sarcasm as he could muster, but deep down I knew his rants were close to what he was really thinking. He did not want anybody to tell him what to do, or pity him for that matter. Most everyone around him had given up and resigned to the fact that was the way he was and if he wanted to kill himself it was his own prerogative, which was just how J.P. liked it. I contemplated his position and decided that for the time being I would let him be."

Cosmo's words flew off of his tongue. He barely stopped to breathe. I listened intently to the saga of J.P.

"He lived in that same dumpy apartment half a block from the beach in Oceanside for the last fifteen years," he went on. "You've been there plenty of times. Disability checks flowed in since the age of twenty-seven and with the low rent charged to him by the owners of his building, J.P. did not need a regular job. He would do odd fixer-upper type of work for friends of friends, he was the best non licensed bartender one could get if you needed someone to take the honors at a celebration in a pinch, and he became quite a collector of random pieces of machinery and all kinds of semi-working contraptions that he tried to refurbish and sell or find a way to collect some cash from by recycling their parts. You've seen all that crap. Who knows how long it will take to go through all the junk he left in the basement of his apartment building.

The air nipped at my skin and bit with icy teeth while I walked onto his porch. I remember being astonished by the cold and wanting to get in and out of there as fast as possible so I could meet up with you and Karana at the show. I kept repeating to myself, "This is Southern California. This is Southern California. There is no way it can be this cold tonight." My breath came out in small, quick puffs of smoke as I approached his door. The stillness of the porch squeezed silent hands around my neck. I couldn't find enough oxygen nor settle my breathing pattern. Some type of boat engine rested on a small hoist with an array of parts scattered below it just a few feet from the door. Oil stains crusted and scabbed over and an apple core next to an empty Budweiser can faded into a dark chestnut. No sounds penetrated from his apartment. No blaring television, no drunken soliloquies or arguments with revolving girlfriends. Not a peep erupted from any of the four units in his complex, just me and my uneasy breathing polluting the air. I tried for one deep, serene breath before knocking upon the door and noticed upon inhalation that I could not trace a scent of cigarette smoke. The absence of the incessant smell at J.P.'s nearly stopped my heart. I knew something was wrong."

Cosmo stopped his story and looked at his Pacifico bottle. He peeled the yellow label with his thumbnail. He took a swig and then looked back at me. I still had not said a word or moved an inch, but my body began cramping and I needed to stand up and stretch my legs. I did not want to disrupt the story during its most poignant moment, but the pause gave me an out so I stood up and shook out the tightness.

"Can't sit still anymore," Cosmo asked.

"Just needed to get up. My legs were cramping up. Sorry about that."

"No worries. Hey, I know this is getting long winded, but I finally feel ready to talk about this stuff, you know. It's finally erupting. And thanks for not digging in and asking me about the whole ordeal up to this point, though I'm sure it has crossed your mind. You are probably the only one who just let me be. If you want we can finish this at some other time."

"No, don't worry about it. Please keep talking. I

might grab myself another beer before you continue if you don't mind."

"Of course. Nab one for me one while you are at it?"

"Sure." I walked to the ice chest and pulled out two brown, near frozen bottles. The night bit my skin similar to the evening Cosmo had been describing and I felt like saying out loud, "This is Baja, this is Baja, but decided to keep my mouth shut.

Back by the fire with new beers cooling our taste buds and warming our bodies I remained standing while I nodded for Cosmo to continue. His gray and black beanie sat low on his head and barely made his eyes visible as he looked into the fire. We made a silent cheer; both took a sip and prepared for the rest of the story.

"You know the crazy thing," Cosmo began, "is that after the silence, the utter stillness, the worry in my heart, I didn't bust in right away and check out what was going on. Instead I turned from the door and took a seat on the concrete steps leading to his apartment. Something was wrong, I knew it, could not hide from it, but for some reason I needed a moment to reflect before facing the music so to speak. I began thinking of his life. The smile he carried no matter how much pain he was in. The favors he completed for anyone, anytime, from close friends to total strangers, always snarling, yet never turning anyone down or entirely failing to finish a task even if it took him months to complete. The formula he used for showering affection, the more obscenities and Charlie horses he threw in your direction, the

more he liked you. I slid my left hand down my right
shoulder and wished for a fresh bruise on his steps.

I shivered, but my mind kept me from rising. If
something happened was it my fault? I was about the
only family member left that he really talked to. Was
I failing him? I tried, I tried so hard, but in the end
that was how he wanted to live; to the fullest. Everything in his life sped on a rapid pace since the day of
his birth. J.P. was born two weeks ahead of schedule
and never used a baby bottle, going straight from the
breast to a cup. He was always a step ahead. Coaches
moved him up a level above his age group during his
entire Little League and Pop Warner careers. He lost
his virginity at thirteen and got a girl pregnant at fifteen which she lost to a miscarriage. At fourteen he
got a job selling newspapers and bought his own car,
a light-blue VW Bug, before he received his license.
While all of his friends sat on the beach daring each
other to go out in big surf, J.P. would paddle out and
take on the monsters by himself. It seemed as though
he sensed the urgency of his life at an early age, never
settling, never compromising, and never putting off
tomorrow what he had in his mind for the present day.

He got married at twenty-three then divorced by
twenty-five. His wife, Linda, could not handle the
atrophy beginning to plague her husband's body, even
though the deterioration at that time was very slight.
As he began to slow just a bit she decided to move
on. I never liked her anyways. She never displayed
any type of personality unless her veins ran heavy
with liquor or something to get her high. J.P. could
always get the best weed and really I think that is

all Linda cared about. Getting stoned and completely wasted. J.P. didn't like me around her much because I had a tendency to challenge her mental skills or any topic other than "hey let's get fucked up," or "I'm so fucking bored." Even though I was in my mid-teens J.P. knew that I saw right through her. She just split one day. J.P. showed me the letter she left behind. It made absolutely no sense and it took everything I could to hold back laughing out loud at her nonsense. Only his downtrodden face quelled an outburst. She did something to him that still mystifies me to this day because she was so opposite of what he stood for.

Then his bones broke down, then his heart, and sitting on his steps it came entirely clear to me how aware he was of his own mortality. He knew he would die at a young age. He totally knew it. Why fight the fate deemed upon him. His bones told him, his heart told him, the warm Santa Ana winds of late September whispered the prophecy into his ears and he decided to live like he was dying instead of lying down and waiting for it to come. I reveled in his defiance for a second, but the thought didn't offer enough solace. It was unfair. He had to be alright, he needed to be alright, and my world could not accept it any other way.

I knocked three times then inserted my key into the lock. The air tasted old. Walking by the kitchen I caught a slight aroma of stale pizza and over fermented beer. My breathing, which pacified during my recollections on the porch, returned to short, rapid gasps. I envisioned the moment in thoughts or in bad dreams hundreds of times, but not one of those visions could do enough to prepare me for dealing with it in actual motion. I looked for the hall light switch and the urge to vomit overwhelmed me.

'J.P. J.P. are you here,' I yelled. The door to his bedroom stood slightly ajar and revealed a dark corner of his un-made bed.

'J.P. you better answer me god-dammit.' The beating of my heart flapped against my ribcage with the pace of hummingbirds wings, yet I could not fly, nor faint, nor let loose of the bile compiling in my throat and instead I held my breath, pushed open the door and collected the view of a large, silent body sprawled in a contorted position, half on the bed and half on the floor. I thought about calling out his name again, I thought about screaming, I thought about kicking his idle ribs to rouse him from his slumber, but I just stood motionless at the entrance to his room.

"He didn't move man. He didn't move one fucking muscle and I just stood there like a useless moron." Cosmo began to cry. Small tears dribbled to his cheeks. Then, almost as if he lifted a two ton boulder from the middle of his chest, he let go and could no longer control himself as the diminutive tears evolved into heaving sobs. The ever steady Cosmo, the master of keeping his emotions in a harmonious balance broke down into a weeping human being.

"He was in a twisted mess," he barely got out. "Arms sprawled, legs in the air, and I couldn't do anything to help him. Not a god-damned thing." I thought I should go over to him for consolation, a kind word perhaps, but I stayed put, somewhat in awe that even Cosmo could reveal a chink in his armor. That he too could let a gush of hurt and pain run freely from his ducts. It felt like watching my father cry for the first time, or a teacher, or a world leader, people whom I thought could keep it together during any situation. Watching them crack emitted a deep scare about the world turning into complete chaos. After the initial shock reality set in and I came to the realization that no one was perfect. Not even my father, or Gandhi, or my fifth grade teacher Mrs. Armstrong. We were all fallible. We were all flesh and blood and at some point we would all show our vulnerability. So I stood agape a few seconds longer until my amazement turned into a profound well of sorrow at Cosmo's loss. He buried his feelings deep into his guts since the day of J.P.'s death and finally, amidst a chilly night, a few beers, and a roaring camp fire, he let them spill over the surface.

I walked towards him and he looked up abruptly.

"I'm all good man," he sobbed out. "It's about time I let all of this crap out of my system. Why do I have to act so sure all the time? So in control, so feigning that I have all the answers. Well I'm not and I don't, that's for damn sure. My uncle died for Christ sake. He treated me like his own son. He was my dad when my father rotted away in prison. It's okay to cry for him. To scream out that it's so unfair that he will no longer take a breath on this planet. Forty-four years old man, forty-four years old." He let it out and I felt relieved for him. Since the day of J.P.'s death Cosmo acted as though it never actually took place. Indifferent and accepting was how his mother described his reactions to me when I asked how he was doing. He held himself together until that point, but he needed to release his pain.

"I know there were odors," Cosmo said regaining himself, "but I can't recall any of them. Death causes the valves in our bodies to give up fortified positions and let loose of the remaining fluids in the organs. The secretions and a decaying cadaver emit a pungent smell as one passes from this world. Not being an expert in forensics or an E.M.T. I couldn't tell if J.P. died just a few hours before I got there or a few minutes before, but I'm sure there was a smell. We hate to think of that, that in death we will cause an extra sensation of discomfort for those who find us or might be caring for us. That we will rot and expunge an awful aroma and add to an already unpleasant scene seems to be another cruel joke played on the human race. A whiff possibly entered my nostrils furthering the urge to vomit, but nothing I can remember or describe. I was too numb.

I did the obligatory check for a pulse on his ice cold body. My first reaction should have been to call 911, but I waited. Perched next to him I stared and watched his lifeless body as though he would get up in a few minutes to go make a Jack and Coke in the kitchen. He twitched, or so I wanted to believe, but nothing moved. Not the curtains, the air, not even my own chest made a disturbance to the stillness of the room while I sat next to J.P. Time stood still. I'm not sure how long I sat next to him, an hour maybe, fifteen minutes more likely as I finally picked myself up off the floor and made my way to the phone.

Forty minutes later the circus arrived. Before they

set foot in the apartment I made a few rounds around the place to search for anything the police might find suspicious. J.P. seemed edgy the last few months and his latest girlfriend told me he was getting into some harder stuff. I didn't find a secret stash anywhere, but I did come across a glass pipe and a lighter in his bedroom. Something told me he was not using it for marijuana, but I couldn't be sure, and so I smashed it into shards in the outside dumpster. The paramedics found his heart medication virtually untouched and automatically assumed negligence as a cause of death. I'm sure that was part of it, but not all of it. If I disagreed they might have investigated and found that some other source of illegal narcotic mixed with a well of alcohol, along with his refusal to regularly take his pills as the final cause to his demise. If that was the case, and I can't be sure if it was or not, they didn't need to know, and as his closest family member I concurred with their initial assessment and signed what they asked me to sign. The police agreed as well and told me an autopsy was unnecessary. And that was that. Another heart attack, but this one did him in. And then my uncle was driven away in an unassuming vehicle by a quiet man from the morgue. I was left alone in his apartment after the parade filtered down the road.

The visions of his contorted body haunt my dreams and I'm sure they will for a long time to come, but I know now that I was supposed to find him. Not his on again off again girlfriend, not some curious neighbor, not the police who could have tainted his image in the position they found him in, no one but me. It was my burden to bear, but it's over now. He is free. His aching bones, his scarred heart, his rush to accomplish what he could in the amount of time allotted him, passed on from this physical world. And I can say for certain, Dane, after purging this story to you and letting myself wail like a baby, that I'm happy for him. I'm absolutely happy. The only sad thing remaining is that he could not make this trip with us."

"Yeah," I got out stumbling for words.

"So here is to J.P. May he rest in peace and hold a place in the lineup until we get there." Cosmo raised his beer, poured a little out on the cool earth, and took a long satisfied drink. I aped his movements as thoughts of J.P. streamed into my conscious. I would never catch a fish with him again, though I think we usually caught more of a buzz than actual fish. He would never again make fun of me on the beach after screwing up a perfectly good wave. And I would never again get a phone call from him while Cosmo was somewhere traipsing around the globe asking if I could help him move some piece of equipment or to meet up with him at one of his favorite dive bars. Tears formed in the corners of my eyes as I took another drink to fight them back. I let the glow of the fire hypnotize my thoughts until Cosmo broke the silence.

"I need to say one more thing, Dane, before I'm done."

"What's that," I said with a crack in my voice like that of a sprouting adolescent.

"J.P. loved you man. I know he acted like a hard ass most of the time and dished out plenty of belittlements and shoulder punches, but that was his way of showing he cared. If he paid no attention to you it meant he probably could care less about you. He told me one day that you were a rare friend to hang on to. He said 'Cosmo, so many people want a piece of you and your time. They want to siphon it out of you like it was their own, but not Dane man. He will just let you be. There are a lot of fake ass-holes out there for sure, but you can tell he is genuine. So don't be a dumb ass and screw up that friendship while you prance around town with all of your cronies numb nuts.'

"He may have never told you anything close to that in person, that was not his style at all, but it was there for sure and another reason why I knew you needed to make this voyage. I would have shared his fondness for you a long time ago, but somehow I felt you already knew. And whether you were aware of it beforehand or not, you were coming on this trip no matter what obstacle got in the way. It may have seemed impossible at the time or even right now, but life could not have evolved any other way.

"You think so?"

"No, I know so."

I felt ready to choke. The air tasted heavy. My bones sagged. "Cosmo, I...."

"There is nothing to say Dane. I know this is kind of a hokey moment between two guys camping alone, but thanks again for being here. J.P. would so appreciate it."

The moon rested almost directly overhead. It appeared only days away from being full. I am not sure how or why, but a satisfied laugh escaped my jaws. I could tell Cosmo was done talking by the look of contemplation that returned to his face. He may have lifted a great weight from his chest, dislodging a huge boulder of burden, and yet, even through his own purged saga he still managed to assist my peace of mind. Up to that point I am not sure I had rested absolutely at ease with my decision to make the journey. The annoying pest so aptly named guilt tugged at my intestines. At that moment it was gone. I knew it might come back, but at least I felt that I could get a decent night's sleep knowing I was supposed to be exactly where I was. The fire lolled me back into a daze as dreams waited in queue among the burning embers.

Chapter 11

A tepid sun broke through the car windows like a rolling wave. It crashed upon my arm and then quickly receded to make room for the next approaching surge. The ebb and flow regulated a comfortable temperature inside the Scout as we bounced down the asphalt. Cosmo did his best to dodge the incessant mine field of potholes which littered the highway. We broke camp early in the morning after a quick session before the wind picked up. Cosmo did not speak any more about the previous night when he revealed the details of Uncle J.P.'s death. He said his piece and we did not need to discuss it further. He hooted and hollered like everything in the world was in perfect balance while we surfed that morning.

I felt good. I enjoyed another pleasant time in the surf. My turns were loose and fluid and I actually felt like my surfing was progressing for the first time in years. The weight Cosmo relieved from his chest during his confession about J.P. seemed to lift an onus from my body as well. Breath came easy; my body light, my motion was almost graceful. Cosmo's MP3 player, which ran out of a docking station because the Scout did not have a radio, came to "Like Eating Glass" by **Bloc Party** on random shuffle and I cranked the volume to compliment my euphoric mood. Music dammed the flow of thought or wonder. It felt crazy how the combination of guitar chords, baselines, pounding drums, and clever lyrics sung to the movement of sound could excite the deepest senses of our souls. Good or bad, elated or melancholy, music could console our joys and sorrows like an understanding friend.

"This was such a good debut album," I said.

"Yeah, too bad the follow up did not pack as much punch," Cosmo returned.

"The second one was not horrible though. It still had a few good songs on there."

"Yeah, it did. But it was just not a start-to-finish album like this one. It did prove that they were above the sophomore jinx, I guess."

We climbed a steep and windy grade. Cosmo flew around the curves like he was driving a roller coaster car. I followed suit and raised my arms around the bends as we sped along.

"I know it doesn't belong on the list of all time greats or anything, but I just really like this one, the debut. I can listen to it all the way through. That's how I classify a good album, listen-ability all the way through, and a bonus factor that it always puts me in a good mood. If I was stuck somewhere I would not mind at all to have this album with me."

"Yeah it has listen-ability alright," Cosmo laughed, "As you put it, the good mood vibe as well, two important factors for sure, I guess you could do a lot worse than to have to listen to this over and over. Probably keep you happy, that's for sure."

I turned down the music. "Well, what if you were stuck somewhere and you could only listen to three albums? Which albums would you choose?"

"Well first of all they are not albums anymore, or at least it's rare to have them on vinyl nowadays, and second of all it depends on what kind of mood I'm in. Am I happy, melancholy, pissed off at the world, got to have some help before answering that question?" When Cosmo and I discussed music we became much like the characters in **Hi-Fidelity**, the novel by Nick Hornby or the movie starring John Cusack and Jack Black, because we could never leave a music topic as simple as naming a favorite artist, or album. Similar to the characters in the story we broke the lists down into a multitude of categories that spanned from favorite songs while camping on a cliff and drinking a beer to the best artists to listen to on the way to a funeral. The picks were ever evolving and made for great discussion.

"O.K ass munch, I know we listen to C.D's, MP3's, on all other types of digital format, but it's just easier to still call a full length release by a band an album. And if you need a mood, how about now, this instant. What are the first three that come to mind in any order? And nothing over, let's say twenty years. No **Clash, Zeppelin, Beatles,** or I don't know, not even anything like **Nirvana.** Have everything a bit more recent or slightly less obvious."

Cosmo shook his head and down shifted into fourth gear. "Like I could ever put **Nirvana** on that list anyway. I can't stand to listen to anything off of **Nevermind** anymore. Good band, good musicians, right time, and the media destroyed them. The songs are good, but every form of media killed their luster for me. Not their fault at all. I feel sorry for Kurt, I really do. They wanted him to be the next Lennon, he just wanted to play music, but the masses would not leave him alone. And to this day stations still play the shit out of that album, and I have to turn the station. I bet Dave, and Chris turn it as well. That's one of the reasons I barely listen to radio anymore, and if I do I usually just listen to Petros and Money on sports radio."

"Gees, sorry I mentioned it."

"Oh, bite me."

"I agree with the PMS show though. I love listening to those guys. They crack me up."

Cosmo gave me a quick smile. "So you want three albums in my current state of mind and less than twenty years old. Hmm, well here it goes with no conscious at all straight from the cuff, in no order: "Swagger," by **Flogging Molly** to get the blood pumping and keep spirits high and glasses full. I know they have grown musically and lyrically since their first studio release, but that first one reminds me of seeing them live. Of all those nights down at the Casbah when we paid five bucks at the door and jumped around spilling beer everywhere. Next I would go with "Being There, disc one" by **Wilco**, because it's so damn good, but wait, the song "Sunken Treasure" is on disc 2. Just say the whole "Being There" album then, discs one and two, because I can't leave that song out."

"Really, I thought you would choose Wilco's debut, A.M., for sure."

"It crosses my mind right now to choose that one, in all it could be there best album, and in speaking of debuts like we were earlier, it could be the best debut album put out in the last fifteen years or so, but I bonded with Being There on a road trip I took to Oregon quite a few years back. The album had come out like a year before the trip and I had not really explored it fully. It was the first trip I had taken in years that did not revolve around surfing. The lush greens of Shasta and entering Oregon, the open road, a different form of traveling, and that C.D. all wrapped into a special memory for me, so that's why I am sticking with Being There. And last, let's see, how about "Thickfreakness" by **The Black Keys** for some plain kick ass rock and roll. I could survive with those for awhile for sure."

"I would poke fun if I could, but that's a pretty solid lineup. I might pick "Rubber Factory" instead of "Thickfreakness" though. Hey, remember when we saw the **Black Keys** at the Belly Up Tavern and you met that gorgeous woman from Brazil," I asked instead of augmenting the question. "I can't remember her name right now, but wow."

"Oooh yeah. That show went off. She was so damn beautiful. Her name, damn, what was her name, it's slipping my mind."

"Sonya?"

"No. It was. It was, umm, Sofia. Yeah that's it Sofia."

"Whatever happened to her?"

"What do you think happened," he asked

sarcastically. "We went out a few times. Got to know each other real well, Brazilian women can be very forward," he shyly smiled. "You know me though. I screwed it up of course. Got all freaked out and cut it short even though it was going good. I have issues man. Scared to just see what happens. I cut the ties before anyone gets really hurt, because I'm so sure that it's bound to occur eventually."

"Yeah you do have issues. No doubt about that. And you may get scared and all, but I don't know how the hell you let her get away. Issues galore brother, issues galore."

"Go on chastise me all you want."

"Don't worry I will." We both laughed as the MP3 searched for a new song.

"This is pretty fun don't you think," Cosmo asked while he turned down the volume on a **Led Zeppelin** song I could not make out. "You know being on the road, surfing, living in the moment, having discussions like these?"

"Definitely, I have not felt this free and easy in so long."

"Been a while since you been down here huh?"

"I guess it has." I looked out of the window and watched the cacti pass. The prickled stalks looked like stick figured Martians. "That old line they always feed you. Time goes faster when you get older, how true it has become. Back at home it felt like I was just here, but being down here now I really feel like it has been awhile."

"So were you sick of it then?"

"Sick of what?"

"You know, sick of being cramped up in that office all day?"

"Of course I was, you know I was, but it's not that simple."

"How do you mean?"

"Well it sucks sitting for eight to ten hours a day doing something I don't really enjoy while the world outside is moving about. I hate that, but at the same time where do I find the balance, you know. The work is easy and it pays me well. Karana and I have a lot of bills to take care of. It works. We live a good life."

"Do you think you would go back?"

"Huh?"

"Huh nothing, back to work at your old job when you return home? You are going to have to find something to do when you get back."

"I know that, but I walked out. I didn't even tell them in person. I just left a voicemail before we took off. Doubt they would want me back."

"Oh please, they would take you back in a second. They would pretend for a minute or two that they were pissed off at you for your behavior, but just as a facade. All you would have to do is flip them a line about being distraught over the whole funeral thing and that you were not of sane mind at the time of your exodus."

"So what are you saying then? Are you telling me I should go back?"

"I'm not telling you anything. I'm just asking a question." Cosmo smoothly took the car around a swooping curve. He flipped the visor down with his left hand to shield his eyes from a burst of sunshine.

My mood soured. I knew he tactically inserted the question to dig somewhere deeper than I wanted to go. The air felt light, I floated, but he instantly changed all of that. I often hated his sudden alterations in the middle of an innocent discussion even though I usually needed his reminders. Sometimes he could not leave well enough alone. Before he began another one of his bloated diatribes I spoke again.

"The balance is hard to find. My heart may not have been in what I was doing everyday, and I may have stewed at my desk from to time to time at my decision to fall in line, but after work or on the weekends, or during my time off Karana and I could afford a fun filled lifestyle. That balance man. Do I give it up? Do I quit, well I guess I did quit already, but now do I go back and find a job where I struggle from paycheck to paycheck and become stressed everyday of my life. I might be happier at work, but maybe home life will become more of a nightmare due to all of new struggles I'll inherit. I was cruising. We went on vacations. We were saving for a house. I could randomly spring for Sushi for a group of friends and it would not hurt the bank account too much. Sounds a tad pretentious I know, but it feels good to be able to do things like that. Don't know what I'll do when I get back, but to be honest I would rather not think about it right now. The time will come soon enough when I have to stare down that fact face to face. I walked out on my own admission, by my own decision, and I have to deal with that, but right now I'm feeling easy, feeling free, feeling in the moment. I would like to keep it that way so let's just drop it."

The Scout huffed up the last S-curve at the top of the pass. Cosmo stared at the gauges. J.P. never fixed them correctly in all the years he owned the vehicle. Just when he got the speedometer to read accurately the temperature gauge would take a dump. Such went the pattern with all the gauges and turn signals in the Scout. Cosmo put in some work before we left and told me that all of the electronics were working in proper order. He looked concerned and completely removed from our recent discussion.

"Something wrong?" I asked.

"She's running a little hot. This incline made her work up a sweat. I think I'm going to pull over when I find a decent place to get to the side."

"Anything serious?"

"I don't think so. We'll just give her a break for a few minutes. I got to take a leak anyway."

I was still a little peeved that he ruined my mood, but I noticed that he had already let it go. He just pried as usual. Made me think, made me work. He found a wide shoulder to pull over on just as we began to descend towards a green valley. It looked as if a vineyard lined the bottom of the hill and its fringes spread out like a gigantic labyrinth. I knew he had finished the interrogation, but I slammed my door when I exited the vehicle a bit more agitated than I let on. Cosmo opened the hood to let it air out and moved carefully to avoid the radiator cap as he scanned over the guts of the vehicle. We rested ten feet off of the road and the shoulder acted as a safe harbor to let the car cool down for a few minutes while she gathered her breath. I opened the back hatch and pulled out a bottle of water from the cooler and a bag of potato chips. I handed Cosmo the chips without saying a word and headed towards a ledge to look out over the valley. Cosmo followed, but stopped short to urinate behind a wild sage bush.

"Had you worked up there for a second," he commented while relieving himself.

He had to bring it back up. It came out with no malice, but I took it that way.

"Whatever," I shouted peering over the edge. My stomach fluttered at the height and I wondered if my body could survive the fall if I took a leap. I did not want to leave the world at that moment. I was just curious about how much the human body could handle. I sat down the water to pick up a rock I could launch over the edge. The rock I chose sat imbedded in the earth. I clawed around its edges to pry it free and caught my right index finger on something sharp that ripped my flesh. Fresh blood ran off of my finger and mingled with the dry terrain.

"Ahh shit," I screamed.

"You alright," Cosmo asked as he emerged from the bushes.

"No, I just cut the crap out of myself."

"On what?"

"I'm not sure, probably a piece of glass. It was right next to a little rock that I tried to pull out of the ground."

"Let me see." Cosmo grabbed my right wrist and looked at the cut. "Yeah that's a bleeder alright, but I think you will live. Put some pressure on it to slow it down."

Cosmo let go of my wrist and I brought my left hand over to slow the bleeding. "Don't we have a first aid kit in the Scout somewhere?"

"Yeah we do, but it will take forever to dig it out. It's under the floorboard in the back and everything we brought down is packed on top of it."

"I can just grab one of those hand sanitizing wipes I guess."

"I've got another idea. It should stop it immediately."

"What is it?"

"Come over here." Cosmo aimed back towards his natural bathroom. He put a hand on the sage bush and turned the corner. I thought he knew of some ancient remedy handed down from a Native American tribe about grinding up sage leaves and sprinkling them into a cut to cease blood from spewing out of an open wound. When I followed him around the bush I saw him squatted near his puddle of piss. "Alright give me your hand."

"What the hell are you talking about?"

"I'm going to stop that thing from bleeding now give me your hand."

"No way, I'm not going to let you put your piss on me."

"Quit being such a baby. It works like magic."

"No way in hell."

"Then you take a leak in the dirt and use your own urine."

"Shit not, that's repulsive. I would rather just search around for the first aid kit and loose a little more blood in the process then bathe my hand in piss." The blood flew out in a steady stream. It throbbed a bit, but the pain did not overwhelm me.

"Suit yourself," Cosmo said dropping his hands to his sides. I realized some of my blood got onto his the front of his T-shirt. "Nothing in that kit will stop it like this puddle of medicine right here, but fine, go ahead, bleed to death. See if I care."

"Does it really work?"

"Hell yeah it does. Just take a piss in some loose dirt. Then, when the whiz and the dirt combine rub some of it in that cut and it will dam it right up."

"Really? You're not jacking with me are you?"

"Dude, come on, you are bleeding like a stuck pig. I'm trying to help. Now if you want it to stop turn over there and get to work."

He left and gave me some privacy. I needed to pee anyways so I could make up my mind while I took care of my humanly duties. It took a while to get my pants undone with one hand, but after a moment I was zipped up and staring at the dark puddle while I held my breath. It was just pee after all I thought, out of my own body. I bent down and scooped up a handful of warm paste and smeared it in with the dripping blood. It stung for a second then it took to my wound. The blood did not stop instantly, but after about a minute the flow dissipated to almost nothing.

I trotted out towards the Scout where Cosmo stared into the engine. "Look, it worked. I'm covered in piss, but it worked."

"Nice job. And you didn't want to believe me."

"It wasn't that; I believed you. I just didn't want to play patty cake with my own urine." I looked into the engine with him. Everything looked normal, not that I would have known the difference, but I nodded in approval. "Where did you learn that trick anyway?"

"I re-read the **Grapes of Wrath** a year or two ago. Tom Joad cuts himself while working underneath his family's broken vehicle and gets his cut to stop bleeding by taking a leak in the dirt. I always wondered if it worked."

"You mean you have never tried it before?"

"Nope, not before today. I really just wanted to see if you would put piss on yourself," Cosmo said while laughing.

"You're such an asshole."

"Oh don't get all huffy puffy. It worked didn't it?"

"Yeah, but that's not the point."

"Then what is the point. The point should be that it worked right. Just like when we stopped at that taco shop in Ensenada. You were munching down what I ordered for you. After diving into your second bite you asked what we were eating remember."

"Yeah it was sesos, brain tacos."

"And after I told you, you immediately slammed down the taco and put a disgusted look on your face. Until that point you loved every bite you took, with the tomatillo tomatoes and the extra hot salsa, but then your mind told you they should be gross when you found out what they were. Same thing here. I could have walked out from the bushes and told you I had just ground some wild herbs together with the soil and that it would stop the bleeding for you. When it worked you would have been awed and appreciative and you would have never known it was my urine that cured you. Now in the know, you think it's disgusting. In your mind herbs are natural, but so is your piss. So funny how are minds twist reality into what we perceive it to be, instead of what it really is."

I wanted to find the rock I tried to excavate from the ground and throw it at Cosmo's head, but he was right. So many times I let my mind tell me what was delicious or awful before I ever took a bite of it, because of some story I heard about it at some point in my life; Or how many times I judged beauty or ugliness through the eyes of the status quo instead of through my own. It may have not been the most sterile course of action, but it worked like a charm, and had he told me it was sage and rosemary I would have thought he told me the most amazing revelation. I let the rock stay in the ground.

"How's the Scout?"

"She's fine. How's your cut?"

"Like you said, I shall live." Cosmo looked right at me and burst out laughing. "Eeew you put piss on yourself. You're so nasty."

"Shut up dick."

"Clean yourself up you dirty tramp." We slammed the hood and got moving down the hill. The Scout cooled down and purred along. We kept sanitizing wipes handy, a necessary luxury while camping in Mexico, and I used about ten of them to cleanse my urine tainted hands. I chuckled at myself. Cosmo took a few minutes before he turned up **Zeppelin**, which he had paused when our discussion escalated, and Plant screamed out an avalanche of sound as we headed towards a jungle of grapevines. We planned to camp one more night before making it to Agua Dulce for the acme of the oncoming swell. I looked for my hawk, but he or she did not make an appearance and then my thoughts drifted towards my job. Damn Cosmo, why did he bring it up?

Chapter 12

A congregation of innocent clouds huddled over a broad mesa to the east as we pulled into a PEMEX fuel station. Since the unusual heavy rain that gushed from the heavens on the first day of our journey the weather had remained calm and warm during the day, but quite cold at night. The possibility of another downpour was highly unlikely for the remainder of our trip, but I kept an eye on the ever changing sky anyways. A young man of about nineteen in a green, long sleeve shirt unscrewed the gas cap and asked if we wanted unleaded or diesel. I stepped out to stretch my legs while Cosmo engaged in a conversation with the young attendant.

The small roadside town consisted of only a few structures, two markets no bigger than a normal sized living room, the fuel station, a handful of dusty houses, and a taco stand all lined the asphalt highway. I took the dirty hand wipe wrapped around my finger and deposited it into a metal trash can. A light trace of red still appeared from the wound, but for the most part the bleeding had subsided. I went to work in the back of the Scout to locate the first aid kit so I could bandage the cut properly. At home I might have gone to get my finger stitched up only because my company offered great medical insurance, but by the look of the wound I could tell that stitches would only be a luxury and not a necessity.

While I sifted through our junk Cosmo walked over to order lunch. When I finally located the medical supplies and wrapped the wound like an ancient mummy I parked the Scout in front of the taco stand next to a familiar black jeep with a lingering tingle on my finger from a shower of hydrogen peroxide. Cosmo was already engaged in conversation with Hillary and Campbell as I approached the faded, red picnic table they occupied. I took the empty seat next to Campbell who sat directly across the table from Hillary. The image of Cosmo and Hillary sitting together set off a silent alarm inside of my nervous system. Something looked too comfortable, too perfect, and yet filled with such explosive capabilities. The ease of their movements and rapport with each other emitted an electrifying chemistry in the air. I noticed immediately, but Campbell seemed more interested in cleaning his fingernails than paying attention to the adhesive connection cementing before his eyes. I was about to tell Cosmo that I was not hungry and that we should get going, but before it came out of my mouth the cook informed us that ten carne asada tacos were ready to be eaten. Cosmo picked up the order and set down the loaded plate between us. Campbell and Hillary had just finished eating when Cosmo sat down, but they were still working on ice cold Coronas. I reached for a taco and Hillary caught sight of the white gauze wrapped around my finger.

"What happened," Hillary asked. She wore a dark pair of jeans, flip-flops, a light-green tank top, and a black sweat-shirt which she left unzipped.

"Ah, sliced my finger an hour or so ago on a piece of glass."

"Are you alright?"

"Yeah, I'm fine. It bled pretty well though."

"You guys want to know how he stopped the bleeding," Cosmo interjected.

"Let it go Cosmo."

"Nah, come on let me tell them. It's no big deal. He pissed on it." I shook my head and let out a sigh.

"You did what?" Campbell asked.

"He put piss on it," Cosmo repeated.

"Why the hell would you do that," Campbell wondered.

"Hey, it's not like I pissed on it directly okay. I peed in the dirt and then used the urine, soaked mud to stop the bleeding like a paste. I was kind of desperate because we were on the side of the road and it would have taken a long time to find the first aid kit, as I just found out."

"Where did you hear about using your pee to stop a cut from bleeding," Hillary asked.

"From the jerk sitting next to you." Hillary looked at Cosmo as he gave off a sinister grin. She smirked at him as if to ask why he would do that to his friend.

"What," Cosmo asked playfully with a laugh. "It was something I read and figured it would be a quick fix for him in our predicament. In a bind it works."

"I would've rather bled to death," Campbell said. "You will wash your hands before you eat won't you." I pretended not to hear the question and leaned over the table and wiped my hands in Cosmo's hair, then continued down to his face. "Huh," I asked trying to sound oblivious. "What's this washing your hands you speak of?" Cosmo threw my hands off of his head. He knew they were clean, but let go into a healthy cackle anyway.

A large motor home pulled into the service station while we consumed our lunch. A man in his late fifties, slightly overweight and wearing a cowboy hat, stepped outside to greet the young attendant in the green shirt. His wife followed him out of the vehicle and instantly began snapping pictures of her surroundings. She aimed at the four of us sitting in the sun, clicked the camera, and then waved in a semicircle. Cosmo and Hillary waved back to the red haired woman and proceeded to strike a pose together like two models that stopped for the paparazzi as she fired off another picture. Campbell finally noticed the camaraderie forming between the two ridiculous looking models that carried on the joke as they curled their lips and made despondent faces.

"You two are like a couple of kids, you know that. You look foolish, grow up Hill."

"Oh, Cam, we're just having some fun, lighten up," Hillary shot back.

Cosmo noticed a shift in the mood between the couple and decided to change the subject immediately. "Are you two getting any waves?" Cosmo asked. "I barely even noticed that you had boards back at

Cuevas and I didn't see either of you surf at all while we were there."

Campbell took a long drink from his beer instead of answering, apparently miffed by the question, but Hillary chimed right in. "We have only tried it two times. It's so hard and these boards are massive. Campbell borrowed them from his friend David in San Diego. He told us they were the best vessels to learn on, but we don't really know what we're doing."

"You should have jumped in the water with us at Cuevas, we would have given you a few pointers for sure," Cosmo responded.

"It was much more fun to watch you guys. You make it look so easy, we didn't want to embarrass ourselves."

A snort came from Campbell as he set down his beer. His deep, black hair looked neatly brushed and the sleek, designer sunglasses disguising his eyes made him appear as if he spent the night in a luxurious hotel rather than in a tent. "Speak for yourself Hill. I'll get it soon enough. I've skied my whole life. It can't be too tough."

"Yeah," Cosmo agreed, "The basics are not terribly arduous if you have someone point you in the right direction, but to progress takes an abundance of self motivation to keep paddling out there consistently. It's not something you do once or twice and then you have it. Surfing is way more involved than that."

"How involved," Hillary asked.

"It can become so involved that you plan your entire life around it. Your job, your travels, where you live, your free moments, can all be affected by it, they can all warp around being near it, being fed by it."

"Sounds utterly enticing, I want to learn," Hillary said.

"We are headed about an hour south after we finish our lunch to a spot that would be perfect to help you guys out a bit. We call it Peppermint Patty's. It's not too difficult to find, because it's just ten minutes north of a well known spot called Cinco Rocas. When you see the signs for Cinco Rocas you take a right and follow the road until you hit the sand then head north for ten to fifteen minutes until you can't drive any further and you're there. Dane, you wouldn't mind helping them out would you?" I waited to answer the question. The ulterior motives behind Cosmo's sudden philanthropy screamed of certain disaster. Each second shared between Cosmo and Hillary drew them closer together while it raised the curiosities of the unknown. Campbell would eventually catch on, but I thought at that moment that he was already too late, and I worried about how he would respond.

"Sure," I said and continued to eat. I wanted to say no, but risked the possibility of revealing the reasons behind my hesitance. It probably would have been better to get it out of the way right then and there if I knew what would happen further down the road, but I remained quiet and let the scenario play out.

"I'm not sure we want to head any further south Babe," Campbell began. "I never even wanted to come down to this dirty country anyways. Hill somehow convinced me to push across the border, but I hate camping. I want to get back stateside and take a nice long, hot shower. We might just head back to where we stayed last night just north of here, camp the night, and then bee line it back to the border in the morning."

The motor home started up and made a wide turn onto the empty highway. A high pitched horn erupted into the air as both husband and wife waved to the four of us. Hillary stood up on the bench and gave one last pose to the moving vehicle as it steadily gained speed. She leaned to the right and put her left pinky to her pouted lips. Cosmo and I applauded her performance as the cook and another man leaning on the wooden shack whistled in approval.

"Such a child, Hill."

"You're just jealous Campbell. Let's follow Cosmo and Dane. I want to surf. You two look as free as soaring eagles out there. It looks so liberating, please."

"Baby lumps, I want to get out of here."

"God I hate when you call me that," Hillary said. She picked up her beer and gazed across the table at me. She offered a playful smile before she took a healthy drink.

"Well what should I call you then, Miss Motor Mouth? Talk, talk, you know this whole trip down here has been just for you and you're still not satisfied with anything."

"Because all you've done is complain. How can I enjoy myself when you try and make every waking moment we spend here as miserable as possible? Look at these guys, just drifting along with the breeze. Let's give into the moment like they are."

Campbell's bottom lip tucked underneath his top one as his cheeks sank in. His face altered into a simmering teapot ready to blow steam out of his ears while he slipped his hands underneath his armpits. He looked directly in front of him as though he was staring right through Hillary and out into the wilderness. Since the moment I sat down Campbell did not sit still. He often tapped his fingers on the table or shifted in his seat. He made exaggerated sniffs through his nose. I noticed a vacant hole on his left earlobe. I tried to picture what kind of earring he would normally clip into his ear and why he was not wearing one at that particular moment. He rocked forward, then back again and raised his sunglasses on the top of his head.

"I don't need your lip Hill, don't need it all. I can't believe you are acting like this in front of company. Sorry you guys have to listen to this big mouth over here." Hillary sank into her hands and then proceeded to drag her fingers through her hair.

"Look I meant no harm in asking the question," Cosmo interrupted. "I just thought we would offer some help if you guys wanted it. If you don't no big deal, I didn't mean for it to cause problems."

"No problems here Babe, but I do have to ask why you would want to help us. Aren't surfers supposed to deter, umm how do you call it, um, kooks like us from getting in the water," Campbell asked.

"What do you mean?"

"Come on Cosmo I've tried surfing once before. Had a guy nearly run me over and then he cussed me out and told me get out of the water before he killed me just because I accidentally got in his way. So much for peace loving, mellow surfers, this guy wanted my blood spilled Babe."

Cosmo held on to his beer bottle though he did not take a drink. "That's a shitty first encounter. Some guys are overly aggressive out there for sure, but let me ask you a question if you don't mind. You are a long time skier correct?"

"Yep, I've been skiing since I was five years old. The back bowls of Vail are my playground. I know those runs like the back of my hand."

"Uh huh, and what do you think of beginners who go to the top the mountain on their first run and cause traffic jams and accidents because they don't know what they are doing. You know who they are, the people who cut off your line and flail right into you as you are going full speed down the mountain. It's dangerous as hell for the beginner and for everyone else who comes upon them on the steep runs right?"

"Yeah I guess."

"It's the same story with surfing. Paddling out into a crowded lineup with no experience is like taking your first driving lesson in the middle of rush hour in Los Angeles traffic. You might want to try a few side streets and un-crowded parking lots before merging into the mess. There is a whole order of motion in a lineup, from who gets the right of way, to wave knowledge, to knowing where to be. Some people don't take lightly to those who barge right in with no respect to how things flow. Just as I'm sure you and your friends would probably not be too pleased with someone who violates similar rules on the mountain."

Campbell rubbed his chin for a second before responding. "That's a great theory Babe and I get your drift, but I'm more of a sink or swim type of guy. Throw me in the deep end and I'll make myself figure it out."

"And that's fine," Cosmo said while setting down his beer, "just don't be surprised when someone reacts the way your surf buddy did on your first attempt, but to answer your initial question I have no concerns teaching people who are willing to learn. The ocean is an alluring force and people are going to be drawn to her powers as long as humans exist. I'm not going to lie, sometimes I want to slap the bumper sticker on my truck that says 'Surfing sucks, don't try it,' because of how crowded it gets out there, but no matter how many deterrents I put up people will come anyway. I'd rather pass along some knowledge in hopes to create a more harmonious element in the lineup than to just give someone the stink eye. It might be an imprudent thought, I know, but education benefits everyone in any aspect of life." With that Cosmo smiled and bit into one of the tacos. Campbell nodded his head and sipped from his beer while Hillary stared into the sky. A yellow pickup truck with at least five people in the bed of it trotted south on the highway. It left a silence and a heavy odor of exhaust fumes as it disappeared from our sight. Digging into my third taco Campbell broke the quiet at our table.

"So you must think you're pretty good then. I saw you move about out there pretty well, you looked like you knew what you were doing, but now you spit out this credo of sorts and offer to bless us with your tremendous knowledge. You must believe that you're pretty hot shit then Babe," Campbell said while he stroked his smooth chin.

"Campbell really, knock it off," Hillary interrupted.

"Hill, I'm just asking him to explain himself. No harm in that. And stop reprimanding me in front of these guys, Jesus."

Cosmo rarely spoke about his surfing accolades and I could tell he felt uncomfortable under Campbell's interrogation. I almost answered for him, because I knew he would not reveal his true abilities and accomplishments in the ocean, but also because Campbell's voice inched closer to mockery with each question he spat out. I hated the way he used the word babe over and over again and his fidgeting became quite annoying. Cosmo could handle his own battle, but Campbell was not making any new friends, nor did he do a decent job of securing the bond with his current one.

Cosmo collected himself and politely answered the question with another question. "Why is that a big deal if I was hot shit or not?"

"Come on man I'm just asking. How good are you," Campbell asked.

"Does that really matter?"

"Hell yeah it does. You're blowing a lot of smoke into the air here Babe. If I'm going to alter my plans I want to know I'm going to learn from somebody that knows what he's talking about. Don't mean to brag, but I'm a kick ass skier, one of the best on our mountain, and it's hard for me to take advice from anyone. Why should I take it from you? If you're just an average Joe out there I might be better off teaching myself instead of listening to someone who might just want to show off in front of Hillary by pretending to know what he's talking about. Get my drift?"

I waited for Cosmo to lay it on him. I knew he usually restrained the natural human urge to paint a pretty picture of himself, but Campbell's rant deserved an entire mural of shimmering colors. I thought he would speak of the contests he won, the many islands he visited, or the number of surf videos he appeared in. Maybe he would tell Campbell of his smooth style and his friendships with a number of guys surfing the Pro tour who spoke of that style and Cosmo's abilities with great respect. Anything, any tidbit would have put Campbell in his place and knocked the cocky sneer off of his face, but much to my dismay Cosmo took another approach.

"I was okay once, but to be honest I could care less if I was the best surfer that ever existed or just that average Joe out in the water, because it was never about becoming the best at something. Surfing is the one thing in my life that has consistently given me pure joy. Attaching a list of goals, or adding on the stress of making my living by it would sabotage that joy. I have left those achievements for other areas in my life so surfing can remain free from the burdens of anything other than absolute pleasure." Cosmo rose from the table and smiled at his combatant. "Who could use another beer? All this talking has made me thirsty."

Though I had wanted Cosmo to verbally abuse

Campbell in any number of ways he managed to do something better. There was no need to justify his abilities to someone who would have not believed him even if he spoke the truth. He cared nothing for Campbell and boasting to him would have only made Cosmo sound just as childish as the man who sat across from him. By taking the high road and not delving into Campbell's game of who had a bigger dick Cosmo drew a mental line that raised the odds to three against one in his favor. No one had to say it out loud, but it became obvious that Campbell had been marooned on a deserted island all by himself.

To save face Campbell followed Cosmo and insisted on buying the round of drinks. I returned to the task of finishing the rest of the tacos on the plate before me. The meat cooled and became slightly more difficult to chew due to the lack of heat. While I chomped down on a bite I noticed Hillary staring at me like a child that wanted a hint about what she was getting for her birthday. She leaned over the table and whispered out of the side of her mouth. "He's really good isn't he?"

I had to finish chewing the massive portion of food in my mouth before I could answer. "Who Cosmo, he sucks something awful. He looks like an elephant on ice skates when he surfs." Hillary grinned and squinted her eyes. The noontime sun illuminated a gorgeous face absent of makeup and lightly brushed by a small group of freckles around her nose. Her long lashes batted at my sarcasm. "What can I say, he's incredible. He has the rare ability to let go in perfect moments of spontaneity and fluidity. I try, I have moments, but often I hear a nagging voice inside of my head that is trying too hard, thinking too much, trying not to fall instead of letting go. Cosmo doesn't have that problem. Even his wipeouts look like they were supposed to happen because he flows right into them. Is that a good enough answer for you?"

Hillary smiled and squeezed the top of my left hand. "I think I love him."

"What?"

"Shhhhh Dane, it's okay, it'll be our secret." She put her finger to her lips as Cosmo and Campbell approached the table. My stomach swayed like a raft in a storm out at sea. The next word out of anyone's mouth could have capsized the entire setting. I could have purged my new secret, Cosmo and Campbell could have resumed their feud, or Hillary could have told Campbell off for good. We sat quiet and it felt like we were watching a time bomb on the middle of the table tick away its final seconds before exploding. I pushed the plate of food to the edge of the table. I could no longer eat and Cosmo lost all interest in the cold tacos. If there was a way I would have snuck out of a secret exit and disappeared from the uncomfortable silence that overwhelmed our table, but unfortunately a miniscule town and sparse desert hills offered no such escape.

I looked across the table at Cosmo. His shaggy hair fell like a pile of spilled needles on the sides of his head. When the weather warmed up I knew he would shave the confusion of dirty-blonde locks to keep him cool, but at that moment it sprawled out in a ragged mess. On most people the style would appear as an atrocity of taste, but Cosmo pulled it off as though he was setting the next trend for how the youth would soon wear their hair, though he probably had no idea what his hair even looked like at the time. I envisioned a young kid walking by and telling his mother that he wanted a haircut just like Cosmo's only to hear the mother tell her son that there was no way she would let him wear a catastrophe like that on his head. After time the young boy would wear his mother down and his hair would ape Cosmo's style, but by then Cosmo would have already evolved with the next season and his hair would have evolved right along with him. Though I wished I could have pulled off the same hair do without looking like a fool I made a comment just to ease the tension in the air.

"Jesus Cosmo you look like shit. When was the last time you peered into a mirror? Your hair looks like a damned crow's nest."

Hillary and Campbell giggled while Cosmo considered my countenance. He studied me for a second then joined the laughter. "Glad I can entertain everyone. I'm here till ten, and don't forget to tip your waitress." He pulled the clear beer bottle to his lips and took a long drink. "Let's get out of here. Hey Dano let's go get in the water." We chugged down the remaining liquid and brought our trash to the garbage can while we handed over the empty beer bottles to the owner of the taco stand. After a brief conversation Cosmo made his way back to the Scout. I leaned on the hood of the vehicle near the passenger door hoping to part ways with our lunch companions. Hillary lifted herself in the Jeep while Campbell stood on the side steps of his vehicle draped over the surfboards that rested on black crossbars.

"You guys following us," Cosmo asked.

"No, I think we're going back to the spot we camped at last night. Not sure what it's called, but it has a nice, long, black sand beach."

"Does the turnoff from the road have a yellow sign with black lettering?"

"Yeah, I think so if I recall."

"That's probably Playa Bruja. I've never surfed there, but it has a decent beach break set up. Good place for you two to get some practice without having to worry about surfing over rocks."

"You guys should come down and give us lessons," Hillary blurted out excitedly.

Campbell ducked his head into the Jeep. "Hill they are headed south let them be. Last thing they want to do is waste their time watching you eat shit over and over. The little dreamer, always thinking everything will roll along smoothly. That everything happens for a reason. These guys are on their own mission, not here to cater to you and not to flow into your little hopes and wishes."

"I just thought it'd be fun that's all since we're not following them, you don't have to be a prick about it."

"Hill, I'm telling you knock that shit off. Next time you mouth off, I swear." Campbell slapped the boards with the palms of his hands and turned his head towards the empty highway. I put on my seatbelt and caught the exuberance disappear from Hillary's kind face. "Hell, I know Hill is a dreamer, and a big mouth, but the offer is open if you want to change your plans a bit. Sounds like you know where it is if you want to join us. Hey Cosmo, no harm, okay Babe. Just checking to see what kind of guys you are. Can't be too careful down here you know."

Cosmo ducked into the Scout. "Forget about it. I'll discuss it with Dano. Maybe we'll see you guys, maybe we won't."

"Well, good luck either way. It's been nice meeting you guys," Campbell said and took a seat in his Jeep. He shifted into reverse and winked at Cosmo through the open window. As they backed away I caught Hillary mouthing words to Cosmo. The phrase "Steal me away" sat in the air like a smoke ring as the Jeep reached the asphalt. I closed my eyes and bounced my skull against the head rest in disbelief, fully aware that those three words were about to change everything. The Jeep spun its tires and in a second they were gone.

"That didn't just happen, did it?" I asked.

"I think it did."

"You're not thinking about actually following them are you?"

"Don't know what I'm thinking, Dano."

"Look, Campbell doesn't do much to make you like him and it's obvious that he and Hillary don't belong together, but that doesn't mean he won't react violently if you step in between the two of them. This spells trouble man. He's edgy, kind of like a cokehead or something. Didn't you notice him at lunch? He acted all twitchy and rushed, kind of ready to snap at any moment."

Cosmo tapped on the steering wheel with his

fingertips. The grit on his face began to look more like the makings of a full beard in the golden sunshine. "Yeah Dano, I know you're right, but there is something about this woman. It's weird, but I feel like I'm supposed to follow her, at least down one road."

"You're just thinking with your dick."

"Ha, ha, God I love you Dano. I'm sure that's how it sounds, but believe me it's more than that. She is rare my friend. That night at Cuevas, I mean I felt like we knew each other forever or in some former life. It's like something is aligning the days to bring us in each others presence." He paused for a second and took in a controlled breath. "This sounds lame doesn't it?"

"Kind of sounds like your mom talking is what it sounds like. You're starting to sound mystic and all fortune teller on me."

"Well I am my mother's child."

"Can't you just let this one go Cosmo? We've followed your urges, your moments of chance and I know we will continue to do so, but let this one pass."

Cosmo looked at the MP3 player as if he wanted to turn it on, but waited to finish our discussion. "So as bluntly as you can put it, tell me what we should do. You always say whatever, or I don't care, but give me a real answer. Obviously our opinions our differing a bit. I don't see the danger. If things don't materialize naturally I won't force them along, but you seem to think trouble waits at Bruja, so tell me Dano, tell me where to point this vehicle."

Most times I trusted Cosmo's instincts over my own. I often struggled to admit to myself what I really wanted much like an oscillating seesaw while Cosmo followed his intuitions full steam ahead, but something felt off. He acted as though he completely eliminated Campbell's existence from his mind like a foolish Romeo. Cosmo was usually much more level headed and his sudden dreaminess alerted my senses to tell him how I really felt.

"Point us south Cosmo. Something might be going on inside of you and I don't want to belittle that, and sorry for this as well, but screw them. They are not a part of this trip. They can only complicate things. Point south and leave it to chance. If the fates somehow have us meet up with them again then I'll knock Campbell unconscious for you if I have to, but for now let's just go south."

A response did not follow as Cosmo hugged the steering wheel. He twisted his head north and then rotated to look south. The Scout rumbled to life with little resistance and choked out a few dark, gray breaths while Cosmo revved the engine. He grabbed the MP3 player and pushed play on shuffle mode then put the Scout into reverse. The little boat curled north with the stern in the lead only to stop in the middle of the highway and follow the Scout in its natural forward motion. Cosmo looked over at me before turning up the music. "J.P. would kick my ass if I ever followed that guy anywhere." He hit me square in the shoulder with a perfect J.P. Charlie Horse and grinned, but I did not feel the pain as a huge sigh of relief took over my senses and we picked up speed down the highway.

Chapter 13

I woke from a nap to find Cosmo missing from camp. I could not recall any dreams from the recent slumber, but thoughts of Karana haunted the nylon walls of my tent. I missed her. I wanted to wake up next to the warmth of her skin and the ease of her breath. The Scout remained idle and Cosmo's tent flaps were zipped down to reveal that he was not resting. I rubbed my eyes and looked out to sea. No Cosmo and no less wind blowing the waves all to hell. None of the boards were missing, not that he would have been out in the mess going on at sea, but I checked anyway. Groggy feet shuffled in the dust to a green and brown camping chair located around our makeshift fire pit. Plopping down I noticed that we needed to collect some more wood before nightfall and I thought Cosmo went to scavenge the hillsides for our evening fire.

I was glad to be rid of the certain calamity that Hillary represented and stretched content arms into the emptiness of the afternoon on the shores of Peppermint Patty's. We gave the spot the name a few years prior while we watched peeling waves break over a garden of kelp patties upon our arrival. The flowing leaves reached out for fins and dangling leashes, but once through the labyrinth of seaweed Patty's produced a clean right-hander over a cobble stone reef. Even after pulling up to a windblown mess I reveled in Cosmo's decision to part ways from the vitriolic couple from Colorado despite the lousy conditions.

On the opposite chair sat a red spiral notebook that toyed with the wind. The cover blew open, succeeded by a peacock fan of lined paper, then fluttered, paused, stepped into an up and down dance of agility, only to clamp shut once again. The dance continued, once in a while it displayed scattered ink that transformed into an occasional word. "Flesh," the pages waltzed, "ambiguous," and into a spirited tango, "demonstrative," and then a tap dance closed. I waited patiently to catch another word, another glimpse, but the notebook remained shut as the wind inhaled. I looked back to the ocean full of whitecaps and thought briefly of home and which day of the week it was. Work came to mind for a second, but I quickly eliminated the sound of ringing phones and forms printers and imbibed the symphony of salty wind as it exhaled. The notebook flew open from a large gust and folded in half. I watched for the dance, but it kept ajar as once again the wind rescinded with an extended inhale. I could not resist and scooted my chair closer to the exposed pages. Instantly a feeling of guilt tore through my shoulders and I scanned the horizon in a panoramic search for any sign of Cosmo.

Not a creature stirred, not even a six foot, two inch incessant voyager of spontaneity.

Where was I to begin? I felt twelve years old again discovering my father's **Playboy** magazines behind a wall of toilet paper stacked up underneath my parents bathroom sink. I knew my dad was at work and that my mom had just put on her Richard Simmons exercise tape, but I was afraid that someone would walk in on me at any second. The lock clicked on the bathroom door. I sat down on the toilet and flipped through colored pages of breasts, dark pink nipples, and triangular shaved pubic hair. I am sure it was a sin, or so they would tell me in catechism on the following Monday night about my impure thoughts and lusting, but nothing, not the guilt of displeasing God, nor the fear of one of my parents walking in kept the pages from turning as I examined each naked leg, every slightly flexed buttocks, and the sex escaping from seductive lips and alluring eyes. Was I stealing something in admiring those beautiful bodies without them knowing? Were they disgusted with me ogling their every curve, their secret patches of hair? Yet they posed, they looked comfortable and proud standing naked in front of the camera, and it must have been their own decision to put their bodies on display for the entire world. Their decision, I pondered that for a second and drifted into a fantasy about curling up next to the brunette wearing a black and red plaid skirt pulled above her bare panty-line, her bushy cavern exposed, a white top tugged down below her left breast, as a new hunger rose from my belly and swelled in my pants. At the time I swore it was love, a profound, urgent love, and then flipped the pages only to fall in love again with a sandy-haired blond.

The initial guilt felt the same as staring at those naked bodies, and yet it brushed aside just as fast as I dove into Cosmo's notebook. The looming questions about whether I had the right or about breaking a line of trust dissipated after drinking in his first paragraph at a random spot in the middle of the notebook. The ramblings spilled forth in raw form contrary to his published writings which came across well refined and scrupulously edited beneath colored surf photos or in an occasional travel magazine, but to me, no matter how brilliant any of his pieces were, something always seemed to be missing from Cosmo's voice in his published articles. He wrote of reefs, jungles, and oceans; exotic foods and tribal cultures in places I could only find after a meticulous search on the internet. One article that appeared in **Surfer's Journal** talked about the two months he spent in the Maldives helping a local friend construct a boat that would charter diving and surfing excursions. He documented the progress of the large craft and displayed almost as much of a keen insight with his camera work as he did with his words. You were there with him sanding decks, taking surf breaks in crystal clear waters, waiting outside of mosques respectfully for his new friends to say their Muslim prayers, and eating a freshly caught open sea tuna with a side of rice. Yet somehow Cosmo, the real Cosmo, was a distant character in the saga. The man with an incessant river of ideas and views, the man so likeable and intriguing painted a perfect picture of the scenes before him, but omitted himself out of those same pictures. When he personally told me the story about the Maldives it came across with layers of passion and heart, self reflection and soul, I was ready to sell everything I owned and get on a plane the next day, but when I read his article the true essence, the human essence in all of its exploratory glory came out diluted on the page and voided of Cosmo's soul.

Much of his published work followed similar patterns. Opening his red notebook meant opening a door to a chamber few people ever visited in a surf magazine or in an online article. I resigned to a lie I told myself about Cosmo leaving it out in the open for a reason. Yeah that was it; he did it on purpose, knowing full well I would peruse his thoughts when I came across them. Relieved by the fib I dug in.

> I have never known a home. Not for longer than a year or two anyways. By saying that I do not mean that I did not know love or belonging, of course, quite the contrary actually for I was showered with love from my family, but what I am getting at is the physical structure of a home. A building with four walls and dual paned windows residing forever in the same spot laced with nostalgic odors and horrid wallpaper. It would almost take two of me, using all of the digits on my hands and feet to come up with the number of abodes I have laid my head down in at night. On a few occasions during my elementary years we moved more than one hundred miles away, but most of the time we stayed in the same town or same

county, just re-locating a few miles down the
road or across the street.

My mom was born a vagabond with a wandering heart. The idea of being in one place for
too long made her sick and she would turn to
fits of panic hysteria or obsessive pill popping
if she sat still for an extended period of time. I
began to read the signs, the twitching, the irri-
tation, the late night insomnia accompanied by
marathon movie watching, all of which directed
me to my bedroom where I packed clothes and
ripped down baseball and surfing posters.

Dad hated it, her self-proclaimed claus-
trophobia, her fear of being idle, the constant
sight of moving boxes, but he hated her feelings
of discomfort even more and so he catered to
the incessant moving about, or more humored
her if you will. Without his influence we probably would have moved every other month and
to no surprise after he went away the amount
of times we moved definitely amplified. Funny,
the place that ripped my family apart, or my
mother and father anyways, is the very place I
clung to with every shred of hesitance a budding adolescent could muster.

My mother describes the tale of my parents
road to ruin that eventually lead to my father's
incarceration with a mystic fervor I cannot
emanate at this moment, maybe at another
time, for now I will just say that my father had
a choice, an option, but he waffled on his decision and because he did not act immediately

like my mom did he lost eight years of his life
and I lost a father when I needed him most. It
still sounds preposterous that he went away for
so long just because of a plant that grows naturally in the earth, but that is a whole different
story altogether, for a different time.

In the summer of 1989, the summer my
mom wanted to leave Green Valley, I almost
ran away from home. Actually, with my mom
leaving to another town in an abrupt manner
she was running away and I was stubbornly
staying put. I stood firm, I wasn't going to
budge, I was staying and she was going and that
was final. Call it a fragile time, call it pertinent
to my character, label it whatever Freudian
state of ego or id that needed massaging in my
early stages of adolescence that some psycholo-
gist would pin on me , but I will only admit to
the fact that for the first time in my life I was
about to become cool.

I had always been the long-haired, freckled
boy who often got mistaken for a girl. At about
the age of nine a gray haired man at a con-
venient store commented to my mother about
what a cute girl she had while I obliviously red-
dened my lips with a licorice rope. Joe Rob-
bins, with spiked hair and sharp blue eyes, who
could already bench press more weights than
I could even count, used to sit behind me and
snip at my hair with cheap elementary school
scissors in science class. "Hey little girl, you
little sissy girl," he teased chopping at the air.

I occasionally pled with my mother about the length of my hair after occasions like these, but somehow after our discussions she would mollify my concerns and the long strands that ran to my shoulders stayed put.

My mother's idea of a hair cut consisted of brushing my hair straight down in my face and then cutting a square window above my eyes and down the sides of my cheeks so I could see. Kids would laugh and tease, but that summer, the summer we were deciding to leave, I watched the hair on the heads of those same kids that teased me start to grow long. I was an all-star on my baseball team and the free-throw champion of our junior high school. I also kissed a girl for the first time. Lynn Gabel. Our tongue dance was a bit awkward, or at least I know that I was all over the place, but she tasted of spring and everything was new.

My status also grew because my cousin from Idaho came down the previous summer to visit and built a six foot half pipe in our backyard. Guys started coming over, guys who I perceived as cool and were popular as well as adored by all the girls at school. After they signed a permission slip that my parents concocted to keep from being sued in the case of any accidents, which at the time sounded so un-hip, we set off skating up and down the ramp for hours. I often won our best trick contests with tiny front side airs and tail stalls. We even got to deny some of the jerk-off, bullies who showed up unannounced without a permission slip. They would get lippy and threaten our little crew and then my father would appear, all six foot six of him and scare them off the premises. They left dejected and I welcomed a sense of pride in my father's raised voice.

It was to be the best summer of my life. My birthday came at the end of the school year and I blew out twelve candles and the end of sixth grade with more wishes than I could account for. As cake passed around on light-blue paper plates a bomb exploded in the middle of the living room. The floor boards shattered, popcorn from the ceiling and busted two by fours with rusted nails showered down in a scattered mess. Smoke devoured the halls and I choked and came to tears when the words left my mother's lips. "We are moving to the coast to live at your uncle J.P.'s for awhile," or something to that degree was all I remember her saying. I wished for one more burning candle so it would make a jagged beam plummet from the roof and pierce my heart after I blew it out. It came so sudden. Without warning I went from making plans with my close friends, to "We are moving right away." It tore me apart. Yet as the tears flowed, my birthday marred, two thoughts persisted immediately; I was staying, and I was going to loose my family.

I planned it all out. I would stay at my friend Mark's house, visit my family on the weekends, and further my rise out of the timid skin of my youth. We continued to skate the ramp quite often and mapped out the upcoming school year. I helped my mother pack her things, while I left my room exactly the way it was, because my father was staying put. He was not around much that summer. My parents' arguments reached a point of no return in their relationship. Dad refused to cease his operation that supplemented our income and mom was convinced that something bad was stirring in the air. She said she felt it in the wind, in her bones, deep in her soul, and she wanted to deal with it no longer.

They called it a break, but I knew better and they both agreed that if I was staying I would be better off at Mark's, because of Dad's enterprise. In retrospect I know that they were doing nothing more than calling my bluff.

The ride to the coast took about forty-five minutes. My mother played along with my little game and let me leave all of my things in Green Valley. She was quiet and reserved, which was quite an arcane disposition for her. I tried to say something consoling, but nothing came to mind over the blasting radio. Only now can I see that my aloofness to any feelings other than my own covertly wounded her heart. I didn't see it at the time nor did it even cross my mind. Everything in her universe revolved around each breath I inhaled. She bled, she fought, and she worked to support my very existence and the thought of hurting her never even entered my thoughts. I was twelve and the world was right then, and only then.

As we unloaded boxes a wind picked up from the sea and climbed into my lungs. I pretended not to notice its effect as we moved from truck to house and back again. It tasted like something I knew, something I loved but could not describe, something I had to have, but I fought, I fought hard. As soon as we finished I asked when we could go back to Green Valley and move my things into Mark's place. No one was heading back that day and I was to spend the night on the coast. My father, who helped with the move even though he did not agree, was going to hang out and leave early the next morning so we made plans to rendezvous the next day.

With everything in order I relaxed. One night away from returning to my coven of security and total independence rested easy in my chest. I moved about so at peace that I never saw it coming. Never caught the sign of my uncle J.P.'s scheming while he asked me to go surfing with him and a couple of his buddies. Without hesitation I jumped into his light-blue Toyota truck.

Oingo Boingo boomed out of the speakers as we cruised along the coast looking for a spot to head out. He only teased slightly at my defiance to remain in Green Valley, probably because I clammed up the moment he mentioned it. Sure, living near the ocean provided many perks, new faces, the beach, but he did not know my heart. He did not see that after three years of living in the same area, though in five different houses, I was finally emerging out of my shell. I wanted no part in trying to rebuild all of the confidence that thrived in my veins. J.P. noticed the shield I erected and quickly let any prodding go. His bones were beginning to ail him and I noticed a slight limp in his step for the first time, but he never mentioned it as we made our way to the sand.

The wind forgot to breathe. The surface of the ocean looked like an aqua sheet of glass lined with pristine hills of water rolling towards the shore. My initial plunge washed over me like a saltwater baptism. It cleansed all thoughts besides the beauty of the moment. No diversions about life in Green Valley, nothing about the rift between my parents or my imminent separation from them, nor a flash about which girl I would like to go steady with, the sea possessed my full attention. Snug waters wrapped around my skin like a mother caressing a babe to her breast. I surfed often during the summertime or on the many jaunts we made to the coast during the school year and I picked it up pretty fast, I liked it, enjoyed it, but never before that day did the ocean speak to me. Never did she cradle me in her arms and whisper into my ears that everything in the universe, my diffident teenage body, the worries of tomorrow, would somehow all be alright.

She spoke and I listened, and for the first time in my life I remember feeling at home. I was where I was supposed to be. I didn't know how to describe it at the time, I just knew it.

I did not speak with J.P. on the way back to his place. After unloading our surf gear I walked straight into my mother's arms and cried like a newborn. I felt her pain, I witnessed my own, and in that moment I acquiesced to the power of the ocean and made a decision to live on the coast. We stayed with J.P. until my mom found a place of our own. We moved plenty of times as the years went on. Apartment buildings, beach cottages, or as roommates of a new friend my mother made, we constantly bounced around in our usual pattern, but my mother promised, no matter how many times we up and left, under any circumstance, that she would never, ever, remove me from the sea.

I have never written of this before nor do I plan on sharing these thoughts with anyone in the future. The ocean is the only home I know. She adorns a welcome sign across the entire planet and takes me in whenever I feel alone. As I have grown into an adult following my mother's pattern of skipping from house to house or gallivanting around the globe, the sea remains my only constant form of familiarity. She has molded my character, my being. She humbles me when I need it, challenges me to push for the near impossible, teaches me to find balance in her ever changing moods, comforts me when I need her, and gives me the gift of life in her healing waters. I may never know a place filled with all of my collected treasures, or a white, picket-fenced front yard with two barking dogs, but that is okay, I would probably get claustrophobic in a place like that for too long anyways. My home will remain at sea, and I will follow her around the planet as long as oxygen continues to fill my lungs.

I closed the notebook and looked out to sea. Cosmo's home, his refuge, and so much of his life made more sense to me. I knew about the absence of his father, but reading his words explained where his deep love affair with the ocean began. It meant much more to him than just a form of exercise or a way of life, in many ways the sea became his father as he struggled through the awkwardness of becoming a teenager. I thought about reading on, because the notebook appeared sated with entries in a myriad of ink colors, but decided to leave it shut. A deep breath filled my body as the ocean pacified its vigor since the moment I first sat down. Then the feeling struck like an ice cube sliding down my spine. I turned around to see Cosmo sitting on a rock a few yards behind me. He looked past me, not through me, but beyond me, into the deep blues of the ocean in an apparent trance. Then, as if suddenly wakened by an alarm clock he leaped off of his rock and headed towards me. Normally I would have trembled in preparation for the incoming ire, yet as he approached something switched, the wind perhaps, the pulses in my heart maybe, I am not sure of the exact cause for the alteration, but I took my eyes from the dust at my shoes to the eyes of my oncoming interrogator and sank back into the folds of the camping chair in a relaxed calm.

Chapter 14

The wind died in sporadic gasps. A banana-skinned
sun hung two hours above its nightly swan dive
into the sea. It looked as though the surf would get
really fun if the wind deceased completely. Amazing,
after all of the power and vigor of the early afternoon
breeze all would pacify into a serene little bay before
night consumed the land. The swell Cosmo hoped for
was to be upon us in the next few days and I wanted
to get in as many sessions as I could to prepare myself
for the large surf, but I needed to shove some food
down my throat before hitting the water. I could not
reach any of the containers from my chair. I knew
better than to stand up and rummage for nourish-
ment as Cosmo approached and pretend like nothing
happened. I could not brush aside the violation I
committed. His notebook sizzled like bacon grease on
my knees as he drew near. I closed it up and handed
him the red-spiral collection of boundless thoughts.
He accepted it, opened it up quickly but did not look
inside, then closed it back up and sat down on the ice
chest across from me.

Cosmo rarely let anger get the best of him. It took an extreme situation for him to loose his head. He was a great negotiator, one who rationalized and compromised for the betterment of understanding. I awaited the scolding I deserved. Cosmo opened a bag of trail mix and crunched down on various morsels. He then took a gulp of water and looked me in the eye.

"Read anything good lately," Cosmo asked. I sifted through his question like a complex algebra problem and looked to see if in his query a hidden algorithm of anger existed in his tone. Through the layers and steps of integers I found no trace of ire. Instead a sense of curiosity seeped through his prodding. Maybe he wanted to see how much I read, or exactly what I had read, and get a genuine opinion on it. Perhaps he really did leave his notebook out for me to read on purpose much like the lie I convinced myself of earlier. Whatever the reason I played dumb at first and pretended not to notice the absence of hostility.

The wind subtracted into a gentle hum and I turned to face him. "Cosmo I'm sorry man. I don't know what I was thinking really. It felt wrong, but I could not turn away. I got stuck in the car wreck syndrome I guess."

"What do you think you did? It's not a personal diary that I lock up with a key or anything. It's a notebook, like a sketchbook for an artist, a scratchpad if you may. Thoughts appear, I write them down, no big deal. And if I was so worried about not letting you read it don't you think I would find a better hiding spot than right here on this chair?"

"I know but, but, you should be able to trust me enough to leave your stuff alone."

"Yeah I should, and I do, but it was nothing I needed to hide so get over it. No harm done. It's not like you were digging through my bags or anything." He took another handful of trail mix and filled his mouth. "So what did you find out?"

I looked out at the ocean. The calm continued and my body followed. I initially thought about telling Cosmo I only leafed through a page or two and more or less skipped around the notebook instead of concentrating on a certain section, but the solace of the moment prompted loose lips to pour out my entire findings. "I opened to the part where you fell in love with the sea. Where you moved from Green Valley to the coast and how the power of the sea kept you with your mom."

"Man I wrote that a while ago. It's so poorly written, I'm almost embarrassed you read it. Oh well, what did you think?"

"It said a lot to me actually. It was a very personal account, something I haven't found in a lot of other material that I have read of yours. I have a question though, but you don't have to answer if you don't want to."

"Go ahead, ask, I have nothing to hide."

"Do you really only feel at home when in the sea or near it, or was that just an analogy or metaphor?"

"Don't know."

"What do you mean you don't know?"

"I mean I don't know for sure. You write things sometimes. Overwhelming urges overtake your body and spill out on a blank page. Sometimes I can't even believe I was the craftsman on some of the things I have written, but I am. Sometimes when writing you can become a multitude of different personalities and conflictions, a blathering contradiction of sorts. So do I feel that the ocean is my home, absolutely one hundred percent, probably not, but it definitely feels like it most of the time. Sometimes it does and on rare occasions it doesn't, but that's the funny thing, the complex vortex that writing becomes, because I could also argue that in writing, in that blissful moment of profound release I exhumed an idea out of my subconscious that I don't readily agree with during my more conscious moments. That in writing those words I realized how important the sea was to me, how much I owed to her magnanimous offerings, or I could have done the complete opposite and penned a figurehead to a time in my life of great flux and called her the sea just to give it a name. Writing can be so comical that way."

He gave a great seminar on the varying aspects of writing, but he did not answer my question. I was searching for a concrete response. "But which do you think it really is, the truth or just a name for namesake?"

"It should not matter."

I thought about that for a second. Did I want to know for my own personal gain or to really discover a new nugget of information about my friend; I could not answer directly. "I guess not in the grand scheme of things, but as your friend I would like to believe that I just got to know you a little better. That the tiny fragment of privacy that you keep tightly sealed just became a bit more lucid to me. So you know what, I am just going to believe it is, that the ocean is your refuge, your peace of mind, your place of absolute home."

The dirt at our feet opened its ears, the rocks leaned in. The environment became our audience as I waited for Cosmo to respond. We were on to something, what we did not know for sure, but thoughts trickled out like a bubbling stream. He shook his head and smiled as if accepting my belief. "I like that, you can stick with that one, but now I have a question for you Dane? Now that we have delved into a personal area about me, it's my turn to ask you something that I have been wondering."

"O.K."

"Have you been writing lately?"

The question hit me in the gut. I could not breathe for a second. I felt like my father just asked if I took the trash out after reminding me to do it numerous times. My chores were incomplete. From the day we became friends in college Cosmo encouraged me to pursue my writing. He told me that I had a gift, but I never truly believed him. I thought he was just being kind. "Not exactly," I finally got out.

"So you are saying that you haven't been writing then?"

"Well not completely like that. I mean, I've been trying to, I think about it ten times a day, but when it comes time to sit down and actually make thoughts appear on paper or across a computer screen I seem to come up with the same pathetic excuses. Stupid stuff like, today is Monday and I need to get into a groove for the week so I will skip it tonight and do some writing tomorrow. I have no inspiration today; I am too tired, blah, blah, blah, all the same old shit and silly excuses. Just lame really, especially saying it out loud right now."

Cosmo took his time, drank in my comments and then asked, "What else?"

"What else what?"

"What other excuses do you have? Get them all out in the open, every wretched one."

"I don't know I use hundreds of them. I can use an upset stomach, Karana wanting me to lay with her while she falls asleep. Most of it is pure laziness and lack of discipline." I paused and looked up at patchy-white clouds morphing into fairytale animals. An overweight ogre clawed its way towards a winged canine with three legs and a spiked tail. A long haired mermaid twisted herself diagonally and revealed a puffy, gray breast. What moral would Aesop attach to a savage ogre, a flying, hobbling dog, and an exhibitionist mermaid? He probably would not touch that one actually, and leave it for a sick and twisted animator to merge into a sadistic, pornographic cartoon. I looked towards the mermaid, but she covered herself and turned her back to me.

"I have been reading a lot," I finally said to Cosmo. "There is never a time in-between books anymore. I have one waiting in queue for the day I finish the last page of the current novel I am into at the time. And the more I read, the more I find authors being entirely too clever. I underline paragraphs, or lines, or dwell on a certain author's usage and end up feeling like a complete idiot wondering over and over again how they came up with such crafty words. For example, I have been really into Hemmingway lately, probably your doing, and I was reading, I am pretty sure **Garden of Eden** or could have been **A Moveable Feast** not exactly positive on which one, but I could not get over a technique he used to describe the lawn area in front of the hotel, or villa, the couple in the novel stayed at. He spoke of the courtyard not as it was, except for a quick glimpse at it, but instead of what it would be like in the next season, of what people would frolic upon it, of what time would do to it and how it would age, and I kept thinking to myself that I could never be that clever. I can attempt it now and look out at the rocks on the beach over there and say that in summertime many of the rocks will burrow like sand crabs and hide below the distribution of sand that occurs from the south shore current, but all after the fact. If I was writing about the beach in a normal state, beneath the glow of a computer screen or at the helm of a scratchpad with pen in hand I probably could only come up with something lame like; the beach was rocky and desolate, not giving it time, or character, or transformation, I am just not that creative on my own."

Cosmo stood quiet for a minute, no doubt pondering an educated response, but I cut him off before he could get to it. "And it's not just the cleverness," I shouted out much louder than I intended, "It's more than that. I mean, o.k., let's say I go on a surf trip to a foreign country for ten days or more, which I have been fortunate enough to do on more than one occasion. I think I'm gaining experience, that the world is teaching me and I am becoming a more cultured and refined human being. And then in some obscure magazine I will read of a daring, early twenty-something, female journalist who spent three months dodging bullets in Iraq, sleeping on dirt floors, and wearing burkas. And that is just one particular story, one courageous woman. Thousands of people experience life in a more profound way than I have ever even come close to. I mean, surfers are generally accepted around the globe and taken in as wandering spirits appreciative of the earth and the gifts given to them. What have I done, what have I really done to gain experience to assist my writing. My efforts are paltry to what I could actually be doing."

I realized that I had been talking for longer than I anticipated. Cosmo did not change expression from the moment I began effusing my guts to the dying wind. His countenance remained stoic, yet highly intrigued. He settled back on the ice chest and stroked the six day shadow that covered his face. He swung his left leg over his right for five seconds, then shifted and leaned forward on both legs. He wore a tee shirt with a gray whale on the front of it which held up a sign that read "Save The Humans." In his forward position he spat in the dust. The saliva formed an oblong ball in the dirt. I waited for something complex, something almost berating, but instead a puckered smile, as though he was happy to taste the tartness of a lemon appeared, and Cosmo broke into a controlled chuckle. I looked at my arms, then my feet, then rubbed my face and nose. No dirt, no crusty boogers sticking out. What was so funny?

"What?"

"What, what?"

"What is so funny?"

"Nothing."

"Then why are you laughing. I hate when you do that. I feel like such a moron. Like you know something that I don't and I'm just a pathetic imbecile at the mercy of your knowledge."

"I'm laughing just because."

"Because why?"

"Because you sound a hell of a lot like a writer to me."

"Huh."

"A writer, you know people who put pen to paper and make something magical happen, you sound just like one, always have."

"How so," I asked, curious about his declaration.

"Umm, hell, let me see. You think everything that you write down sucks and question every word you print. You over think too much, but you have amazing ideas. You are tortured by thought and the complexities of your surroundings. Sorry for the prognosis, but you have writer written all over your face, for lack of a better term. It's cemented in your soul. Whether you aim towards it as a profession or continue to furtively fill empty pages with your thoughts for only a few to read you will succumb to the torment of putting down your passions and fears on paper for the rest of your life. You have always had something to say, but more times than not you keep quiet. Writing is your release, a part of you that you will always need."

He was toying with me, or was he. I felt I should prod him further. "If I'm such a writer then how come I can't make myself sit down and write more often? I'm not asking for everyday, but at least a couple times a week."

Cosmo stood from his chair and stretched towards the heavens. "I'll tell you why. You need help. You need someone to kick your ass and stay on top of you so you can stay on course."

"Oh really. I do huh. And do you think you are the one who can do it smart ass."

"Of course I can, but that's not the point. The point is to get you to stop making excuses, to step up and be a man and go after something because you want it. And I'm going to make you start at this moment."

"Bullshit."

"Bullshit nothing, I'm starting right now. I have an assignment for you?

"A what?"

"Don't say what like an illiterate imp. I have an assignment for you to complete by tomorrow night," he mouthed out painfully slow. His tone irritated me.

"What am I eleven years old? O.k. dad I swept the driveway what's next? You want me to clean my room and then feed the dogs?"

"Stop being so immature and if I was your dad I would have kicked your ass a long time ago. I would have lit a fire underneath your procrastinating ass in hopes that the heat would get you to live life by your passions again. As your friend I want to help you with that."

His comments impaled a deep wound. For months and years I wanted to change my everyday existence, but instead I sat. I stayed in the exact same place waiting for something to change when I should have gone out and hunted down the change myself. I wanted to challenge Cosmo, but it was time for me to eat crow. "Well, Jesus Christ Cosmo, how am I supposed to respond to that?" I grabbed a handful of trail mix and returned to my seat." And what if I refuse your little assignment?"

"Don't do it, see if I care. Go ahead and be a callow ass who will not accept some genuine assistance and perhaps a new perspective. Wallow in your own ignorance if you wish, but I think you might like it."

"What is it?"

"Are you on board then?"

"I don't know. What is it first?"

"You've got to be on board. I'm not wasting the time."

I thought about his demand. He sounded arrogant, but that was the pride section of my brain speaking. Deep down I knew he was trying to help. I stood up and pulled my left heel towards my butt. I put it down and then duplicated the movement with my right heel. Stupid pride, the swell and stench of it sickened me. "Alright, what do you have for me?"

"Glad to see you're over yourself."

"Piss off."

"Ha ha. So here it is. I want you to sit down and construct a page or two or ten, doesn't matter the length really, on why you are so afraid to write, so afraid to put it all out there. Make it an essay, make it a poem, make it sound like a cheesy birthday card. I don't care about the format at all, just let go of reservations and put something down."

"That's it?"

"Yep, that's it."

"Then what?"

"We're not there yet Speedy Gonzales. Just write the assignment before you. Tomorrow night, or the next night depending on how the day goes, wherever we eat dinner or make camp for the night you read it out loud and we will go from there. That's it and that's all."

It was my turn to laugh. He at once became overly serious. "O.K. Mr. Mitchell, report coming right up sir." We took multiple classes with Mitchell in college. He commanded his classrooms with a stern, yet comical authority. I saluted and then flipped him off.

"Just have your pages by tomorrow night."

"Yes Mitchell sir." The ocean roared in the background. Each pounding breaker rumbled through camp. I wanted to surf, but one more question lingered on my tongue. I knew it would bite, but the moment propelled me. "Hey Cosmo can I ask you one more thing?"

"Sounds like you are going to ask anyway, so go ahead."

"When is the last time you talked to your Dad?" A range of emotions swept across his face. He went from surprise, to anger, to an apparent sadness and I wished that I had restrained my stupid mouth.

"Why do you ask?" he said, and dropped his head to face the ground.

"There was mention of him in your notebook. I'm sorry I should not have asked." A loll came to the ocean and silence devoured the air. Cosmo took his gaze from his feet and caught my eyes.

"It's been a while." He got up and walked towards the rock I spotted him resting on while I pillaged through his notebook. Cosmo grabbed two dried out yucca plants by the tail like slain dragons and pulled them back to camp. I walked over to lend him a hand thinking not about my assignment, but about the great rift in Cosmo's teenage years that altered his life forever. I thanked the oceans and the dying winds for the continuity in my family, the love my parents held for one another, and the blessings granted upon me in a world with such common tales of tragedy.

Chapter 15

Occasionally when Cosmo slid into a loose tongued intoxication fringing upon hallucinations, where seemingly all mystic and cosmic phenomenon appeared possible, he liked to tell a story about how his life was changed by a Palm Reader. He also would boast that if he ever had a daughter he would name her after the very Palm Reader who made such an impact on his life. I heard the story a few times in one on one conversations with Cosmo, and also from his mother, who confirmed the tale with tenacity. I found the saga somewhat amusing coming from his well read and educated vocal chords the first time I listened to it. I wondered how a man who read deeper into everything, who never jumped too quickly to claim anything as a certainty in a mad-scientist approach towards life could speak of a Palm Reader with such conviction. It bordered the ludicrous, but each time I heard the story the more feasible his words became, and it often lead me to feel more acute to the welling pockets of sorcery alive in the universe.

Cosmo did not always live at the beach. Three

years of his boyhood were spent in the town of Green Valley on a small, two acre orange grove. It was always difficult to picture a merman of the sea surrounded by rolling hills and jungles of citrus trees, but Cosmo spent fourth grade on through sixth grade in the small farming community. Two gas stations filled empty vehicles on opposite sides of town. Daddy Bear's restaurant, Fat Matt's Ribs, and Coach Wagon were the only sit down establishments to grab some food at, and three mini-markets which also posed as liquor stores took post at scattered positions. One video store and a few random boutiques lined the main highway, but any major shopping took place down a steep grade twenty minutes away.

Cosmo starred in sports, constantly elected to all star teams which often stole large chunks of his summers. He rode his bicycle everywhere; to visit friends, to the local market to get a Slurpee, and to adventure around the dense brush and incessant groves which teemed with curiosity to a boy with a twinkle of exploration in his eye. Bike jumps and endless games of cops and robbers echoed through the groves of his youth. The trees took posts like uniformed soldiers. Green leaves, oval globules of fruit, and dark brown trunks protected Cosmo from the world at large. He romped, he roamed, and he gallivanted as the king of the oranges in his one man territory.

He became an expert on eating oranges. Juiced, peeled, cracked with a straw through the middle, or perhaps even peel and all, Cosmo consumed a healthy dose oranges in his youth. Cosmo and his friends often emerged from a day of frolicking in the groves dripping with orange juice and strings of pulp from relentless orange fights. The semi-rotten fruits with a slight firmness worked the best, because they flew through the air without emaciating and then imploded on a victim upon impact. At any moment in Cosmo's wanderings about the planet the scent of orange blossoms creeps nostalgically into his veins and his fluids regress into pumping the same blood as the wild prince of his orange kingdom, covered from head to toe in dust and orange stains.

Life felt like no more than an orange in the palm of his hand, peeled to the sweet nectar of existence. He never questioned why his mother rarely entered into the rat race of the work field or why his father, who worked in construction, spent more days around the house than driving to a job site. For three years Christmas mornings glistened as toy-child diamonds underneath exotic pines. Ample piles of plastic joy exceeded his usual mound of gifts. With a new swelling of presents at his feet Cosmo could think of no reason why his Christmas morning treasures grew to large childhood fortunes besides the secret he kept uncomfortably on his lips.

The small grove bowed in a u-shaped pattern with an island that rose in the center of it which displayed a moderate sized, ranch style home. Green fingered ice plant protected gentle slopes. Out of the back-door exit and through a sidelined garden teeming with lettuce, tomatoes, carrots, cucumbers, and various squashes and herbs, sat a cinderblock staircase which led down the island to the orange grove and a large aluminum barn. The front half of the barn contained a two sectioned room, one half filled with various pieces of farm equipment, PVC sprinkler remnants, and a number of garden tools, while the other half acted as a chicken coop. One of Cosmo's daily chores consisted of collecting eggs from squawking hens scratching in the hay. Every so often his friends would accompany him on his duties and over and over again the same question arose about what hid in the other half of the barn. Cosmo bit his lip at the query while his mind pondered the emancipation of his secret, wondering if sleep would come easier, or if the tension would ease from tight shoulders, but always he straightened his shaky voice and assuredly spoke with the arrogance of an actor and said" It's my dad's office. "

The exact day Cosmo became fully aware of the secret he could not recall, for it came to him more through osmosis than a singular discovery, but he was pretty sure it occurred around the age of ten. He heard the terms early on: Marijuana, pot, weed, smoke, bud, all definitions he bracketed together to describe the odd looking green plants that grew in his dad's office. At large family parties he witnessed funny looking pipes or contortedly wrapped cigarettes stuffed with the green weed, lit on fire, and then inhaled into adult lungs. They held long breaths and then released a large cloud of skunk-sprayed smoke into the air. He wondered to himself why adults smoked the non-assuming plants and why they were kept a secret. He noticed the red, lazy eyes, and either a loss of enthusiasm or uncontrollable giggles on all of those who indulged in the secret. He wondered if it would work with tomato leaves. They were green as well. What if Cosmo and his friends crumpled up tomato leaves, artichoke leaves, or even squash leaves and lit them on fire. Would they inhale and encounter in similar mannerisms as those he watched use the green pot? Would they discover a new phenomenon and then need to call the growing of their particular vegetables a secret? But the vegetables were not a secret, only the skunk smelling pot was. As a bright kid Cosmo listened closer to every detail at his parents parties about the secret plant. It became apparent that pot only appeared in private places; at a party, at a family friend's home, at an uncle's house, or somewhere off the radar from the rest of the planet.

The eighties delivered Nancy Reagan's "Just say No" campaign and Cosmo heard about the terminologies and dangers of various drugs in school. The word drug always flashed a red alarm. It filled his head with police sirens, dead corpses rotting from gun wounds, evil, tattooed men with goatees dangling to their knees making deals with switchblades and handguns in dark alleyways, but nothing like that happened in Green Valley. Not in his peaceful environment where he moved about like a prince sheltered from much of the outside world could drugs ever exist. His mystified brain stumbled over the notion that his father's office could attain drugs. Drugs, am I a convict, he thought. Am I ready to for a life on the run laden with relentless crime? His fear heightened when his friends visited because he no longer wanted to be asked the dreaded questions that would one day lead to a jail cell if he ever let the secret spill from his lips.

Under the blaring August heat of a Green Valley summer Cosmo thought his life was over. He wondered if God might reach down and snatch him between Thor-hammered fingers and terminate his miniscule existence, or worse, his father would discover he broke the promise he vowed to keep forever. Nothing in the world could have been more frightening. Cosmo would have rather had the devil himself impale a fiery pitchfork through the center of his loins than to even hear his father's voice raised in anger. "It's not my fault dad, it's not my fault" he repeated through a salty reservoir of tears for consecutive nights following his blunder.

In all fairness it was not his fault. The responsibility of such a young child to cover up his father's secrets proved too massive of a burden for him to bear. He felt like a liar and a convict all in the same breath and should have never been weighted down with the secret to begin with. Plus, Cosmo did not give it away as though he was telling someone the temperature outside or the score of the Charger's game, he held much tighter to the grips of his dedication. Instead Don, the neighborhood bully and three years Cosmo's elder, already developing toned muscles and slight traces of facial hair, Don the antagonist who tripped kids in front of him and then walked over their backs when they were on the ground beat Como's arm repetitiously while he yanked his hair and kneed him in the thigh until the words "My dad grows pot in the barn" came dejectedly out of his mouth. The tears poured, not as much from pain as from a relief of a profound incision that troubled the deepest caverns in his soul, mixed with a glaring fear about what might follow next after the hidden vault encased inside his body was beat open. "I am a coward for not fighting back, I am as free as a soaring eagle," he thought. Only three fates awaited his defeated heart, God, Devil, or his father.

Dread flirted with his psyche in wonder if Don had told anyone about the barn. Did the Cops know? Was he going to jail for being the informant? All thoughts and whispers tormented Cosmo's restless hands which nervously required constant motion. He contemplated informing his father to warn him for what might beat down their oak door at any second, but his fear overwhelmed him. He felt lost at sea, isolated from any other human being with working lungs.

His tension eased a week and a half after his confession. Don bullied his way up to the house and demanded to see the secret room. Caught unaware, playing near the barn, Cosmo panicked as Don dragged him by the shirt towards the door at the north end of the barn. "My life is ending," he thought. "This is all I was meant to accomplish in this short life. Goodbye mama. Goodbye dad, and dad, I guess it was my fault." He tripped and broke free of Don's clutches. Both of his knees skinned to the first shock of white and then to cherry syrup red as blood oozed down his legs. His pride raped from his intestines, Cosmo laid in a heap of spaghetti noodles underneath Don's cruel laughter and tight, auburn crew cut. All strain, all festering inside his sizzling innards boiled to the surface and he kicked Don in the right shin just below the knee and rose to his feet.

"You are not going in," Cosmo shouted.

"What, are you going to try and stop me with that sissy kick of yours? Kick me again sissy?" Cosmo reared back in his best soccer form as a center forward and struck Don in the stomach with a pounding blow. Don bellied over and let out a scream of pain, which then turned instantly to laughter.

"Is that all you got you little pussy. Say your prayers because you are going to die," Don yelled in a rage.

"Then you are going to have to kill me Don because you aren't going into the barn. I will kick until I can't kick anymore and score one hundred goals on your face. And I will swing with these arms that will hit seven hundred home runs one day until I can't swing anymore." Cosmo roared with exultation and gloated at the cowardice that came upon Don's face. In the commotion he did not notice the shadow which enveloped his slender frame. Raymond, Cosmo's father, brushed Cosmo aside and growled words from a leonine voice which reduced Don into paralyzed prey. Cosmo's own fear of being next in line to meet the executioner eased for a brief second while he listened to Don's whimpering voice turn into full blown tears. Don ran home and received a visit from Raymond later that evening. Raymond talked to Don's parents about picking on small children and sewed up any differences about the secret hiding in the barn.

Cosmo's fate turned completely around by his father's reaction. More than anything, Raymond pleaded apologetic words to his courageous son. He asked for forgiveness for the burden pressed upon him and praised his efforts of defending himself. A new Cosmo emerged, relieved and liberated from the mass that weighed down his soul.

During harvest season one year later a strong Santa Ana wind blew through the deep, green leaves on the ranch. Tumbleweeds floated about like inflated beach balls on random, swirling courses. Cosmo's mother and his aunt Rebecca on his father's side were both elbow deep in assisting Raymond to prepare the latest crop. In the chaos and drawn out hours of clipping away at plants with razor sharp scissors Cosmo's mother Madeline realized the house was out of food and decided to go down the hill to do some shopping. She piled into a powder-blue VW bus with Rebecca and set off to take care of household errands. A while later they exited the Alpha-Beta supermarket with a large sack of pinto beans, a fifty pound bag of dog food, cases of Budweiser beer, numerous paper bags filled with groceries, and an enticing urge to visit the Palm Reader located in the same shopping center as the Alpha-Beta.

I always thought of Madeline as somewhat of a mystic, a spiritual healer, though she never claims any of those titles for herself. Porcelain angels protect her shelves, her house, the people she loves, along with burning candles and charmed stones. She is in direct contact with energies most people do not ever see or feel, but they exist, I am learning, if we open our hearts and minds to more than the glowing televisions that numb our minds. She is an angel, of that I am convinced, disguised as a human being and sent to our planet to aid the world in discovering how to use our hearts. A bit eccentric yes, but still every bit the compassionate sage the world could use plenty more of. Her inviting blue-eyes mingle together with a smile that dig straight into one's soul, and on a warm and gusty afternoon during trimming season Madeline and Rebecca walked with their open minds in through a Palm Readers front door.

The two sisters' were greeted with broad statements about their radiating energy. The woman introduced herself as Rosemary and made them sit down to a cup of tea. "Sit, sit," she said. "I am sensing strong vibes from the both of you." A bit skeptic, Madeline sipped her Jasmine tea and studied Rosemary's movements. She did everything in a semi-chaotic, yet deliberate manner as she reached out for Madeline's hands. Rosemary squeezed the hands tightly then looked up with a terrified expression.

"What's the matter," Madeline asked.

"Stop," Rosemary returned and let go of her hands.

"Stop what?"

"Stop what you are doing in your life and get out before it's too late."

"What are you talking about," Madeline responded.

"This is no time to play coy. You know what you are involved in and you need to cease this instant. You have a son, yes?"

"Yes."

"Just barely a teenager?"

"Thereabouts."

"You need to be there for this child. He needs a

mother, a strong woman to help guide him. He is special. He shares your gifts of the heart. The world needs people like you filling its chambers of broken spirits. We are the dreamers who teach the world to love and enjoy our gift of birth. Your son will be one of these prophets, but you must stop now or his life, your life, your husband's life will be ripped apart. Torn from each other's arms and redirected from your natural born paths in life." Rosemary paused momentarily to catch her breath and sipped a cup of tea with the bag draped over the side. She aligned eyes with Madeline and continued. "Look at me and listen. I know the road will be difficult and not easy to liberate yourself from, but you must for peril lurks on the avenue you now travel upon. Any monetary value is not worth the risk of your souls. The winds of alarm are screaming vociferously outside our doors and you must take notice and follow the breezes towards a new path."

The room fell silent. Rosemary rose from her shawl-wrapped table and disappeared behind a jungle of beads hanging from a doorway. Madeline and Rebecca took their first glances at one another. Madeline constantly felt the waves of danger swelling in her stomach concerning her husband's underground source of income many times before, she sensed it, aware, and intuitive of possible calamities, but hearing the words spoken out in the open by a complete stranger nearly stopped her heart from beating. Madeline wondered if she was transparent. Did Rosemary really possess the gift of foresight and intuition or did Madeline unknowingly give away her secrets due to the haste in which she left for town. She smelled her clothes and then checked her hands to see if the sticky marijuana resin left behind pungent clues for Rosemary to follow. The scent could not be traced, but she thought about the possibility of her nostrils becoming acclimated to the aroma and because of her dulled senses she might not have been able to catch a slight hint of it. Either way Rosemary's words slammed into the air like a seal of approval, a ticket in hand to depart from the perilous station in life she grew accustomed to. Without conversation Rebecca embraced Madeline's hands and gently nodded her head in approval as if saying, "It's o.k., now is the time to go and you will be alright."

Rosemary returned with a knobby, turquoise stone and placed it in Madeline's trembling hands. "This stone will bring you strength and give you energy when your body feels too tired to fight. Be strong, my beautiful, peaceful warrior, and always, when feeling lost, remember your gracious heart, and above all think of your son, he is of the cosmos."

Without mention of the experience with Rosemary, Madeline returned home overloaded with groceries. She resumed her trimming duties and after she finished for the day she informed Raymond she was out for good. She hurled out her plans without hesitation or worry of the outcome. Madeline exclaimed the desire to watch her son evolve into a fabulous human being through her own eyes instead of through glass windows and weekend visits in prison. Their lives were more important as a family and meant something to the universe. The safety of that unit accounted beyond money or capital gain and they could survive penniless and scraping by if necessary. She also assured without pity that she was going, with or without Raymond, and Cosmo was going with her.

Raymond sat like a stunned boxer in the corner of their kitchen. Slowly regaining his wits he questioned her sudden decision. He knew she wanted to get out eventually, but what brought it about so rapidly. A new crop waited to be cashed in and would put them in a very comfortable position. He loved his wife with every inch of his massive frame, but he needed time to sort everything out. The friction in the air was nothing more than his pride, for deep down he knew his wife was right. They made some money, they never got greedy and tried to expand to unfamiliar sources, and Raymond told himself never to stay too long. He wanted nothing more than to take his son to the coast and teach him to become a great surfer. To live by the sea and extract the juices of its many offerings called to Raymond as a life long destiny, and he was so close. Just one more transaction could make his dreams a reality. He turned to his wife and asked for the rest of the summer to finish and then he would quit for good.

"Please Madeline we are so close to our dreams. This last crop can give us a huge down payment on a beach home. Just ride it out with me. Give me until September. That's three months. That's all I am asking for."

"I can't give it to you Ray, it's now or never. I have been feeling it in the air. Something is about to switch, bad energy has filled this house for months. Today only confirmed my suspicions."

"What suspicions. And why is today so damned important. What did you get an anonyms tip or something."

"Something kind of like that you could say."

"From who Madeline?"

"It doesn't really matter Ray, and if it does then you are missing the point. The point is to go, now."

Raymond took a deep breath to soothe the agitation building in his throat. "Yes it matters. Do we need to make a mad dash in the middle of the night? Are the cops on the way to kick down the door?"

"No it's nothing like that. Your sister and I visited a Palm Reader while we were out shopping. I had never seen her before, but she seemed to know everything about us. She knew I had a son and that we were doing something we probably should not be involved in. She told me to get out. She justified every feeling I have had over the past year. I'm not taking any more chances Ray, and if you can't accept that, then I'm sorry, but we will move on with out you."

"What," Raymond screamed out. "You're telling me that you want to leave because some psychotic, phony gave you some generalized information that you decided to fit into your own story. You were just searching for words that you wanted to hear Madeline. That woman, who ever she was, doesn't know shit about us. And now you are going to trust some loony over your husband who has never led you astray. Have I Madeline; have I ever led you astray?"

"No Ray, no you have not."

"And I'm not going to now. Just give me the

summer and we can forget about all of this telepathic bullshit. We'll get out on our own, together."

"See Ray, you are missing the point. It doesn't matter where the source came from, the fact is that I know it's time. It could have come from a look on an old woman's face, an electricity from the odd Santa Ana's we are getting in June, or yes, from a palm reader. I love our son and I want him to have his parents. I am leaving as soon as I can get everything together. I do wish that you would come with us."

"I don't believe this shit. A fucking palm reader and you want to leave me. And where would you go if I don't agree with your abandonment?"

"I have not thought it through yet or pictured our world without you, but I would probably call my brother J.P. and see if we could stay with him for awhile."

"So this is for real. You're telling me you really want to go."

"I don't want to go Ray, I have to. We have to dear, it's time."

Raymond stormed off to the barn. It took three weeks for Madeline to finally walk out of the front door. Each day Raymond tried to convince her to stay, but in late July she climbed into her VW bus and left for the coast. I only learned of Cosmo's reluctance to leave Green Valley after reading his red notebook. In September Raymond did not leave as promised and kept up his work on the ranch. Two months later a knock came. Raymond did not answer and turned up the volume on his television. Within seconds the door broke from the hinges and came crashing to the floor as twelve agents stormed the house armed with shotguns. Raymond did not move from his recliner and kept his eyes fixed on the Los Angeles Lakers winning a game handily over the Portland Trailblazers. Raymond went down, so did his partners. He received a five to ten year sentence and served eight of them.

Cosmo became a man without his father. He never disowned him, he visited often and sent letters, but he never forgave him. It was not the marijuana that bothered him, for Cosmo could never see why a plant that grew naturally in the ground could ever be considered illegal, but it was his father's inability to act. Life offered Raymond a choice, whether ridiculous sounding or not due to the palm reader involved in the scenario, it was a choice, and Raymond chose his crops over his family, or at least, that is what Cosmo chose to believe. After learning of his father's incarceration Cosmo made an oath on two things; one, never to smoke marijuana under any circumstance, and two, never to be afraid to act when the energies of the universe propelled him forward to take advantage of a moment. Cosmo learned to trust his intuitions. They were not always correct, but they led him down a trail few dared to follow, a trail without hesitation or worry of what the masses thought about his actions. He lived out in the open, intrepid, and always blazing his own path. I knew he might never slow down long enough to raise a daughter, but I could see his reasoning for wanting to name her Rosemary if that day ever came. The story probably gained embellishments over the years, but it did not matter. The babbles of a mystic and the openness of his mother's heart, along with her inner strength, spared Cosmo his life.

After hearing the story I wondered if Rosemary smelled a heavy dose of marijuana seeping from Madeline and Rebecca. They were in the middle of trimming season after all, and perhaps they did not do a good enough job covering the odors with body sprays and fruity lotions. Or there is the possibility that a tiny pot stem clung obliviously to one of their garments as they charged down the hill and perhaps Rosemary caught sight of it. But that was just my mind in skeptic mode, gripped tightly to all things tangible. I prefer the universe in its impossibilities and apparent chances for magical occurrences. I like it better to believe in the energies we emit being just as alive as our physical bodies, out in force flirting with the world. All that exists we cannot always see with our eyes, it travels in energy and soul, and I am content in believing that the energy can be read and telepathically inspected, but for sure, can be felt if we slow down for a minute and open up our hearts.

Chapter 16

Light is too powerful to drink in. It feels as if the earth swallowed the sun and vomited its entire luminescence through a single crevice in its skin. A concentrated pocket of energy rushes up the bottomless, cylinder pit only a few feet away. Mud crusted eyes shield the sting of illumination as a lame body crawls like an injured serpent toward Lola's miraculous hole in the planet. The sky squeezes out any remaining light from above. The atmosphere comes for me. A pathetic victim targeted to disappear into the catacombs of nothingness.

The pit roars. What stirs below? Perhaps death and the fiery pits of hell, but hell feels upon me already? A wave of slime washes over my legs and under my belly as though I am floating on top of the river Styx. I close my mouth so I do not imbibe the lethal concoction of flowing muck. Cerberus waits, waits to gnash and claw and yank me into depths of the inferno, yet another alternative does not appear. The landscape vanishes. The mountains, deserts, rocks, trees, structures, and living beings are no more. Nothing left but the light coming from a gouge in the earth. Maybe I deserve to evaporate from existence, to breathe no more, but something keeps me alive. Can I do it? Can I make it past the eyes of Satan unharmed and escape on the other side of the world? Before I can answer the question Styx pushes me over the edge.

I flap, but I do not fly, I fall, I fail. The rapid descent pushes all of my limbs above my torso. I plummet at a rapid pace, but I make no progress. No further down the hole. The edges reach out for my fingers attempting to bite them off. Mud flies from my eyes and I try desperately to keep them open against the surging air. I scan for the fire, the horns, the screams emanating from tortured souls bound to a life of servitude and pain in the dismal chambers of Hades, yet I hear nothing, see nothing, the light overpowers all. Maybe I never fell into the hole after all and the emptiness outside swallowed me whole. A lost soul devoured inside the intestines of a violent storm primed for decimation, but I keep falling. A large stone pushes its way into the middle of the hole. I just miss it. Then another stone, followed by another, speeding by like a cluster of asteroids. One just below to my left, one to my right, I do not see the one in the center. A large smash and darkness overcomes.

The tar pit boils. Legs kick, arms flail, toes wiggle, but the useless mass of flesh makes no progress. Branches run long just a struggle away, boulders protrude, land beckons, but the task appears too insurmountable. The body sinks steadily. Even if rescued by a dangling appendage the chances look bleak. The monsters of the earth, the demons of the underworld await his escape. They lick their chops, they snarl at one another for a prime piece of real estate. The mighty T-Rex, the giggling hyenas, the fat goblins, the coiled snakes all hiss and roar. Why fight the rotting ooze just to incur a violent slaughter upon the volatile shore. Just give up. Swallow the potion shoved down his throat. Eat it, he has no choice. He closes his eyes and let's go into the bowels of death.

Choked spasms, limp body, the elements conquer. Never again would he breathe. Never would he sing, or swim, or run, or think, or dream. The emptiness consumes after all. The emptiness of death, of nothing, of becoming mere sediment at the bottom of a bowl of tar obsesses what thought remains. One more moment, one last word, anything, but his head ducks below the surface. The steaming muck begins to emulsify his tongue and his teeth. No voice left. Soon the brain and the heart would erode. Soon he would exist no more. Why does he quit the fight? Why does he let his body fade into the slime instead of dueling for one last breath, one last second of life? He vomits black tar. He screams, but no sound escapes.

The sinking stops and he hits the bottom. Death does not take him. The scathe of the Grim reaper turns south away from his lifeless shadow. For what purpose, what possible reason does he still exist? He could not end it himself. Life awaits him, needs his presence for some future purpose. His body twitches and claws. His feet circle and create a ruckus. The chaos propels him towards the surface. He springs upward. A sudden burst of adrenaline shoots him directly in the heart. The fights, the beasts, the hounds of hell no longer exist. He sees only life. A dolphin kick and he erupts out of the syrupy, thick lake.

A limb reaches out. He tows for a coven of rocks. The monsters do not see him. His dark camouflage makes him a blob, a lump of nothing essential. He maneuvers, ducks, hides, scampers, and puts distance between he and the tar pit. He makes it. Where he is he does not know, but he sprints alive and free as the hungered beasts gnashing impatiently at the black lake wait for him to emerge. He falls to the ground and kisses the earth, embraces the soil, and sings to the grass. Laughter effuses from his guts. He rolls to his back and looks for the sun. A shadow envelops the sky. He draws to his knees and feels the beast's breath on his shoulder. He did not go unnoticed. He opted for life. Life snarled and sat poised to make him honor that choice. The fight stares him straight in the face. He cannot escape, nowhere to run, nor hide, the challenge comes simple and plain, life or death, and he is tired of dying.

Chapter 17

I remained in the water and prayed that the Jeep was a mirage. My eyes closed and reopened just in time to watch Hillary greet Cosmo with a kiss on both sides of his cheeks. Campbell extended his hand and then climbed a knobby tire to take down two, long surfboards strapped to the roof of their dusty vehicle. Two clenched fists pondered the ability to strike a man for defending his pride and the last connecting fibers of an eroded relationship. I made a promise, but I never thought I would have to honor that oath when the Jeep and the Scout set off in opposite directions, yet there on the shore, after breakfast and a long morning session as noon crept up the beach like a silent assassin, the black Jeep appeared on top of the nearest sand dune like an albatross chained around the veins of our journey.

I looked at the duct tape that covered the deep slice on my finger and wondered if Cosmo would ever fall in love again as he talked with Hillary. He typically avoided involved relationships due to his incessant roaming, but once he dated a news journalist for nearly seven months when he was twenty-five, which turned out to be the longest relationship of his life. Her name was Vanessa and she worked as a field reporter for a local television station in San Diego. She was gorgeous in an exotic way, and looked Scandinavian mixed with the radiant, dark skin of a Central or South American and highly adventurous. Cosmo loved her daring, her risk taking, her willingness to up and leave at a second's notice. Their relationship was intense and highly passionate, almost explosive as profusions of animated energy overwhelmed nearly everyone in their presence. Cosmo met his match in many ways, but Vanessa's lust for being the best, being first on the scene, no matter what, no matter who she stepped on to get her story or who she destroyed in the process by reporting an incident before she got all of her facts straight created a devastating chasm between the couple.

Vanessa worshiped the big lights. She wanted CNN, 60 Minutes, or Fox. Cosmo did not mind her ambition at all, in fact he encouraged it, but he could not stand the lack of ethics she displayed with increased frequency as their relationship went on. Cosmo watched with a heavy heart the damaged trail she left behind on her way to the top. Her reporting, while insightful and well delivered, often ruined lives in her effort to be the first one to report a story or make a splash by adding outrageous headlines just to draw attention to her name. She made graphic claims and catastrophic allegations to grab the public's interest, then simply would tag on a "supposedly" or "so alleged" to keep her free from any repercussions.

It sickened Cosmo. He told her she was no better than the people who stalked celebrities and published idiotic articles in the supermarket check stand magazines, and that put an end to their connection.

Vanessa moved on and made her rise to the big lights as a regular anchor on a nationalized news show, while Cosmo altered his opinions of love from the moment of their parting. He took the break up hard, but not as much as for losing Vanessa as it was the disappointment he incurred after discovering her true character. They were perfect for a small pebble in time and after that pebble rolled out of his hands he felt that maybe all any human being ever needed was merely that precious pebble, a brief instant of perfection, and not the giant boulder of forever which could only lead to regret. After much contemplation he found he could believe in nothing more than moments. A slice of life, an instant of aligned energies, a celebration of discovery between two consenting adults, and when the magic faded or the moment passed, then on to the next adventure. It was not a game to Cosmo because he truly believed in his manifesto and convinced many of the women he encountered after Vanessa to believe in it as well. "Why burden each other with hauntings from the past or flaws in character," he would say. "Let the perfect energy of the moment lead you into an amazing experience and then let the moment go. Why do we always want to hang onto something incredible and turn it into forever? Don't blame and destroy each other because you cannot be perfect to one another, no one can, but a moment can remain pure and perfect forever. Indulge in the moment, then let it go."

In our brief encounters with Hillary she exuded an aura spontaneity that ran akin to Cosmo's credo. As I sat still in my wetsuit I could not help but think that she could hear the far off music that guided Cosmo's nomadic footsteps. The arcane rhythms, the mind bending melodies, and unique chord changes propelled her body as Cosmo assisted her and Campbell to the beach with their big boards. An odd rumbling spoke out over the hushed desert behind them. A fast moving storm headed straight for the sand and three unsuspecting victims. Perhaps they heard it too, not one of them oblivious, but I wanted no part of it and remained sheltered in the curls of the sea.

After twenty minutes of catching chest high waves all to myself Cosmo re-joined me in the line up. He informed me that Campbell and Hillary would be ready for their lesson in about an hour and that Hillary was dying for some more entertainment. They both made themselves comfortable on the warm sand as spectators. The proper point at Peppermint Patty's was not working due to the direction of the swell and we were forced to ride a beach break a few hundred yards south. The waves broke fast over the relatively flat beach, which propelled them to form rapidly closing hollow tubes. The spot was shifty and only a few of the abundant barrel rides available allowed either of us to make it through the aqua curtains before they closed out, but that did not stop Cosmo and I from trying to stuff ourselves into as many oval pits as possible.

A tube ride stood as the most difficult facet of

surfing to describe to someone who never enjoyed the experience of being cradled by one. When the crest of a wave crashes over from top to bottom a crystal room of cascading water forms its own oval galaxy. Cut off from the world yet tapped into the universe all senses thrive on getting through the liquid cavern before it shrinks up and crashes down all around you. Almost every surfer around the globe, no matter how many airs they boost or snap reverses' they turn, describe the act of getting barreled as their favorite aspect of surfing. Just one glimpse down a sacred tunnel can spread through a surfer's veins like an infection. It is a rare view and an orgasmic rush comprehensible only when explained internally through personal experience. While the barrels were not large, they were racy, and Cosmo and I each lodged ourselves into a number of thrilling cylinders that sped over the sandy bottom beneath us.

We went in when hunger called. We ate green grapes, dry turkey sandwiches, and sipped on a chilled white wine that Hillary brought out from a cooler. The cold pleased my teeth. During our meal Cosmo broke down the basics of surfing. He explained how waves were constructed by strong wind surges and massive storms in the ocean, how the tides ebbed and flowed due to the gravitational pull of the moon, and how the three main types of surf breaks which were, beach breaks, reef breaks, and point breaks contrasted from one another. He then spoke of safety and how to fall to the sides or the back of the board during a wipeout so the board would not smack anyone in the head. Campbell paid little attention to the lesson, but

Hillary listened to every detail and a serious look of determination came to her childlike face for the first time in our presence.

After Cosmo's instructions on the sand of where to position while paddling and how to stand up properly on the board he surprised me when he grabbed Campbell's board and led him into the surf. Hillary picked up her board by the nose while I grabbed the tail and we made our way into the crumbling whitewash close to the sand. She was fearless and listened to every suggestion I offered to her. On her fourth whitewash wave she made it flawlessly to her feet in a secure, crouched position and rode the wave until the fins stopped in the sand. A smile erupted from such a pure location in her soul that it swept me into a euphoric state right along with her. She screamed with every decibel she could summon from her five and a half foot frame. The shrills skipped off of the water and into our eardrums like a pleasing melody. Cosmo yelled back as he sat chest deep in the water and tried to get Campbell to accept his help, but Campbell thought he could do it on his own. He told Cosmo that anyone could have caught the miniature wave Hillary rode to the shore and that he was waiting for a much bigger one. Campbell splashed and flailed until Cosmo took charge and pushed him forth on a small bump. Campbell gave a feeble attempt to do a push up then replanted his body back down on his belly and rode the wave in on his stomach while he mocked the size of the mound of water that propelled him.

Hillary paddled back out and embraced me in an ecstatic bear hug. A familiar buzz entered my pores as I remembered the two summers I worked at a surf school with Cosmo while I was in college. It was the most fun I ever experienced at a job. Playing in the sun, the sand, surfing, and teaching people of all ages to respect and enjoy the ocean and the art of wave riding all while collecting a paycheck at the end of the week felt too good to be true. I made people around me noxious when I skipped off to work everyday with a glowing smile while they climbed into their vehicles and inched along in morning traffic like vapid zombies. Hillary's joy brought me back to the smell of coconut sunscreen and a fit, dark-brown body the color of Mowgli from the Disney version of the **Jungle Book**. I knew underneath my wetsuit a pale-shouldered man with an increasing waistline took the young jungle boy's place. He used to frolic the beaches and the hills as a boy carefree and in the present moment, continued the march quietly through the odd years of teenage awkwardness, and emerged out in the open on the sands as a young man, but at some point he vanished. My journey with Cosmo was just as much of a trip to put J.P. to rest as it was to rediscover the whereabouts of Mowgli on the shores of the Pacific, to capture the shaggy haired, happy-go-lucky, wandering Mowgli who turned into a listless adult. I cringed at his disappearance, but only for a second as Hillary's exuberance outweighed my thoughts.

"That was simply incredible. I think that's the best thing I have ever done in my entire life, ever, ever. Thank you so much."

"You're welcome, but there's no need to thank me, that was all you girl. All I did was give you a little push. You're a natural. You have a nice, strong stance, good balance, and the most important thing of all."

"What's that?"

"The stoke, look at you, you're glowing. That's what surfing is all about, that smile right there."

"I don't want it to end, ever," Hillary exclaimed. She splashed cool water on her face and let it drip from her cheeks.

"Hopefully it never will." My first face wave on my uncle's single fin, pin-tailed Dick Brewer on a glassy morning resurfaced. The thrill of moving on top of a flowing collection of water sent me into a tizzy. I vowed I would surf everyday for the rest of my life after the initial rush I drank into my soul, but as I aged it became more and more difficult to dive into the ocean as often as I wanted. I managed to get in the water more than a part-timer would make it into the lineup, but for the first in my life I found myself making excuses not to surf instead of creating the excuses I used to come up with to steal any moment possible to paddle out and catch a few waves. Somewhere along the line I forgot my first wave. If I carried it with me, if I had let the spirit that filled Hillary's entire body at that moment stay fresh in my mind I would never make another excuse to stay away from the ocean's graces ever again. I did my best to imprint my first wave to memory when Hillary broke my trance.

"This is so amazing, so absolutely amazing honey," she said in pure adulation of the moment. "So, how are you guys going to get me out of this? Have you guys talked about it yet?"

"Talked about what," I asked puzzled by her question.

"About helping me ditch that pompous ass over there."

"What," I said taken back. "You mean Campbell?"

"Of course Campbell silly, who else? I almost didn't get in the Jeep with him when we left you guys at the taco stand, but somehow I knew we would meet up again. It's fate, or a crazy energy of some kind. I knew it the moment we pulled up that I would be rid of him today."

"What happened, did you guys have a fight or break up or something?"

Hillary licked the salt from her lips and stretched out on the board. "We've been over for a long time Dane, honey. We actually broke up two months ago. He's tried to win me back, but we are all wrong for each other, he just hates to lose. He convinced me to get in the Jeep with him. I needed to go somewhere, anywhere. He came into the bar that I work at on the mountain the other day when I was in the shittiest of moods and he mentioned he was taking a road trip to Southern California. I don't know, it sounded fun at the time and I walked right out of the door with him. He said the trip would be our chance to see if we could rekindle anything from our past and all it has done is further secure my decision to leave him. When we reached the ocean in San Diego though, I became intoxicated with it and I convinced him to keep heading south to follow it. The brilliant blues, the stretch into eternity, I can't get enough. This is the first time across the border for me. I would have left him sooner, but I wanted to keep going, keep exploring this wonderful peninsula and he was willing to keep driving."

I ushered her over a small wave in a confused stupor. A question burned on my tongue about whether or not Hillary and Cosmo had set up the meeting the night they talked by our campfire and emptied out a bottle of almond tequila. I almost did not ask, but I had to.

"Did you and Cosmo set this all up beforehand?"

Hillary looked me in the eye to reveal her earnestness and said "Of course not. Cosmo and I bonded for sure, but we left it at that. I have no idea where I am or how to get around this place, neither does Campbell, we have just picked dirt roads that looked inviting and headed down them. Cosmo and I agreed that if we met up again then we were meant to do something about it and now here we are all together, albeit, with an exaggerated tantrum I threw this morning on my part. The moment you pulled into the gas station by the taco stand I knew my life would change forever. It already has. I am more alive at this second than I have been in the last two years, my first wave, a new country, and the positive vibration that radiates from the both of you. I was so meant to find you guys, or maybe you were meant to find me, not quite sure, but it was supposed to happen either way, for that I am sure."

Shocked by her confession I told her I was going in. Campbell could have cared less about Cosmo and me, but he seemed like a prideful man. A man who would not take a couple of scraggily surfer's stealing away his girl lightly. In the thrill of Hillary's first wave I forgot about the impending disaster that waited to punish us all. I resented her immediately. It was not her fault, but I knew she would change everything. I plopped down on the beach like a ten year old and pulled the warm sand close to my body. Campbell tried one more wave, but teetered and fell over before he could get going. He came in and dropped his board in the sand. Cosmo swam over to Hillary and pulled her into position for an incoming wave. They laughed like two people who had known each other for years. "Oh brother," I thought as Campbell approached. I wondered if I would have to punch him in the face like I had promised. He was at least ten years older than Cosmo and I, but still in great shape and taller than the both of us. He stripped the top of his wetsuit and revealed the toned physique of someone who spent many hours in the gym. Cosmo sure knew how to pick his adventures.

"I think Hill likes that mouthy friend of yours more than me," Campbell said as he watched the two of them play like school children in the sea. I let out a forced laugh. This is going to get very ugly I thought.

The side shore wind that greeted the morning softened with the aging of the day. Campbell straddled the width of his board and dug holes in the sand at the sides of his legs. Two words, I searched for at least two words that I could put together and say to him while we sat in silence and watched the drama unfold before us, but they never came. It almost felt like Cosmo and Hillary had already made up their minds and did not care if Campbell watched the sparks fly between them. I finally decided to ask a simple question.

"What prompted you two to come south and meet up with us," I finally got out.

Campbell knocked some of the sand off of his hands and looked me in the eyes for the first time. "Hill threw a fit. Our little surf session didn't go too well on our own. She said that she has liquid dreams, and that the ocean calls to her, or some random bullshit like that. She went crazy and told me she was going to walk down here to find you guys so she could learn to surf. She's a damn tenacious chick, I'll tell you. I didn't want to leave her by herself down here you know, even though I should have. Damn chick hasn't put out the whole trip; you know what I mean Babe."

A flock of pelicans soared just above the surface of the water in a v-shaped pattern. Their wings stretched wide, but did not flap as they glided without effort towards South America. Hillary rose to her feet on a wave for three seconds before she splashed sideways in the water. The ride did not last as long as the wave I pushed her into, but she acted just as excited. She tackled Cosmo with a spirited hug into the shallow water. It took a few seconds for them to surface. Who knew what type of flirtatiousness went on in their underwater wrestling match, but they resurfaced with clenched hands and tried to take each other down in hysteric cackles. I sighed louder than I meant to and Campbell looked over at me.

"What the hell," Campbell asked as though he finally understood how strong the connection between Cosmo and Hillary radiated in front of us. He threw two scoops of sand towards the water and stood up. The two wrestlers began to make their way in. Cosmo collected the board under one arm and retaliated fire with Hillary in a playful splashing fight with his free hand. Then, as if they both forgot where they were, Cosmo dropped the board and the two wet bodies pulled each other into an intimate embrace. They did not start kissing, but the act was imminent.

I did not know what else to say besides letting the truth come out. "Isn't it obvious Campbell? It's been obvious since the first time they met. You should have never followed us."

He stared at the water and the disappearing pelicans. He was a handsome man. His features straddled the line between being well manicured and carrying just enough roughness to keep from being called a pretty boy. The pelicans vanished as did Campbell's usual arrogance. He looked defeated, not melancholy, but absolutely destroyed that he lost to someone like Cosmo. I almost felt bad for him, his wounded pride, his uncertainty of what to do next, but he quickly erased my empathy when he opened his mouth.

"She's just a low class slut anyways. She had nothing and I gave her everything and then she wants to bang some loser like him. He's got nothing either, just a big mouth like she does. They think they are so smart, so mystic, so cool because they follow their dreamy intuitions, but they don't know shit Babe. The real world doesn't work like that, not at all. It doesn't cater to dreamers, it crushes them. I know what works, what's real, and they don't have it. The world will eat them alive Babe. Stupid idiots, I swear." He turned and started towards the Jeep. I stood up quickly after his sudden movement.

"Are you alright man," I asked, but he did not respond. "Where are you going?"

He stopped and turned around. "I'm a sore loser Babe," he said and kept walking towards the Jeep. I ran to the water to warn Cosmo and Hillary that Campbell was up to something. I told them about our conversation, but they seemed not to care and floated their way up the sand. After ten minutes we noticed Campbell emerge from behind the Jeep. My heart sputtered as I watched each agitated step make its way towards us. I hated conflict, I shrank from its challenges, yet Cosmo and Hillary stood their ground with smiling faces like valiant knights. I grasped for their courage as the forces collided.

"Well aren't you two cute."

"Campbell look..." Cosmo began.

"Shut your mouth; don't say a word to me, not one fucking word. You hear me." Cosmo nodded his head. Hillary stepped in between them and put a hand on Campbell's arm. He brushed it off immediately. Hillary smiled and folded her hands behind her back. She squished her lips together as if in thought before she addressed Campbell.

"I'm sorry Cam, I am, but you know we're over, we've been over. We don't belong together. We both know it. Don't take this as a bet or game that you are losing. Take it as life following its rightful course and we can both part on our separate journeys."

Campbell had changed out of his wetsuit when he went to the Jeep. He put on a pair of jeans, a tee shirt, and a fresh North Face jacket. An edge came to his face. He looked much more like the twitchy Campbell that we ate tacos with the day before. "You don't get to tell me how I should take this or how I should feel. You don't deserve that."

"But Campbell, we've done nothing wrong. We haven't secretly had an affair or anything like that. And besides, you and I are not even together, you know that, you know I don't love you. Don't make this about your pride."

"I'll make it about whatever I want. You're nothing but a small town whore, you know that, I shouldn't care one rat's ass about you," Campbell said and stuffed his hands into his jacket.

"And it's obvious you don't care about her Campbell. So why don't you stop with the insults and we can all go our separate ways," Cosmo said.

Campbell jerked his hands out of the black and gray jacket and shoved a nine millimeter pistol to Cosmo's head. It happened so suddenly that I almost thought I was dreaming. "Didn't I tell you to shut your mouth? Huh, didn't I? Answer me you back-stabbing piece of shit."

"Yes you did," Cosmo said. He dropped his hands towards the earth and took in a deep breath. He did his best not to act alarmed with a gun aimed at his head, but I could not tell if he was putting up a façade or if he really did not fear the weapon pressed against his temple. The murderous swells rose and fell in twisted increments. A splat of blood, a slippery catastrophe of loose intestines, a pierced chasm of smoked flesh, and a collapsed pile of limbs face first in the sand. The rotted skin, the decayed organs, the attracted flies and lurking scavengers primed to devour. Where to run? Where to flee? The sand would sink like wet cement. No escape, no rescue, only three victims at the mercy of Campbell's temper.

"Campbell please stop," Hillary protested. "Let's talk about this, you and me okay. Leave them out of this. It's not their fault, it's mine, my choice. You are not a violent person and you know that. I didn't even know you had a gun."

"There's a lot you don't know Hill. I borrowed it from David when we picked up the boards. You don't think I would come to this God forsaken, dust bowl without some protection now do you? Nothing but lawlessness down here, you've seen it all on the news. Dead bodies here, kidnapping's there. But the law is in my hands now. I'm your sheriff, I'm your God." Campbell twitched erratically in his movements. His hand could not hold the gun steady. The weapon shook as though he was still riding on the bumpy, dirt road that led to Peppermint Patty's. Every so often he sniffed and pinched his nose with his free hand. "What did you two think, that I would just sit here and watch you seduce each other right in front of me? You might as well have screwed each other in the sand. But, you're not so tough now are you Cosmo? Where is that mouth of yours? It's killing you to keep it shut isn't it Babe? You want to say something so bad. Something witty, something clever, something you think will calm me down, but I'm beyond your foolish witticisms."

He paused and rotated his neck. A smile came to his face and he continued. "You know all I have to do is squeeze. No one will care, no one will find you, any of you. The coyotes and the buzzards will have you picked clean weeks before anyone even knows you're gone. You will erode in the dust. The desert will swallow your bones. So what do think of that there tough guy, open your mouth now and say it Babe, say something clever and wow me. Wow me you worthless surf shit," Campbell asked of Cosmo as he took another swipe at his nose.

Cosmo softened his eyes. His shoulders relaxed and at once I knew the answer to my earlier question; he was not putting up a façade. "I've never claimed to be tough," Cosmo began, "because I'm not. You could kick my ass from here to Cabo San Lucas without much effort, that's a fact, but another fact that you should know is that I'm not afraid of you or your gun. All you can do is kill me. You either will or you won't, but I can die today, I don't mind really, it's a spectacular day to die. In the next few seconds either outcome will take place, I have no power over it," Cosmo said and took another deep breath. "I can't pacify you Campbell. I'm not going to try. You must deal with your loss the way you must and I wouldn't blame you either way. I'm prepared to accept the consequences. So here I am. Take a look at me. Life has called us to this moment. You must tell us how this moment will end."

"Campbell, your nose," Hillary interjected. A streak of blood ran to his lips.

"Yeah right Hill."

"Honestly, your nose is bleeding," Hillary responded. Campbell took the sleeve of his jacket to his nose and cleared the red stream. "I thought you were done with that crap."

"As I said Hill, there's a lot you don't know. And what do you care anyways. What do you care if I shove shit up my nose? You obviously didn't care enough about me when you let you let yourself fall for this false guru right here. What a crock of shit he is. You're scared, you're pissing in your rubber suit right now Cosmo. I can taste the fear, oh, and it's delicious. It's so sweet to listen to you babble to keep yourself from crying like a little bitch. And you Dane, you stay where you are Babe. Don't think I don't see you over there. Not that you would do anything anyway. All bark and no bite the lot of you. I love to see you cower instead of fighting back Cosmo. You dreamers are all the same, convinced that words and ideas will make a difference when it's only action that counts."

Cosmo tried to hold it in, but failed miserably as a smirk came to his face. "I couldn't agree more. Words mean nothing if action never follows. Hillary and I have acted, you're acting right now in response to our action. It is all a domino effect set in motion the moment we came across the two of you at Cuevas. The pieces are falling all around us. Action is how you define it. This is as tough as I can be. You have the gun. You hold all of the cards. This is my action."

Campbell looked at Hillary. He drank in her wet hair, her wonderful curves molded in the black, rubber suit, and the disappointed look that crossed her teeth. He ducked from her gaze and spat near Cosmo's toes. "No, this is action," he said as he forced the gun further into Cosmo's skull. His finger trembled near the trigger. I could not find air. Hillary covered her mouth. Cosmo took his eyes to Mars, to Ursa Minor, as though it were night. Campbell pulled the gun six inches from Cosmo's face. With lightning quickness he smashed the barrel of the weapon near Cosmo's eye. The impact made a sickening thud as Cosmo fell to the sand. "Action. What a waste Hill, a complete waste this whole trip has been, what a waste all of you are." Campbell pointed the gun at me and strutted towards his Jeep. "You stay put. He got what he deserved." His threat did not matter. I was frozen.

Hillary dove into the sand at Cosmo's side. A lump formed just below and to the edge of Cosmo's right eye accompanied by a warm trickle of blood. Campbell started the Jeep and proceeded to toss out a backpack, a duffel bag, and a brown guitar case. After heaving the guitar like a hammer throw he kicked the duffel bag into the air and an assortment of clothes and colored underwear fanned out across the sand. Hillary screamed a few curses in his direction, but he just laughed and decided to take a shot with the pistol that landed near the rear tire of the Scout. In his mind he had just won and we let him drive from our sight without another word.

"Cosmo are you alright honey. I'm sorry, this is all my fault. All my fault. God I never meant for this to happen."

Cosmo put his teeth together in a subdued hiss. He softly touched the swelling under his eye and checked the bright red coloring that painted his fingertips. "Could have been worse. Oh man that was intense. For a second I thought he might actually do it," he said as Hillary helped him into a sitting position. "He popped me pretty good though. How bad is the cut?"

"It's a nice gash. Does it hurt," Hillary asked.

"Hell yeah it does. At least it's not a bullet though." I finally found air, but my organs still slam danced into one another. I walked over to help Cosmo off of the ground. He smiled as I pulled him up. "Geez Dano, what did you say to piss him off," he said and started laughing. The motion quickened the blood flow as a steady stream ran towards his chin.

"We need to clean up that cut Cosmo. We need to stop it from bleeding," Hillary insisted.

"Yeah okay."

"How about I piss on it for you, I've heard it works miracles," I said surprised to hear my own voice.

"What idiot told you that?"

"Some lunatic who thinks he knows everything. He's probably full of crap, but I could sure go right now since I didn't piss my wetsuit a few minutes ago." The three of us took stock in one another and realized that our journey had transformed in the lingering dust from Campbell's Jeep. We were a trio. She was ours to look after from that moment on. I could not tell what I felt, but I knew it was not happiness. The new couple walked to the Scout so they could patch up Cosmo's eye and I collapsed back in the sand. I searched for serenity and the ease of my heart and instead fell into impatient thoughts. I grabbed a beer from the ice chest to calm my nerves and chugged it down in a few, brief gulps, before I zipped up my suit and returned to the sea, unsure if I was ready for change.

Chapter 18

We stayed on at Peppermint Patty's for two more nights and waited for the sea to come to life. The swell Cosmo predicted lost its way somewhere in the incessant Pacific while we bided our time in small beach break surf at Patty's. At low tide we could actually surf the main point for about an hour and a half before it would shut down again. Cosmo spent a lot of time helping Hillary in the shallows. She improved rapidly. Propelled by her new love for surfing and the excitement from her blossoming relationship with Cosmo she floated about with a graceful ease.

The puppy love that radiated from the new couple upset my state of being. Cosmo so often urged me to run from love, from marriage, from the arms of a good woman, because of the disasters that would follow, and yet there on the sands of an isolated beach in Baja he sewed himself into a passionate affair. I kept to myself. I read, I took wandering hikes, I struggled to write Cosmo's pages, and I thought about Karana. We met on a rainy night and I drove away from her on a rainy afternoon. I wondered if it was just coincidence or if a layer of symbolism needed consideration about the significance of rain. I took to profound contemplation. Maybe everything Cosmo said was bullshit. I could not understand why I took his every word to heart. My world was turned upside down. J.P. was dead and still not put to rest, I felt that Karana was probably in the process of leaving me, I had no job, no future, and a madman almost put a bullet in Cosmo's brain. As I pondered all the negatives I could think of Cosmo and Hillary acted as though it was Christmas morning and they were ten year old kids who unwrapped each moment with unbounded enthusiasm. It depressed me deeply.

The day after Campbell sped off a group of middle-aged men in a Dodge Ram pickup truck drove up to our spot at high tide. The wind howled straight onshore and churned the waves into a butchered mess. Cosmo handed each of them a beer as we talked about approaching swells and the current conditions. After they finished their beers they took three cold cans from their ice chest and returned our gesture. They were camping at Cinco Rocas to the south of us. The driver said that Rocas was fun, though a bit crowded for his tastes that far south of the border. We all pounded the second round and they went off to collect anything they could burn in their evening fire. I almost wanted them to stay so I could rid myself from feeling like I was in the way all of the time. It repeatedly came across Cosmo and Hillary in the middle of a deep kiss or during some flirtatious game that I constantly interrupted. I thought about taking the guys up on their invitation to surf with them down at Rocas and indulge in the generous feasts they boasted about, but instead I remained a loner at Patty's with the two lovebirds.

We decided to take out the boat and launched it at the south end of the beach. The wind picked up soon after we made it out to sea which cut our trip a bit short, but not before Cosmo and I each reeled in a few healthy sized sea bass. We cooked them up over an open fire with black beans, corn tortillas, and as always, ripe avocado. Our avocado supply remained sated because Cosmo stopped often at roadside fruit stands to stock up on them. The buttery texture of the green fruit complimented nearly every meal we consumed on our trip.

Before nightfall on the last night at Patty's I found myself sitting at the waters edge with my shoes off. Exhausted surges of sea water inched up and licked my toes. Lost dreams haunted skeleton bones in hushed cemeteries. They moaned in the wind. They rattled rooftops and tapped on darkened windows. They accumulated into an expanse of isolated territory, uncharted, unexplored, and scantly tangible in the cataclysmic abyss of the mind. Failure to act, to live, to search, to believe, to reach out and grab a hold of a speeding comet transformed coveted dreams into horrific nightmares. The broken dreams imposed their weight, their heavy onus, their ever present guilt of what could have been.

Spoiled fantasies washed in with the lapping tide. Bits of indecision rode on rotting macrocystis. Words left unsaid, steps not taken, crashed in the tumbling sea foam. I skipped a stone that made three feeble jumps and then sank into the sea. A brief splash, a glint of potential, and then a plodded fade into the pits of anonymity. Lost in the silt, the benthic creatures, the webbed stalks of seaweed, the absence of light, the near translucent rock burrowed amongst the masses never to resurface again. Was I the rock? Was I the vanishing act in the middle of the thriving masses? I thought so. At one point in time I dreamed the impossible dream. I was willing to give up everything upon a moments notice to follow an unexpected adventure. I wanted to change the world one heart at a time, one soul at a time, one moment at a time. Moments, diminutive fragments that changed history in a microsecond. Each moment, every moment, required the ultimate care and consideration. Life could alter in a moment, life could end in a moment, and at one time all I wished for was to live in the exact moment before me. Then somewhere along the line I began planning for the future. I put dreams aside to accumulate, to amass, to act according to providence. Every buried dream came to my feet and bit my ankles with each stalking breaker. So many ideas, so many hats I wanted to wear. Dane the baseball player, a bloated version washed by. His disappearance occurred junior year of high school when he did not agree with the philosophies of his new coach. He did not work, he did not fight, he ran. Dead and bloated they all fell. Dane the surfer, he flopped by. He created excuses on a daily basis, a fabricated mantra that worked as a shield to disguise his cowardice. He lied to himself and instantly believed his lie as doctrine. He did not push himself, he did not progress, he cowered in fear. Dead and bloated they all fell. Dane the director, the writer, the artist, the actor, he looked pale at my feet. He never trusted his worth. He pretended to be shy and hid behind a delusional blanket of spinelessness afraid to fly, to sing, to scream out his boiling passions. Dead and bloated they all fell. Dane the humanitarian, the philanthropist, the teacher, the Indiana Jones adventurer, he choked on the saltwater. He held on too tightly to tomorrow, to his possessions, to his warped sense of responsibility. Dead and bloated they all fell, all of them.

Who was left? Who remained to take in the cool ocean air? Dane, the ex- contract buyer, a man with a nice car, a good chunk of change in the bank, an amazing woman who fell in love with the dreamer he once was, he was the only one left. He would lose that woman, he would loose himself, his entire world, if he could not revive any of the bloated corpses that landed at his feet. But which one, which broken desire could he mend into a new life. A life with color, with passion, a life with grace, he had an opportunity to create a new life, but did not know which way to turn.

I picked up another rock and instead of chucking it across the water I gripped it firmly in my hands. My fingers curled around its body and formed a dark cave for the rock to nestle into. I peered into the cavernous flesh. A heartbeat thumped, an artery of quartz pumped iron blood, and stone dust released a sigh into the wind. I heard its plea. It did not want to be hurled into the chaos of the churning seas only to disappear upon entry. There, alone in its element it radiated all of its magnificence across the beach like an unfurled peacock fan. It would find its own path, its own way, and if the time arose it would march into the sea on its own terms. It found its home, it knew its place. I wished for such an answer and picked myself up from the cold ocean water. Dreary steps led to a pad of paper and I began to write.

Cosmo's assignment did not surface immediately, I just wrote. Words splattered like a bucket of paint dropped on the asphalt from a tall building. A profusion of thoughts in a jumbled, yet mellifluous mess poured out in a feverish pace. Some would have called it therapy, some a release, but I felt it as necessary. My hand flowed along alive, content yet searching, born right there on the sands of the Pacific. A free breathing pattern entered and before I knew it I melted right into answering the question Cosmo challenged me with. The moment I finished I walked right over to where he was reading with no concern that Hillary sat right next to him and started to read out loud.

"I am afraid of my pen
Petrified to push a plastic body and metal tip
Across blank sheets of paper
Effusing ink, spilling emotion
Releasing a cornucopia of thoughts
Which dominate daily routines
They taunt at the office chair, they swim out
    at sea
Alive, trudging down well traveled highways

Always spinning, always speaking, yet my pen
    does not move

Bukowski leans in over my right shoulder and
    scoffs
"Hah, you're not a real writer"
He gulps a cheap scotch and spills a few drops
    in my hair
"A real writer will write, no matter what
Until the early hours of morning, drowned in
    words
Drunk in loss and love and the piss stains of
    life"
He sets down his drink next to a spiraled
    notebook
The amber liquid refracts streams of light from
    the desk lamp
Into fanged shadows that nip at my fingertips
He continues "Even if what you write is shit
Just an inebriated mess of sophomoric garbage
And you would rather wipe your ass with the
    pages
Instead of having someone read them, you are
    writing nonetheless
Honing the craft, being who you want to be,
Hah, you are no writer"

Bukowski storms off and at once I want to get
    smashed
I make a few scratches, crumple them up and
    sink into an uncomfortable chair
The door breaks open

A husky man with a graying beard charges for-
   ward like a bull
He grabs my shirt and pulls me from my seat
"You want to write then get off of your ass
The world will teach if you explore her limbs"
Hemingway chugs a beer from a thick stein
"All this sitting around will do you no good
The walls are not going to talk, the wood floors
   do not care
You need to live your life boy"
He grabs my throat "What if this is your last
   breath?
Did you live? Did you experience? Did you
   wade in the waters off Corsica?"
In the commotion he knocked over the rest of
   his beer
He lets go of my neck and I collapse into a
   puddle of ale
"You are too much of a pansy to leave this
   room"

Offended I get up to look out of the window
Darkness swallows the backyard and any celes-
   tial glow
I mope at my ineptitude
A glass chimes on a dark, maple coffee table
I glance up to see a man seated in my blue
   recliner
Right leg crossed over the left and eying his red
   wine
"You spend too much time feeling sorry for
   yourself to ever be a writer"

Neruda sips the burgundy liquid and folds his
    hands together
"You hurt, so do I, so does the world
Babies starve in their mothers arms, mass
    genocide plagues the globe
Political leaders misdirect nations on personal
    trails of greed"
He sighs and brings his hands to his forehead
"The earth needs a voice, a spirit to bring
    about change
And you wallow in the pittance of your own
    selfish heart"
He finishes his glass and rises to his feet
"A shame you cannot see beyond the skin cov-
    ering your bones"

The fear swells
I ponder the blank page before me, the depths
    of my mind
Nothing comes, nothing forms on the empty
    canvas
I hear chuckles and heightening conversation
Bukowski is drinking straight from the bottle
The three Wiseman trample over me like a
    stampede of bison
Mocking my attempts with a collective toast
    as they roam
Leaving me in a pile of splintered bones and
    torn flesh

Cosmo put his book down on his lap. He cocked
his head to the left, but did not say anything. I almost

turned and walked away immediately after reading, but I stayed even though I already knew what he would probably say.

"Did you just write that Dane," Hillary asked. "That was beautiful honey. Don't you think so Cosmo?"

Cosmo rubbed the grit on his chin. "I liked the content. Nice wording, good picture you painted, but what do you think of it?"

"What do I think of it, you know what I think of it Cosmo. It says what you wanted me to say. That I am a coward. That I feel everyone, from my past, from my future, from my present, leaning over my shoulder on everything I do, each decision I make. Instead of letting everyone, or everything inspire me I do the opposite and let them silently scrutinize me. I let them hold me back, I hold myself back."

"Dane, don't be so hard on yourself, I thought it was wonderful," Hillary said. Cosmo wanted to say something, but I dropped my pages and walked away. I felt dramatic, but I was not in the mood to discuss the words any further. I was happy enough that I got something down on paper. It did not solve anything, but at least I created a mirror. I so often kept much of what I feared bottled up in my brain. In those pages I witnessed a portrait of myself, a reflection of damaging flaws that required serious soul searching.

"Thanks Hillary," I said with my back turned. My voice just above a whisper as the crickets began their love songs. I felt relieved and open. Cosmo wanted me to release my own fears, but I also understood that what he really was doing for me was to get my pen moving. They were only two pages of poem style writing, but they were honest. I wanted to be more honest with myself. We were packing up in the morning to head to Agua Dulce because the swell had begun to show signs of life and in the terms of being honest with myself I knew I feared a really large swell. Cosmo would push me to my limits, I would have no way around that, but as I walked towards my tent I thought that when the time came I would only let him down. Honesty served an acrid meal and it did not sit well in my guts. I almost regurgitated its contents at my feet.

Chapter 19

The engine roared over a peaceful afternoon. Light gusts brushed alongside the car windows and raced towards a barren desert. Another growl erupted into the air as two rear tires twisted further into a pit of mud. Cosmo climbed out of the Scout to check out the impending mishap. Tire treads filled with a slick mixture of mud and river silt. We tried to cross a stagnant puddle of water which rested at the bottom of a small hill and the beginning of a steep incline. Cosmo hit the gas to plow through the water and buried the tow hitch half way through the large mud pit. Luckily we packed two shovels in the Scout in preparation for a similar instance and we went to work digging out the buried connection between the boat and the Scout. Covered in mud and sweating from a snuggling sun we freed the tow hitch and were ready to get back on the lightly treaded road, but the puddle made different plans. Once stopped, the Scout trenched itself deeper into peril with each spin of its wheels. The mud acted like magic grease in a cartoon and did not allow our vehicle to make any progress.

Cosmo dug out the tires while I went on a scavenger hunt to find rocks and any form of wood we could place underneath the wheels for traction. Rocks of all shapes and sizes littered the khaki terrain, but I could not locate any wood. We made a path of stones and cleaned off the treads with a wire hanger then tried to liberate the Scout once again, but after catching the first rock in an apparent escape the subsequent stones sunk in the mud and the tires excavated a new grave. Frustration overwhelmed us. We planned to make it to Agua Dulce well before nightfall and the predicament threw a curveball at our intentions.

Hillary acted unfazed by the delay. She turned up the music and danced on the hood of the Scout as though being stuck in the mud was our daily blessing. After her recital she made chicken sandwiches and cracked open beers for her dirty men who tossed aside mud in agitated frenzies. Engrossed in our work, Cosmo and I failed to notice the old Ford pick up truck heading towards the Scout. We were blocking the road. We knew of only a few homes along the road and that a traffic jam was highly unlikely, but we also knew that the road we blocked served as the only way in and out of the area. Hillary tapped Cosmo on the shoulder as a man approached our mess.

"What we got here? Looks like you boys been wrestling with the hogs," he said. Cosmo and I emerged from behind the Scout to apologize for being in the way. We were surprised to hear English with a southern edge to it coming from the man. "Names

Jerome, I live a few miles back that way. Boys need sum help, looks like."

"Can't seem to escape from this mud," Cosmo said. "It's almost like quicksand. The Scout can usually get through anything, but we cased the tow hitch trying to get through the mini pond here. We dug it out, but then the tires could not free themselves from this stuff. I am Cosmo, the dirty guy to my right is Dane, and the pretty lady is Hillary."

"How y'all doing? Been a while since I heard English. I've been here three years now and my Spanish's still awful. Good to talk in my native tongue." Jerome stood about six feet tall. He wore a thin mustache that barely made it to the corners of his mouth. On his head sat an olive-green, mesh hat with the word "Army" in gold lettering. "Been stuck in this type of mud myself, had a devil of a time getting myself out too."

"Sorry for the inconvenience Jerome. We'll try and get the Scout out of your way as soon as possible, I am sure you have somewhere to go" I said. I turned to head back to work when Jerome's voice stopped me.

"Ain't no need to apologize. This mud can alter everything you were planning. Sides, I was just on my way to make a few phone calls. Gets lonely out here, wanted to hear someone's voice other than my own. I have a tractor back at my place, an old John Deere. She puffs and pops, but she'll get the job the done, save you boys some time. One of y'all want to ride back with me, sometimes she gets a bit cranky and might need sum help turning her over."

"I'll go," Cosmo volunteered immediately.

"Sounds fine. Take us about half an hour or more

to do the round trip. I've got no food for you on me, but I can bring something back if you're hungry."

Hillary smiled and looked at Jerome. "Thank you so much, but we just ate sandwiches. I think we can tough it out for awhile." Cosmo and Hillary shared an innocent moment of silent goodbyes which erupted into full blown laughter as Cosmo headed to Jerome's truck. On their way I heard Jerome ask about the cut near Cosmo's eye and what kind of name Cosmo was anyway.

Hillary and I made ourselves comfortable on the hood of the Scout with our backs planted against the warm windshield. Jerome's mention of using the phone reminded me of the message I left Karana just a few hours earlier before we began the trek towards Agua Dulce. The answering machine could not substitute for the real thing, but at least I heard her voice. It let me know she was real, actual flesh and blood parading through her life back at home. Hillary wanted to know all about Karana, what she did for a living, what she looked like, and what she thought about letting me go on an adventure into Baja with someone as free spirited as Cosmo. I began in generalities, but the more I talked, the more comforting Hillary's kind face and attentive ears became, and I found myself revealing profound details to the borderline stranger. While we waited the resentment I built up towards her faded away. We became friends. She carried Cosmo's ability to flow with whatever life threw at her. She mentioned Campbell only briefly as a mistake that led her to the very moment in life we were sharing. "Campbell might have been all wrong, I knew it, but he got me out of town and now here I am stuck in the mud with two adventurous men in the middle of Baja. I can't wait to see what happens next. With all of that energy radiating out of Cosmo I don't know what to expect at all and I love it. Must be so exciting for you on this adventure, never knowing which way you will turn next."

I laughed with a true gush from my belly. It took her no time at all to catch on and let herself go into our journey while I still struggled with plans, and days, and timelines. My earlier resentment when she joined us was nothing more than plain jealousy in witnessing how easily she slid into our random travel habits. It was pleasant to hear another voice, an understanding and caring voice that added a soothing dynamic to the constant banter between Cosmo and me. I nodded in agreement and fell back on the windshield.

"So," Hillary asked after a good minute of silence, "Karana actually told you to up and leave just like that. She sounds awesome."

"Well," I began trying to find a way to put it "It wasn't just hey go with Cosmo, I mean she knows me so well. It was a build up. It was something I needed to do a long time ago, but I never had the balls to do it. Many things were aligned to get me here and yet I still have fought it every step of the way, whether verbally or internally. Karana knew I needed something, anything to open my eyes. To see outside the miserable shell I have ensconced myself in over the past year or so. I'm trying to see from out there, from the other side. Sometimes I catch it, but only for a glance and then it disappears."

Hillary scratched the side of her nose. "Sounds like a familiar story, the escape part anyways. I would have never paid much attention to a guy like Campbell, but he caught me at a time in my life where being treated to great material excess felt good. It was wrong, but for a while I could not help but enjoy myself. The gifts, the expensive dinners, it was all new to me and somewhat thrilling. It took only a few months to realize that we had nothing in common and that I was merely holding on to that oh so familiar dream of so many little girls about being a princess. Yet, he only treated me that way with the macho man display of his wealth. So I left him, but he couldn't let go. He walked into my work the other day when I was feeling overly rooted, bored, and in need of an escape of any kind. I got in a Jeep Wrangler, you bolted from a train, and now here we are living in today's adventure."

I studied her for a second as she leaned against the windshield with her eyes closed. She drank in the sun like a smooth glass of wine. "How do you do it Hillary?"

"How do I do what sweetie?"

"I mean, how do you act so at ease, so at peace in this moment. You barely know us. This trip could be a total disaster and yet you already look just as willing to accept the moment as Cosmo does. I'm trying, I'm really trying to catch that glimpse, to totally feel at ease, but I still fight the unnecessary fretting about what is going to happen next. I can't do it, I can't completely let go. I'm, I'm......"

"Shhhhhhhh," Hillary mouthed and put her finger to my lips. "Don't try so hard Dane, just be."

"Just be?"

"Yes, you poor, sweet thing, just be."

Jerome putted down the incline towards the mud pit with Cosmo perched on a side step and holding on to a steel bar underneath the tractor's lone seat forty-five minutes later. With long, iron chains and puffs of smoke spit into the air out of the tractor's exhaust Jerome pulled the Scout free. With the fast approaching sunset we explained our need to get on the road and find a place to camp before night fell. Jerome knew where we were headed and confirmed we would never make it there before dark. With a humble grin he offered for us to stay with him for the evening. "I got a whole chicken that will take me days to eat and I make my own tequila. Got a fresh batch ready to be tapped into if you like." Hillary spoke for us and said that we would be honored to stay with him. I knew the oncoming swell enticed Cosmo to decline the offer, but he tossed his longings aside to accept Jerome's sincere generosity.

Jerome and Hillary went to work in the kitchen while Cosmo and I took seats on wooden stools placed on the living room side of the kitchen's countertop after we took turns cleaning up. We brought our cooler of beers into the house and spoke of our journey. Jerome chopped vegetables while he listened to our tale and silently nodded with each turn of events. He moved with a direct purpose. Each action in a regimented order, first the carrots, slowly peeled then chopped into identical pieces, then onions, cut thinly into sliced ovals then each oval diced separately from the next. He directed Hillary with step by step instructions down to the last detail. As Cosmo approached the mud in his story Jerome interrupted to begin his own tale.

"Sounds like y'all are having a good time and I hope your uncle gets a proper sendoff in the little town you mentioned." He cleared his throat and then continued. "Now just to free your heads, because I'm sure y'all been wondering and asking yourselves what the hell a seventy-one year old black man is doing in the middle of nowhere in a land that only speaks Spanish. Well I'll tell you, I just had to get away. Just don't understand the world no more."

We listened closely as he told us about his life. The aromas from the kitchen taunted our senses. The quaint home contained two bedrooms, one bathroom, and a large living room area that smelled like a campfire. The house felt like a mountain cabin in the middle of a forest of pine trees instead of a modest house surrounded by large cacti and desolate hills. Limited decorations adorned the walls except for what appeared to be a few family photos scattered about the house. Each window was blanketed with dark curtains, which blocked out any incoming light. Cream-colored tiles ran the length of the house and several Oriental style rugs that Jerome purchased while in the Army took positions in the living room, the bedrooms, and the dining area in the kitchen.

Jerome spoke with a soft cadence, methodical, yet demanding of attention. He began in Georgia, where he was born in secret behind an aluminum barn. His father disappeared two months before his birth never to be heard from again while his mother struggled to raise him on her own. His mother Della could not read, but that did not stop her from telling her newborn son stories of enchanted lands and magical realms as she recalled them from memory. As Jerome turned eight years of age Della contracted a malicious pneumonia that kept her bed ridden for three weeks before she passed away. She could not afford medicine or a doctor and told her young son that it was just a cough that would pass after a decent rest. The cough never ceased and neither did the image of Della holding his hand in a bath of sweat and tears as she left the earth. After her death Jerome went to live with various relatives who could not control his increasing temper. He was upset with the world, he hated a man who did nothing more than contribute a poisoned seed into his suffering mother, and any time someone around him would cough his heart would ache for the loss of his mom.

"At sixteen I faked my age and joined the Army," Jerome continued. "My mother always spoke of other places, far off places around the world, and the Army felt like my chance to find some of them. Seemed like the only way to get out of Georgia and make myself into a man. I saw the world, I fought in Korea. I had friends, black friends, white friends, Latino friends all bleeding the same color blood die all around me, in my arms. Many times I wished for my own death. I would crawl into any rice paddy; I charged the front lines praying for a bullet to spill my brains out the back of my skull. People back home tried, I don't blame them none, just, none of them was my mama and I didn't have a daddy or brothers and sisters.

I was alone in the world, a cruel world full of war, bigotry, color lines, and people wanting to kill you, so I figured might as well happen on the battlefield, then at least then my life might be worth something, but the bullet never came. I stayed in the Army for twenty years. I retired in California. California is a crazy place. I remember the first time I saw a black man jump on a tiny board and paddle into the sea like y'all do and I knew that something was different in California than anywhere on the planet. A black man where I come from would have not part of that mighty ocean on such a small object."

"I enrolled myself in college and shortly after graduation I became a school teacher in my mid-forties. My wife was a teacher as well. She taught second grade, I dealt with the seventh and eight grade rambunctious teenagers. My angel, she was the best thing to ever happen to me. She taught me how to let go of my hate, my anger, and I loved her like there was no tomorrow. She fought hard, but died of ovarian cancer ten years ago. I hung on at school a little while longer then moved down here. I like the quiet. No bombs going off in my head, no screams of anguish coming from our bedroom back home where my wife made her fight, nope, me and the hills, my little farm, and the ocean breeze wrapped around me and an evening tequila."

Jerome ducked his head into the gas oven and pulled out a large bird smothered in his secret sauces. He set the pan on top of the stove and said we needed a few minutes for it to cool down. The four of us sipped on our beers lost in Jerome's story. Cosmo wanted more and asked Jerome a question to keep him talking.

"Did you just up and move one day Jerome," Cosmo asked. "I mean that is a big step to come to another country without speaking the language or knowing much about it."

"I had enough. As I told you earlier I just don't understand the world no more. Seemed as good a place as any to get away. Been down here a few times with friends on fishing trips and decided it was a good place to be forgotten. The worlds gone crazy, everything's spinning out of control. I knew the exact day I had enough. A kid comes to class with a gun in his backpack. He yells at another youngster in class that he'd been having problems with and pulls the gun out with intentions to shoot him. I tackled the kid and got the gun away from him. In the process the kid broke his hand and his pinky finger and his parents filed a lawsuit. The school district backed the parents and left me out to dry. Over twenty years of service, a gun about to destroy who knows how many lives, and I get let go. I went home and didn't know what to do but cry. I cried for five days straight. A strong and resilient man who endured atrocities at war, utter hatred in the south, his mother and wife dying before their times, sat in a room and cried like a baby. I thought I was tough, but nothing could console the hollowness left in my heart after the incident at school. The world was full of too much hurt and didn't make sense at all. I sold my house and crossed the border with no plans to ever return."

"Are you serious," I said stunned by the incident.

"Jerome that is so awful," Hillary added. "I can't even imagine."

"And it wasn't just the gun incident neither," Jerome continued while carving up the chicken, "The whole worlds in for a big shake up. You got tsunamis washing out hundreds of thousands of lives, catastrophic hurricanes, tornadoes in places they ain't supposed to be, cold where it's supposed to be hot, hot where it is supposed to be cold, not to mention every time the winds even pick up in the slightest half of California goes up in flames. Nope the Bible speaks of it, a day of reckoning, Armageddon. I believe it's upon us. Leaders don't get along. Whether it's Bush's fault or not he is hated around the world. The Middle East is a time bomb waiting to explode. Figure if it's time for the world to come to an end might as well die in peace. So here I am all alone in the quiet desert and it suits me just fine."

Jerome and Hillary doled out the meal on blue, ceramic plates. They piled on portions of chicken, fried potatoes with rosemary, bell peppers, and onions, steamed carrots with honey, and flaky biscuits. We made our way to the dining room table anxious to dig into the tantalizing feast. Jerome was the last to sit down and placed a bottle without a label on it in the center of the table along with four glasses when he joined us. "My new concoction," he said while he poured generous amounts in each of our glasses. "Now this ain't any shooting tequila, no sir. This here is sipping liquor. Take your time with it, hopefully you'll like it." We all thanked him and clinked glasses in a cheers to our generous host. We let the conversation die down while we tore away at our food and sipped on the homemade tequila that tasted of singed oak and sweet nectar.

Stuffed to the point of explosion we cleaned up our mess and headed into the living room where Cosmo got the fire going to keep everyone warm. Hillary softly plucked away at her worn down guitar as we sunk into Jerome's two sofas in food comas. I was to take the green sofa to sleep on while Cosmo and Hillary were offered the guest bedroom that had never been used. I was about to nod off in a seated, upright position when Cosmo broke the silence that christened the peaceful room.

"Do you really think the apocalypse is coming Jerome, that the world is coming to an end as so spoken of in the Bible."

Jerome placed his hands on top of his salt and pepper hair then lowered them to scratch through the scruff on his face. "It seems that way to me. All signs point to it. Not just weather wise and climate changes, but all of humanity. Our pride, our greed, our sloth has taken hold of all the souls on this once beautiful planet. Everyone in it for themselves and can't trust no one. People will sue you for trying to help them out of a car wreck or for tripping on a sidewalk. They would rather shoot you in the face than lend you a hand. How did we get this way? The Devil crept into all of us and we don't even see it. Yep, sounds like the end to me."

Cosmo thought for a second and massaged his left shoulder. I could tell he wanted to debate the topic of the apocalypse further with Jerome and he paused to find the most tactful way to go about it without offending his gracious host. "You know the Mayans inscribed on their calendar that the end is in December of 2012," Cosmo began. "Nostradamus also speaks of an end that some historians link to this same time, though he used no dates to actually call out 2012 as an exact time. The Mayans, according to which interpretation you listen to, predict it more as a shift than an actual end of the world that will take place. That major events will shake up the pre-existing way man and the planet have interacted. Then some historians say the opposite, that the Mayans precisely mapped out the end of the world and that we will all perish on December 21st, 2012."

The fire crackled in the dimly lit room. Hillary put down her guitar so she could place her full attention on the simmering conversation. I bit my tongue and hoped that Cosmo would not take it over the edge and insult Jerome's obvious faith. Of all the discussions that got Cosmo going religion headed the top of the list. Jerome was not pushing his beliefs, he only stated them, and I gripped tightly to the cushions of the couch and wished for Cosmo to be kind to the man who pulled us from the mud and fed us an exquisite meal at his table. I held my breath.

"Don't know much about the Mayans to be honest. Of course I have heard of them, their calendar, their being far advanced for their time, I just don't know if they got it right. Now, me and Jesus, we get along. He makes me feel right when I get lost. When I read about him in the scriptures I can lay down my head peacefully at night. All the Mayan calculations and mystic predictions don't seem real to me. I will take my chances with God and Jesus."

"You have a strong faith don't you Jerome, a firm belief in the Christian religion?"

"Of course, of course, don't you son?" Oh shit, I said under my breath. Jerome released an opening that usually sent Cosmo into a litany of stored information from his arsenal that he loved to fire into a warming conversation. I clutched the green cushions with tense vigor.

"Jesus, he always sounded like an amazing man. A kind, healing man, who brought hope and inspiration to his people, but to be honest Jerome, I don't have faith in any religion." Jerome turned to face Cosmo. I expected a rise in his voice, but he remained calm and delved deeper into the discussion.

"So you're saying you have no relationship with our Lord, God and savior. You have no belief in him at all."

Again Cosmo took his time to answer. It became obvious that his stalling techniques were used to search for the right words to avoid sounding combative. He respected Jerome a great deal. "I get that opinion a lot when I tell people I have no faith in religion. Thing is though, I have no problem in believing in a higher power, a creative force that exists somewhere in the heavens. You call that form God, some call it Buddha, some call it Allah, some call it Itzamna, and many countries formed their own religions around their own Gods. The early Egyptians had their Gods, the Greeks and the Romans created theirs, and so has modern civilization. If any of those doctrines makes sense to someone on how they should live their lives then more power to them. I just don't believe any human being can know what that creative source is, so I stick to my own credos. I am not a nihilist, I believe in right and wrong, and being a good person. If this is wrong then I am wrong. I can live with that, call me a searcher. Somewhat of a wandering chef who gathers ingredients from all forms of beliefs, all walks of life, from humans to insects, to the mountains to the frigid rivers that make their way to the seas."

Jerome sifted through Cosmo's words and took a sip of his tequila. He placed his glass down on an end table below a bamboo lamp and brought his hands to his knees. "Sounds a bit complicated and a tad crazy son, but I like it. Maybe if I was younger all that craziness might be something I would like to chase after, but at my age I am willing to rest any of those concerns on faith. It might sound dull in comparison, but I don't mind that anymore, the serenity fits me quite nice, kind of like an old pair of shoes."

Cosmo could have kept digging into the discussion to find a pocket of scalding lava waiting to erupt, but he evened off. He fell under Jerome's charms and looked at the man through the eyes of an adoring grandson or a student listening to his favorite professor. That was where Cosmo made his mark as a person I truly admired as a friend. He could spew facts out for hours, quote passages from a multitude of novels, but his true gift came in his acceptance of people for who they were. He liked to mix it up for arguments sake, but when all was said and done he just wanted people to be themselves. To be comfortable with who they were and find that same comfort in the person sitting next to them who might have quite different beliefs. Jerome was exactly that man. He rested comfortable in his own bones and accepted the two scraggily surfers and one beautiful woman sharing space in his home. There was no need for Cosmo to go off on one of his tirades about the hypocrisies of religion, the blood shed in the name of a faith, or any other hot button he liked to press when confronting divinity. Jerome was content where he was and equally content with whom we were which Cosmo respected with ample fervor. Cosmo smiled in appreciation and let the topic go as Jerome finished up.

"And if that is what is in your heart, then God bless you. You seem like a nice young man, all of you got a nice stream of genuine goodness flowing about you. I'll say prayers to God and Jesus to keep you safe on your journey, y'all can pray to whoever you like. But thanks for humoring an old man, I sure have appreciated your company, but it's getting way past my bedtime. Y'all sleep tight and I'll see you in the morning."

Jerome pushed off the couch with his hands on his legs to ease himself up. He patted Cosmo on the back on the way to his room and reached out for my hand, which I shook in great thanks. Hillary gave him a warm embrace as though she was saying goodnight to her father and Jerome disappeared down the hall. We did not talk as the fire eased in ferocity. A few minutes later Cosmo and Hillary made their way to the guest bedroom and I snuggled up inside my sleeping bag on the green sofa feeling blessed for the opportunity that allowed our vehicle to become stuck in a puddle of mud. I fell asleep with visions of myself dancing on the hood of the Scout as Hillary had done just a few hours before. She knew it instantly, Cosmo reveled in the challenge, but I took my time to understand that each moment could lead to an unforgettable encounter. What began as a mess turned into an evening I knew I would cherish for the rest of my life. I needed to dance in the moment not after it had already passed.

Chapter 20

The smell of fresh coffee roused me from my coma on Jerome's couch. The aroma flooded the house like a sudden downpour. At first I thought I was at home rising to the familiar scent of brewing coffee that Karana would start each morning before work. I used to hate the drink, but loved the smell. Karana changed all of that. We spent many Sunday mornings making breakfast with fresh ingredients from our garden while we sipped on a freshly brewed pot of java. I would come home from an early morning surf session while she took advantage of a few extra hours of sleep and we would convene in the kitchen and pretend we were on vacation in some tropical part of the world, cooking banana pancakes and slicing ripe avocadoes. It was our relaxing time, a time when the world slowed down for the both of us. I could never sit still, her work devotion demanded more hours of her time than it should have, but on Sunday mornings we created an escape from our worries, from the world at large, and fell into the peace of each others company. The intention was not there, I just missed her, but I felt slightly disappointed to see Jerome working away in the kitchen instead of Karana running a million miles an hour trying to get to work on time.

The three travelers slept in much later than we anticipated. Cosmo and I were typically early risers, but something about the comfort of Jerome's home, his kind way about him, his potent tequila, and a good night's sleep underneath a roof made us catch up on some extra sleep time. The swell was rising by the minute, but Jerome would not let us leave until we shoveled down a hardy breakfast complete with pancakes, bacon, eggs, and strong, black coffee. Jerome also gave us three bottles of his tequila to keep us warm on the rest of our adventure. We left J.P.'s boat on Jerome's property at his insistence to ensure a less burdened journey to Agua Dulce with plans to pick it up once we decided to continue south. It gave us a content pleasure to know we would see Jerome at least one more time.

The road to Agua Dulce was not much of a road at all. After Jerome's we passed only two more homes and the road appeared as though it ended at the last of the houses, and in a sense it did. A tractor never blazed a path beyond that point and only pure discovery alone led vehicles to push further west. The first and only time that I went to Agua Dulce with Cosmo and J.P. I thought that J.P. was going to kill us as he pushed the Scout to its limits over boulders and large collections of brush. We made our own path and bounced our way into a dream scenario. A sublime cove tucked away from the rest of the world adorned with a perfect right hand point break that could handle swells from two feet to twenty feet. As Cosmo pushed the Scout as J.P. had done before him a silent excitement buzzed through the vehicle to reach the perfect surf and the large waves Cosmo hoped for. I caught the buzz from Cosmo and definitely from Jerome's coffee and wanted to feel just as exuberant, but along with that joy came an overdose of fear. Cosmo predicted that Dulce would produce the largest waves of the swell due to the angle in which it pointed out to sea. I wanted to push my limits more than anything, but thinking about it as we tromped through our own made up road sent my heart into panic fits. Paddling out into big surf with Cosmo was like riding up in an airplane with him as my tandem jumping partner for a freefall towards the earth. He would never let me back down, even if he had to shove me over the edge, and covertly I prayed for the waves to not become ridiculously huge.

Though the rolling hills of Baja lacked the booming growth of vegetation that overtook the hillsides of California at the onset of spring, patches of green life penetrated the sparse terrain and spoke of the shift in the seasons. The air warmed with each mile we headed south and every day that we extended our journey. The gradual change made me long for the imminent summertime sunshine, soothing seventy degree ocean water, optional shirts, optional shoes, and the smell of the dry desert winds that would collide with the coastal beaches back at home in Oceanside once summer began. We passed a thriving green yucca that sent its phallic stalk twelve feet into the air aware that in those dry summertime months the plant would drop its vibrant greens and replace them with a faded, sandy-beige. Cosmo laughed at the wheel like a pirate confronting a storm, Hillary shrieked with delight after every exaggerated bump we hit, and I sat like a deaf mute and held on to the outside of the car door through the open window and thought about the alterations of life, the progress, the setbacks, the cycles that would continue years after my bones became the dust that erupted from our tires.

When the Scout made its last bounce and steadied itself on a ledge overlooking the sea below we imbibed a glorious sight. The waves fired around the point and wrapped into the protected cove twenty feet below us. Cosmo exited the Scout like a king welcoming his court. He raised his arms to the skies and then bowed to his kingdom. The lapping seaweed applauded, the encroaching breakers set off bass drums, a line of gulls fanned the air in mad sprints as Hillary and I joined the freshly crowned majesty of Agua Dulce.

The wave set up as a right hand point break, which basically meant that a point of land stuck out in the ocean, and as waves met that point they wrapped around it and followed the stretch of land as it angled towards the shore. Typically point breaks were classified among the finest and longest waves in the world to surf. Jeffery's Bay in South Africa, the Superbank in Australia, Raglan in New Zealand, Pavones in Costa Rica, were just a few of the many world class breaks coveted by surfers around the globe. A pilgrimage and catching a wave at one of the glorified breaks passed along in surfing families and communities as tales of visiting one's Mecca, or perhaps one of the wonders of the world.

Almost every surfer has a legend about a secret break that no one else on the planet knows about. The vow is never to tell, never to expose the exact location or definitive landmarks to anyone in hopes that the break will remain pristine and vacant of all human involvement. A righteous vow indeed, but somehow as years pass so do stories and surf breaks can only remain hidden for so long. To my knowledge Cosmo and I were the only two people in the world who had ever surfed Agua Dulce, with J.P. being the only other human being we had seen step upon its shores, but this was only a vision through my own eyes, reality favored the certainty of other groups of surfers who stumbled upon Dulce's perfection at some point in time or another, though if so their traces remained near non-existent and their commitment to the vow stood as downright admirable.

Cosmo scrambled to get ready. Instead of tying a towel around his waist to cover himself while changing into his wetsuit he stripped bare in front of nature and his two companions. His white buttocks glowed against the tan of his back. Hillary walked over and slapped him on the ass while he turned his wetsuit inside out and exposed his body just as he was created. It mattered to no one. By that time I knew Hillary had already seen him naked and I had witnessed similar behavior many times in the past in front of much larger audiences. He did not care and neither did the hills or the beckoning sea that roared below us.

After watching the waves it became apparent that the swell was building right before our eyes. Cosmo hypothesized that the monsters rose to double overhead faces and climbing. Surfer's measure waves in a variety of facets. By the face of the wave, by the back of it, from height in feet, to height according to body size, any number of concocted formulas can expel from a surfer's mouth when trying to calculate the size of a wave. A wave in California could be described as fifteen feet tall, and then conversely, the same size wave in Hawaii would get labeled in the six to ten foot range as the Hawaiian's measure more from the back of a wave and Californian's from the front. I was particular of measuring from a wave to human scale, more or less describing how many of my bodies could stand on top of one another to get an accurate detail of the face of a wave. Cosmo's agreement that the waves probably equaled a solid double overhead meant that I could take another one of me at around six feet tall and place that other body on top of my head to get an approximate measurement for the size of the waves. It would have been just as easy to say ten to twelve feet, but I believed it always added more perspective when I gave the wave scale.

Hillary went to work setting up camp as though she sat in front of an easel ready to create a painting. She hummed and moved about with the soft breeze that swayed her back and forth from the Scout to our designated pad where we decided to make our home. Her blue and green sarong danced with her hips. In the matter of a day I went from resentment, to acceptance, to jubilant that she became a fellow member on our voyage. We were becoming our own little tribe and I relished her company, I only wished Karana could have joined her on the cliff as Cosmo and I made our way to the ocean.

We had to scale a rocky hill to make it to the shore. A natural path, though not well worn, had been cut from the run off of the heavy winter rains. The trail was not easy to follow, especially for Cosmo, because he carried a little scoop of J.P. in his right hand, but we managed to make it to the bottom without incident. I wanted to talk over a strategy with Cosmo about how to take on Dulce, but before I could get a word out he bowed his head at the toes of the sea and then belly-flopped on the top of his board. After three awkward strokes with a clenched right fist Cosmo let J.P. loose to fend for himself. Somehow I knew J.P. would not have a problem.

I charged after Cosmo with my heart on alert. The size comparison we agreed upon was just an approximation and I wondered how the incoming walls of water would look from a prone position on my belly. Because a point break offered near perfect waves that rarely broke in front of each other while following the land, paddling out would have normally consisted of stroking through the channel away from where the waves were breaking in an arced line. Once we reached a distance equal to the appropriate take off zone we would angle into the lineup and maneuver for position. With the large surf before us the paddle would have expanded into a much longer journey to get around the heaving breakers, and although the arduous paddle seemed exhausting it remained a much better option than trying to go underneath successive big waves. When the surf gets really large at a point break sometimes the channel closes out and the paddle can become absolute hell. Fortunately some breaks also offer jump zones near the tip of the respective points where a simple launch into the water can bypass almost the entire paddle and Dulce offered such an area. The only precautions resided in proper timing between waves to make our jump and any rocks or shelves we needed to clear during the leap. With our jump behind us we made it into the lineup after a mad-sprint paddle to the outside without incident.

I paddled straight for the shoulder to get a full view of what we were dealing with while Cosmo headed right into position. A set approached, not as large as we had seen from the shore, but definitely over head high. Cosmo looked like he was too far inside and stroked for the shoulder as he angled into his first wave. The lip sucked him up and then let him go on an elevator drop towards the bottom. He hit the flats with a slight wobble and appeared as though he might pull off the amazing drop, but the lip tackled his head and down he went. I waited for him to resurface cradled in the safety of the shoulder. A few seconds later he busted through the water and let out an unreserved laugh as though he had just heard the funniest joke in the world.

"Yeehow, that one kicked my ass," Cosmo shouted while he made his way back towards me. "It's sucking up a bit right next to the point. It should get real hollow Dano. Barrels 'o' fun Dane the Mane, I can't believe we are rolling up to this. We have to be the luckiest fuckers on the planet." I laughed, but it was a fake laugh that attempted to disguise the fear lumped in my throat as I paddled towards the peak with him.

I was upset with my apprehension. Dulce broke nearly perfect. Sure the drop was steep and the waves grew larger by the minute, but after conquering the size and precipitous entry the wave offered a perfect, empty canvas to play with for as long as my legs felt like they could ride. I did my best to shake it off like a dog scratching at a flea and concentrated on the surf. Cosmo took off on a clean one. I watched him disappear down the face and as I turned to witness the wave peel into the cove his board, nose first for just a fraction of a second which was quickly replaced by his fins, carved off of the lip and sent water flying into the air in a flash of lightning. He continued down the line in perfect harmony and waltzed with his partner. A step below sight, a resurgence of spray, a dip around a leg kick, a twirl out of his partner's hands, then a spin back into her arms, Cosmo knew his partner well.

Inspired by the display I paddled into my first wave. I took off close to the shoulder determined to feel my way instead of jumping in head first like Cosmo had done. I teetered a bit on the drop, but found my feet soon enough. The wave was just a little over head high and perfect. I cruised down the line a bit hesitant and more or less tested the wave out. I performed one strong turn towards the end of my ride and Cosmo shouted as loud as he could.

"Yeah Dane the Mane, just let it rip here brother.

The wave is perfect. Don't be shy, you can show her your balls." I laughed and finally it did not feel forced. We surfed for hours, not sure how many, but paddling out with my arms burning from another long ride I watched Cosmo drop into the biggest wave that either of us had seen all day. Our assessment from the cliff came out a bit exaggerated and the double overhead sets we thought we saw came out to be just a foot or two overhead, but as Cosmo flew towards me in mid bottom turn the mountain above him was definitely at least double over his head, probably bigger. Cosmo put his hands up as the wave cascaded down around him and then slotted himself into a perfect tube. From the side angle I watched as he calmly took his right hand and dragged it along the speeding cylinder of Mother Ocean's belly and then emerged from her blessed womb with a visceral howl, reborn, refreshed, and pulsating with every living organism in the sea.

I waited for him in the channel. My arms ached and my belly grumbled, but I was in absolute awe of the perfect ride I had just witnessed. After I congratulated him we decided it was time for one more before we went in to devour some food. My fear waned the longer we surfed after I realized it was not as big as we originally thought, but Cosmo's mammoth ride sounded the alarms once again. I had been out in surf as large as Cosmo's wave, but never in a barrel that big, nothing that hollow. Our whole way out Cosmo told me to be patient and to only take a wave that he hand selected so I could experience a ride just as amazing as he had. The butterflies stirred and performed drunken flights in the pit of my stomach. I was not sure I could handle such a wave.

We sat for fifteen minutes and let medium sized waves peel perfectly to shore. Cosmo karate chopped the water and sent a large chunk of it towards my face. I drank in the comfort from the saltwater shower as it spilled down my body. I searched for tranquility, for a clear mind, for a relaxed breath, and then Cosmo pointed to the horizon.

"I'll take the first one," he half shouted in between paddles. "Let the second one go by and take off on the third one. The third wave has pitched over better than any wave in the last four sets. Just stay calm, relax on your bottom turn and set a line. That's all you have to do, the wave will do the rest."

With my heart in my throat I paddled over the first wave as Cosmo disappeared towards shore. The second wave approached and it looked bigger than Cosmo's previous tube ride as I let it pass by unmolested. In position for the wave of my life I turned around and started clawing at the surface of the sea. The wave accepted my presence. I thought about the significance, the stories I could tell, the elation I would feel while my arms kept moving. The wave stood up and I looked down. My thoughts turned. I thought I was too late, too far inside, too unprepared to make the drop, too afraid of what would happen when I wrecked. In reality I could not have been in a more perfect position, but my heart went from beating rhythmically in my throat to bleeding profusely on the center of my tongue. Last glance and I pulled back, only to see Cosmo drop his head to his board in disappointment in the channel before he turned and made his way in.

Eventually I caught a smaller wave and found my way to the sand, but I could not climb the hill back to camp. The thought of coming up with an excuse made me wish that I would have drowned out at sea. I could not face him. Everything was perfect, every-thing set, and I let my old fears, the fears I thought I had shed since walking off a train, rule over me once again. All of the freedom of the road, the liberation of my thoughts, the emergence of a man I wished I could be vanished suddenly in a cresting wave. My gift wiped clean on the round rocks of the shore and sucked back to sea. Perhaps it was too late for me, too late to teach an old dog new tricks. I was a coward living in fear of everything that I really wanted. How sad that I would forever remain that way.

Chapter 21

S ince the day Cosmo and I became friends during
our second semester of junior college I wondered
why I could not be more like him. He was different
from anyone that I had ever met. While most people
talked about the things they wanted to try and made
excuses for not trying them, Cosmo contrarily went
out and attempted whatever filled his heart at any
particular moment. It was as if the filter that ninety-
nine percent of the adult population placed between
their thoughts and their actions had been surgically
removed from Cosmo's brain. His curiosities carried him like a child from one activity to the next
and he gave each moment his full attention. I mar-
veled at his complete disregard for fear of failure, or
more acutely, his lack of fear about what anyone else
thought about his actions. He looked at each day as
an empty canvas waiting to be sated with an effusion of life and he did not want to waste one dab of
paint. Watching him charge the rise of each new day
I could not help but think of a quote he revered in a
discussion about **Walden** by Henry David Thoreau

in a Literature class we took together. Thoreau said "If a man does not keep pace with his companions, perhaps it is because he hears a different drummer. Let him step to the music which he hears, however measured or far away."

Cosmo definitely marched to the beat of a different drum and I did my best to catch the sounds that bombarded all around him, no matter how faint they were to my own ears, but something always held me back. I was always a step behind, over thinking and not acting. Sure brief moments occurred. During our college years and the early stages of our friendship I pondered the world at large, I discovered the adventurer buried deep in my soul, and I started putting my thoughts on paper. The high I received from pouring out the inner workings of my heart carried me into boundless dreamlands where I unearthed a pure joy of which I had never felt before. I would loose myself for entire nights drunk on words. I was alive, I wanted to make a difference, and I desired to take as much from everyday as I possibly could, but that young Dane, that early twenties kid with such a lust for life had come to be a missing person in the onset of my thirties. I looked for him in the reflections of the sea, but did not recognize the man that scowled back at me.

Who was to blame for his disappearance, for his infrequent arrivals? For years I secretly placed responsibility on my parents like most children. The pathetic, natural instinct of children as we grow up strives to blame our parents for something, anything we can. A believer in almost any faith will claim that the only perfect being in existence is the deity heading their religion. Humans in contrast cannot overcome our flaws, no matter how holy or philanthropic we aspire to be, to attain a level equal to our Gods. In that case no single parent can ever perform a perfect job of raising their offspring, because a perfect human being does not exist. A dominant personality trait displayed in a parent strikes forth as the cause, and a defect or an excuse spills out of the child as an effect. Why the blame? No one is perfect. If our parents love us why are we so hard on their trivial shortcomings? We are all flawed, no one is perfect. Maybe it relies on the simple act of being born. Why do we exist at all? What does it all mean? Why were we created?

Cosmo blamed his father for not listening to his mother's telepathic visions and because of this ignorance his dad spent eight years in prison. Karana faulted her mother for marrying a man she never really loved to begin with. She said that an honest conversation could have saved many years of walking on eggshells and avoided silent, apathetic dinners. That left me. What did I have to complain about? Nothing with much valid merit, but as children we are always in some mode of denial and on occasion I listened to words spill off of my tongue laden with a skewed sense of blame bestowed upon my parents in place of taking responsibility for my own inconsistencies.

My parents met at San Diego State University during the mid-seventies. They often exaggerated about their encounter and early courtship. I gained a closer version of the truth about how they met through stories from my grandparents on my father's side. Donna majored in English, excelling in Poetry and in reading a vast array of the classics. She adored the Romantic Era, delving into Keats, Tennyson, Byron, Whitman, Thoreau, and Dickinson. She liked to recite the final lines in **Ulysses** by Tennyson, or passages from **Sonnets From The Portuguese** by Elizabeth Barrett Browning. I still remember my mom singing out to me:

"How do I love thee? Let me count the ways.
I love thee to the depth and breadth and height
My soul can reach, when feeling out of sight
For the ends of being and ideal grace."

At first I thought she stole the lines from a Bugs Bunny cartoon where Bugs fell in love with a motorized rabbit circling a dog track, and so it came as a surprise to me when I studied the sonnet in college to find that Bugs did not create those memorable words and instead they sprouted from a young heart bursting with love in the 1800's.

Donna respected many of the Romantics, but she truly idolized Mary Shelley. More than anything she admired Mary's age and the circumstances under which she created the story of **Frankenstein.** Just in her late teens Mary took a vacation with her poetic husband Percy Shelley to meet up with their friend and fellow writer Lord Byron in Switzerland. Persistent rainstorms kept them indoors for much of their visit and so the group turned to reading and discussing ghost stories around the fire. After a late night conversation they challenged one another to see who could come up with the scariest tale among them. That night Mary encountered a nightmare of sorts and came up with the basis of what she thought would be a simple short story. Not only did she create the best story amidst two literary giants, but she also managed to incorporate the fears of the industrial revolution and the danger of man's impact on the earth at just eighteen years of age. To this day my mother thinks it is blasphemous when someone refers to the stitched and square headed monster as Frankenstein, especially around Halloween. "Frankenstein is the doctor for Christ's sake," she says. "Doesn't anyone care about the facts anymore? The damn monster is called the Creature not Frankenstein." To no surprise, I was never the creature for Halloween.

Lost in a world of Romanticism I found it kind of amazing she met my bookish, scientific father at all. He was a graduate student specializing in entomology. While an undergrad he took several courses from his favorite instructor, Professor Mesner. He did well in all of Mesner's classes and by the time of graduation for his bachelor's degree Mesner had taken Dale under his wing and insisted he apply to graduate school. To that point in his life my father only wanted to come out of college with a degree. Before the prodding of Professor Mesner he never really considered completing a master's degree or going on to receive a doctorate, but he respected his professor and decided to continue his education. While busy with his graduate studies, Dale made time to perform some student teaching for a few of Professor Mesner's classes. Even though he was an entomology major Dale felt comfortable enough to fill in for a variety of Science classes. While going over notes he prepared for a lecture about the tides in Mesner's Oceanography class a young woman interrupted his silence and entered the room well before class began. She touted brown hair streaked with blond kisses from the sun and a glowing smile. Her deep tan radiated an aura of adventure and she smelled of coconut as she made her way to a desk at the back of the room.

"Hope I am not bothering you," she shouted out as her narrow hips settled into an empty chair. "I just need to catch up on a few things and I knew it would be quiet in here." Dale caught himself tongue-tied and took a few seconds to gather his wits before responding. He desired to be alone to mentally prepare his lecture before class began, but he would never admit to the urge in the presence of such a lovely woman.

"No bother, no bother at all," he stumbled out. The pattern continued for the next couple of weeks and their conversations assented into full blown discussions about life, politics, music, and poets. Donna fought for the Romantic's while Dale preached about the beat poets in San Francisco. Dale finally built up the courage to ask Donna to do something after class. His idea of an afternoon out consisted of nature hikes and long walks where he would bring along a notepad and a pen to classify the various types of insects he came across; and not just, "I saw a butterfly," but full scientific names down to Family, Genus, Species. I grew up knowing that the monarch butterfly carried the name Danaus plexippus and not to confuse it with the oh so similar viceroy butterfly or Limenitis archippus as predators often do, because the monarch is often a poisonous snack to its prey due to its intake of milkweed. I doubt observing insects ever sounded cool, but Donna loved the outdoors and the idea of a hike sounded way out of the ordinary compared to most of her dates who took her to dinner and a movie with the hopes of taking a rumble with her in the back seat of a car after the movie reel finished spinning.

My dad definitely leaned toward the nerdy side, but he exuded an ample amount of charm and a disguised sense of humor. The two kept hiking, whether on the cliffs of Torrey Pines or back in the mountains of Julian they marched right into a love affair that led them to the altar within one year. Two and half years later I was born, followed by my sister Drea who came into the world three years after me.

They are warm, caring, and trusting parents. They do somewhat odd things on occasion that come across as interesting only to themselves. For example, our names, they all start with the letter D. Drea is short for Andrea, but after calling me Dane, along with their names of Dale and Donna they felt it necessary to be an all D family, hence Drea. We also never purchased a real Christmas tree during the holiday season. Instead of opening a new baseball mitt under the fragrant smell of pine needles like most children my age I often sat beneath the redolence of citrus leaves or the non-aromatic palm tree. Long before they had children they decided not to kill a tree every year and instead would purchase a living orange tree, a lemon tree, a peach tree, or one year even a banana tree which we would all go plant in the back yard as a family after the New Year began. It seemed unfair and weird at the time, but after living thirty years on the planet I could finally appreciate their yearly custom, especially when I saw their backyard filled with fruit and vegetation giving back oxygen to the earth and providing organic food for their bellies. They can be taken for borderline hippies in their liberal views about the world or their consumption of natural foods and homeopathic cold remedies, though they do not look much the part of beaded, long haired free spirits. My father looks every bit the professor. A neat beard, glasses instead of contacts, somewhat on the preppy side in his clothing style, though he likes to wear flip-flops instead of shoes, and he carries his lightweight backpack wherever he goes. Mom on the other hand can be traced back to her roots as a peace loving flower child a bit more than my father. She often touts long, Native American looking skirts and wears little to no make-up. She hangs charms, wears herbal fragrances, and burns Primo incense throughout the house. Her high school students adore her. As a teacher of college prep literature Donna possesses a rare ability to translate her passions of the written word to unruly teenagers who not only pay attention, but often times send letters of gratitude and make personal visits to my parents home after they are graduated and far removed from high school. They carry an ease about them, as individuals and as a couple, which I took for granted as an ignorant teenager, and there, if I could break it down to its very core was where my blame was placed I guess, if I could actually validate any reason, in their ease of how they dealt with me.

They never really pushed me to do anything. I never wanted the little league father who screamed and yelled from the bleachers, but I hoped for some words of encouragement to keep with it when I decided to quit playing baseball during my junior year of high school or when I told them I no longer wanted to compete in surf contests. Dale and Donna never tried to influence the classes I took in high school to better prepare me for my future. I skirted around Trigonometry, I avoided human anatomy and physiology because of its workload, and I did not take college prep Literature, a class my mom taught at a neighboring school, and instead took an English class where we watched movies every other week in place of reading. Granted, many of the books in the upper division literature class were on our bookshelves at home and I familiarized myself with many of the classics, but my parents failed to motivate a rise of excitement inside of me to take on a challenge. They believed that I would find my own path, that as an intelligent human being I would figure out what direction my life should take and follow a true line. Anyone within earshot of my complaint would probably come close to vomiting when hearing my pathetic attempt to place blame on my parents for such trivial discrepancies. A whole army of children from broken homes and war torn countries would give anything to receive even half of the love, dedication, and freedom my parents devoted to me. I never felt ungrateful or burdened with resentment, but for my entire life I struggled to find the fortitude to stick anything out, though I did finally make it through college. It seemed easier to quit when the going got tough and just move on to a new hobby, or sport, or way of thinking. Human beings always want what they do not possess. Children with overbearing parents wish for some space to discover their own dreams. Yet I wished for the opposite, perhaps a nudge of firm guidance to direct me towards a goal and achieve it. Maybe I did not possess the intelligence they constantly gave me credit for. Maybe I needed a little whipping into shape. I never wanted to work for a major financial cooperation, but as the job fell into my lap my parents simply agreed with my decision to take the position. They exerted an over abundance of faith in me above and beyond what I deserved. Dale told me I was just doing what I needed to do at the time to get where I wanted to go next and he trusted I would not loose sight of my dreams. I let them down, I betrayed their faith.

Regardless of any blame I felt entitled to dole out I made every choice on my own. I drifted into things instead of searching for them or fighting for them with every clawing fingernail on my functioning hands. Secretly my parents probably shared tacit disappointments in their glances at one another during one of my phone calls or when we ate Sunday evening dinners at their place. I did not drain society or their pocketbooks, I made a good living and I enjoyed many comforts, but I knew they envisioned much more for me. Their number one vision being, that I would enjoy the work I did everyday, that I did not go somewhere just to collect a paycheck, that I would give back the unique perspective they passed on to me with my very existence. That is where I needed to take the blame. That is where I needed to stand up and hold myself accountable.

Wonder percolated. My exit off of the train to follow Cosmo down the coast of Baja flickered as a positive step. Internally I heard my mother applaud each leg of the journey, anointing the voyage as one laden with Romanticism or being overly Beat Poet, Kerouac like, but what did I really want to do. With a new bound freedom to choose any path I wished to pursue I needed to find out what kind of man I really wanted to be.

Blame got me nowhere, especially when I could see beyond it, for all it became after its identification was a feeble excuse, and my excuses ran out long before our trip to Baja even began. It was time to stop making excuses and listen intently to the embers burning in my heart. The adage said "time waits for no one," and I knew it would no longer wait for me. Time flashed a quick smile and disappeared in a crashing wave. I could blame no one for my missed opportunity, my hesitation, no one except the dejected man who sat quietly and looked out to sea unwilling to climb the cliff and face his friends.

Hunger finally guided me to camp. Cosmo read from one of the many books he brought along while Hillary wrote in a journal. The air was still, the hills quiet, and I felt as though every living organism glared at me as I set my board down and climbed out of my suit. They all knew I was a coward, the rocks, the crickets, the coyotes, the shrubs; and they all scoffed and turned away. Hillary looked up from her writing and offered a friendly smile. She pointed to a sandwich on the hood of the Scout which I devoured in a few, quick bites. I wondered if she knew. If she did, it did not seem to bother her in any way, not that it should have in the first place, but I felt paranoid. Cosmo finally looked up from his book. He took a long gaze in my direction with no malice or glee. "What happened," he asked.

Shaking my head I looked to the ground and said "I, I don't know."

"Oh," was all Cosmo said in return and then he ducked back into his book.

Night lurked in the growing shadows. The three of us worked in fluid unity to prepare for the approaching darkness without much talk. We got the fire going, food ready, lanterns turned on, and settled into our warm clothes. I hugged close to the fire to kill the shiver in my bones. Cosmo passed a bottle of tequila around. He opened the bottle while we were making dinner and had steadily taken swigs since. I took my first sip from the unlabeled bottle and almost spat it out. Nothing was different from the tequila we drank the night before besides the bitterness in my mouth. Everything tasted sour, the tequila, the avocadoes and rice, even the juicy mango we ate for desert left an acrid flavor on my tongue. I kept the tequila down without shooting it out into the fire and fell back into my chair.

I wished for rain, for hail, a downpour of molten lava, for lightning to strike, anything to disrupt the quiet evening and the low hum of Cosmo and Hillary as they gently spoke to one another. After a few minutes I received my wish, just not in any form that I was ready for.

"Explain something to me Dane, please," Cosmo asked calmly. "What stopped you out there today? You were flowing, everything was perfect and you backed out, why?"

I did not feel ready to talk, but I knew there would be no way out of it. "I told you I don't know. Something switched in my head and all of a sudden I was pulling out. It's killed me every moment since. Sorry for wasting it." Cosmo stared into the fire and took another hit of tequila. I could tell the drink was starting to affect him. I wondered what Cosmo would emerge from the generous intakes of liquor. Would it be the philosopher, the educator, the entertainer, or the blunt devil's advocate who side-stepped nothing. Something told me that I was not going to get off lightly.

"That's it, that's your excuse."

"What do you want me to say Cosmo. Do you want me to say that I chickened out? That I'm nothing but a big pussy? Is that it, is that what you want to hear? Because if it is then let's get it out of the way right now. I'm a chicken shit, pussy alright. I'm not you o.k. I want to be as free, as fearless, but I'm not. I'm not as free, I can't let go like you can, I never have been able to."

Cosmo shook his head. "Why is that always your response Dane? Why do you always have this vision that I'm so free and you're not and because of that you can't accomplish the things you want to? No one is free until we're dead, plain and simple. Then and only then will we be truly free from our vices, our fears, our failures. The best we can do is limit as many of those hindrances once we have identified them and get rid of them. You say I'm so free, but I only appear that way because I don't use my burdens as an excuse. You are just as free as I am. How long are you going to let these excuses rule your life, huh? Until you are old and wrinkled and dying in some sterile hospital bed wishing a genie would come along and grant you one last wish to be young again so you could do all of the things you wished you could have when you had the chance? Is that it? Well wake up because that shit only happens in crappy movies."

Words did not come to my tongue. I sat and took my medicine among the blaze of the fire. Hillary grabbed the bottle from Cosmo and handed it to me.

"I don't see what the big deal is Cosmo," Hillary interrupted, "it was only a wave."

"No it wasn't just a wave, it was Dane's life. It passed right by him. Did you see it Dano? It was all there for you. All the potential, all the possibility, but you would rather just sit there and watch life pass you by rather than jump in and see what you are capable of. What's your problem? If you fail you fail, so what, at least you tried something. And if you are trying you are not failing, because attempting always leads you somewhere, maybe not where you originally planned, but exploration always yields something positive. Someone is more of a failure if they know what they want and never strive for it. The journey, the trying, is just as important as the result, more important actually because of all that inspires you to get there. Once you're there, who cares really, it's just a destination, then on to the next one. Take the journeys, see what's out there, and what's in here," Cosmo said pointing to his head. "Clear that crap that holds you back, the crap that makes you live in the past, or over worried about your future. The crap that makes you live in the land of "What If." Cosmo's voice evened out as he continued to speak. I sifted through his comments, but could not get over those two words, "What If." They haunted me like a ghost that did not know how to pass on to the next transformation. Stuck in limbo, not living, not dying, simply a meaningless shell of what was once a human being. I was not sure where it came from, but the words escaped before I could deter them.

"What if, what if, what if I died? What if drowned right there?"

"What if my aunt had balls then she'd be my uncle. What if Woodrow Wilson never had a stroke? He might have been more willing to compromise in the negotiations for the League Of Nations and the world might have never experienced World War II. I'm tired of being too nice to you Dane, tired of watching your excuses destroy you. And you know what Dane? Are you listening over there, you know what?"

"What," I barely got out.

"It's not okay. It's not okay at all. I have met countless people across the globe, you know that, and out of all that mess and confusion your friendship has meant the most to me, and god-dammit if it has not also at times frustrated me the most. This is life, right now, right here, this is all we have. Here we are and nothing's changed. Just because you walked off of a train doesn't all of a sudden make all of the disappointing elements of your life dissipate like a morning fog. It's more than that Dane and you know it, you just won't let yourself fall completely into it. Your heart, your feelings, your outlook are more powerful than you know. Wasting all of that does a disservice to the world. You have become a sea anemone; prodded and poked you reel in all the beautiful and colorful aspects thriving in your system and instead of fighting through you quit or let the moment pass you by. I can't go on watching this. Everyone else let's you get away with it, your complacent idleness, because you are a nice person, not upsetting or inspiring the human race, but I can't. Not anymore. The rest of the world can take that role, but you know that you're not contributing to the heartbeat of the world and that you're wasting the innate gifts that compose your core, and that is unacceptable. I don't think I can watch it anymore. You have to make a choice, do you want to live, or rot away in a slow, miserable death. Because what does this ordinary life bring, this complacent life, well I'll tell you, it brings nothing but a wasted existence, it brings you a more steady paycheck so you can buy a bigger coffin to bury yourself in. Don't succumb to it Dane. Pull yourself into the present and live. Die living, don't live just to die."

Hillary stood up and put her hands out like a traffic cop. "You guys this is getting out of hand. Come on you're friends."

Cosmo paid no attention "Think about your pages Dane? You probably haven't even thought about exercising the demons from them have you?"

"No I haven't," I shot back. So much of what he said I needed to hear, and I did hear it, I consumed

284

the message deep into my guts, but he also awakened a sleeping ball of fire. We bickered back and forth. My voice rose, Cosmo drank more tequila. I no longer cared about whether I was right or wrong and spoke as words spilled off of my tongue. I said a few cruel things that I did not really mean, but I was rolling. He took a weak moment and turned it into a metaphor for my entire life and I could not let him get away with that. I was much more complicated than that, I laughed. Hillary called us childish buffoons before she retired to Cosmo's tent. Her guitar took her place on the vacated chair she left behind.

Cosmo and I jawed into the night. We went in circles, but the words kept coming and neither of us wanted to back down. Before long I forgot about the wave and my shortcomings, I let go of the blame I bestowed upon my parents and the blame I placed upon myself and lived in the exact moment breathing fire back and forth with my greatest opponent. It was a typhoon of thought and nonsense, and as the storm touched down I found myself wrapped in a navy-blue sleeping bag buzzing from the ignited conversation ready to prove Cosmo wrong, even if it killed me.

Chapter 22

A stench of pooled excrement erupts from the beasts massive jaws. Gnarled teeth, some up, some down, all razor sharp drip with frothing saliva. The scarred face takes on a mixed form of tyrannosaurus rex and a starving wolf, with the loose snout of a large elephant seal. The massive frame blocks out the sky, the surroundings, and shakes the ground with each clumsy step. Sharp claws lacerate brush, lusting with a raged passion to sink into his weak flesh and spray blood out of his pumping veins. David and Goliath ready for battle, or at least the beast stands primed, displaying perhaps two weaknesses with its pencil thin calves and awkward steps.

Tar comes off in blotches. He looks for a weapon of any kind. A stone, a branch, a venomous snake to place under the monsters steps, but nothing shows. A steep wall of earth cradles his back and denies any further distance between him and the creature. He faces the impossibility of destroying his enemy with such diminutive hands, such flat teeth. It cannot not be done. He chose a violent death, a one-sided brawl, instead of a quiet departure at the bottom of the tar pit. He knows that after a few narrow escapes and futile attempts to wound the monster nothing would remain besides a mangled carcass for the scavengers to pick apart after the beast ate its share.

A swipe hits the bank above his head and he rolls out of the way. Chunks of earth fall to the ground from the powerful blow. He runs through the beast's legs and tries to race for the open pasture ahead, but the monster clips his ankles with its tail and he lands hard in the dirt. He pushes himself to a standing position as blood flows from his freshly scraped knees and elbows. The beast turns towards him and lets out a guttural howl. The decibels almost crush his ears. He wants to quit. To stand there in a puddle of fear and let the beast devour him whole. Just end it quickly. Murder the nagging worry and definite pain. End it you putrid beast.

The beast stares him down. It curls its claws and gnashes its teeth. He does not move. He no longer wants to run, to delay the inevitable slaughter before him. A steady finger points to the frothing monster in defiance and he releases a bellowing shriek of his own. It echoes off the bank and reverberates in his ears like a symphony. He does not know where it came from, the visceral battle cry that energizes his entire body, an unknown chamber in his guts perhaps, an untapped lobe in his brain, but the emancipated yell births a wealth of courage which makes him feel invincible. The world stops ticking. The horizon goes silent. The beast stands still on its slender legs and he screams again.

Let them all hear. All the creatures of violence still waiting on the shores of the tar pits let them come. "I am not afraid of you," he shouts, "I am not afraid of any of you." A warped sense of peace enters his veins and he laughs at his previous fear. He only possesses the moment in front of him, that very instant. The past does not matter, the future disappears, and he marches straight for the beast. It collapses at his feet with a loud thud and melts into the soil. They all vanish. He stands alone with the hills. He becomes the hills, the pasture, the wind, the seas. He can hear the heartbeat of the world. Thump thump, thump thump. Two hands rise to the skies in exultation and he takes flight on the tail feathers of a giant bird.

I wake in Lola's clutches. She delicately corrals my tumbling frame in her talons and soars through the hole. She swerves around the boulders, the roots, the possibility of hell, and darts towards the exit. We eject into the atmosphere at the speed of a hurricane. She dances and banks and returns to my cloud. Lola eases her grip and deposits my body on to the pillowed fluff. She appears to smile and turns into the wind.

I leap after her. I fly, I soar. I make death defying loops around the moon. We dance amongst the cosmic dust of the stars, we chase descending meteors. Lola moves one flap faster, one streamline ahead. I reach for her, pine for her feathers, but she avoids every futile lunge with expert navigation. I do not want to lose her. She keeps apace, taunting my efforts. Why would she shun me now? I fell to the earth and crawled through the sludge of the universe. I battled with the manifestations of evil just to find her and yet she remains distant, far from the reaches of my inclinations.

I dive below a rush of storm clouds and find a green island lost at sea. I perch upon its sandy shores and try to figure out where I went wrong. Where did I fail? Why did the treacherous path I so recently conquered lead me to utter isolation and loneliness? What was the point? I approach the water and immerse my body into its turquoise splendor. An orange sun peaks in the sky and it occurs to me that my road led me exactly to this moment where cool water drips from my hair and coarse sand massages my feet. I am where I am supposed to be. The adventure is my prize and a new journey waits as soon as I inhale another breath.

I breathe deep. I accept my place, my existence, my unique self. I exhale towards the sun and a mess of feathers tackles me from behind. I look up and imbibe my future. I grab Karana's hand, she smiles and we turn into the lush hills of our island.

Chapter 23

A heavy fog drooled on our camp over night. I woke up with a purpose. Ready to prove something, anything, to the world, to the hushed, tan cliffs, to the imposing seas, but most of all to myself when I snuck out of camp with a board under my arm, determination guiding resilient steps, and silent enough to escape unnoticed by the snoring Cosmo in his nearby tent. He drank a lot more of Jerome's tequila than I had. The previous day impaled my innards. A constant loop replayed in my mind, the perfect form, the half-hearted paddle, the passing wave, and worst of all, the look of disappointment on Cosmo's face as the epic right-hander peeled into the bay. Each time the scene commenced I died on top of the large wall of water before I ever caught sight of Cosmo's glare. Death seemed a better fate than to deal with my own cowardice, yet I awakened after each vision still breathing, still licking my wounded disposition as a craven onlooker.

The excuses no longer added up. How could I continue to justify staying in the same place? Never pushing the boundaries of my abilities or even trying to elevate them to a higher plateau. Crested on the precipice only to falter the wave crushed my ego as well as my entire existence. Cosmo had every right to lay into me afterwards. My futile arguments bounced desultory circles around the fire, half for anything I actually believed in, but pathetically half of the time just for something to say. How it stung. Not just the wave, but the metaphor it represented for my entire life. The words complacent, inanely content, scared to live, hurt more than any physical death I could have ever imagined. I sat on the verge of so much more than just following the herd, the next panicked flock, and yet I pulled back and sat idle and watched possibility roll into the future without me. The acceptance of the fact brought me to an all time low, a rock bottom of sorts, to not only define those apprehensions of which I lived with, but to actually feel and understand how far those aspects handcuffed every molecule in my body. The acceptance compared to what some referred to as seeing the light. Whether the sinner falling to his or her knees at the benevolence of their God, or the alcoholic hitting an ultimate nadir and coming to terms with their vice, a sense of utter hollowness overwhelmed me when Cosmo ranted and I replayed my weaknesses over and again.

And so our conversation went, Cosmo made some valid point while I internally kicked the shit out of myself. Yet, after a time towards the end of our roundabout the emptiness transformed into something else altogether. Organs flared and began to burn. A tingle from the wind licked my fingertips, and suddenly instead of looking at it as a crutch or excuse blanket I continually draped over myself, the ultimate low I incurred became a spark. I exchanged verbal blows with Cosmo like never before. Not as a student to teacher role I usually resigned myself to in full discussions with him, but as his equal or even his victor, spitting out debates and comments with raised voice and flushed passion. Not in anger or provoked ire, but in a search for truth and as a small act of defiance. I hit my pillow swimming in a new hope from the fresh ignition as Cosmo's words repeated in my head; "When you focus on the negative, i.e., you will never make that wave, you will never be able to leave your job, you are bound to the exact life you are living, then the only results you can ever receive will end up negative or stay exactly as they are. You cannot do the exact same things the exact same ways and expect different results. That is pure lunacy. You are blessed with a similar talent level I have in so many areas, if not more, but the only difference is that I believe in my talent and expect success, while you question your skills and your worth in this world. This perpetual questioning gives birth to a valley of ambiguity which swallows you in its catacombs. Lost in a pit of oblivion you can never succeed, only fail, as you wallow, watch, and not contribute to the world. You are not your fear, Dane, remember that."

I thought about his words as I made my way towards the beach. I never thought of myself as a negative person. Not upsetting, not idle, but riding the flow of life's daily motions seemed not to cross any negative poles. What was wrong with that, I mean why was anything above and beyond that necessary? Why ruffle feathers? Why stand out from the crowd? Any of those acts seemed somewhat like attention mongering. Those were my thoughts as I trotted along, bordering regression and frightened about my upcoming spar with the sea. Doubts for sure, festering, teasing, but they were not enough to halt two cold feet from scaling down the twenty foot, jagged cliff and continue on the black and gray sand adorned with large patches of multicolored beach rock.

As I made my way down to the beach more of Cosmo's words tugged at my nerves. "Not going for that wave was near sacrilegious," he stated. "She offered a gift and you refused. That is what you were out there for. But you have a problem Dane. You build up an event in your mind before it even occurs and don't allow for a natural ebb and flow of actions to take place. You rarely let yourself get caught in the moment. Let go man. Just let it go. Empty out that scurrying brain of yours and let a blank page be written in the exact moment you experience it. Clear your head, your soul, and just let go." I could let go. What did he know anyway? He held no clue of how much I could let go. He did not know everything. Sleep on Cosmo I thought, I am about to prove you wrong.

I stretched out on the last hexagon shaped patch of sand available before the shore gave way to large chunks of land. The sun remained hidden beneath the morning fog which was dense enough to produce tiny brushes of moisture as it ran up the beach. Greened yucca plants and khaki earth stretched down hillsides and clashed with moistened boulders and a foamy sea.

Eons of existence displayed art exhibits on layered sediment that eroded away from the cliff. The landscape followed the natural path of evolution, unspoiled from human stain and carved out its own identity from the vigor of the sea and a nudge from the elements. I pretended not to see the plastic laundry detergent bottle wedged in between two lavender beach rocks and became swept into a space of time before man and all of the clumsy mistakes of his hands.

Hands are such funny objects. Fingers move and point and curl and grasp all of the solid masses they come across. Sturdy appendages with opposable thumbs separating human kind from nearly every other species on the planet, and yet, under microscopic view these magnificent workers, these miracles of science, are nothing more than a collection of atoms and molecules, all moving, all spinning, all changing. My skin, though minute, was slightly altered from the night before. A new shell, a new body, a solitary Adam beneath the mysteries of the skies and the power of the ocean sat and stared at the sea wanting nothing more than to re- write his own existence. The painted scene did not equal the splendid glamour of Eden, but perfect waves rolled, and a new universe, a one man universe, spread out on the magnificent seascape. I did not need Eve and an apple for temptation; I sat determined, ready to take a bite out of the day with my own gnashing teeth and my ever changing hands.

Blinded by daydreams I hit the water without properly surveying the early morning conditions. I knew I screwed up when I began paddling, because at once a sickening feeling as though I left the stove on or that the front door might have been unlocked crept into my stomach. I thought about turning around to reassess the situation, but after a quick glance towards the shore to take in its welcoming safety I returned focus to the tip of my board and stroked out to sea knowing all too well that the slightest hesitation would have stalled the mission permanently.

With a fortunate flat spell I made my way out into the lineup with relative ease and paddled deep into the channel. I took a moment to reflect before making my way back into the impact zone. My missed opportunity wave surfaced and stirred my guts, but I paid little attention. Things changed overnight. I breathed as a new man with a clean slate and a boiling passion. I would prove them all wrong. The old reservations, Cosmo, everyone who said I was exactly what they thought I would be would realize that Dane compiled of so much more than they could have ever imagined. They might not witness the act in person, but somehow they would all know. They would feel the rush and know that I faced my fears head on. Head on and alone. It stood as my moment.

About five minutes after entering the lineup a few perfectly formed waves passed through without much more than a glance from me. My mission required only one purpose, to catch the biggest wave Dulce could manufacture. Hollywood would have inundated the cliff with spectators and television cameras, yet, in an isolated section of Baja the rocky beach and vacant cliff remained void of helicopters or a bikini clad cheering section as I paddled out the back in hopes of an oncoming set. I used my 6' '11" board a year prior during a session in Oceanside where I probably could have easily handled the swell on my 6' '6", but decided to test it out just to get a feel for the board. Paddling upon the yellow body of my 6' '11" I wished I would have brought something bigger.

Finally a set approached, easily double overhead and throwing, and I turned around to take a look at the third wave in the bunch, but decided something bigger pulsed on the horizon. I am not sure where the urge came from, but at once I scratched out to sea. I felt scared. Something told me danger lurked and that I should return to shore. I thought about it, but I knew I would never make it out of the impact zone in time to evade the incoming set. With no escape route possible or rescue boat on standby, petrified limbs plowed through the water like a broken winged duck. Flailing and splashing I somehow made progress as what I feared came into focus. It looked like a mountain coming out of a smoked curtain of fog. A mountain moving at a rapid pace armed with teeth and ready to throw five ton boulders upon my head. If time gave me a gift and stopped its ever moving hands I am sure I would have cried, stopped right there and broke into a spastic childlike temper tantrum full of snot and spit, but instinct propelled me to push over the mammoth structure of water before it pounced upon my helpless body. My broken wing exhibition mended into a graceful and speedy glide up a wave larger than I imagined for my heroic journey. The lip crested over. The only chance to escape a perilous freefall backwards was to punch through the collapsing peak. With one last horrified effort I knifed a hole in the top before it completely spilled over and made my way down the back of the monster gasping for oxygen.

I paddled out another twenty-five yards and attempted to gather myself as a loll overcame the horizon. Cosmo came to mind. Everyone came to mind. I thought to myself, I cannot back out now, not again. Remember a blank page. Make my mind a blank page. I tried to clear everything and let the moment flow through my veins. With open eyes it did not seem possible. My lids closed and waited for nothing to come. On my way towards a meditative, empty bliss a shiver ran through my body. Eyes opened and collected an approaching set; it was time.

To wait any longer meant losing the nerve and suffering my own craven humilities all over again. Nothing resonated in my consciousness except the speed of my flapping arms. Feeling that I reached an opportune location to make a clean drop my board spun around and at once I paddled into a convulsive fit which aped something close to rage. Spit exuded from my mouth, steam from my head, fire from my nostrils, or at least that is what it felt like. I let go. Of the past, of the future, of my life, and experienced my board gaining speed. Before I realized it I stood on two feet and descended an avalanching cliff. The velocity beneath my limbs seemed impossible as I reached the bottom of the ledge. I tried not to look up as I began a bottom turn, but I did it anyway. The wall of water enveloped the entire sky while the board skimmed the surface below me and sat on a rail to set a line for my ride. With more time to think I probably would have straightened out and skipped lodging myself into the forming, hollow tunnel due to my awe and trepidation, but with my course already set the wave swallowed me whole.

In the past I rode through a few good sized tubes where I actually stood almost straight up and down without hunching over too much to fit inside of the opening. Not bad for local waves at home. Then I would watch video footage of Pipeline in Hawaii or Teahupo'o in Tahiti and witnessed waves so hollow that a semi-truck could drive right through them and realized an entirely different level of getting tubed existed. Dulce did not equal the ferocity of Teahupo'o, but the opening was larger than anything I had ever witnessed and I slotted myself in perfect position to come shooting out of the other end.

The cave dimmed and an enticing silence consumed the tunnel. The possibility to make it out rested on a large amount of faith to hold my line and trust in my abilities. Blank page, keep the blank page I thought, as I painted my own universe, but suddenly the page smeared with an onslaught of squiggly lines. I tried to discard the scribbled mess for a new sheet, but my knees buckled and before I knew it the lip sucked up and lofted my body upside down. Head over heels and staring into a frothing pit of exploding force everything in my mind finally went blank. I became a rag doll or a raptor caught in the clutching jaws of the T-Rex in **Jurassic Park**, tossed and swung about with an absolute loss of control as the lip buried me deep into the sea with such a display of pressure every bone in my body felt like they would shatter into a million pieces of ravaged shrapnel. I attempted to fight, but nothing worked. The blank page became an empty slate of darkness, a Stephen Hawking black hole, and the only message transcribed across my moment of letting go screamed of my ultimate demise.

Chapter 24

I often glanced at my fingers and cringed. A quick survey registered two broken middle fingers, a broken pinky on the right hand, and two dislocations on the same left hand ring finger. Then onto a broken collar bone and two broken wrists, four cracked ribs, a broken ankle, and a slew of scars which required stitches. The cracked and re-fused bones whispered of arthritis and the mended flesh tattooing my body often told epic tales of how they came into contact with a patch of asphalt, a surfboard fin, or a bouncing ball. Sadly I followed the example of my ailments many times and engaged in full fledged battle wound conversations where I lifted shirts, pulled up pant legs, and brushed hair aside and revealed past accidents in dramatic fashion with my voice filled with the grit of a captain Ahab sailor of the seas.

On occasion, and I could never figure out why, I divulged into my injury sagas around women. Whether I talked privately on a night out with a date or during a backyard party the list unfolded itself in gory detail. Perhaps it came out to invoke compassion for the incidents I encountered, maybe to unveil a certain amount of bravado, or maybe just for something to say when fear kept me from delving into anything else. Maybe a mixture of all of those aspects played a prominent role along with the opportunity it presented to reveal another side of myself, but I knew that being reserved and shy unfairly anointed me as an inactive and boring person. Caught in a contemplative and pensive mind I probably thought that bringing up dramatic stories would allow for new avenues of discussion to arise when a woman assumed I was nothing more than an idle onlooker.

Sports accounted for a majority of the injuries. Surfing delivered a few nasty scars as well, and after that, just being somewhat accident prone tallied numbers for the rest of my medical records. Some people said accident prone was the wrong definition and that a few cuts and breaks were inevitable when I was such an active person. I liked that, but I knew deep down that I was a borderline klutz.

I found it amusing to think of all of those scars and fissured bones years later, because for some silly reason I used to long for them to happen. In fantasies, instead of coming out of my shell or triumphing over some powerful evil and saving the world I often fell into pathetic dreams about receiving a near fatal wound, which upon my recovery elevated my meager reputation into legend status. Not only did I hope for something tragic to happen, I prayed for it. I made wishes on falling stars. It seemed a much easier route to gain attention than to actually go out and do something incredible.

One day I would fantasize about getting slammed in the head by a flying baseball bat and then being knocked unconscious. The next day I might get a broken arm and a few stitches defending one of my childhood crushes from a foul mouthed bully. In a particular daydream I used to take a bullet wound to my right shoulder during an apparent robbery at a friend's birthday party while saving the day. Then, rudely, a bell would ring, or someone would tap me on the shoulder, and I would wake from my dreams only to see my science teacher at the front of the classroom erasing a green chalkboard. I then shuffled out into the hallways as the same un-cool kid I had always been.

The reality of getting injured along with its subsequent aches and pains did not spawn any of the lofty results I desired in my inane visions nor did they give a sudden boost to my popularity. A group of beautiful women never revived me after passing out and I never made the local newspaper after a mangled accident. The secret love letter never arrived after a two day stint in the hospital from a reckless skateboarding mishap. I began to wonder if anyone would ever miss me if I disappeared all together. If instead of just a bullet wound to the shoulder the gunman aimed true and struck me through the heart. Would I be missed after I was dead and gone? Even sillier thoughts no doubt, and as my gangly teenage body accumulated injuries through an active lifestyle in which I hoped in some strange way would enhance my persona, I began to realize they did nothing more than inconvenience my life. Fresh stitches required a hiatus from the ocean for seven to ten days; a broken bone altered everyday normal function, and I eventually learned that getting hurt was never as glorious as I perceived it in my dreams.

WHEN YOU ARE about to drown there is no noise. The previous chaos of splashing and flailing dissipates, the power and rumble of surging waters eases into a gentle hum, and at once all becomes still. Light fades like the setting sun ducking below the horizon, allowing nothing but darkness to consume the liquid tomb enclosing in on all sides. Oxygen becomes sparse, used up amid convulsing for the surface and the length of time submerged under water, while the carbon dioxide count begins to rise. Alarmed and searching for air the mouth opens and tries to suck it out of the sea, spawning pernicious gasping and choking. Slowly the lungs fill with liquid and the early stages of asphyxia commence. When all hope, all effort to find up from down disappears the body discovers a warped sense of complacence. Drifting in limbo, ready to sink to the bottom and die, or apt to give one last fight and surge for the top , the motionless puddle of flesh hovers like a jellyfish and awaits its fate; either succumbing to ones fears or triumphing over them, and an eerie quiet overcomes.

It was without a doubt the heaviest wave to ever tackle my insignificant body. I could not help but thinking that I was finished. My last breath spent in spastic convulsions in search for the surface of the sea. I tried to prove something to myself, to people who were not even watching and I ended up getting myself killed. Brilliant strategy, to think I could outwit the forces of our Mother Ocean. She kicked my ass. The more I fought the more futile my actions became. The force upon my body proved too powerful to overcome. I knew my leash or the leash cord snapped somewhere in the middle of my spasms because the pressure yanking on my leg disappeared. Up and down, sideways, no ways, direction lead nowhere as the sea dragged my helpless body just above the ocean floor like a lassoed calf roped by the hooves.

A weird thought poured in as the saltwater churned like a billion gallon washing machine as I realized that perhaps it was not such a bad place to say goodbye. The sharp blues, the cool of the sea, the algae covered boulders beneath my stammering feet appeared as a welcoming tomb. The confines of which were much more pleasing than a wooden box buried six feet below a perfect, green lawn and I could have died knowing my bones would swim forever in an aqua wonderland.

Death loomed as just an illusion. The possibility of drowning was nothing more than fear teasing with my mind rather than an actual chance of coming close to perishing underneath the vigor of the sea, it only appeared that way. I was not surfing forty foot Jaws or a huge day at Maverick's. I did however experience the longest hold down in my surfing career. The urge to laugh out loud at the pathetic individual who craved sympathy from a near death experience or a fresh wound across the forehead filled my thoughts. What a worthless engagement. To wish for injuries or death to enhance ones stature was nothing short of blasphemy. I wanted to live. I wanted to rise from the sea floor and kiss the welcoming sky. And I wanted, more than anything else in the world at that moment, to pull myself back on top of my surfboard and paddle into another set wave and scream down the line.

A phantom curled its fingers around my throat and squeezed. A familiar face, a face I knew, rotted and littered with worm holes held me below the surface. It wanted me to give up, to die, to succumb to my fears. I kicked and hit nothing, my punches made no contact. The specter played with my thoughts. "Just give up. You'll never make the surface for the fight is too hard. You haven't the guts anyways; just stay here with us and you can swim forever." The ocean jumped from behind tombstones, skeleton surges ravaged my limbs, and blood caked demons swam against the levelness of my head. I craved life. I wanted to fight and the best way to battle through my predicament was to find serenity in the sprawling chaos. The ghost squeezed tighter. It scoffed at my paltry, mental attempts and went in for the kill. I let go. I accepted my place, my moment, my exact location beneath the rumbling ocean, and ceased my spastic impulses. The ghoul pressed, twisted, constricted, but the pressure was gone. It no longer had control. That face, that familiar face, panicked at my sudden ease and released its grip. Its rotted face became devoured by the deep. Calm nestled in.

I swam to the bottom and grabbed hold of a large, round rock for a few seconds and the energy of the ocean passed over me. My feet took the place of my hands on the rock so that I stood on its crest. Feeling the need for an added push I crouched down low enough to where my chest almost touched my knees and exploded off of the rock towards the surface. I sank much deeper than I thought, probably swept towards the channel during the tumble, but the swim energized my body and I twirled like a sea lion in realization that I contained enough oxygen left in my system to make it to the surface. Light showered down like a brilliant, cascading firework and I finally pierced the skin of the sea.

Oxygen tasted like a meal. It poured into my mouth in a variety of bursting flavors. A sleepy sun peaked through the morning fog and kissed the back of my neck, the wind danced lightly on the water and I was alive, pulsing, thriving, and aware of every molecule working in my complex system of veins and electrical surges. My wreck and prolonged tumult dragged me well inside the impact zone, but at an angle that almost deposited me out in the channel. The shore looked much closer than I expected and with a strong effort I could make it back to land before the next set rolled in.

As I swam I felt the remains of my leash lag behind me. With the Velcro wrapped tight just above my ankle I pulled the black cord out of the water to see that it was still intact which meant that the leash string that connected the leash to the board ripped in the commotion. My board, I wondered if it had made it to shore in one piece. I scanned the rocky shoreline to find my vessel while I stroked for land. As I approached the welcoming safe haven a figure was fishing something out of the water. He bent forward in a black, rubber suit and gathered a white length of Styrofoam and held it above his head. Cosmo looked like Zeus calling the thunderbolts himself with my surfboard aimed towards the heavens.

"You alive," Cosmo asked. He extended a hand after putting my board down to assist me out of the water.

"I think so."

"That wave was sick mate. I thought you were coming out of that barrel for sure."

"I blew it. I fully had it." I found a seat in the same area of sand I had stretched out on before my wipeout. I took in a few deep breaths and gathered my senses. "My blank page was there. I was locked in. God it was beautiful. And then, I don't know, my mind just scrambled and the next thing I knew I was plunged underneath the force of Niagra Falls. I'm not sure it was fear, because I don't remember feeling afraid, I just recall being so focused and in tune, and then, then I just began thinking about how I would feel after I made it out. Instead of thriving through my ride and experiencing every amazing wonder it had to offer, I began thinking about the finish line before I was even half way through it, so stupid."

Cosmo bore lines of sleep on his face and I waited for him to yawn. Instead he scooped up a handful of sand and then let it escape in between his fingers. I wondered if I would I receive a Kung Fu lesson about the hourglass of time blowing into the wind with no ability to stop it or would he comment on how my life should be lived similar to the escaping sand and let it flow with ease. The grasshopper awaited his daily words of wisdom.

"Your board didn't get too banged up," Cosmo began, "pretty incredible. You just need a leash cord and a bit of resin up by the nose and it will be ready to be back on the sea in no time. That wave you caught was definitely the biggest one of the set. You charged it Dane."

"How long have you been down here?"

"Not sure, fifteen minutes maybe. I'm hung over and I feel like an ass. Tequila man, it got me going. I was brash last night, way too harsh. I'm so glad you started back at me. I deserved it. I hate that I try to make everything a god-damned metaphor for how one should live their life. It was just a wave. Yeah, you probably could have caught it and a few of your hidden demons could have been the source for you not catching it, but maybe not. Maybe you just didn't catch it plain and simple. And then look at the result. You probably felt some inundation of rage that fueled you to paddle out alone in the large surf out there with the words "screw you Cosmo" chanting from your vocal chords. When am I going to learn to just shut my slanderous mouth?"

Odd, I did not get a lesson and instead he passed out a roundabout apology. I did chant those words though, not exactly to a tee, but in a varied form they did come out of my mouth, but I was over it. The previous night's heated exchange propelled me into a state of focus and determination. I did not make my wave, but I attempted it, and I sat on the sand next to Cosmo still breathing precious intakes of oxygen. He was right about so many things, he came up with a wealth of correct answers and opportune bits of advice, but in that moment I realized the equality of our friendship. I so often looked to him more as an older brother than a friend. I relied upon his advice and considered his word law; as if he knew all the answers I had questions to, and in the over glorification I often wondered if he ever received reciprocation. For so long I convinced myself that I did nothing more than take from Cosmo while I gave nothing in return, but in the tone of his apology, the fear of his offenses, I sensed the silliness of my thoughts. He did not need to say it out loud, we both could read it in the air. I decided to shut up and let him pull from my silence.

"Were you scared shitless," he asked. "That wipeout freaked me out just watching. I was getting ready to come after you until I saw your head surface."

I did not answer immediately. If I responded right away something along the lines of stupidity getting the best of me probably would have escaped out of my mouth, but that was not true. I did not feel scared or stupid. I felt more alive than I ever remembered. The biggest wave of my life, the heaviest wipeout of my life, and the world felt new. I tackled a great well of fear by not just dropping in, but by being in the situation to begin with. I walked out of a life set in stone to participate in the exact moment that we sat on the shores of Dulce's splendor. The person locked in mere fantasies emerged out in the open and shook hands with my timid self. I beamed, adventurous and alive. I charged a wave that I never dreamed of actually taking off on. I wanted to do it again.

"I want another one." Cosmo did not respond, but a quirky smile curled into the grit growing on his upper, left lip. I ran back to camp for some duct tape and a spare leash cord while Cosmo waited for me on the shore. The urge to tell him of my discovery of our unique equality and the self appreciation of my accomplishment stood on the brink of eruption, but I decided against it as I wrapped tape around the one inch gash in my board assured he already knew.

We made the jump and short paddle in relative silence. The waves pumped in, but they never equaled the size of the set I paddled into just an hour before. Cosmo and I scored a handful of epic rides that day and I ended up making it out of a healthy sized tube, though it did not equal the girth of my earlier wave. We came away with no photographs or video footage of the session. Our tales when retold will be taken in with apprehension because we brought back no proof of the size or perfection Dulce blessed upon us, but it does not matter. The imprints on our memories will last forever and I will always remember the day, March eighth, as the day Dane Dylan Edwards for the first time in his life felt absolutely comfortable in his own skin. I let go of any lingering worry wasted on how much longer our journey would take. At that moment our trip could have lasted forever.

Chapter 25

Onshore winds blew hard for the next three days. We surfed early in the morning before salty gusts reached full speed and late in the cool evenings when it decided to take a rest for the night. The swell dwindled each day until it became almost too small to ride at all. Hillary made it out to the point on the last day at Dulce and caught the wave of her life. Cosmo angled her down the line and she cruised upon the face of a wave for the first time. She was elated beyond words.

Something switched in my body. My hands felt new, my feet floated above the ground, my mind was a lucid gathering place for thoughts to flow in and out without wasted worry or overzealous enthusiasm. It was not a feeling of a second lease on life, because I really had not come that close to drowning, but more of an appreciation for every second allotted to me. I actually failed in what I originally set out to do, but in failure I found everything. I picked myself up and kept on going. It was alright to try and fail. It sounded so simple after the fact, but I had to experience it firsthand for it to really make sense. Most things I wished to attempt would not kill me or erase my existence if I went after them with true intentions. I knew I might not reach what I originally set out for, but Cosmo was right, the destination was usually never as important as the journey itself. I wanted to share my insight, my glowing ease, but I was afraid that mentioning it out loud would put an end to my personal version of enlightenment.

On our last night at Dulce I woke to the sounds of Cosmo and Hillary wrestling in their tent. A full moon illuminated the sea below us and I stepped outside to take a walk in the well lit night. Hysteric giggles transformed into soft moans. I tried not to listen, but their infection for one another screamed into the night. Earlier in the evening we entrenched ourselves into a heated discussion about which bands or artists gave the most compelling live performances. Hillary got to witness our music battle mode we often fell into. After a roundabout of various shows and venues Cosmo and I ended up both agreeing that one of our favorite artists to watch live, hands down, was Steve Poltz, especially when he played with the Rugburns. Hillary had never heard of Poltz or the Rugburns before and did not seem convinced by our result, but Cosmo took care of that.

"What do you want out of a live show Hill, what makes the money you fork over worth the price of admission?"

"Hmmm, a strong performance that at least parallels or surpasses what you hear on a recording. Yeah, a show that makes you feel something, makes you move."

"Well put, Hill," Cosmo said. "Poltz and the Burns always surpass their recordings and connect with the audience, but there is a level beyond at their shows. When I go to see live music I want to see someone who loves what they do. Someone who absolutely loves playing music, Poltz is that guy. He was born to entertain with his guitar and his voice; it comes out at his shows, always. Over the last fifteen years or so of going to performances around the area I have never been disappointed when Poltz and the Rugburns take the stage. It's fun, it's rocking, it's heartfelt, and there is something so true and pure about it. They have stayed on a level where music is what it should be. Talking about it never does enough justice though, you just have to experience it for yourself."

"I hope I'll get the chance soon," she said and smiled brightly. That smile ended our night in a hurry.

On my walk away from their lovemaking I though about how just a few days before Hillary traveled under the dictatorship of a man with an elitist attitude to living out a dream underneath the stars with a man she had been searching for her entire life. What luck, what fortune I thought as I distanced myself from their increased passion, but then quickly corrected myself. It was not luck at all. Luck was an inane word to use after the opening of such portals in my vision. She followed her desires down the twisted Rockies, across the deserts of Arizona, through the pleasing climate of Southern California, and into the desolate territory on the Baja Peninsula all on a chance that something wonderful waited for her somewhere along her journey. It was not luck at all when she was out searching, out living, out seeking her glowing dreams.

Her zeal for life reminded me so much of Karana, of how Karana went after what she wanted instead of waiting for it, of how she thought life should be lived and not loathed. I heard a distant moan and at once became the loneliest man in the universe. My body craved Karana's curves, the intoxicating chemistry of her skin. I needed her.

I knew Karana was incredible from the moment I met her, I just did not know how to fall in love at the time. For years I longed after women who were impossible to fall in love with. They rode on wavelengths completely opposite of my own, yet I fell for them anyway. It was a difficult road. Nothing came easy. Each day I struggled, I fought emotions, I blinded myself with stubborn eyes that believed they could make that which did not make sense actually possible. I always thought I could be a ridiculous storyline in a sappy movie where the fairytale always comes true in the end.

That was my idea of love, an impossible dream, an arduous journey of suffering that could only be relieved in a glorious moment of recognition. When I met Karana I did not know how to react when love came so easily. It occurred without strenuous effort and the simplicity of it all was frightening. It flowed as natural as water running downhill. I felt like I missed something. I did not know how to accept it without all of the hard work, the worry, the pining, the convincing, and it took some time for me to fully appreciate the uniqueness of our connection.

The exact moment of definition fell into an abyss of possibilities. A stirring began, the mixture of excitement and a perilous voyage into unmapped coordinates in the soul combined to offer a vague recognition of what could possibly be, but I do not think I meant the words, "I love you," with one hundred percent conviction until Karana and I went camping for the second time. Our first trip went off smoothly. We camped at a state park a few miles south of Oceanside with a few of Karana's co-workers. On the second trip we were alone.

While finishing school Karana worked two-part time jobs, one as an after school tutor at Lincoln Junior High School, and the other as an assistant for a local surf magazine. The publication was up and coming and ran by one of Cosmo's close friends. Cosmo was at a stationary point for a few months and stayed close to home. He spent much of his time helping his friend Charles get the magazine moving. He worked on articles and contacted many of his connections in the surf industry to see if they would buy ad space for upcoming issues.

Cosmo invited me to a party he and Charles threw for the success of their latest installment of the magazine. Karana had just removed her sweater when Cosmo introduced us. She looked comfortable in a pair of jeans, black flip-flops, and an off red top. She held a glass of red wine in a large, oval goblet. I knew nothing of wine, but asked her what type she was drinking. It was an Australian Shiraz. Though I had quit the baseball team in high school I continued to play volleyball and it turned out that Karana played it as well. We talked of the sport, of the ocean, of her migration from Washington State to California. We drank more, Karana from her goblet, me from the keg and our discussion bore a hole into the profound. She was easy to talk to. She wore a pleasant smile of white teeth and an attentive ear. There was no act, no trying to feign something she was not and I could not believe how natural and comfortable I felt in her presence. I wondered if it was the drink, but I remember thinking that she was the most beautiful woman on the planet. It was not her attractiveness, though she looked fantastic, it was her grace, her humor, her passion, and her caring heart mingled in with her good looks that made her desirable on multiple levels. All of the proper combustions exploded in my chest and we knew that something different, something special, emanated in our first encounter.

We began dating. It went smoothly form the beginning. On our second camping trip we forgot to pack the tent poles and we had to sleep in the back of my truck underneath the heavens. No friends or colleagues. It was just the two of us and I was content. The sea sang us to sleep as Karana snuggled tight against me and I gazed up at the Big Dipper. This is love, I thought. I knew it. It was a comfort I never even knew existed. I woke her up with a kiss on her ear and told her that I loved her. I had said it to her once before and thought that I had meant it, but in the bed of my truck I no longer wondered if I the words were true, I knew they were with every atom in my body.

I FOUND A clearing above our camp and sat down on

a large, granite rock. I inhaled the calm. The moans from the two lovebirds were gone. Though I wanted Karana with me more than anything at that moment I realized my journey would have taken a different course if she had come. I needed to awaken on my own terms. I had to find me, to open my own eyes, to discover the missing Mowgli who had been removed from my dreams. If the man I was prior to the trip kept plodding along and exchanged vows with her at the altar he would have ruined us both. She knew it and that is why she pushed me along.

We had not set a date for our wedding. It was the answer she was looking for, one of the topics we were arguing about before I left. I wanted to marry her, I knew she was the right one, but I always circumvented the finality of picking a date. Maybe it was Cosmo's manifestos on the atrocities of marriage or perhaps my thwarted sense on the impossibility of love that had held me back from going through with it, but underneath the glow of the moon and the cool of my rock I could have married her right there alone in the dark. I called out her name and prayed that she heard me.

Chapter 26

A low rumble from the Scout brought me from my dreams. Cosmo woke up early and broke camp down while I slept. Hillary helped me fold up my tent while Cosmo checked under the hood of the Scout when I got up. I inhaled my last scent of Dulce. The spot brought on many realizations. I gave thanks to the earth under my feet. I was alive, awake, and grateful to the land and the sea that cradled me into a blissful state of being. Cosmo made us hurry because he had a surprise for the two of us and we needed to get moving to reach it on time. We picked up J.P.'s boat at Jerome's and said our goodbyes. He gave us two fresh bottles of tequila and in an instant we headed south.

My hawk no longer visited my sleep and I ceased to look for her gorgeous feathers. Her job was done. The cacti grew in height the further south we went. They rose from the desert like green-armed sky-scrapers. Tumbleweeds and rocks rolled beneath their limbs no bigger than working ants. We stopped at the tallest cactus within a reasonable distance from the road and fired off a few pictures. We took turns standing underneath the massive succulent and got back on the road.

I ate the wind. I floated on a euphoric air as we entered the town of Gurrero Negro. The small town marked the entry into the State of Southern Baja. We ate an early lunch at an idyllic restaurant that made us feel like we were eating in one of our Grandmother's homes. The grilled sea bass melted like butter. Spicy rice with nopales complimented the flavorful fish as we ate on a round table over clay tile. Cosmo would not tell us what he had planned while we savored our meal and Hillary and I did not prod him further. After lunch we drove two minutes up the road and checked into a hotel. My room contained a single bed no more than four feet wide, a squatted, leather chair, and a bathroom with a shower. I set down a pair of clean clothes on my new bed and peeled off my shirt. I could not wait to get in the shower, but before I was completely naked Cosmo broke into the room and said we had to go.

Back in the Scout we let adventure guide our thoughts. Cosmo was in a Hip-Hop mood and played the "ATLiens" album by **Outkast** as we headed towards a splendid lagoon. Another two miles up the road I caught sight of a structure on the edge of the lagoon with a small fleet of boats anchored in front of it that looked just like the one we towed behind us and figured it would have been our destination, but instead Cosmo pulled over on the side of the road and drove around a few sand dunes then stopped the vehicle. He took the keys from the ignition and shoved them into his pocket. "Wait here," he said and exited the Scout in a rush. He disappeared behind a sand dune and Hillary and I broke into laughter.

Ten minutes later Cosmo returned. We locked up the Scout and grabbed my camera. I gave Hillary a piggy back ride as we followed Cosmo to the shores of the lagoon. A man waited near a small boat beached in the mud. I let Hillary down and Cosmo pulled a tattered tee shirt from his shorts pocket. He ripped the shirt into two lengths and proceeded to blindfold Hillary. He then repeated the routine on me. Seagulls squawked just above the lagoon and the aroma of decayed sea foliage mixed in with a warming sun. I bumped into Hillary as Cosmo led us to the boat.

"You guys, say hola to Antonio."

"Hola, Antonio" we both repeated.

"He will be our captain for the next hour and a half. Please, don't ask what's going on. Just let your imagination travel. Your blindfolds will come off in about twenty minutes."

Neither of us hesitated to agree with him. The mystery excited us both. In a few minutes we were on the water. I barely heard the boat motor as it purred in the salty lagoon. I tried not to think about what waited for us when we opened our eyes and instead thought about what Antonio looked like before Cosmo blindfolded me. I remembered that he stood about an inch or two shorter than Hillary. He appeared thin and wore a black bandana like a scarf around his neck. He spoke Spanish to Cosmo in a low voice. I recognized a few words, but the anticipation kept me from concentrating.

The motor stopped. Splashes of water lapped against the boat. I could not see it, but the water felt close and I knew the walls of our boat were no more than a few inches above it. Cosmo told us to hold on for ten more seconds before we removed our blindfolds. He began a quiet countdown when a loud noise interrupted the air. It sounded as though a large train surfaced from the sea and released its brakes. The decompression hissed as Cosmo reached the number one. I peeled away the shirt and took in the sight of a gray monster no more than five feet from the boat. I nearly fell overboard as I stumbled backwards. Gnarled barnacles littered an area just below its eye while it opened wide jaws and revealed straw-like baleen. It bobbed on the surface for a few more seconds and then dove in the dark-blue water. Hillary and I looked at each other with the same stunned expression. Before we could talk another gray whale surfaced with its calf while Antonio navigated with a wooden oar. The little one tried to ape its mother's movements while the mother made sure to keep her body between her calf and our boat. Still awed, I looked across the inlet and noticed a litany of gray behemoths on the surface all around us.

The mother dwarfed our little boat. She could have wiped us out with one swipe of her tail. I had always heard about the sizes of whales. Thirty feet, forty, fifty, on to the one hundred foot blue whale and the scale never seemed real. Much like the size of the waves we rode, the massiveness of a whale could have never been understood until I sat no more than five feet from a forty foot, serene traveler of the oceans.

We rocked on the water in Scammons Lagoon where the gray whales migrated to have their young. When the ice in the northern Pacific began to push southward around the month of October the whales headed south on a 12,500 mile round trip voyage. The pregnant mothers usually arrived first with the rest of the pods arriving shortly after. The miracle of life, nursing, and mating took place in the salty waters. Though the mother made me miniscule in proportion to her size she also translated the pure wonder of our planet in the powerful breaths she casted into the air. The magnificence of her leathery body gave me such an appreciation for life and prompted the urge to give thanks for the opportunity to witness the majestic creature perform her motherly duties. I felt a part of something much greater than myself. I was a piece of the planet, a part of it, no longer separate from its natural cycle. We all had a role to play, from the tiny benthic crustaceans that gave their lives to feed the massive mammals, to the sea eagles who hunted for fish from high above, to the sea lettuce on round boulders, to the funny looking human with outstretched arms reaching out to say hello to a childhood dream.

On her next surface the mother nearly bumped the boat and the three of us placed our hands on her rubbery skin. She felt like a wet gym mat. Hillary began to cry. Cosmo tried to give the whale a hug. I found tears on my eyelashes. I attempted to hold them back for a mere second then brushed it aside and gave in to the beauty of the moment. The little one stuck close to its mother's side. She turned a bit and let us grasp a better view of her new creation.

Antonio instructed us not to touch the calf through Cosmo's excited translation. We drank in one more look of mother and child before they dove below the surface and Antonio paddled along.

We watched the whales for another forty-five minutes. They spy-hopped, they blew out large clouds of mist from their blowholes, and one whale even breeched three times. I snapped a multitude of pictures in between mystified trances. Early afternoon clouds formed above the lagoon and before we knew it Antonio informed us that it was time to go. After he cleared a path through a forest of gigantic bodies with the wooden oar Antonio put the little motor back in the water and we headed for the shore. No words passed. Hillary held Cosmo tight as the wind off of the water played in her hair. We helped Antonio beach his craft and Cosmo gave him a wad of cash. As we navigated through the dunes towards the Scout Cosmo stopped and looked back at the lagoon. The clouds moved fast overhead. He extended his arms about shoulder high and then bowed like a maestro after a riveted performance. He turned back around and smiled at the both of us.

"Most people will never experience something as amazing as that, not even if they happened to be riding right along with us. So many people would have watched, but would have never really seen or heard what was going on out there because they could not shut their mouths long enough to hear it. It happens all the time. At the sea, near a waterfall, they are there, but not really there. That was beyond words and you two noticed that." He shook his head and grinned. Then he wedged between Hillary and me and put his arms on our shoulders. "I'm ready to say good bye to J.P. now."

We went back to our rooms. I called Karana. I heard her voice for the first time since I walked out of our living room. I pictured the way her wet hair coiled when I left her while we talked. There was too much to say in one conversation. I said I would tell her everything when I got home and went on as best as I could about the whales. She listened to our plan. La Escondida was three hours from Guerrero Negro. We were to spend at least two days there for J.P.'s final sendoff and then turn around for home in much more of a straight line than we had traveled on the way down. She asked if I still loved her. I could hardly answer the question the way I wanted to, because I knew I loved her much more than the day I left. I found a better place in my soul to love her from. A place where I could love her how she was meant to be loved. I attempted to explain this through the static on the line and the clumsiness of my words, but I knew it did not come out the right way. She seemed pleased enough with my answer and we both agreed it would make more sense when I could sit down and say it to her face to face. When I hung up the phone I was aware that I was not going to lose Karana, ever.

Chapter 27

The heart beat the same. Oxygen flowed in through the mouth, down the windpipe, and into the lungs. Carbon dioxide discarded from the body much like any other human being on the planet. Glands secreted sweat, veins pumped fluid, and muscle fiber thrust skeleton bones in motion. Feet scuffled, organs performed, and bodies lived. Each frame wrapped in skin penitent to hunger, thirst, breath, and excretion. Two feet walked towards a bed in Taipei while two feet rose from the sheets and set down on a tiled floor in Los Angeles. Both needed rest, both needed to rise, both were biologically from the same species, yet each one, each pulsing human being frolicking upon the earth differed drastically from one to the next. With duplicate lifelines necessary to sustain life one body from Asia and one body from North America became two entirely different people.

Long ago the continents cracked and drifted apart leaving the vast oceans to divide populations into separate evolving units. Unique vocabularies formed, body hues developed on the amount of sun or a lack there of, and each land mass created its own race of people. People who adapted to their own lands, their own cultures, and began scribing a history of mankind in their respected kingdoms to become promising nations. They created their own Gods, they made their own rules, and nothing else existed beyond the fringes of their country and the shallows of their coastal seas.

Then man began to wonder. What existed beyond the sunset? How far did the expansive ocean spread? What rested on the other side of the gigantic mountains? And the migrations began. Land journeys across continents. Ocean bound treks down coastlines, then to as far as the wooden ships would carry them. Strange tongues, strange customs, strange foods and the world became an endless chunk of possibility. The ships became crowded, the masses followed, the new arrivals wiped out entire local civilizations. They forced their ways. They warred in the name of their gods, they slaughtered in the name of their gods, they reshaped the world in the name of their gods.

Races combined, melting pots formed, and mankind grew wings. Planes took to the skies. Travel became immediate. What once took months and years took only a matter of hours and days. The once endless chunk of possibility became a globe with boundaries and borders and limits. The globe shrank. People could connect with one another thousands of miles away instantly through wires, through keyboards, through satellites. Humans became one again, the initial clan on an unbroken mass of land unabated by the perilous oceans or the thundering skies.

Somehow time skipped over La Escondida. The heart beat the same, but the desire differed from much of the world. The ever changing globe, the technological advancements, the hustle and bustle to accumulate more, to build larger, to expand further had not yet corrupted the tiny village of just under one hundred people. The nearest telephone required a half an hour ride down a dirt road, or a hike for two hours. The internet, even in Spanish, came across as a made up word. They owned a few trucks and beaten down cars among them, three boat motors to attach onto their hand made fishing boats, a few generators that ran on gas to power refrigerators, and two old and cracked A.M. F.M radios, but for the most part the world beyond the borders of their small community remained quite foreign. No light switches, no running water, no televisions, and little influence outside of their circle.

They fished for food. They cultivated the land. Crops of tomatoes, corn, beans, and peppers nourished their bellies. They raised chickens. Collected fresh eggs and roasted mature birds on special occasions over open pits of fire. They traded fish for necessities, for clothes, for masa to make tortillas, for sacks of rice. They worked during picking seasons in neighboring fields and collected fruit and vegetables for large companies to ship to the United States, to Canada, to Asia. A few men made trips to the California every year to pick avocadoes and oranges in northeast San Diego. They would return home with green bills and stories of people of great waste and excess. The families cared for each other. They worked much like a tribe. They raised each others children, they shared clothes, they shared food, and they shared responsibility for one another.

They could have pooled money together and relocated closer to telephone poles and power lines, closer to small markets and water that came out of pipes in floods, closer to the land of moving asphalt, moving bodies, dissipating families, but the edge of the sea was their home. The men woke in the morning with a longing for salt, the cool of the ocean, the peace of hours on the water. Calloused hands labored on ancient equipment with skill, with innate technique. Men were made at sea after a big catch and men were lost at sea when she was angry, but she was always forgiven. If you took, you must give back in return. The women were strong. They balanced the children, they balanced the meals, they balanced order, they balanced their men, and they balanced the crops. The sea did not burn in their lungs as it did for the men as a desire, as a need, but instead gave them a sense of gratitude for life, for love, for strength. They prayed each morning for the safety of the men and for a bountiful catch. They prayed for protection and offered thanks. The ocean was home. The ocean was life and to leave her meant the undoing of a rare culture.

How long before the reaches of the planet spoiled the people? How long before society told them they were poor? The world waited to taint their image of life. Soon they would be sniffed out and the world will hold a mirror before the village and tell them what was beautiful, what they had to have, how they had to live. The children would be told they needed food that rotted their teeth, toys that made them lazy, and clothes with particular logos. The wants would change. The people would change. The community would break. Families would spread apart and the village would dry up.

A sepia photograph, a penciled sketch, a snow globe replaced with dust, any way possible to catch La Escondida in its pristine state and keep it preserved before the world took it away seemed like a necessary cause. The world would try. Visitors would try. But the people were strong. The people with blood in the roots, blood in the soil, blood in the sea would hold tight. They would clutch the land and the ocean of their souls.

I watched from afar as Cosmo told Manuel of J.P.'s passing. He did not say a word and turned to the sea. He then chanted an ancient prayer and bowed his head. J.P. spent a lot of time in the village. He hid from the world in the comfort of his adopted community. He always brought tools, vegetable seeds, clothes, and extra fishing gear. The people adored him like a folk hero. The children ran from his large frame when he exited his vehicle and roared at them like a monster only to gather at his feet by the light of the fire after dinner. He never wrote it down anywhere, but Cosmo knew the small craft we towed behind us was meant to end up with the gentle people that J.P. loved so dearly.

After Cosmo told Manuel of the gift the whole community circled around the muddy offering. Hillary took pictures of smiles, of climbing children, and of grateful mothers. Manuel then quieted everyone down and told them about J.P. and the ceremony we planned to commence. The crowd grew silent and slowly dispersed from their gift after the dismal news. Manuel wore an ivory cowboy hat that J.P. gave to him on his birthday and a pair of faded jeans. His torso was covered by an old O.P tee shirt that probably arrived in one of J.P's sacks of clothes he brought down over the years. Manuel rarely smiled, but always appeared to be happy. Without an explanation about what would happen or how it would happen he put a hand on Cosmo's shoulder and said "Manana."

We set up camp on the bluff about one hundred yards from the patchwork homes behind us. An intermittent wind pushed our tents around, which made the task more difficult than usual to erect them. On the way out of Guerrero Negro we stopped at a market and stocked up on supplies. Cosmo purchased large sacks of rice and beans and plenty of drinking water for the villagers. Hillary uncorked a sweet red wine. She filled three paper cups and we drank the wine in our camping chairs after we finished setting up our temporary homes. The wine tasted like crisp sangria without chunks of fruit bobbing in it. We waited for the sunset and listened to the wind. The clouds that formed during our whale watching excursion the day before persisted and blocked our view of the sun, but just before it touched down the magnificent life star penetrated a hole in the gossamer lining just above the water and said goodnight. Manuel approached our camp and insisted that we eat dinner with his family. We brought along beverages and Hillary carried her guitar.

The small home was pieced together by a random assortment of materials. The walls were made with pieces of plywood, two old garage doors, and metal sheeting. A few of the beams and studs appeared to be hand planed while others looked like standard two by fours. We sat down at a hand made table and rested our feet upon carefully chosen stones that rested over the earth like tile. J.P. consumed many meals in the same home. The walls were always evolving and Manuel added a number of rooms over the years to accommodate his six children. His oldest daughter was twenty-three and still unmarried. She fell in love with J.P. as a girl and held on to a child's wish that he would one day come and rescue her from the isolated village. Manuel once told J.P. of his daughter's innocent crush on him and asked if he would one day want to take her hand in marriage. J.P. then told Manuel that their friendship meant the world to him and he was only capable of breaking his daughter's heart. Her name was Imelda and she did not say one word during supper.

Manuel's wife Luisa prepared a wonderful meal. We plowed through rice and beans, homemade tortillas, and toro, which was a large tuna. The tuna meat was brown on the inside and looked much like the dark meat of a carved turkey. Luisa dressed the fish with jalapenos, cilantro, and onions. We drank beers, sipped on Jerome's tequila, and chased Manuel's youngest children around the house. Hillary played her guitar for a few minutes and then passed it on to Manuel. He plucked away at rhythmic tunes and taught us the words to a few of his favorite songs. The house sang and swayed to the music. No one mentioned J.P., but we did not need to. He was there with us. Dancing, singing, and enjoying the night. Manuel was saddened by the news, but accepted the circle of life. For fifteen years J.P. was a part of La Escondido's circle and just like the ebb and flow of the tides Manuel knew the circle eventually had to change.

They met in Ensenada. Manuel needed a ride back to his village and J.P. had enough alcohol in him to want to leave at that second. A few hundred miles later J.P. discovered a place that he fell in love with immediately. The simplicity of life and family, the ease of the days as they melted into one another, and the calm of spending hours on the sea to put dinner on the table made absolute sense to him. He vowed to move their every time he returned from the affable village. Much in the way Jerome found solitude in the quiet hills near Agua Dulce, J.P. felt like Escondida was a great place to be forgotten. We toasted to his life and his memory and instead of mourning we celebrated.

Chapter 28

Flames were about to dance upon the Pacific. The water, asphalt black after nightfall, would become illuminated in orange fans of light while glowing embers sparked off into a sincere requiem. People gathered at the toes of the sea armed with unlit candles and patient faces. Who knew the actual time, five, or maybe six in the evening, not quite sure for it seemed irrelevant in increments of hours, minutes, and seconds. Time instead revolved around the sun, her rise, her apex, and her fall which she commenced before us, bending low to kiss the ocean goodnight. Preparations took all day. Fishing, cooking, organizing, laughing, and cleaning up consumed the little village as their hearts poured into every ounce of work needed to be done to proceed with the night's ceremonies. Excitement moved dirty feet through menial tasks marred with the foreboding word of goodbye, but the night was a celebration after all, sad yes, but better to venerate life than to wallow in melancholy. A lesson gathered in broken Spanish translations.

A satisfying calm swallowed the dusk underneath

a clear sky. Cosmo and I hiked up the hill behind the village to take in a view of what the saints of La Escondida created for the evening, although once on top we could not see their actual accomplishments. We could not see their sweat and their hustle. We could not see the large pots of food and stacks of clean dishes. We could not see their humbleness, kindness, and giving. We could see movement and bodies dressed up in bright clothing usually reserved for Sunday services. We could see the gift we towed down from Southern California as it was pulled towards the water. I could see Manuel sitting near his daughter Imelda on a small stone wall waiting for the festivities to begin. And I felt love, I felt peace, and I knew I was supposed to be there, right there at that exact moment in time.

I already tasted the food spicy and delicious. I almost felt a vague sense of a hangover after the tequila bottles came out in hordes by the light of the fire. So much I felt, so much I was in tune with. The salt in the air, the scurry of a field mouse circling underneath a green yucca plant, the cool beer as it hit awaiting taste buds, the glide of a flock of pelican's skimming above a glassy two foot wave all came into focus. My body rested at ease with all five senses thriving, pulsing, and engulfing the gifts of the evening. Thanks were given to whoever listened, but I wondered why it took death and a promise to an isolated village to come to such a place in my being. Even in my celebration on a cacti littered hill above the sea, even in a halo of bliss, a duplicitous tongue of fear lashed callused heels and caused me to question;

how long would I be awake? How long would I feel so free? I tried my best to quell pangs of worry, and Cosmo, as if sensing my unnecessary fretting broke the silence.

"Tonight should be quite a party."

"Yeah, I am looking forward to it."

Cosmo sipped from a red Tecate can and then gazed towards the sea. His eyes squinted at the dissipating sun. In the spontaneous thought to take a walk before nightfall we both forgot to grab sunglasses from our tents below. He brought his right hand up to shield his forehead as a visor from the glare and I emulated the motion and looked out on the horizon. No large vessels, no fleet of fishing boats, no helicopters screaming up the coast, just the ocean, patchy gray clouds, and a papaya sunset.

"We should probably head down in a bit," I got out. I finished my beer and let out a small burp in satisfaction.

"Yeah, looks like it's about that time." Cosmo tossed me a new beer from the pocket of his black, hooded sweatshirt as I crushed the depleted can underneath a pair of dirty shoes. He cracked open a fresh beer for himself and foam spilled over the top from our charge up the hill.

"Here is to our journey," he said raising his can towards me.

"It has been incredible man; I mean I can't believe how eye opening it was."

"Don't go talking in the past tense yet. It's not time to start thinking about the trek home or to begin sorting through the pictures you like and dislike on your digital camera. We are still here and there is a raging celebration we have to tend to. Don't forget that."

"Okay, okay, wrong tense I know. You are right punk ass, as usual." We clinked cans and a splash of liquid sloshed back at me. I dodged it in time sucking my chest and legs into a vertical cylinder and my footing gave way. Cosmo reached out to grab me before the fall, but he missed with a usually sure, swooping right hand. A half second slide on loose pebbles sickened my stomach. The hill was not a face on Mount Everest by any means, but it did rise with a steep incline and a tumble from my position might have turned me into a dust covered avalanche for at least thirty yards. Hundreds of cacti, green and yellow-tanned yuccas, sharp cuts of eroded boulders, and scattered tumbleweeds adorned the path, but just before the perilous trek began my left foot caught a small, round lump of earth followed quickly by my right. The violent images faded as fast as they came and I found myself composed and smiling on top of the saving pile.

Cosmo grinned and shook his head. "Nice catch," he said and broke into a slight chuckle. "Are you purposely trying to kill yourself on this trip or do you just love adding a flare to the dramatic? You don't have to create another episode to keep the rest of our trip going you know, we can just go down the hill and party. Damn that was close."

"Yeah, I guess it was," I said eyeing the hazardous path I almost departed upon. A deep breath came in and soothed my rapid heartbeat into a gentle murmur.

"Did you mind flash back to your wipeout at Dulce at all," Cosmo asked."

"Not really. The funny thing is, I feel pretty calm. Not that I didn't get a stab of panic or anything, but it's just that in that brief moment of worry I slowed everything down. It was almost like watching an instant replay from a Chargers game with L.T. tiptoeing the sideline before going in for a touchdown. You know how they slow it down and zoom in on where his foot actually lands near the sideline, in or out, frame by frame, well it kind of felt like that. I had an initial rush, then it eased and I watched everything in slow motion until I ended up standing on my platform here. It's like, after the wild order of events from our entire trip everything seems clearer. If clearer is any type of vocabulary word to use, but I feel different and alive, almost in unity with all of my senses. I wanted to talk to you about it after our big day at Dulce, but I didn't want to spoil the pureness of being that has overwhelmed me since. I didn't want to curse it."

"Are you awake?"

"Aha, wide awake."

I looked back down the hill then took a drink of what was left of my beer. A layer of foam coated the initial sip, but underneath the liquid was cool and pleasing on the tongue, though Tecate always tasted better with a little lime. A few seconds before I might have been mutated into an undecipherable mess of limbs and tissue, possibly never able to walk again or at least broken and cut up pretty badly, and yet somehow I was standing completely unscathed in the descending sunlight with a friend who taught me more than anyone else in the world. I thought I had about used up all of my good luck tokens for a while. I turned back towards Cosmo and asked "How long will it last?"

"What, being this awake?"

"Yeah."

"I don't know. Maybe the rest of today, maybe the rest of the trip, perhaps the rest of your life, I can't tell you that. Almost everyone experiences a moment in our lives that changes us, or rattles the very core of who we are. Some of us forget these occurrences as quickly as they ran through our bodies, complacently lapsing back into reiterated patterns. And yet some of us mark these moments and really take a look at the lives we are leading, soon after altering what we only previously dreamed of changing."

I bent forward and stretched towards my toes attempting to loosen up my back. "What category do I fall in? Or wait, maybe I don't want to you to actually answer to that." Deep down I did want Cosmo to answer though. I wanted him to tell me I was someone who would take the elements of our trip, the recognition of who I wanted to be, and would apply it to the rest of my life, would fight for the liberation that filled my soul and make it endure, but I was alarmed by what he might come back with. Fangs of the cool evening impaled deeper into my skin as cooking fires and bonfires began to flame below. We needed to go down the hill for the events to begin. I could barely make out Manuel because of the fading light. He must have wondered where we wandered off to, though Hillary knew where we were. Cosmo's silence clamped down with the cold and I wished my mouth would have stayed shut.

"Since you asked I'll say it," he said after what seemed an hour of silence, but in reality could have lasted no longer than a full minute. Cosmo took his gaze from the ocean and directed his eyes toward the left side of my face that I presented to him. "You are going to hate it, but I'm going to say it anyway, because you did inquire. Only you know the answer to the question you posed. How long, what category of person, are just questions of posturing and the need for some type of self-reassurance. You know what type of person you are, but as long as you need to ask these questions I have no idea what the fate of your illumination will be. Waves of elation need to be ridden just like waves in the sea. You cannot dwell on when it is going to end or how good you are going to ride it, you just ride it. Any attempt to toy with this cycle almost always brings the wave, whether physical or mental, to a close much faster if we are too preoccupied on the outcome instead of enjoying the pleasing motion we are fortunate enough to be set upon.

"This trip has awakened you; that I know. When you retell of our adventures many people will look towards your death-defying escapade and think that your near drowning episode acted as the most poignant and life altering occasion on this journey, but I will always be of a different opinion and I think you already might be of that same opinion as well. That altercation was just a singular incident, a profound incident for sure, but still just one incident. Everything about this trip from walking out on your job, to meeting Jerome, Hillary and Campbell, to the emancipation of your surfing, to expressing your fears on paper, to experiencing the whales, to the ease that fills your body at this moment, everything has been a release and a true commitment to following your heart, leaving your wipeout as just a branch on the tree of experience that has sprouted, not the entire tree."

Cosmo held the red Tecate can to his lips but did not drink. The can turned in his hand and he closed his left eye. His open eye stared down the can into the amber liquid. I waited for a big sigh, a let's get going, but instead he twirled the can back to his mouth, took a drink, and continued.

"I'm not perfect nor do I give perfect advice. Maybe I have it all wrong and I'm just polluting the air right now with a bunch of wasted nonsense. That is for you to decide. You're wide awake now and if you go home and just pick up the exact pieces you shattered before you left, life will become even more miserable for you, and for Karana. You know that though Dano, so don't let it happen. Stay awake. You must understand, that what is different now, is you. It was never your job holding you back or the fear of this or the fear of that, it was you holding you back. You have always had the capability to do anything you wanted, to be happy in any situation, the power has always been there and now you are aware of it, you are tasting it. You know what it feels like. The difference now though, is that you know you don't need a dramatic exit or a freefall from a massive wave to open yourself up to channel it. It is there always."

The crickets began to sing on the right side of the hill. The tunes played sharp in the crisp air and cut into to the silence perched on Cosmo's teeth. I thought about how many of the melodious insects would successfully attract a lover. The charm of it all, serenading heart strings to the wind, to caution, to the world with a reckless drive towards passion. I wanted to sing out loud in a voice full and deep. Let it boom and reverberate off of scattered clouds and reach Karana wherever she was. At happy hour with her friends, staying late at work or resting in the comforts of the home we made in our modest rental, whatever space she consumed I wished for my feeble lungs to fill with enough power to reach her in any-thing as beautiful as the offerings emanating from the tiny legs around me. All of a sudden it felt possible and without thinking my mouth opened up.

"And I want to rock your gypsy soul
Just like way back in the days of old
And together we will float into the mystic"

Van Morrison erupted from a foreign throat. The voice sounded confident and free. It may not have rivaled Van's version, but it sounded true and sated with life. I scanned the hills, the brush, the darkening skyline, and found no stranger singing the potent lyrics. Where did the voice come from? Who broke the silence in between Cosmo's synopsis of my state of being? I turned to him and realized he had been staring at me, for how long I did not know, with an amused look curled into his right lip. He gave his head a playful shake and broke into an approving chuckle.

"Whoa Mr. Morrison, where did that come from?"

"I'm not sure. Your words were soaking in, silence hit, crickets started chirping, and then Karana seeped into the moment and I felt like singing to her; weird. I have always wanted to sing that song to her you know. Belt out that line, 'I want to rock your gypsy soul.' She loves that song. Funny thing is, and I know this sounds odd, but I kind of think that she did hear it. Sorry to interrupt the moment, I took in every word, every last detail and then the song just came out. I didn't mean to be rude and disrupt the flow you were on, I mean, here you are on the night we are going to scatter your uncles ashes out to sea and you are giving me advice. I don't know what........"

"Shut up."

"Huh."

"Shut up. I have a feeling that you are going to be just fine Mr. Morrison. There is nothing left to be done here. Let's get down this hill while we can still kind of see." His grin widened as he turned and lead the way back to camp. A sense of satisfaction guided his steps across the awkward terrain. Perhaps after how many days it took to carry out our mission he displayed pleasure for the upcoming moment of finally fulfilling our task, maybe I amused him like a circus clown and he grinned at my red nose, but somehow I thought my outburst and apparent confidence pleased him. The moment, that exact moment, the cool air, the last peak of sun flowed through every vein in my body. And maybe that was it. Cosmo could sense it from me, he heard it in my voice and perhaps that had been his wish for me all along. His speech about staying awake and riding out waves of elation erupted before him. He could see me riding, gliding, free-flowing across the canvas of the evening. Cosmo maneuvered with speed and great dexterity, and as we neared the village the chocolate-peanut smell of Mole along with seasoned tuna and grilled carne asada entered my nostrils.

HILLARY, COSMO, MANUEL and his family, and I motored out over the small waves on J.P.'s boat. We barely stayed above the water. Five more boats from the village followed close behind and formed a con-torted circle two hundred yards out at sea. Cosmo spoke briefly and then I followed with a few words of my own. Manuel went next and everyone bowed their heads. It was not a spectacle of any kind, it was simple and perfect. We brought J.P. where he wanted to be set free and let him loose on the sea. The remaining ashes sprinkled down and rested lightly on the sur-face before free diving out of sight. The candles fell. They burned bright in the quick night. The tears were gone. Only Manuel's oldest daughter Imelda sobbed. J.P did not let us cry. We had already done enough of that. Instead we gave thanks for his life, his spirit, his unwavering sarcasm, and motored back in the dark-ness to celebrate his time on earth.

While beer bottles and red cans piled on top of one another and the tequila bottles exchanged hands with greater pace I walked to the bluff for a moment of solitude. I only said a few words on the boat and I felt I needed to tell J.P. another thing or two with no one around. I took slow drinks from my beer and quietly thanked him. His body was not present, but his spirit drove us down the coast, down into our souls, down into the heart of what we truly were, and I would have never been able to reach such a place without him. I poured the rest of my beer over the edge of the bluff and returned to the party that screamed behind me. My shoulder throbbed and I rubbed it as I walked towards liquored voices. It was J.P. slugging me in the arm. He gave me one last Charlie Horse to erase any lingering sadness. Cosmo caught me massaging my arm on the opposite side of the fire. We made eye contact, a brief nod of acknowledgement, and then broke into elated smiles.

Chapter 29

I surfed with Cosmo the morning after J.P. died. We barely spoke, but the ocean offered a soothing ointment for our souls. The morning after we put his ashes to rest we found ourselves in a similar position on the shores of La Escondida. The ocean smiled an ominous grin as we stretched on the cool sand. A lifting vale of haze slithered on the skin of the sea and grew dark at the far reaches of our eyes. No words passed between us. Cosmo never showed his teeth. They remained sheltered beneath quiet lips and tired eyes. My head rang from the sting of too much tequila. Cosmo was hung-over. The thought to speak panged and quickly died as I looked out at the small surf in front of us. Escondida did not offer a great wave to surf, but we could at least get in the water and ease our pounding heads. As I pondered the small waves a chest high set stalked the beach and brightened my mood.

"Doesn't look too bad out there," Cosmo finally said.

"Yeah, there's a couple." I wanted to keep talking, but nothing came out. Instead I rolled on to my back and pulled my bent right leg into my chest.

"Thanks for coming Dane. I couldn't have made this trip with anyone else."

"No worries man, of course." I paused a second. "I'm sorry about J.P., truly."

"I know, thanks, but let's not talk about it. He's at rest, we should just be happy for him now." I nodded my head in recognition and proceeded to lay flat on my back. We were both finished stretching, but neither of us got up. We sat in front of the shoreline and watched wavering sea-foam accumulate near our feet. It was thick and impeding, and we could have grabbed it from the sand and swirled it around our fingers like cotton candy.

"Hey Dane, you and Karana fit pretty well don't you?"

"Yeah," I said caught off guard by the question.

"I'm glad to hear it. She is a beautiful person. You two belong together. Ready to set the date now, I'm sure."

"Funny you mention it. I was actually thinking about that this morning. I thought an early fall wedding would be nice if she still wants to go through with it."

"Oh she'll want to go through with it alright, for sure."

"So does this mean you are through trying to talk me out of it?"

"Oh give me a break; you know I can be full of shit at times."

"There's some earth shattering news there."

"Yeah, yeah bite me, but when it's right, it's right. To marry not out of circumstance or foolish misguided passion, but of love, honest and sincere love and respect, man that is so beautiful it almost makes me want to cry. I'm happy you've found it. You have experienced, lived, loved, lost, and have come to this point with full recognition of who you are and who Karana is, and that is how it should be. I only see the two of you making each other stronger and better people, not only to each other but to the entire human race as well." Words did not from well on the tongue, but I managed to mumble out a thank you.

"As for me," he continued, "I feel my path will always lead me astray from that area in life, but who knows man, the sledgehammer can come from anywhere and knock me to my knees. I mean, I said at one point in time that I would never listen to country music, but hell if I haven't sucked down beers listening to George Strait or Kenny Chesney." We laughed at the change in both of us. "Funny the curves of life," Cosmo said. "You know it's right, but do me one favor. Don't be ordinary. Don't let your relationship get stale, let it evolve, let it travel, don't let it limit you. Don't look at all the couples out there and acclimate along with them, be yourselves and invent your own path; don't let society predestinate it for you." He brushed off his hands. "Oh yeah one more thing, when you have kids teach them how to swim right away. If the apocalypse does come the Mayans foresee a world covered in water."

"O.K.," I said laughing.

"So take care of each other," he said.

"Of course."

"Always."

"O.k."

His tone suddenly turned serious and I knew that he was trying to tell me something. I tried to read the majestic philosopher who always seemed a level ahead of me. It was there, overtly palpable in his words. Then it hit me like a cement truck, he was leaving, and for an extended period of time. I should have seen it coming. Instantly I wrestled with a jabbing threat that I might not ever see him again. I panicked. I wondered if I would regress from the progress I had made. Was I adjusted enough to take off my training wheels and ride the obstacles of life with my own hands and feet without my teacher nearby? Was I ready?

"You ever hear of rogue waves," Cosmo asked.

"What?"

"Rogue waves, have you ever heard of them before?"

"Wait, where are you going? How long, what about Hillary? You are leaving aren't you?"

"Easy Dano, yeah I'm going. I'm not sure how long or where exactly, but I'm starting in Cabo. Manuel has to drive there for some business and I'm tagging along. I'll buy a ticket and then disappear for a while. Could be weeks, months, years, not sure, but I need to sort some shit out. You and Hillary can take the Scout back to the states."

"She knows then? You are not just going to bail on her without telling her are you?"

"No Dane I've already talked to her. She knows, she gets me, who knows maybe she can be that sledgehammer one day, but I've just got to go." He took his gaze from the ocean and turned his head towards me.

"I need to tell you a few things. I've been hard on you during the trip, maybe too hard, and I know some of it has surfaced from my own failures. You have something Dane, something I wish I had, but have lost. I have hardened like the dull pavement oblivious souls tread upon everyday. At a time I was a sponge, a penetrable foundation, but years and hours have clotted my openness. I've become a cynic, a skeptic, a disbeliever. We are lost as a people and right now I do not possess the tools to help steer us in the right direction. I know this because I have let people piss me off too much as of late. No one wants to think for themselves anymore. Herds of cattle, blind sheep, we never take a step on our own, mooing, baaing, as we spit and shit and trip all over one another. Watching human beings is like watching a pee wee soccer game. There is an entire playing field, a vast open pasture to roam upon, and yet, when the ball drops every player in this game of life gravitates to the same spot. A clouded huddle of bodies all lured on a singular path. No room to breathe, to run, to live, as arms flail and legs swipe and bodies fall to the turf. Scraped and bruised the fallen will get up and jump right back into the fray of elbows and violence only to get knocked down again in the confusion. Someone wiser will scream to liberate from the pack, to open up to the empty spaces and discover an entirely different way to live, yet words pass through ears like a speeding train, a sudden impact of noise and metal, then gone, forgotten on a track towards San Francisco and we run right back to the pack."

He took a breath and continued. "Human beings

can't stand alone and everyday we get fatter, lazier, and less adept to breathing air. No one wants to take responsibility for themselves. They want someone else to fix it, they want to blame anyone and everyone, but won't do a damn thing on their own. I use to want to change things, to be part of the solution, but how do we fight pure and utter lunacy? Jerome made so much sense to me. I got what he was saying. I want to disappear too. I've lost my compassion, but not you Dane. You still have it, have right there in the middle of that thumping chest. I envy it. I've been so hard on you because you need to share it. You exhale an aura of well being and kindness that the world needs. Keeping that person bottled up is like keeping the world on pace to its own demise. It's people like you who possess the grace and understanding to alter this road to ruin. I use to be one of those people, but I've lost him. You have helped me understand that on this trip Dane. You have made me realize what I have been missing. I need to go and find him again, and who knows, maybe upon my return I might even go and look up my father in Northern California."

I just sat there and listened. There was no way of stopping him. When he set his mind to something he followed it with full conviction. Though it stung I accepted his sabbatical and gasped at the vacancy I already felt. We let his words sink in and sat in silence. The crashing waves purred on the sand. After about a minute I changed the subject.

"O.k., so you were talking about rouge waves."

"Yeah right rogue waves, do you know what they are."

"Vaguely, but I don't remember much about them."

Cosmo crossed his legs and leaned back on the palms of his hands which imprinted the stale, gray sand like a Plaster of Paris casting I made in the seventh grade. He looked composed and in control. "They begin as wide wavelengths, collected and unitary, wandering the ocean in search of their identity. They possess great potential with their mass of attributes and unique qualities, but do not know what they truly are. From all angles they appear adjusted, full, alive, but they are no ordinary wave and a fate of sorts must cross their path with a confrontation to draw forth the true nature of their existence. They are altered when they come across an island, a sea mount, or a rock cropping that stands firm and confident in the depths of the sea. When the two collide the wave begins a metamorphosis as part of its previous identity washes upon the shore. It gives away a part of its previous self to meet a challenge that will transform it forever."

He paused for a second and released his legs from their crossed position and straightened them towards the sea. "Some waves get annihilated after the encounter with such a profound source, but the rogue wave gathers itself as its resilient span wraps around the island and reforms again more powerful than ever before. It retains the basics of its former self, but is changed forever as it rolls along the turquoise skin of the sea."

I licked my lips and then responded. "So if I get you right, you are saying that a rogue wave hits an island, is almost destroyed, then re-composes itself, forming together in the wake of the opposing coast of the island, stronger, more developed, and becomes a more powerful and enlightened source."

"Exactly Dano."

"And so then are you saying that I am this rogue wave. That I have been a drifting wave in search of an island to challenge the very essence of who I am, and that you, or this trip in general have been that island. Have I needed to break myself upon you and the elements to see if I could pull out the true nature of who I am?" Cosmo smiled and stood up. He picked up his board and walked towards the water.

"Just as you have been my island as well Dano," he said and ran into the sea.

HILLARY AND I said goodbye to Cosmo and La Escondida that afternoon. She was at peace with Cosmo's journey. Their connection was strong and reassured her that they would reunite later on down the road. She told me that even if they never saw each other ever again she would not take back a single second of our adventure. I felt the same way. We stopped and got two rooms at a small hotel after a full day of traveling. The next day we crossed the border and I dropped her off at Lindbergh Field in San Diego. She was going home to Colorado to gather a few things and then she planned to return to the coast. She said she could not stand living away from the ocean. The sea infected her veins and she would return to the cure as soon as she could pack her car.

I headed for Oceanside, Karana, and a new life. I

planned to propose to her all over again as the man she hoped I would find. As I hummed along Interstate Five I knew I had found that man. He emerged from the influence of a liberated voyage, an old friend, new friends, and the magnanimous sea. And the more I thought of it the more I realized how much I owed to the ocean. Much like Cosmo found his home in her waters I knew she had humbled me, taught me, cradled me, awed me with her magnificent creatures, and pulled me from the depths of my own self loathing. Surfing brought me to her, but the activity took a back seat to her affect upon my life. I realized myself in her. Not the picture I foolishly attempted to paint, refined, and right, and good, but the actual mirror to my entire being displayed upon her skin. My fears, my weaknesses, my imperfections, my talents, my courage emerge in every embarrassing and glorious detail to sketch exactly who I am when I am in her presence. And when I am lost in her, entirely fazed into her depths, I am everything I wish to be. I am beautiful, I am wise, I am emancipated. To find myself I only needed to visit her shores, take in her intoxicating aroma, and loose myself in her waters. How did I ever forget that?

Breinigsville, PA USA
05 July 2010
241136BV00003B/2/P